MW00332380

Six

Jane Blythe

Copyright © 2018 Jane Blythe

All rights reserved.

No part of this publication may be reproduced, transmitted, downloaded, distributed, reverse engineered or stored in or introduced into any information storage and retrieval system, in any form or by any means, including photocopying and recording, whether electronic or mechanical, now known or hereinafter invented without permission in writing from the publisher.

All characters and events in this publication, other than those clearly in the public domain, are fictitious and any resemblance to real persons, living or dead, is purely coincidental.

Bear Spots Publications
Melbourne Australia

bearspotspublications@gmail.com

Paperback
ISBN: 0-9945380-8-1
ISBN-13: 978-0-9945380-8-6

Cover designed by QDesigns

I'd like to thank everyone who played a part in bringing this story to life. Particularly my mom who is always there to share her thoughts and opinions with me. My awesome cover designer, Amy, who whips up covers for me so quickly and who patiently makes every change I ask for, and there are usually lots of them! And my lovely editor Mitzi Carroll, and proofreader Marisa Nichols, for all their encouragement and for all the hard work they put in to polishing my work.

NOVEMBER 4ᵀᴴ

"You didn't have to leave Laura and come," Detective Ryan Xander told his brother, Jack, as they sped toward the river.

Almost fifteen minutes ago his wife had received a phone call from the man who had been stalking her for over six years. The stalker had fixated on one of their friends—Ryan's partner, Detective Paige Hood—and decided that the two of them were having an affair. Convinced that the only way to make Sofia's marriage safe, the stalker decided he had to kill Paige.

Five years ago, the stalker had attempted to beat Paige to death. Thankfully, she had survived, and for all these years the stalker had laid low.

Until tonight.

Tonight, he had returned, attempting to run Paige down with a car. Ryan had managed to push her out of the way, but the stalker hadn't left. He had followed her out to a crime scene and then called Sofia to tell her that he was going to kill Paige tonight.

Ryan had immediately called his partner and managed to get through to her. He had warned her and found out where she was. But then there had been a loud crash, a splash, and then the call had been abruptly cut off.

"Of course, I had to come," Jack said. "Paige is my friend. Laura is safe at the hospital, and besides, she's out of it. They had to sedate her, and her parents are with her. If she knew that the stalker had tried to kill Paige again and I didn't come with you, she'd be furious with me."

Jack's wife Laura had been abducted and held hostage just a

couple of hours ago. She had sustained injuries and started having contractions over a month early. The doctors were hoping to delay labor to give the baby a chance to develop further, but right now it was a wait and see situation.

"Plus, the stalker is dangerous. Just because he's fixated on Paige right now doesn't mean he can't shift that focus to someone else. And since he thinks you're cheating on Sofia with Paige, he could easily decide he has to go after you, too, in order to ensure Sofia's happiness," Jack warned.

"Then you should be careful as well," Ryan informed his brother. "He saw you comforting Paige earlier while she was crying; he thinks she's after you as well."

Jack shook his head in disbelief. "We were just talking about Rose and how we both miss her."

Rose had been his brother's partner and Paige's best friend. She had been murdered four years ago by the same man who had tormented Jack's wife, Laura.

"Paige said she was on this road," Ryan said as they turned the corner.

"What exactly did you hear?" Jack asked.

"I was talking to her and then there was a loud crash. I think he rammed her car with his. Then it sounded like a splash, and I lost the connection," Ryan explained. Images of Paige lying beaten nearly to death when he'd interrupted the stalker's first attack on her were flashing vividly through his mind. Last time Paige had managed to survive the attack, but there was no guarantee that she would this time.

"You think he forced her car into the river?" Jack asked.

"Yes, and this time of year the water would be freezing."

"Unless she was badly hurt, she could have gotten out of the car before it sunk."

"But, if she got out, the stalker would probably have been waiting for her and shot her or something." Ryan had a bad feeling that his partner wasn't all right.

"Ryan." Jack cast him a serious glance. "If she was trapped in the car, she might already be … gone. It's been fifteen minutes since your call to her got disconnected; the water's cold so she's going to get hypothermic, and the car will sink quickly."

Ryan knew that.

That's what was scaring him.

He scanned the road for signs of either their friend Xavier's car, which Paige had been driving, any other cars, or signs of an accident. It was storming, and between the wind and the rain and the fact that it was four o'clock in the morning, visibility was pretty much nonexistent.

Ryan spotted something up ahead in the beam of the car's headlights. It looked like muddy tire marks in the grass. "Jack, pull over just up there," he instructed his brother.

Jack complied, and a moment later they were shedding their jackets, grabbing flashlights, and jumping from the car. Up close he could see that it was definitely tire tracks, but there was no sign of Paige.

Inspecting the water, he hoped to see the car. If they didn't, if it had already sunk completely, they would never find Paige in time. Already the chances that she had succumbed to either hypothermia or had drowned were high.

Then Ryan saw something.

It looked like the back end of Xavier's truck.

"Jack, look." He pointed.

"Yeah, I see it. Let's go."

Sliding quickly down the wet slope, Ryan barely noticed the pounding rain. He did, however, notice the freezing water as he plunged into the river.

It temporarily stole his breath and froze his muscles. Adrenalin, however, was pulsing through his body, and he shook off the paralyzing cold and started to swim toward the car, his brother at his side.

Both of them were good swimmers and reached the car—

about ten yards from the bank—quickly. There were no signs of Paige in the water. Not that it necessarily meant that she hadn't gotten out of the car. She could have escaped only to have hypothermia take over and been washed away down river.

Diving down, Ryan found the water wasn't too deep. At the moment, the car's back wheels hadn't reached the bottom of the river. Once they did, only five feet or so would separate the roof of the car from the water's surface.

They both shone their flashlights into the car and immediately saw Paige.

Her eyes were closed, and she wasn't moving.

He thumped a hand on the window, but she didn't rouse.

Her seat belt still held her in place, and Ryan assumed she had either been unconscious when the car hit the water or her seat belt had jammed, trapping her.

Thankfully, Jack had been more prepared than Ryan's panic had allowed him to be. His brother pulled a Life Hammer from his pocket and used it to shatter the window.

His lungs were beginning to burn, desperately crying out to take a breath, but Ryan wasn't leaving without Paige.

He yanked on her seat belt, but it didn't budge. Shaking his head at Jack, his brother used the tool to quickly cut through the seat belt, then Ryan pulled Paige out through the broken window.

Swimming them both to the surface, he gasped in several deep breaths before he started for the bank. Jack was already almost to the edge. Maneuvering Paige so he could slip an arm across her chest, Ryan swam them both back to the riverbank.

Paige was completely limp in his arms. He feared she was already dead and was desperate to check, but right now they both needed to get out of the freezing water. For the moment, his adrenalin was helping to mask the cold, but Ryan knew that couldn't last indefinitely.

When his feet found the muddy bottom, he swung Paige up into his arms. Water streamed off them, mixing with the rain that was pouring down.

"Here, I'll take her." Jack held out his arms, and Ryan passed Paige to his brother, then followed him out of the rushing river.

The cold water was beginning to get to him, making his muscles stiff and sluggish. Paige had been in there much longer— a dangerous amount of time.

Jack laid Paige down on the grassy bank, and Ryan dropped to his knees beside her.

"I'm going to get an ETA on the ambulance." Jack stood and headed for the car.

Ryan pressed his fingertips to Paige's cold throat.

Nothing.

He held his cheek over her mouth.

Nothing again.

"Come on, Paige; don't you dare die on me," he muttered as he commenced CPR. He struggled to keep his panic in check as he pumped on her chest, hoping to keep oxygen circulating through her body. Paige couldn't die. He couldn't lose his partner. She was his best friend; he couldn't imagine not seeing her every day. Tilting her head back, he covered her mouth with his and forced air into her lungs. "Come on, Paige, breathe."

"Here, I'll do that." Jack knelt back down beside them.

"Ambulance going to be here soon?" He glanced up.

"Any minute now." Ryan paused in chest compressions and Jack pinched Paige's nose closed, put his mouth over hers, and breathed into her.

"Breathe, Paige, breathe. Please," Ryan begged as they continued with CPR. It felt like hours since they'd dragged Paige from her submerged car. Where was the ambulance?

"Ryan, I think she's got a pulse." Jack was hunched over Paige, his cheek over her mouth, his hand on her neck.

Before he could check, Paige began to cough and splutter. As carefully as he could, mindful of the fact that she'd just been in a car accident and they had no idea of the extent of her injuries, he rolled her onto his side. Water streamed from her mouth and nose as she continued to choke on the fresh air.

"Breathe in, Paige." He brushed her wet, matted hair back from her face. "Come on, breathe in. There you go." As Paige sucked in a few gasping breaths, he eased her back down. His partner's eyes were open, but unfocused, and Ryan didn't really think she was seeing anything.

"She's like ice." Jack's hand was pressed to Paige's cheek. "We should get her to the car and out of these wet clothes. I've got a thermal blanket we can wrap her in while we wait for the paramedics."

Agreeing with his brother that Paige was too cold and definitely hypothermic, they needed to keep her warm until help arrived. She was breathing again, but hypothermia could still kill her if she didn't get treatment quickly enough. Picking Paige up, he followed Jack as they scrambled back up the bank.

In the car Jack turned on the engine and got the heat blasting, while Ryan laid Paige down on the back seat and yanked off her soaked jeans and sweater.

"Here." Jack handed him the blanket.

He wrapped it around Paige. "Where are the paramedics?" he demanded. "They should be here by now. She's too cold. She's not even shaking; her body isn't even trying to generate heat. And she probably has water in her lungs and maybe internal bleeding from the crash, or head injuries. She needs help. Now." Ryan knew he was ranting but he was scared. Paige needed immediate medical attention.

"I'll call again." Jack picked up his phone.

"Ryan?" The voice was so soft he almost didn't hear it.

"Paige?" He looked down at his partner, whose eyes were struggling open. "I'm right here," he assured her.

"You got here in time." Her voice was hoarse and ragged, and her eyelids were fluttering as she fought to stay awake.

"Of course, I did," he admonished gently. "There was no way

I was going to let anything happen to you."

"I thought I was going to die. Did you get the stalker?" Paige gave up and let her eyes stay closed.

"Don't worry about that now, just rest, focus on your breathing." There was no need to stress Paige out. They needed to keep her calm until help arrived. "From now on, you don't go anywhere on your own—not even the bathroom. You are under twenty-four-hour-a-day protection." Even though he meant it, Ryan had hoped that the command would provoke Paige into responding, but she didn't reply. "Paige?" he gave her shoulder a gentle squeeze.

"So tired," she whispered.

"I know, honey—try to stay with me, though; help will be here soon. Can you tell me where you're hurt?"

"Everywhere. My chest hurts." They'd probably cracked some ribs performing CPR. Paige's teeth were chattering and her body was beginning to shiver. It was a good sign. It meant her body temperature was slowly rising and her body was now attempting to generate its own heat.

He slipped his hands under the blanket to grasp Paige's. "Can you feel that?" She nodded. "Can you move them?" She gave his hands a slight squeeze. He moved his hands down to her feet. "What about that? Can you feel that?" Another nod. "Good, move them for me." She complied. Sensation and movement intact, hopefully that ruled out any neck or spinal injuries.

"How is she?" Jack appeared beside him.

"A little better, I think. I hope," Ryan added. "Ambulance?"

"The storm caused a tree to fall down, blocking the road. Hopefully, it won't be much longer," Jack replied.

"Did you call ...?" Paige broke off, wracked by fits of violent coughing.

"Shh, don't try to talk ... concentrate on your breathing." Ryan attempted to calm Paige, her breathing was still labored; at the very least, she needed oxygen and heated blankets. "I haven't called Elias yet. I didn't want to worry him until we found you. Once the ambulance gets here, I'll let him know what happened and that you're okay."

Paige coughed a few more times, shuddered, and went completely still.

He frowned. "Paige?" His fingers went straight to her neck to check for her pulse. She had stopped shivering, and her breathing seemed to be getting worse, not better. "Jack, we can't wait any longer."

"I agree. We'll drive her to the hospital ourselves." Jack climbed into the driver's seat.

Ryan slid Paige onto his lap, hoping his body heat would help to warm her. Realistically, he knew that was pretty pointless. His clothes were still soaked, and his own body was shivering relentlessly, but he couldn't not try to do something. Grabbing his and Jack's discarded coats, he wrapped them around Paige, who was completely unresponsive now.

"Jack, drive quickly."

* * * * *

4:20 A.M.

Faith was so tired.

It was a weird kind of tired. Her brain felt all stuffy. Like someone had packed it with cotton wool. Her limbs felt weird too. Heavy and useless and kind of numb.

Her whole body felt fuzzy.

She recognized the feeling.

She'd felt it before.

Someone had drugged her.

At that realization, panic sliced through her, cutting away some of the fuzziness.

Faith tried to make her brain work properly. To think things through. Maybe there was a logical explanation to why she felt like she'd been drugged.

Only, Faith couldn't think of a single one.

As her brain slowly began functioning again, she started to become aware of her surroundings.

She was lying on something soft—most likely a bed.

Immediately, fear overwhelmed her. Had she been raped? She was a young woman and she lived alone; it was a definite possibility.

When she attempted to move her arms and legs, Faith found that she couldn't. They were bound. Not with something hard though, it didn't feel like duct tape, or plastic ties, or even handcuffs. She was tied up with something soft, maybe strips of cloth.

Garnering up enough courage, Faith tried to open her eyes.

And found she couldn't.

She had a blindfold on. Again, it was soft, probably the same as whatever had been used to bind her.

Without thinking, she tried to scream.

But again, she couldn't.

She was wearing a gag—not a good one; the material went between her lips, cutting into the edges of her mouth. She could make some sound, just not enough for anyone to hear her.

How had she not noticed all these things the second she returned to consciousness?

Probably because this was all so surreal.

These things just didn't happen.

You didn't just wake up tied to a bed with a blindfold and gag on.

And yet, there was no denying that this was real.

She really was lying here tied to a bed with a blindfold and gag on.

Her biggest fear was that she'd been raped.

It felt like her clothes were still on. That had to be a good thing. And it didn't feel like she'd been touched down there. That had to be a good thing too.

But if whoever had done this to her hadn't raped her, then what was he planning to do?

Maybe he was waiting until she was conscious before sexually assaulting her.

She didn't have any enemies and she couldn't think of a single person who would want to hurt her.

Faith lived a pretty normal life.

She had a boyfriend, a job, friends, and a house. She liked to paint and ride horses. She didn't know any crazy people. Did that mean that whoever had done this was a stranger?

What kind of stranger would break into her home and tie her up?

The answer to that was beyond terrifying.

It would only be someone violent and vicious, who intended to hurt her and probably kill her.

And kill her how?

Fast or slow? Painfully? Was he going to rape her first? Or torture her?

Faith's fear was mounting so quickly it was now nearly overwhelming.

She needed facts.

Facts would help her to remain calm.

If she couldn't use her sense of sight to figure things out, then she would have to use her other senses.

She didn't think she was still in her home.

It didn't smell like her home. She always had scented candles lit and the smell would linger long after the flame extinguished. And right now, she couldn't smell any of her favorite scents. When she inhaled deeply through her nose, Faith could smell cold and damp and dirt. Not only was she not in her own house, but it smelled like she wasn't even *in a house* anymore.

It didn't feel like her home either. The bed felt different. She was a restless sleeper and found she slept a little sounder on a really good quality mattress. Hers had been expensive, but a good investment. It was so soft it was like sleeping on a cloud. What she was lying on now was nowhere near that soft. It felt thin and cheap. And the air was as damp and cold as it smelled. If it hadn't been for the fact that someone had tucked a blanket around her, she would have been too cold.

Faith knew she wasn't in a house. She was in some sort of barn or shed or maybe even a basement of some sort.

That meant that someone had gone to all the trouble of setting up a bed, then taking her from her home, transporting her here, and tying her up.

None of that could be a good thing.

People who went to that much trouble always had a reason.

But what was the reason?

Who had done this?

It was driving her crazy that she didn't know.

If she didn't know who had abducted her and why, then how was she going to get out of here?

She couldn't do this anymore.

Her panic was rising rapidly once again.

It was like her fear had manifested into hundreds of tiny bugs, crawling all over her skin. Faith hated bugs. Hated the feel of tiny scratchy feet on her flesh. And right now, that was exactly what her terror was feeling like. The hundreds of imaginary bugs felt like they were growing to thousands and then millions until her whole body felt covered with them.

She squirmed, trying to rid herself of the sensation, but it was completely useless. It was strangling her. Swarming up her body from her toes toward her mouth. She screamed through the gag, the sound nothing more than a muted moan of distress.

Losing complete control of herself, Faith began to thrash desperately. She wanted to be away from here. She wanted to be home. She didn't want to be hurt. She didn't want to die.

She had faced death, stared it in the face eight months ago and survived. She had thought the worst was behind her. She was finally starting to move on. To live again. And now she was going to lose it all.

It wasn't fair.

She didn't want to die.

Abruptly, she went still.

Her violent thrashing loosened the bind on her left wrist.

Not a lot, but enough to allow her to move it a little.

Enough that if she worked at it she may be able to free it.

Enough to give her hope.

If she could free her left wrist then she could untie her right wrist. And then her ankles. And then she'd be free.

* * * * *

4:27 A.M.

It made him feel good to watch.

Faith was so pretty. He could watch her for hours. He *had* spent hours watching her in the eight months since they'd met.

Poor Faith had been a mess back then. She had been so scared and so sad and had needed so much tender loving care and support. He had been more than happy to offer it.

He couldn't deny his attraction to her had been immediate.

She was petite, of Chinese descent, with gorgeous almond-shaped brown eyes and long, shiny black hair. And Faith wasn't just beautiful; she was smart too. And funny and kind and sweet. She was amazing.

He knew he was very lucky to have this time with her.

He wasn't good with women.

He never seemed to get it quite right. He always said and did the wrong thing. He scared women off. He didn't mean to, but he always seemed to even when he was trying his best not to.

Perhaps Faith could help him with that. Teach him how to talk to a woman. He'd dated a few times, but it never really went anywhere.

Maybe it was because he came on too strong? He really wanted a serious relationship. He wanted commitment and marriage and a family. Only, he didn't know how to get it.

He had some time to try and figure it out. Faith would be staying with him for a while. Because of that, he'd tried his best to make sure she'd be comfortable during her stay. He'd set up a bed for her to rest on and made sure there were blankets so she didn't get cold. He'd had to restrain her; it may take her a while to come to terms with why he was doing what he was, but he'd made sure to use some of Faith's silk scarves so the binds wouldn't cause her pain.

He was glad that he would get to spend some time with her. Glad but also a little apprehensive. He thought that he and Faith got along well. She always talked nicely with him, but what if he had read her wrong?

Or what if she was angry that he'd brought her here?

He was hoping that, once he had explained his reasons to her, she would understand.

It made perfect sense.

His motives were pure.

There was so much crime in the city. He had to do something to put a stop to it.

The police didn't try hard enough. They let so much crime go unpunished. They needed some motivation to do better. Didn't they know that people were counting on them?

Well, he was going to do something about it.

He was going to push them into doing better.

They should be anyway. It was their job, after all. Their job was to protect people and to keep them safe. So why were there so many innocent people being hurt?

It was unacceptable.

He didn't want to see it anymore.

He was making it his life goal to see crime eradicated.

He was The Protector.

Faith would understand that. She would understand why he'd had no choice but to bring her here. She wouldn't be angry with him. She'd be proud.

* * * * *

4:32 A.M.

"How's she doing?" Jack looked at him in the rear-vision mirror.

"She's still breathing," Ryan replied. Beyond that, he had no idea how serious Paige's condition was. She hadn't woken up again, hadn't stirred at all, just lay there in his arms. Thankfully, they were only minutes away from the hospital where their younger brother, Mark, was waiting for them. Given that they still didn't know who the stalker was, Ryan wanted to limit the number of people who had access to Paige.

"We're almost there." Jack was speeding as fast as was safe in the bad weather.

"Come on, Paige, hang in there," Ryan murmured to his partner. With the heater blasting, the temperature in the car had risen enough that he was no longer all that cold, although his clothes were still quite wet. However, the heat hadn't seemed to touch Paige. She was still so cold, and she still wasn't shivering. It was like her body temperature had dropped too low, and now her body just wasn't capable of warming up on its own.

"Ryan, she needs twenty-four-hour-a-day security from now on," Jack spoke up. "I know she agreed earlier to let Xavier stay with her and Elias at night, but I don't think that's enough. She shouldn't be at work until this is over, and we need to discuss with her the possibility of a safe house."

14

Ryan agreed. The only problem was he wasn't sure Paige would. She was a cop; she didn't think she needed protection; she thought she could handle the stalker on her own. They needed a lead, but so far, they had zero clues as to the stalker's identity.

"Maybe it might be best if you two weren't partners anymore," Jack continued gently.

"What?" he growled at his brother. Ryan knew Paige sometimes thought about asking for a new partner, but he'd thought that was because she was uncomfortable that he'd seen her close to death, and she had somehow got it into her head that that meant he could no longer trust her to have his back.

"I know you two are close, but we're talking about her life here. You know I love Sofia, she's like a sister to me, and I'm not blaming her, she's not responsible for her stalker's actions. But the facts are that Paige's life is in danger because of Sofia and you," Jack reasoned.

"There are no guarantees that the stalker would leave her alone just because we stopped being partners. He still thinks we cheated on Sofia, so he's probably not going to stop going after her," he objected. There was no way he was going to stop working with Paige; he didn't want a new partner, and he didn't need one. What they needed was to catch the stalker. That was the only thing that was going to keep Paige safe.

"It's not just about you, Ryan. You're not the only one who cares about her. Paige and I dated; she's important to me too. And to all her other friends and her family and her husband. No one wants to see anything else happen to her. We don't have any leads on the stalker, and right now our focus has to be on her safety, and I'm not sure that her remaining your partner is going to ensure that."

Was he being selfish? He and Paige had been partners for close to ten years now. Even thinking about having another partner depressed him. But his brother was right. He wasn't the only one who cared about Paige. She had a husband who loved her, parents, siblings, nieces and nephews, friends—a lot of people who would be devastated if anything happened to her.

"We're here," Jack announced.

For the moment everything else fled his mind as he balanced a still-unconscious Paige in his arms as he climbed from the car and hurried toward his younger brother. Mark was a trauma surgeon and worked at this hospital. Mark also didn't look like he was too pleased with them.

"Why was she on her own? The stalker already tried to get to her twice tonight."

He ignored his brother's frustrated questions, since there was no good answer to them. "She's really cold, Mark," Ryan told him.

"Give her here." Mark held out his arms and Ryan passed him Paige. "Give me a rundown of what happened," he demanded as they headed for the door.

"We found her unconscious in her submerged car. The seat belt had trapped her. We got her out of the river, but she wasn't breathing, so we performed CPR." Ryan paused as Mark muttered and started walking faster with Paige. "She started breathing again so we got her to the car and out of her wet clothes. The ambulance was taking too long, and she was too cold, so we drove her here ourselves."

"Has she regained consciousness?"

"Briefly."

"Was she lucid?"

"Yes, and I got her to tell me if she had feeling in her hands and feet. She did, and she could also move them. She said her chest hurt; we probably cracked or broke some ribs performing CPR. Other than that, I don't think she's badly hurt, Mark. It's hypothermia I'm worried about," Ryan said anxiously.

"You two wait here," Mark ordered as they entered the ER. "And, for goodness' sake, change out of those wet clothes before I'm treating all three of you for hypothermia."

"We should have gotten her here sooner," he murmured as he watched his brother carry Paige away.

"We got her here as quickly as possible," Jack reassured him. "We did everything for her that we could; now we just have to trust Mark to take care of her."

"Yeah," he agreed distractedly. Guilt was swamping him. Again. Four and a half years ago he'd left Paige alone, knowing someone was after her and that she was distracted, and she had nearly been killed. Tonight, he'd done the exact same thing.

"I'm going to go grab some scrubs and change then go check on Laura. You should change too and then go and tell Sofia what happened. She's going to be out of her mind with worry."

"Yeah," he agreed again, knowing he should but not wanting to tell his wife that, once again, Paige had been almost killed by her stalker until he at least knew that Paige was going to be okay.

Watching Jack hurry off, Ryan attempted to rouse enough enthusiasm to go and get out of his wet clothes. He almost welcomed the chilly numbness it brought as it distracted him a little from his near all-consuming guilt.

"Ryan!"

Turning, he saw Paige's husband, Elias, rushing toward him. The sight brought back a horrible sense of déjà vu. Although, maybe that was a good thing. Last time, Paige had survived; hopefully, this time she would too.

"Where is she?" Elias demanded.

"Mark has her."

"How bad is she?"

When he'd called Elias from the car, all he'd told him was that the stalker had run Paige's car off the road and into the river and to meet them at the hospital. "She wasn't breathing when Jack and I pulled her from the car."

Elias gasped. "She's not dead, is she?"

"No," Ryan assured him. "We did CPR, and she started breathing again. But she's hypothermic."

"This is a nightmare." Elias began to pace, nervously running his hands through his thick, dark hair. "Did you at least catch the stalker?"

"No, I'm sorry."

"Well, do you at least know who it is?"

"No. I'm sorry, Elias. But we'll get him."

Elias arched a disbelieving brow. "Paige can't go on like this; it's going to kill her. She still has nightmares at least once a week, and some nights I wake up and she's not in bed. Do you know where I find her?"

Assuming that was a rhetorical question, Ryan kept silent and allowed Elias to get his anger out of his system.

"I find her in the library, curled up in a rocking chair, crying her eyes out."

"I didn't know it was that bad." Ryan was upset Paige hadn't confided in him.

"Paige didn't want you to know. She didn't want you to worry about her. Ryan, I'm serious—she can't go on like this, or it *is* going to end up killing her." Elias' brown eyes were filled with unshed tears.

"We will find him," he said because he couldn't think of anything else to say.

Guilt flashed across Elias' face. "We argued," he said softly. "I was angry with her because she wouldn't come home after the car thing. I yelled at her. I was so angry with her for not taking her safety seriously enough. She hung up on me. Now I might never get a chance to apologize and tell her how much I love her."

"You know Paige knows you love her," Ryan reprimanded gently. "And she isn't angry with you. She wanted to make sure that I called you."

Elias' gaze shifted to something behind him. "Mark, how is she?"

"Her body temperature dropped very low, her pulse and respiration rates are low. To manage her breathing we put her on a ventilator. To get her body temperature up we're using heated blankets, warmed fluids via an IV, and we may have to irrigate body cavities with warmed fluids as well," Mark explained.

"Can I go and see her?" Elias looked desperate to see his wife.

"Yes, I'll take you to her. No, you can't," Mark snapped at Ryan before he could open his mouth and ask to see Paige as well. "You can go and get out of those clothes like I told you to. Then you can go see your wife."

Mark led Elias off and Ryan reluctantly grabbed some scrubs and changed in the bathroom. He couldn't put off telling Sofia what had happened any longer. As soon as he opened her door, his wife's terrified silvery-gray eyes all but jumped at him.

"Paige?" was all Sofia said.

"She's alive, but she's badly hypothermic." Ryan perched on the edge of her bed and relayed the events of the last hour.

"Ryan, I don't know how to make him stop. I feel so helpless. How do I stop him if I don't even know who he is?" Sofia begged. Unfortunately, he didn't have an answer to that.

"Paige will have security on her permanently from now on," Ryan soothed, pulling his wife into his arms and holding her tightly. He could empathize with Elias; he knew what it was like to see the woman you love lying unconscious in a hospital bed.

Burying her face in his shoulder, Sofia cried for a few minutes then resolutely pushed away. "I have to figure out who he is. I'll go through the old recordings of the voicemail messages he left me. I'll figure it out."

Ryan wasn't sure that would help, but he was pleased that Sofia had something to do that she felt was constructive so she didn't let herself get bogged down with blaming herself.

"Tell me she's going to be okay." Sofia stared desperately at Mark as he entered the room.

"We'll have to wait and see," his brother replied.

"Mark, can you please take this thing out?" Sofia asked holding up the arm that still had the IV attached. "I feel much better—

fine, really—and I'm not lying in bed while Paige and Laura are here in the hospital."

"Okay," Mark agreed. His brother cast him a surreptitious glance as he set about removing the IV. "So, you finally changed your clothes. I thought you had some sort of death wish. Why would you leave her alone?" Mark growled. "You knew he wanted her dead, and yet you left her alone, and he almost succeeded in killing her."

"You think I don't already feel bad enough?" Ryan asked quietly. "I thought she was safe where she was. I didn't think he'd follow her to an active crime scene that was crawling with cops. Look, Mark, I know you're angry with me right now, but just make sure that you don't let anyone you don't trust near her. He's been following her around here all night. It makes sense that he could be a doctor or nurse here at the hospital."

* * * * *

1:51 P.M.

"Xavier."

Turning in the direction from which his name had been called, Xavier saw crime scene tech, Stephanie Cantini, climbing from her car. She was in her mid-forties, with curly, light brown hair and hazel eyes, and was one of his favorite crime scene techs to work with.

He had to stifle a yawn as he waited for Stephanie to reach him. Xavier was tired. It had been a *really* long night.

His partner, Jack, had called him last night to ask him to come to the hospital where his wife had stumbled upon a kidnapped teenager. Things had eventually worked themselves out but not before Jack's wife Laura had been held hostage and injured, as had one of the kidnapped girls. He had spent the last few hours sitting in the surgical waiting room while Eliza Donnan underwent life-saving surgery.

"Have you seen Paige?" Stephanie asked as she reached him, her hazel eyes brimming with concern.

"Yes." Xavier was feeling guilty about Paige almost being killed. She had been driving his car at the time, and he had given her the keys because he had ridden back to the hospital in the ambulance with Eliza. He knew how dangerous the stalker was—and how persistent. In fact, he had volunteered to move into Paige and Elias' house until the stalker was caught so she wouldn't be unprotected at night. It hadn't been a big deal. Since his girlfriend of five years had moved out of their home, there was nothing tying him to it anymore. Leaving Paige alone, even if he'd thought she was in a safe place, had been a mistake. A mistake that could cost Paige her life.

"Is she doing okay?"

"Mark says she's improving—her core temperature was rising."

"Is she awake?"

"No, Mark has her sedated."

"Why was she on her own if the stalker had already tried to kill her once last night?"

"She wasn't supposed to be on her own," he muttered.

"You're mad at her?" Stephanie asked understandingly.

"A little, which makes me feel bad. She's fighting for her life right now. I should have stayed with her and not gone with Eliza." If Paige didn't survive or suffered permanent damage, he was going to be battling his guilt for a long time.

"How's Laura?" Stephanie asked.

"She's sedated too. She lost a bit of blood from the neck wound, but so far, they seem to have been able to stop her contractions." Laura was thirty-four weeks pregnant with her second child, and the stress of her abduction and attack had caused her to start having premature contractions.

Stephanie shook her head. "What a night!" she exclaimed.

"At least everyone other than Malachi came out of it alive."

Casting a glance at the house they stood in front of, he said, "Let's hope that Faith Smith is as lucky."

Faith Smith was twenty-three years old—a pretty, petite, young Chinese woman, who worked as an IT specialist at an elementary school. A couple of hours ago her boyfriend had returned home from a business trip to find her missing. With some signs that Faith hadn't left of her own free will they were treating it as a kidnapping until they knew otherwise.

"You working this one solo?" Stephanie asked as they headed inside.

"For now, at least," he replied. "If things settle down with Laura, then Jack will be back, but right now he wants to stay with her, so, for the moment, it's just me."

Xavier didn't mind working on his own. He had for a while after his last partner had gone on maternity leave, it was just that right now he seemed to be constantly finding himself on his own.

He was the only one of his friends not married, and with Annabelle moving out, he really wasn't even sure if they were still in a relationship or if it was over. Annabelle had claimed that she wanted to change and that she wanted to learn how to trust him and not shut him out. But he had never done anything to give her cause to doubt him. That was Annabelle's issue, and he had worked hard to help her overcome it.

He loved her and he wanted a future with her. He was thirty-seven years old, and this was not how he had envisioned this time in his life. By now he had thought he'd be married with kids, and yet he was virtually on the cusp of ending a five-year-long relationship.

Maybe it was time for him to accept that he was always going to be alone. His first marriage had ended after the stillborn death of his daughter and his now ex-wife, Julia, landing in jail. Why should things with Annabelle turn out any better?

"Xavier?" Stephanie poked him in the side.

"Yeah?"

"You are a million miles away. Which I guess makes sense given everything going on with Paige and Laura. And with Annabelle," Stephanie added sympathetically. "Right now, you need to be focused, though. Faith Smith is counting on you. So, as I was asking you, why do we think this is an abduction? Faith is an adult, and she's only been missing a few hours."

"Boyfriend came home at lunchtime and found the back door wide open and no sign of Faith. Her wallet, keys, car, and phone were all still here."

"Signs of a struggle?" Stephanie asked as they paused on the porch.

"That's all I know," Xavier replied. When his lieutenant, Belinda Jersey, had called to give him the case, she hadn't offered many details. Or perhaps she had, and Xavier had just been too distracted to take much notice. Still, he preferred to enter a crime scene for the first time with a fresh slate, so he didn't make assumptions based on information he already had.

"I'll go check out the back door." Stephanie, with her case in hand, disappeared around the side of the house.

Before heading indoors, Xavier took a moment to study the front yard. It was small but immaculate. The yard was ringed by a perfectly manicured hedge, and in the middle of the rectangular lawn was a topiary tree done in the shape of a penguin. Either Faith was an avid gardener, or she used a company.

Stepping inside the little house, Xavier saw that the penguin theme continued. He spotted a penguin clock on the wall, a penguin cookie jar on the bench in the kitchen, a pair of penguin gumboots, a penguin umbrella by the front door, and several penguin pillows on the couches.

The downstairs of Faith's house was basically one room. On a small table by the door sat a handbag, a set of keys, and a cell phone. A desk sat under the front window to his left. Directly in front of him were the stairs leading to the second floor. There were two white leather couches positioned in a V shape around the TV. The kitchen split the room into two halves—the living room at the front and a dining space at the back. There was a small room in the back, left corner of the room, which Xavier assumed was the laundry room.

Despite the penguin paraphernalia, there weren't many other personal touches. The furniture was sparse, and a couple of abstract paintings hung on the white walls. There were no photos anywhere that Xavier could see, which he thought was odd given how readily she displayed her collection of penguins.

As he surveyed the room, a few things immediately stood out to him.

There didn't appear to be any obvious signs of a struggle. He noted a book was lying open facedown on the coffee table. It looked like Faith may have set it down in a hurry, intending to return to it.

The table was set for six with glasses, bowls, and spoons. An empty tub of cookie dough ice cream sat on the kitchen bench alongside two empty bottles of soda. As he moved closer he saw that five of the bowls were dirty; coated in sticky ice cream residue.

That left one empty spot.

Faith had been expecting one more visitor.

"Steph?"

"Yeah?" The CSU tech looked up from the back door where she was dusting for prints.

"It look like a break in?"

"Nope. Why? You thinking she knew him? Let him in herself?"

"That's exactly what I'm thinking. The table is set for six, but one place was never occupied. She didn't clean up, the dirty ice cream bowls and glasses are still on the table, and the trash is still on the bench. Yet there is no other garbage about and no other dirty dishes. It doesn't look like the party ever finished ..."

Her eyes widened. "You think he kidnapped all five of them?"

"I don't know," Xavier replied, although he did indeed think it was a possibility. "Maybe he just came in late. The others had left, Faith was still expecting him, she would have let him in, probably never even considered him a threat."

"Could still be a stranger. Maybe everyone leaves, there's a knock at the door, she assumes either someone left something behind or maybe that the person who never turned up finally arrived, she opens the door and gets surprised by someone."

"Maybe," he said slowly. "But I don't like that empty spot at the table. If someone had canceled, they would have called, and she wouldn't have set a place for them. She was expecting someone who never turned up, and then just hours later, she's reported missing."

"We need to know who she was having over for ice cream last night." Stephanie was staring at the table. "They could be victims too."

"If he took five people at one time, he had to have made sure he'd have the upper hand. He was outnumbered; they could easily have taken him down. If it were me, I would have drugged the drinks. Then all I had to do was wait until they all passed out, bring the car up the driveway, then carry them out one by one."

"I'll get on the drinks immediately." Stephanie set about bagging everything on the table.

"To get Faith and the others—if there were more victims—to the car, he had to be physically strong. If they were unconscious, they would have been dead weight, and some could have been men."

"If there were multiple victims, he would have needed something big enough to transport all of them." Stephanie's eyes had gone bright with enthusiasm. "We'll check the driveway. We could get lucky and get tire treads."

"Most importantly we need to know if this was a single or multiple abduction." Xavier was already prioritizing things in his head. "I need to talk to the boyfriend. He might know who Faith was hanging out with last night, and if there was anyone who had a grudge against all of them."

Xavier was hoping that this was just someone with a grudge against Faith Smith. Because to abduct five people simultaneously was extremely brazen and confident. And an overly arrogant kidnapper was an enormously dangerous thing.

* * * * *

3:00 P.M.

Where was she?

How could she just disappear?

He knew there was no way that Faith would just walk off and not let someone know where she was going.

That meant someone had done something to her.

But who?

Bobby Kirk had been driving himself insane asking himself these same questions for the last three hours.

Ever since he'd let himself into his girlfriend Faith's house only to find the back door open and Faith nowhere to be seen.

Immediately he had known that something was wrong.

Faith had been through a traumatic experience eight months ago and was vigilant about her safety. She would *never* leave the back door open under any circumstances.

He needed to be doing something.

This waiting was killing him.

It felt like wasting time.

Faith was out there somewhere, and she needed him. He itched to be looking for her. When the cops had showed up at Faith's house, they had ordered him to come back and wait here for a detective to come and speak with him. He lived right across the street from her, and he had reluctantly agreed only because he didn't want to do anything to waste their time. He wanted them focused on Faith.

But that was over three hours ago.

He had waited long enough.

He was going to go and start searching for Faith himself.

Bobby was just gathering his things when there was a knock at his door.

All but flying to the front door, he flung it open so hard, it banged into the wall; Bobby barely noticed. "Who're you?" he demanded, hoping this was the detective he'd been waiting for.

"I'm Detective Montague," the man replied. "May I come in?"

Bobby wanted to say no. He wanted to order this man to stop wasting time and go and find Faith, but instead, he sucked in a deep breath and nodded. He led the detective through to the living room. "Drink? Something to eat?" he asked only out of courtesy and hoping the other man would decline.

"I'm fine," Detective Montague answered.

"Do you know where Faith is?" Bobby had to force it not to come out as a growl.

"No, we need your help to figure out what happened," the detective replied.

"I don't know what happened," he snapped, wanting to unleash all his pent-up frustration and helplessness on this man since he was the only person within range.

"When was the last time you spoke to Faith?"

"Before I got on the plane."

"And when was that?"

"Yesterday, early evening."

"You know I have to ask for proof that you were really on a plane when Faith disappeared."

"You think I would hurt her?" Bobby exploded.

"It's nothing personal," Detective Montague said calmly. "Statistics are that the significant other is often the perpetrator. Don't you want us to eliminate you as quickly as possible from our suspect pool, so we don't waste time on you that could be spent finding out what happened to Faith?"

He harrumphed because he didn't have a comeback for that. He *didn't* want the police wasting time investigating him because Faith may not have a lot of time. Without a word, he snatched his keys from the table in front of him and stalked off toward his car where his bag and plane ticket still sat in the trunk.

Outside, he froze.

His gaze was drawn against his will to Faith's house.

It was abuzz with activity. What looked like crime scene people were walking around with cases and collecting evidence. Cops were standing about talking, and when he glanced up and down the street, he could see a pair of cops knocking on a door.

"Don't watch that; you'll drive yourself crazy," a voice spoke softly behind him.

Turning slowly, he saw Detective Montague had joined him in the driveway. "What's happening to her right now?" Bobby desperately wanted the cop to tell him that Faith was perfectly fine and would come walking down his drive any minute now.

"I don't know," the detective answered honestly. "But you can help me find out."

Deliberately, he shoved away thoughts of what might be happening to Faith at this second. If he thought about it, he'd lose it. And that might cost the life of the woman he loved. Retrieving his plane ticket from his car, he handed it to Detective Montague and then headed back inside. Sinking down into one of the couches in the living room, he looked the detective in the eye. "How do I help you find Faith?"

"When you talked to her on the phone last night, how did she sound?"

"Normal. We didn't talk for long, just confirmed our lunch plans for today." Bobby wished that he had savored every second of that phone call. It could be the last time he ever talked to Faith and he had hurried her off the phone. Already late for his flight, his focus had been getting on the plane, getting settled, and then attempting to get some sleep.

"Did she mention any plans she may have had?"

"No, she was just going to chill out and then have an early night."

"She didn't talk about having visitors?"

At first, he didn't get why the detective was pushing the issue of whether Faith was having people over, but then he remembered Faith's table. When he'd entered her house earlier today expecting to find her waiting for him, he'd seen that the table had been set for six, although the significance hadn't hit him at first. When he'd searched the house and been unable to find her, he'd realized how unlike Faith it was to leave dirty dishes lying about and that had only served to heighten his panic that something awful had happened to her.

"Mr. Kirk? Did Faith mention having some friends over last night?" the detective repeated.

Slowly, he shook his head. "She didn't say anything."

"Was that unusual? For her not to tell you she was having friends over?"

He bristled at the implication that he and Faith weren't close. It was a sensitive topic. "If it was planned, she would have told me."

"Was it usual for her to have an impromptu gathering?"

Bobby was about to say no, but that wasn't quite true. It was possible that Faith would invite people over last minute. Especially one particular group of people.

"Mr. Kirk?" Detective Montague prompted. "Would she have invited friends over last minute?"

"Not friends," Bobby replied softly.

"Family?" The detective's unusual eyes, one hazel and one bright green, surveyed the room, clearly puzzled about why Faith's family hadn't come running right over.

"No, not family."

Confused, he asked, "Then who?"

"Her support group," he replied.

"Support group?" Detective Montague repeated. "Was she a recovering alcoholic? Drug addict? Gambler?"

"No, Faith didn't even drink, and she would *never* take drugs. She wasn't interested in gambling. She worked hard for her money and she wouldn't waste it on something frivolous," he explained, hating that he had to waste time explaining the woman he loved to this detective. How could the police find Faith when they didn't know a single thing about her?

"What then?"

Bobby sighed. He hated talking about this. Hated it because it had caused Faith so much pain and anguish. "Eight months ago, Faith was caught up in an armed robbery. She was working as a bank teller, four men came in, they had guns, they intended to rob the bank and run. The silent alarm was tripped, and the police showed up almost immediately, so the robbers ended up holding everyone in the bank hostage for sixteen hours. Faith wasn't physically harmed, but they made everyone strip down to their underwear. They thought it would make the hostages too embarrassed to try anything stupid. SWAT came in, rescued everyone, all eleven of the hostages were uninjured, and only one of the four robbers was killed."

The detective nodded. "I remember that. I didn't know Faith was one of the victims."

"Well, she was. I didn't know her then—not well, anyway. Obviously we're neighbors and I'd nod hello if I saw her, but we hadn't spoken. Faith's whole life was turned upside down. She quit her job, she broke up with her boyfriend, she was lost. I arrived home from the airport late one night and saw her sitting in the middle of her driveway crying. It was raining, and she didn't even notice that she was soaked. I brought her over here, dried her off, made her some hot tea and we talked for hours."

"You started dating after that?"

Giving a tight nod, Bobby was used to people disapproving of his relationship with Faith. Her family were the worst. "I would *never* hurt Faith. I know we aren't the most conventional of couples, but I love her. I want to spend the rest of my life with her," Bobby told the detective. He couldn't have the police wasting time investigating him when time was the one thing Faith didn't have.

"Faith's family doesn't approve of you?" Detective Montague asked even though it was clear he already knew the answer.

"They think I'm too old—I'm forty-nine, Faith is twenty-three. I'm divorced with three grown kids; Faith has never been married. I'm white; Faith is Asian. They don't like anything about me. I don't care, but it hurts Faith's feelings. She wants her family to support our relationship because she knows we're committed to the long haul. They think I'm a bad influence on her because she quit her job, but that was because she couldn't go back there after the hostage situation. It had nothing to do with me. Faith had never known what she wanted to do. She dropped out of college after only eighteen months and worked as a jeweler for a couple of years before moving to the bank."

"What does she do now?"

"She works at a school in the IT department, but she really loves it." A small smile lit his face as he thought of how happy Faith came home from work each day. "She's thinking of going back to study something related to kids, maybe teaching or play therapy or even child psychology."

"What about this ex-boyfriend that you mentioned she broke up with following the hostage situation? Could he be a threat to Faith?"

He considered it for a moment. "I doubt it. I've never met him, but the way Faith talked about him, he didn't seem like the kind to harm her. Apparently, he was quiet, kind of shy. She implied that neither of them was all that into the relationship, but their parents had set them up. I don't think he cared enough about Faith to hurt her just because she broke up with him."

"How long were they together?"

He shrugged. "A couple of years, I think. But, like I said, their parents set them up, and neither Faith nor Matt were into the relationship, but neither of them had the guts to tell their parents that and break up."

"We'll still need to talk to him. Do you have his name and contact information?"

"No, but I'm sure you can get it from Faith's parents when you talk to them."

"So, Faith has been attending a victim support group?"

"Yes, her therapist had recommended she try it out, but she hadn't when we first started going out. I convinced her to give it a go. She was reluctant at first, but I pushed. She wasn't comfortable talking to me about it, and I didn't want it to eat her alive, so I thought this was the perfect compromise. I kept pushing, and she finally agreed."

A flash of something, understanding maybe, crossed the detective's face. "Did she find it helpful?"

"Yes. I noticed a change in her almost immediately. She was more at peace. She didn't have as many nightmares. She was calmer, more in control. I think it really helped her to talk with people who truly understood what she was dealing with."

"Do you know the names of anyone in her support group?"

"No, none, sorry. I didn't ask questions. Faith wanted to keep that part of her recovery private, so I didn't intrude. Do you think that's who she was meeting with last night?" Bobby would guess it was as Faith didn't have a lot of friends, and she would drop everything for anyone in that group if they needed her.

"What do you think?"

"I can't think of any other friends she would agree to meet with on such short notice."

"What about her family? You said they weren't happy about your relationship. Would they have cause to do something to Faith?"

"No," he replied immediately. Bobby didn't like Jing and Miriam Smith, but he knew they loved Faith and would never hurt her. "Her dad doesn't keep good health, and her mom is blind. Neither of them would hurt her."

"What about your family? You have an ex-wife and three kids; how do they view your new relationship?"

He was unable to stop anger bubbling inside him at the thought of how his family had treated him since he told them he was seeing Faith. "My ex threw a fit, said I was embarrassing her, but she was the one having affairs—that's why we got divorced. And the divorce was final ten years ago. She's already been married and divorced again twice since then. My kids are all older than Faith: twenty-four, twenty-five, and twenty-six. My son is the one in the middle. He thinks it's cool, me being with a younger woman. He's been the only one who's supportive. Both my daughters have cut off complete contact with me. I love my kids, but they're all adults, and I love Faith. I don't care what anyone else thinks. I'm complete when I'm with her, and I intend to ask her to marry me."

Bobby couldn't allow himself to think that the engagement ring that was hidden in the spare bedroom closet would never be slid onto Faith's finger. He would get her back and he would propose and they would spend the rest of their lives together.

"Okay, Mr. Kirk, I have one more question, and it's a difficult one, but I need to know. Is there a chance that Faith may have harmed herself?" he asked gently, his eyes full of sympathy.

Even the suggestion that Faith would do that horrified him. It had never even crossed his mind. Bobby knew in his heart that Faith would *never* do anything to harm herself. She just wasn't that sort of person. Faith was a fighter. She didn't give up—ever. "Definitely not," he answered decisively.

With an expression that clearly displayed doubt, the detective pushed the topic. "Are you sure? She went through a major trauma, she quit her job, ended a long-term relationship, maybe she wasn't coping, decided to end things."

"No," Bobby repeated firmly. "Faith wouldn't do that. She was happy. *We* were happy. She was planning for her future, a future that excited her. There is no way she would kill herself."

"Okay." Detective Montague nodded, although Bobby had the feeling the detective was simply pacifying him. "I have to go, but I'm going to leave you my card. Call if you think of *anything*, no matter how small, that might be helpful."

"Wait." Bobby stood to block the detective as he went to leave. "I need to ask you a question, but I need you to promise to answer me honestly."

"Sure." Detective Montague's eyes were kind and sympathetic. Bobby knew the detective didn't believe he had done anything to Faith.

"What are her chances of surviving?" Bobby had to know. He had to know if he was ever going to be able to hold the woman he loved in his arms again. Whether he would get a chance to propose to her, to marry her, to give her the children she longed for.

"I'm sorry, Mr. Kirk, but I can't answer that for you." Detective Montague's face and tone were pained. "I wish I could. I wish I could give you some sort of definitive answer, but I can't. Faith's chances of survival depend on who took her and why. We will do everything we can to find her and bring her back to you alive and well, but I can't offer you any guarantees." The detective paused and drew a deep breath. "All I can tell you is to keep faith."

Bobby could do that.

He *would* do that.

He would put his faith not only in Detective Montague and his colleagues but also in Faith. She was a strong woman. She had survived hell once before, and she could do it again. If anyone could, it was his Faith.

NOVEMBER 5TH

2:36 A.M.

A presence beside her bed had her eyes fluttering open.

Eliza wasn't surprised to see Detective Xavier Montague sliding into a chair at her side.

This man had saved her life multiple times, and she had known him less than twenty-four hours.

She had been grabbed off the street five years ago—kidnapped by a man named Malachi, then brainwashed so he could keep her under control when she kept trying to escape.

When freedom had finally come tantalizingly within reach, she had been too afraid, too messed up inside to believe it.

If it wasn't for the man who sat beside her, she would still be cowering in a corner, terrified of Malachi and what he would do to her. But Xavier had helped her find strength she hadn't known she had and courage to overcome Malachi's brainwashing and help the police end his reign of terror.

However, she'd been seriously injured in the process.

Malachi had plunged a knife deep into her shoulder, nicking an artery and almost causing her to bleed to death. Xavier had been at her side, keeping pressure on her wound to slow the bleeding and then donating blood in the ambulance.

He had saved her life.

He was her hero.

He had been the first face she'd seen when she had awakened in intensive care. He'd told her she was going to be fine and that the family she hadn't seen in five years had arrived and was waiting to see her.

Then, he'd had to leave, but now he was back, and Eliza couldn't deny that she was a little bit relieved.

Seeing her family again after all those years had brought up so many conflicting emotions. She loved and missed them and was thrilled to be going home as soon as the hospital released her. And yet, on the other hand, she felt odd and uncomfortable around them. She was sure that they must have thought she was stupid for falling for Malachi's tricks and then allowing herself to be brainwashed.

She didn't feel that way with Xavier though.

With him, she felt at peace.

Eliza knew why Xavier made her feel so comfortable.

It was because he reminded her of the man she had loved.

She had been only eighteen when she was kidnapped, but she had already been lucky enough to find her other half. George Holden. She had thought that he'd have forgotten all about her in the years she'd been gone, but apparently, he hadn't. He was coming to see her. Eliza was almost more nervous about that than anything else. She didn't know if there was still anything romantic between them, or if after everything she'd been through, there ever could be, but even if there wasn't, she knew George would make a great friend.

"Sorry, I didn't mean to wake you." Xavier realized she was awake and reached over to take her hand.

"You didn't," she assured him. Her voice still sounded weak, but her doctors were pleased with how the surgery had gone and assured her that she would make a full recovery, although she would probably need quite extensive physical therapy to regain full use of her injured shoulder.

"How are you feeling?"

"Better." Really, she hadn't felt this good in a long time. The morphine drip in her arm took care of most of her pain, and the knowledge that she was no longer Malachi's prisoner was freeing. Malachi was dead. He could never hurt her, or anyone else, again, and that made her feel light. She had a chance at a life that she'd never thought she'd get.

"You're not in too much pain?" Xavier's eyes were full of concern.

It was so sweet of him to care. "No, I'm fine. Sore, but it's manageable. Mostly I'm just tired."

"Then you should get some more sleep."

Eliza was tired, and sleep sounded like heaven about now, but there was something she had to ask him first. Something she had to sort out. She needed to know that it was taken care of before she could properly relax. "I need to ask you something."

"Anything." He smiled at her.

"Maegan and Bethany ... they have their families, but what's going to happen to Hayley?" Two of the three girls who'd been kidnapped along with her, fifteen-year-old Maegan and nine-year-old Bethany, had already been reunited with their families.

"Well," he began, his tone gone serious, "she'll probably enter the foster care system. Her parents are deceased. Her only living relative is her grandmother, but she's old and keeps poor health. She can't care for Hayley."

"I spoke with her earlier. I had to know that my sister was safe, that she'd be looked after. She offered me custody." Eliza could feel tears filling her eyes. She loved Hayley, couldn't love the five-year-old more if she truly were her sister, but ...

"That's great," Xavier offered her an encouraging smile. "Then Hayley can stay with someone she already loves and trusts."

Tears began to spill down her cheeks. Eliza could feel them rolling slowly toward her chin. "I can't take her. I'm still messed up. I feel better, but I'm in no place to be raising a traumatized little girl." She was so afraid that she was being selfish. She would do anything for her sisters. Had done anything for her sisters. Had risked her life for them time and time again. Walking away from the child was the hardest thing she had ever done, and she was only doing it because she truly believed it was in Hayley's best interest.

"That's okay, honey," Xavier assured her. "We'll find her a good home."

Knowing she had no right to ask, she asked it anyway. "I was wondering if you would want to take her. You're everything that I would pick in a parent for her. You're strong and smart and kind and courageous. I'm sure Hayley's grandmother would be happy to give you custody. I was wondering if you would take Arianna too."

Eliza's heart broke having to ask someone to take her baby. Her feelings for Arianna were mixed. She loved the child because it was her child, but the baby was the product of rape, and she wasn't sure she could ever completely set that aside while looking at her daughter. She wanted Arianna to grow up in a home where she was loved unconditionally.

"Oh, sweetheart, that is so sweet of you. And I would have loved to raise your daughter and your sister, but I'm not in a good place right now. The woman I've been involved with the last five years ... she's ... well ... we're just not in a good place. I don't know if we're going to last. After everything they've been through, I would hate to get them settled only to unsettle them all over again."

"That's okay." Eliza tried to smile. How could she expect someone to take on the responsibility for Hayley and Arianna when even she couldn't?

"Hey." He hooked a finger under her chin and tilted her face so she was looking at him again. "I might not be in the best place to be taking on two little girls, but I know the perfect person to raise them. If you trust me."

Eliza nodded. She trusted Xavier implicitly.

"Remember my friend, Paige? The short brunette with the curly hair?" He continued when she nodded. "Well, unfortunately, she was attacked a few years ago by a man who's stalking a friend of ours and decided that Paige was hurting her. He tried to kill her and almost succeeded, thankfully, she survived, but her injuries were severe, and she can't have kids. She wants to be a mother so badly, but she's already had a few adoptions fall through. Paige is a cop. Her husband, Elias, is a firefighter. If I had to pick someone to raise a child of mine, I would pick them in a heartbeat. Paige is sweet and kind and compassionate and caring. She and Elias would make fabulous parents. But Arianna is your daughter. It's up to you."

Eagerly, she nodded. A weight had been lifted off her shoulders. Paige and Elias sounded like the perfect people to raise Hayley and Arianna. With a home for the girls sorted, Eliza felt herself becoming overwhelmingly tired. "I'll tell Hayley's grandmother. I'm sure she'll be thrilled. My dad is a lawyer; I'll ask him to draw up the papers immediately. I want to know that they're settled as soon as possible. Xavier, do you think they'll let me visit sometimes?"

"I'm positive. Sleep now, Eliza," he said softly.

"They can take the girls now," she said sleepily.

"Paige is here in the hospital. The stalker tried to kill her again, but I'm sure Elias would love to take them home. Are you sure about this, Eliza?"

"Positive."

"The stalker still wants to kill Paige, and he might try again," Xavier cautioned.

"I don't care. It's not her fault. Besides, you'll find the stalker, keep her safe." Of that, Eliza had no doubts. To her, Xavier Montague was like a superhero. Paige and her husband sounded like just the people she would want to raise those precious girls.

Content, Eliza drifted off to sleep.

* * * * *

7:42 A.M.

If she wasn't asleep before Mark came back, he was going to sedate her again.

Paige knew this and yet she still couldn't calm her brain enough to let her sleep.

Every time she closed her eyes, she was back in that car.

Strike that. She didn't even have to close her eyes to feel like she was back in the car.

Images of being stuck in the river kept assaulting her.

Relentlessly assaulting her.

She could feel the car bumping her about as it was rammed from behind. She could feel the freezing water slowly rising inch by inch from her feet until it reached the roof. She could feel her lungs screaming out to take a breath. She could feel her mouth opening against her will and water running in to fill her lungs.

Gasping and disoriented, Paige tried to force herself to remember that she was safe now.

Ryan and Jack had found her in time. They had pulled her from the submerged car and brought her to the hospital. Paige didn't remember anything after passing out in the car. It was all a blank until she woke up here at the hospital with Mark at her side and a tube down her throat to help her breathe. Mark had filled her in on what happened. Explained that she was hypothermic but they were treating her and optimistic about her prognosis.

To discover that she'd come so close to death again was terrifying. The stalker truly wasn't going to let her live. She would never have left the crime scene to come back to the hospital if she'd thought there was even a chance that the stalker had followed her there.

Panic was starting to flow through her—almost physically flow through her like it had invaded her body.

She was struggling to draw a full breath, which was ridiculous given that she had a tube looped from ear to ear delivering oxygen to her water-damaged lungs.

She was still cold—ice cold—despite the couple of heated

blankets that she was swaddled in. Right now, though, the blankets weren't helping her. They were making her panic grow. They reminded her of the water that had covered her just like a blanket, fully and completely until it had become her coffin.

A sense of claustrophobia so intense it made her feel physically ill swamped her and she shoved at the blankets, threw them off her and to the floor, yanked the IV from her arm, and climbed from the bed.

Immediately, she realized that was a mistake.

Getting up this soon had not been a good idea.

She should have listened to Mark and stayed in bed.

Light-headed, she swayed and nearly passed out.

"Whoa. I got you."

Strong arms suddenly wrapped around her, catching her as she collapsed, then lifted her up and set her back down on the bed. At first, Paige thought Mark had come back, but then she realized the voice was her partner's.

Keeping her eyes clenched shut as she fought violent waves of nausea, she attempted to breathe through it until the sensation passed. Not that there was anything left in her stomach to dispel. She'd already thrown up several times since she'd first awakened a couple of hours ago.

By the time she had the nausea under control enough to attempt opening her eyes, Ryan had already wrapped her back up in the blankets and was putting the nasal cannula back in place.

"I'm okay, Ryan," she tried to assure him although her voice came out as a weak rasp and wouldn't have convinced anyone, let alone her partner, who knew her well, that she was okay.

"You just about passed out," he contradicted. He eyed the blood trickling down her arm from where she had ripped out the IV. "I'll go get Mark to put another one of those in. I think you're still supposed to be getting fluids."

She grabbed his hand as he moved to stand. "I just want to go home, Ryan," she pleaded. She had made the same plea to Mark to no avail. "This place is making me claustrophobic." Paige had never suffered from claustrophobia in her life. She wasn't used to the feeling, although she suspected that she was going to become intimately acquainted with it.

"You are not going anywhere. You are staying right here in the hospital where Mark can keep an eye on you," Ryan informed her. "You almost died last night. No, no, let me correct myself. You *did* die last night; Jack and I had to perform CPR on you."

Mark hadn't told her that. Her chest ached, and Mark had told her that she had a couple of cracked ribs, but she'd thought it was from hitting the steering wheel as she was thrown around inside the car. Instead, it must have been from Ryan and Jack's lifesaving efforts. Tears filled her eyes. She was never going to be safe. The stalker was relentless. Her luck couldn't last forever. He was going to end up killing her.

"Hey." Ryan turned her face so she was looking at him. "He is *not* going to hurt you again, Paige. I won't let him. I am not leaving your side until we know who the stalker is and have him safely in custody. I want you in protective custody in a safe house until this is over."

Ryan looked at her as though he was waiting for her to argue. Only this time, Paige had no intention of arguing. She was so weak she couldn't even stand up and so tired she couldn't stay awake for more than a few minutes at a time. She couldn't protect herself, and if the stalker came after her now, she'd be a sitting duck.

"You're not going to fight me on it?" Ryan asked, surprised.

"I'm way too tired," she murmured. She wasn't just tired, but cold too. Those sixty seconds or so out of her little warm cocoon had her shivering again.

Ryan pressed the back of his hand to her cheek. "You're still cold. I'm getting Mark."

Before Ryan could move, the door swung open. "Did you tell her?" Xavier asked.

"Not yet. She was stupidly out of bed when I came in, almost collapsed. Could you go get Mark? She ripped out her IV and she's still too cold."

"Sure thing." Xavier disappeared again.

She stiffened instinctively. At the moment it seemed all she got was bad news, so she didn't have high hopes for anything Ryan had to tell her. "What's wrong?" she asked.

The smile he gave her was warm and his blue eyes were twinkling. "Absolutely nothing. It's good news, nothing for you to worry about."

Relaxing slightly, Paige let her heavy eyes fall closed and concentrated on trying to still the tremors wracking her body. She didn't bother opening them when she heard the door open and footsteps crossing to her bed.

"What happened?" Mark asked as he picked up her arm and set up a new IV.

"I came in, and she was standing up. She collapsed but I caught her before she hit the ground," Ryan explained. "Why is she still shivering?"

"Because it takes a while to recover from hypothermia. That's why I'll be keeping her here in the hospital for at least the next few days," Mark replied, voice tight with controlled anger. Then his tone gentled. "Paige, I need to check your temperature." He popped a thermometer in her mouth, and while he waited, he began to clean the blood from her arm from where she had ripped out the IV, placing a Band-Aid over the small cut.

"Is her temperature back up to normal?" Ryan asked when Mark removed the thermometer.

"No, it's still too low. She's not warming up as quickly as I'd like. What am I going to do with you?" She could feel him leaning over her. "Why'd you get up?"

She forced her eyes open. "I keep getting claustrophobic," she explained.

His blue eyes were full of sympathy. "I'm sorry, Paige. I wish I could help you out with that, but right now I need you still wrapped up in the warmed blankets, and I'm still giving you fluids, so I need the IV. And speaking of warmed blankets, I'm going to go get some more." Mark paused at the door when he realized Ryan hadn't followed him. "Why were you in here anyway?" he snapped at his brother.

"Would you prefer to have come in and found her passed out on the floor?" Ryan asked quietly.

Mark ignored that. "I told you to stay outside. She's weak, and she needs to rest to get her strength back."

"Xavier and I have to tell her something."

"Can't it wait?" Mark demanded.

Clearly her partner and his brother weren't getting along at the moment. If Paige had to guess she would say it was her fault. Mark was probably angry that Ryan had left her alone and she'd been hurt. But that wasn't her partner's fault. She had made the choice to leave the cemetery on her own. It was no one's fault but hers that the stalker had almost succeeded in killing her.

"No, it can't wait," Ryan replied.

Curiosity piqued, Paige looked from Ryan's grinning face to Xavier's. "What's going on?"

"Eliza wants you to adopt Hayley and Arianna," Ryan blurted out, his grin growing.

Surely, she must have heard that wrong. "What?"

Xavier perched on the edge of her bed and took her hands. "She can't raise Arianna herself because of how the baby was conceived. She's worried that she won't be able to set that aside and give her daughter a happy home. Hayley's grandmother offered her custody of Hayley, but she knows she's not in a place where she can be raising a child. She wants both the girls to have a real home and parents who love them. She asked me to take them but with things with Annabelle the way they are right now, I didn't think that would be fair to Hayley and Arianna, so I told her about you. She was thrilled. She wants you to have both the girls."

Paige had had her hopes raised too many times already to get them up again. "Does she know someone is stalking me and keeps trying to kill me?"

"She knows." Xavier nodded.

"What about in a few years, once she gets her life back, what if she changes her mind and wants the girls back?" Paige knew that would kill her, to get attached to the children, raise them as her own, only to have to give them up in a few years.

"She won't. All she wants is to be able to visit them sometimes, keep in contact with them, be the big sister she's always been to Hayley. Paige." Xavier squeezed her hand. "The papers are already being drawn up. Hayley knows, and she's thrilled. She really likes you. Once the papers are ready, you and Elias, and Eliza and Hayley's grandmother will sign them, then they'll be filed with the courts, but the girls are yours. Elias can take them home now."

It seemed too good to be true. She looked to Ryan, and he nodded. "It's all sorted, Paige."

"But they won't be safe with me. What if the stalker hurts them? I can't put two innocent little girls at risk," she protested.

"Paige, you're going to need to take time to heal and time to get the girls settled. You could take maternity leave, go away someplace for a while so you're out of harm's way until the stalker is caught. I was thinking that Sofia and I haven't had a vacation in ages. We could come too, and that way, I'd still be there to protect you if the stalker managed to track you down. As soon as you're released from the hospital we can pack up the four kids and get away. Sophie is the same age as Hayley, so it'll be a great way for Hayley to learn how to make friends and play with kids her own age. And Ned loves babies, he'll be fawning all over Arianna. It'll be a blast, you and Elias and Sofia and I and the kids will have a fabulous time."

Of that she had no doubt. She got along great with her

partner's wife; they were really good friends, and she adored Ryan and Sofia's five-year-old daughter, Sophie, and two-year-old son, Ned.

"Hey, maybe we can make it a family thing and convince Jack and Laura to come with Zach. And, Mark, you and Daisy and the kids could come too." Ryan looked to his brother, offering an olive branch.

He accepted it. "I do have some vacation time owed." Mark smiled. Then he grimaced jokingly. "But nine kids? That doesn't sound like a vacation to me." Mark and his wife had four kids: eleven-year-old Brian, who'd beaten leukemia when he was younger; eight-year-old twins, Elise and Eve, and five-year-old Tony.

"Xavier, you're in, too, right?" Ryan asked.

"Wouldn't miss it for the world," Xavier replied.

Paige had always felt a little jealous when she saw her friends or siblings with their children. It made her feel guilty because she didn't resent her brothers or sister or friends their families. It was just that seeing them so happy with their children made her think of everything she'd lost and thought she'd never have. Only now it seemed like, by some miracle, she had it—everything she'd ever dreamed of. "This is really happening?" She hardly dared to believe it was true.

"It's really happening," Ryan promised.

Turning wet eyes to Xavier, Paige asked, "How can I ever thank you for this?"

"You don't need to thank me." Xavier squeezed her hands. "Those girls deserve the best and you're the best. Hayley wants to come and see you. Only if you're up to it," Xavier added with a glance at Mark.

"I'm up to it," she replied immediately. Of course, they all knew she wasn't, but she didn't care. Nothing would stop her from seeing those girls. Her girls.

"Just for a moment, then she needs to rest." Mark smiled at

her.

Xavier left the room and a moment later the door swung open and Hayley rushed into the room like a tiny little tornado. "Paige, did you know that Eliza said that Arianna and I can go and live with you?" The little girl rushed the bed.

Struggling to hold back her tears, she didn't want to give the already emotionally sensitive child the wrong impression that she wasn't thrilled to pieces. "Yeah, I heard."

Hayley's expression turned serious as she studied her. "Did you get hurt?"

"Yeah, something like that. But see my friend Mark? He's taking really good care of me, and he'll make sure I get all better really quickly," she assured the little girl.

"Good because I can't wait to go home with you. I never had a real home, you know."

"I know, but we're going to fix that." Paige smiled at her, unable to believe that this amazing little girl was really hers.

"Paige?" Hayley climbed up on the bed and Paige helped to pull her up and then hugged her tightly.

"Yeah, honey?"

"Do I call you Mommy from now on?"

"That's up to you, sweetheart. You can call me Paige or Mommy or whatever makes you feel the most comfortable. It's okay if it takes a little while before you want to call me Mommy, and it's okay if you never want to call me Mommy." Although Paige would adore for both the girls to call her mom, she wouldn't push them—especially Hayley. She hadn't grown up like most children. She'd never had a mother, and Paige wanted the child to do whatever made her comfortable.

"I want to call you Mommy right now, is that okay?" The little girl's blue eyes looked anxiously up at her.

Unable to hold back her tears any longer, they trailed down her cheeks. "I would love that." She kissed the top of Hayley's head.

"Are you crying?"

"They're happy tears, baby," she assured the little girl. "Because I'm so happy that you and Arianna are going to come and live with us."

"That's good." Hayley snuggled her head down against her chest and closed her eyes. "I'm happy too."

Cradling the little girl in her arms, Paige met her husband's eye. Elias stood at the foot of her bed, holding a sleeping Arianna in his arms. Her husband had the same look of shocked joy on his face that she knew she must have.

At peace for the first time in five years, her own eyes drooped closed, as her exhausted body and mind hit the end of the road and she fell asleep.

* * * * *

10:29 A.M.

Xavier was distracted this morning.

Although this time it was a good distracted.

Every time he tried to focus on work he found himself thinking of the look on Paige's face when he and Ryan had told her about the adoption.

A part of him wished that it had been possible for him to keep Hayley and Arianna. To take them home, raise them with Annabelle, and give them the family they deserved. But he knew he'd made the right choice. For everyone. Especially the girls. And Paige really deserved some happiness.

He had agreed to go along on this big family vacation thing of Ryan's, but the prospect of spending time with four happy families while he was all alone was pretty depressing. He wanted what Jack, Ryan, Mark, and now Paige had. He wanted a family. If he could shake some sense into Annabelle, he'd do it in a heartbeat.

Xavier knew that she still loved him.

He knew that she wanted a family and a life with him.

What he didn't know was why she kept fighting it.

Rousing himself, he decided he couldn't spend any more time trying to figure out what went on in Annabelle's pretty head.

Instead, he looked at the four photos laid out on his desk.

Four other young women in their late teens or early twenties had gone missing the same night as Faith Smith.

Xavier had already cleared Faith's family.

Having spoken with Bobby Kirk, he didn't believe Faith's boyfriend had done anything to her. Still, he'd confirmed with the airline that the man had indeed been on the flight he'd claimed to be on. He may not have approved of the relationship given the massive age difference and the fact that both families were adamantly against it, because despite what Faith and Bobby thought, having your family's support meant a lot. But it wasn't his place to judge.

Although judging Bobby Kirk was exactly what Faith's parents did. Jing and Miriam Smith hated their daughter's boyfriend. Blamed him for everything they saw as a fault in Faith. But Xavier didn't believe they had anything to do with her disappearance. They were genuinely terrified at what might have happened to their only child.

He had also counted out Faith's ex, Matthew Xing. The quiet, intelligent, young Asian man that Faith's parents had so carefully picked out for her had already moved on and married in the eight months since Faith broke up with him. Matt had backed up what Bobby had already told him. Neither he nor Faith were into the relationship but neither one wanted to be the one to disappoint their parents. He'd been relieved when Faith broke up with him because there was another woman he was interested in—his now-pregnant wife.

Given that Bobby's family were so vehemently opposed to his new love interest, Xavier had paid both the ex-wife and all three grown kids a visit. As Bobby had mentioned, his ex had been remarried twice, both times to much older and wealthier men since their divorce. Her dislike of Faith seemed to be based more on the fact that Bobby had found someone he truly loved rather than that Faith was so much younger.

Bobby's son was supportive, although a little too supportive in Xavier's mind and he wondered whether the son actually had a crush on his father's woman. If he hadn't had an ironclad alibi—he was a fire fighter and busy putting out a blaze on the other side of town at the time Faith disappeared—Xavier would have been interested in him.

Both Bobby's daughters were mortified that their nearly fifty-year-old father was dating a woman younger than them. They had mocked Faith, claiming she was a gold digger, although neither seemed to have spent any time around her. But the majority of their anger was directed at their father. They felt betrayed, let down, replaced. Although they were both grown women they seemed to have believed that their father should have ended his relationship with Faith on their say-so. However, Xavier suspected that if either of them had planned revenge, it would more likely have been directed at Bobby than Faith. At the moment, he didn't consider either of them viable suspects.

Interviewing family had taken most of the rest of his day yesterday and had yielded no real leads other than the possibility that it was linked to the trauma survivors support group.

That possibility was intriguing.

What reason would someone from the support group have to hurt another member of the group?

At the moment, Xavier couldn't come up with one.

Perhaps someone had unrequited feelings for Faith. Pressured her to break up with Bobby Kirk, and when she wouldn't, lost his temper and took his anger out on her.

Perhaps someone had infiltrated the group for the express purpose of getting close to the already emotionally vulnerable attendees for sinister purposes. Sociopaths were manipulative and often smart, and a group of traumatized women would be a ripe pool of victims to choose from.

Or, then again, perhaps it was simply random and had nothing to do with either Faith Smith or the support group.

It all hinged on whether Faith had been taken alone, or if the people she'd had over for ice cream were also victims.

Hence the reason he was staring at these four photos. Were these missing young women taken by the same person who took Faith?

Ruby McBrady was twenty-one. She was a tall, pretty, blonde college senior with amazingly bright green eyes. She had been reported missing by her boyfriend when she never made it home after her shift at the supermarket where she worked after school.

Mackenzie Willows was a blue-eyed redhead, age twenty-five. She owned and ran a nightclub. She had been reported missing by her husband when she disappeared from their nightclub and then never returned.

Ava Burns was a college freshman, a beautiful nineteen-year-old with dark skin, dark eyes, and dark brown hair. She had been reported missing by her parents when she never returned to their house to pick up her three-year-old son after her classes and they couldn't contact her on her phone.

The last young woman to go missing the same night as Faith was one he'd met before. Vanessa Adams was now a twenty-two-year-old librarian. She still had the same large brown eyes and ash-blonde hair she'd had when he'd first met her. Back then, she'd been a little chubby, but in this current picture, she was thin. Too thin.

Vanessa Adams and her family had been victims in the case that brought Annabelle into his life. A man out for revenge on his neighbors had set about killing families and leaving one person behind. Starting with Annabelle's family, he worked through several others. The big finale was supposed to be Vanessa's family. Only he and his then-partner had interrupted him. Not in time to save the entire Adams' family but in time to save the then seventeen-year-old Vanessa and her father, Barney.

And now, Vanessa was missing. The young woman had been through enough. She had watched her grandparents, mother, and younger brother slaughtered in front of her eyes, and then Ricky had slit her throat in an attempt to buy himself time to get away.

He had saved Vanessa's life that night, putting pressure on her wound so she didn't bleed out before help arrived. Xavier felt responsible for her. Even if Vanessa's disappearance had nothing to do with Faith's, he would find her.

Xavier was still intrigued about the mystery guest who never arrived at Faith's house that night. He needed to find out who it was. And he needed to find out if Ruby, Mackenzie, Ava, and Vanessa knew Faith Smith. Since Vanessa had also been a victim, it was plausible that she was now in a support group. That meant two of the five young women who went missing on the same night had both been previous victims of crime. Maybe Ruby, Mackenzie, and Ava were too. He would interview their families and friends today. If they all attended the support group, then it was reasonable to believe that they were victims of the same assailant.

He picked up his phone, intending to call the relatives of the four missing women and set up interviews with them. Instead, he found himself contemplating calling Annabelle. Maybe she just needed him to come running after her one more time. Just once more to assure herself that he truly did love her. Yet he had already gone running off after her more times than he could count. He had proposed twice and been turned down both times. What more proof did Annabelle need that he loved her and wanted her?

No, the ball was in her court now. She'd asked for space and he'd give it to her. If she didn't truly want to be with him, then he was fighting a losing battle trying to convince her he wanted to be with her.

SIX

* * * * *

Just a little more and she'd be free.

Faith had been working on freeing just that one hand since she'd first woken up. She didn't know when that was, but it felt like well over twenty-four hours, maybe even closer to thirty-six.

Her persistence and perseverance had paid off. She was close. Very close.

It hadn't helped that she had to pause several times and try and hide what she'd been up to.

Every time *he* came.

She didn't know who he was. He never spoke, and with her blindfold on, she couldn't see a thing.

The man came often, taking off her gag and giving her food and water. The first time he'd come he'd virtually given her a heart attack. She had been so focused on attempting to free her hand that she hadn't realized anyone was in the room with her until she'd felt the cold metal of the gun pressed against her head.

Startled, she had thrashed violently for several minutes, until she wore herself out. A couple of minutes had been all the fight she'd had in her. That was a worrying thought. But the drugs had left her drained and shaky and she hadn't eaten or had anything to drink, so she didn't have a lot of strength.

The mystery man had simply waited until she exhausted herself, shoved the gun into the side of her head so she remembered it was there, and took the gag off. The implied threat of the gun made it clear that she should keep her mouth shut, and although every molecule of her body screamed at her to yell for help, she didn't. Instead, she ate the sandwich and drank the water he offered her.

Part of her had wanted him to take her to the bathroom. She

had already been forced to urinate three times. Faith had tried so hard to hold on, but there was only so long she could do that before her body just had to release itself. She had been humiliated but there was nothing she could do about it. She had to poo twice as well. That had been substantially more mortifying, and she had held it in for as long as possible, but the inevitable had eventually happened.

As awful and degrading as this all was, she had bigger problems right now than being embarrassed.

Which was why only part of her had wanted him to let her use a toilet. If he untied her and took her someplace else when he brought her back to the bed, and she had no doubt he would, he would tie her up again. And that time he might make everything too tight.

While she had been working on loosening her hand, Faith had been trying to figure out who might have taken her. The last thing she remembered was having ice cream with her friends. They'd been chatting, laughing, encouraging one another.

And then nothing.

Faith couldn't remember a single thing after that until she woke up here.

Had her friends gone home before she was taken?

Had one of her friends done this?

Had her friends been taken too?

If they had, was that a good or a bad thing?

She fought off tears. She had to stay strong. She had to fight. She had to get back home. Bobby was waiting for her.

Her boyfriend was the only good thing to have come out of the bank robbery. Those sixteen hours had been the most terrifying of her life. But she had stayed strong, calm, in control, even helping to calm others. She'd known that hysteria and panic would make the four hostage takers more likely to harm them. It wasn't until it was all over that she had fallen apart. Paramedics at the scene had taken her to the hospital where she had been sedated and treated for shock.

When she'd managed to pull herself back together she had realized that life was too precious to waste, so she'd started making some changes. Quitting her job and breaking up with her boyfriend had been the first.

Bobby had been the biggest.

That her family hated him upset her but not enough to make her give him up. She loved him. Completely and deeply. She wanted to spend the rest of her life with him. She didn't care that he was old enough to be her father or that his kids thought she was a gold digger. Faith had found the engagement ring that Bobby had hidden in the closet of his spare bedroom. She couldn't wait for him to propose and for their lives together to begin.

What must Bobby be going through right now, wondering what had happened to her? What would he go through if she never made it back to him alive?

She couldn't do that to him. Couldn't put him through that. She had to fight.

And with that, her left wrist came free.

Immediately her hand went to her face, tugging at the blindfold until it came off. It took a moment for her eyes to adjust, even though the light in the room was dim, and then she surveyed her surroundings. No wonder she had been able to smell dirt earlier. The walls, floor, and ceiling all seemed to be made of tightly-packed dirt. She was in a small room, maybe eight feet by eight feet. There were no windows, and the only furniture in it was the bed she was tied to and a chair beside it. On the far wall was a door. Faith knew she had to get to that door.

Without wasting any more time, Faith ripped off the gag, debating whether to call for help. The man who took her could be nearby. He could come back with his gun and shoot her. Deciding it would be best to keep the element of surprise, she kept her mouth shut and attacked the knot at her right wrist.

Faith had thought that once she had one hand free the rest would be easy. However, working with the use of only one hand, and one that was stiff and heavy after hours of insufficient blood supply, made the task seem impossibly slow.

Once again, perseverance paid off and eventually her right wrist came free. Briskly, she rubbed her hands to try and restore circulation, then she set to work on her ankles. Now that she had both hands to use it didn't take her long to get free.

Launching herself off the bed, Faith ran as quickly to the door as her numb legs allowed. She half expected it to be locked, but it wasn't.

On the other side of the door was another room, about the same size as the one she had just left. Again, all the walls, floor, and ceiling were made of packed dirt. There were two other doors and a set of steps leading to one more. Attached to the walls were several sets of chains, but Faith didn't have time to worry about what her abductor intended to use those for.

She headed straight for the stairs. Her legs were still leaden, and she had to lean heavily on the handrail to drag herself up the rickety wooden staircase. At the top, she all but flung herself at the door, but bounced off it.

It was locked.

Despairingly, she beat her hands against the heavy steel door.

That was unfair.

She'd gotten free. She'd gotten this far. She couldn't be trapped.

"No, no, no, no, no," she screamed, thumping wildly on the door, no longer caring if the man with the gun came back and shot her. If she didn't get out of this room, she was dead anyway. "Help! Can anyone hear me? Is anyone out there? My name is Faith Smith. I need help. Someone kidnapped me. I'm trapped in here. Help me, please, someone help me!"

Faith continued to scream pleas for help through the door, alternately banging on it and twisting the handle, until her voice no longer worked properly. Breathing raggedly, she sank to the floor and leaned against the door as she struggled to control herself.

No one was coming.

That was clear.

Wherever this underground bunker was, it was obviously not near any people.

As her breathing calmed, pain in her hands became more noticeable. Glancing down at them, she saw they were bruised and bloody. Faith winced as she attempted to move them. Had she broken something? That wouldn't be good. If she had broken hands she wouldn't be able to defend herself against her abductor when he returned. Her only hope at escaping was somehow managing to knock him out or injure him so she could run. With broken hands she couldn't do that. And if he tied her back up she'd never be able to get loose.

With a final hiccupping sob, Faith wiped at her wet cheeks. The salty tears stung her injured hands. Despite the pain, the fear, and the panic that all pounded inside her, she wasn't ready to give up. She would search this place from top to bottom for a weapon, then figure out a plan. Perhaps she could hide under the stairs. They weren't enclosed, but if she kept the door to the room where she'd been held closed, when her attacker came back, he would have no cause to think she wasn't still tied up in there. Then as soon as he was down the steps his back would be to her and she could run up as fast as she could, lock him in here and then run for help.

Satisfied with her plan, she stood, then immediately froze.

She could hear something.

Muffled screams.

She had wondered whether her friends had still been at her house when she'd been abducted and had been taken too. Maybe they really were here.

Running down the steps, she eyed the two doors. Left or right?

It was hard to distinguish which direction the sounds had emanated from.

Picking right, Faith threw open the door, then gasped as she looked at the bed. The room was identical to the one she'd been held in, and on the bed lay Ava Burns.

"Ava." Faith ran to the bed.

Ava strained against her bonds and tried to talk through her gag.

"Hold on." Faith pulled off the blindfold and then the gag. "Are you okay?"

Ava gasped several breaths before nodding.

"Do you know if anyone else is here?" Faith was wondering whether the rest of their friends were also in the basement.

"I don't know. Where are you going?" Panic edged into Ava's voice as Faith moved away.

"Just to see if anyone else is in here, then I'll come and untie you," Faith promised. She'd untie Ava now, but the knots were tight, and it would take her several minutes. Before she did that, she needed to know if the others were here and if any of them were hurt.

There was another door in here in addition to the one she'd come in through. Opening it, Faith wasn't surprised by the scene she was met with. This time the woman in the bed was Vanessa Adams. Only, Vanessa wasn't moving.

Staggering to the bed, Faith still felt unsteady on her feet, she pulled off the blindfold and gag. Vanessa didn't stir. She slapped lightly at her face. "Vanessa?"

"Vanessa's in there?" Ava called through.

"Yes, but I think she's unconscious."

Leaving Vanessa for the moment, there was nothing she could do for her friend right now, so she went back to Ava. She had to get her free, then with two of them against this man they actually stood a chance at getting out of here.

With her damaged hands, it was difficult to make any progress with the knots. Her knuckles were bruised and bleeding, her fingers shaking and uncooperative. Every time she thought she was winning, her hands spasmed and she was forced to pause.

"What happened? Did he hurt you?" Ava asked.

"No, I hurt them on the door."

"I heard you. I didn't know anyone else was here. What's wrong with Vanessa?"

"I don't know. Maybe he did something to her."

"Do you know who he is?"

"No. He never talks when he brings me food."

"Same." Ava nodded. Her eyes closely watched Faith's every move as she struggled to undo the silk scarf binding her right wrist. "He has a gun." Ava's voice trembled.

Faith knew why Ava was so scared of guns. The same reason she herself was. Because they'd both had bad experiences with guns before. "I know, but he doesn't know I'm free. I'll undo you, then we'll see if anyone else is here. There was another door, and Mackenzie and Ruby could be in there. If all of us get free, we can take him; we'll have the element of surprise."

"Think anyone is looking for us?"

"Yes," Faith replied firmly. Of this she was one hundred percent positive.

For several minutes she worked in silence, wishing she hadn't lost it earlier and hurt herself so badly. She had allowed her fear to get the best of her, and that could cost her her life, and her friends their lives. She wouldn't make that mistake again.

"What do you think he's going to do to us?" Ava asked softly.

"I don't know. There are chains in the walls out there. Maybe he wants to keep us here for a while. So far, he hasn't hurt me, he's fed us and given us water, and all our clothes are still on."

Ava paled. "You think he might rape us?"

"I don't know, honey," Faith replied softly. "Got it." With one last tug the scarf came undone and Ava's right hand was free.

"What's the last thing you remember?" Ava asked as she

helped to work on freeing her left hand.

"Eating ice cream at my house. I think he drugged us."

"I agree," Ava said immediately. "I definitely felt like I'd been drugged when I woke up."

"I'm sorry, Faith."

They both started at the voice.

Both she and Ava had been so consumed with getting Ava free that they hadn't heard the man approaching.

"Please let us go," Faith begged. This was the first opportunity she'd had to plead for her freedom, and she intended to make the most of it.

"Not yet." The masked man stood still in the doorway, his whole demeanor seemed calm, unfazed, unhurried.

"Don't hurt us, please." Ava fought desperately with the scarf binding her left wrist.

The man seemed genuinely distressed that they would even suggest such a thing. "I'm not going to hurt you."

"Not going to hurt us?" Ava screeched. "You drugged us, abducted us, tied us up. If you don't want to hurt us, then let us go. I want to go home. I have a son. He's three years old; he'll be wondering where I am. Please, please, please, let us go."

"Shh, Ava." The man took a step toward them, and Faith edged farther away. "All in good time. I'm sorry, Faith." He sounded genuinely remorseful.

"Sorry for what?" she was asking as a burst of fire suddenly shot from her shoulder through every inch of her. Her body jolted violently, and she lost all control of her limbs, falling to the floor. Her body spasmed several more times before she slumped limply against the dirt.

Vaguely, she could hear Ava screaming her name, but Faith had lost the ability to talk. Her whole body ached, she felt nauseous, and like everything around her was happening at a distance.

Then she felt herself rising.

Someone was carrying her.

Faith tried to protest, tried to fight, but her body was uncooperative.

"Relax," the man carrying her said. "You'll make it worse if you try to fight it. It'll pass, just try to relax."

She expected the man to return her to the bed, but he set her down on the floor instead. A moment later something cold and metal snapped around first her right wrist and then her left.

"You hurt yourself." The man sounded sad.

She felt rather than saw or heard him move away from her. At first, Faith thought he had gone for good. But then he was back. Gently, he bathed her hands, rubbed on some sort of ointment, and then bandaged them. He took care to hurt her as little as possible.

It all felt so odd. So contradictory. Why would he kidnap her and her friends if he genuinely meant them no harm?

Before Faith could ponder that she felt herself fading.

"It's okay, Faith." He spoke softly, almost soothingly. "You'll understand soon. You'll understand why I'm doing this. You'll understand."

Understand what? she wanted to ask.

And how did he know her name?

Did she know him?

Before she could ask any of those questions, she faded off into unconsciousness.

* * * * *

8:44 P.M.

Something was wrong.

He hadn't seen anything on the news about Faith and the other missing girls.

Had he done something wrong?

Messed up somehow?

Maybe he hadn't been clear enough with his intentions.

The Protector was baffled. Well and truly baffled. He had thought that five missing friends who all disappeared from the same house on the same night at the same time would have been front page news, but there'd been no mention on TV at all.

He would have to do something about that.

His intentions had simply been to keep the women here until the police realized how inept they were and lifted their game. Then he intended to send Faith and the others home.

But maybe that wasn't enough.

Maybe the police needed more motivation.

Maybe they needed to see firsthand how badly victims of crime suffered.

If that didn't make them stop crime, then nothing would.

He'd show them.

He'd show them the suffering.

Make them understand.

He was already moving toward the door when he stopped himself.

No.

That wasn't the plan.

He had to stick to the plan.

The police would figure it out. They weren't stupid, after all. They'd get it. They'd realize what he was trying to tell them. They'd agree. They'd do better. He knew they would.

Maybe he was just being impatient.

He wanted this *so* badly.

It was almost making him giddy.

The very thought of a perfect world where crime didn't exist, where no one got hurt, where everyone lived in safety and happiness was so intoxicating. No wonder he was getting impatient.

But he could wait.

After all, he had Faith here.

Safely tied back up after her attempt at running.

He didn't blame her, of course. How could he? She just didn't understand. She thought he was a threat. She thought he was going to hurt her.

That knowledge made him sad.

Sad, but not too sad.

She'd soon learn. Soon learn that all he wanted was the best for all of them.

Maybe it had been a mistake to keep the women separated. They'd probably be calmer if they were together. So, he'd chained Faith up in the middle room and then brought in the others.

It was of course riskier to keep them all together, but he wasn't afraid. They were all safely attached to metal chains embedded in the thick dirt wall. And besides, once they knew what he wanted, they would see him as the hero he truly was.

While he waited for the police to figure it out, he could take the time to get to know Faith better.

That excited him almost as much as the plan.

Faith was so pretty.

Faith was so sweet.

Faith was so smart.

Faith was his dream girl. But she was taken. Taken by a good man and he would never interfere with that. All he wanted from her was to learn. Learn how to get a woman like her to fall for him, so one day he could live happily ever after with his very own Faith.

NOVEMBER 6TH

8:53 A.M.

"Jack, you should have gone home, slept in our bed, gotten some proper rest." Laura Xander reprimanded her husband when she opened her eyes to find him still right where he'd been when she'd fallen asleep the night before.

"Do you really think I'd leave your side after everything you've just been through?" Jack moved from the chair to sit beside her on the bed.

No, Laura didn't. She knew Jack was as shaken up about what had happened to her as she was. Instead, she asked, "What about Zach?" Their eighteen-month-old son had been at his grandparents' house the night they'd brought her sister-in-law to the hospital after she collapsed. It wasn't that Laura didn't trust Jack's parents to take excellent care of her little boy—she adored her in-laws and loved them very much—but she hadn't seen her son since the afternoon of the third and it was now the morning of the sixth. She missed him. She wanted to hold his chubby little body in her arms, have his sticky little lips kiss her cheek, smooth his silky soft blonde hair.

"Mom and Dad brought him around yesterday. He spent most of the day here, and then they took him back to their place," Jack assured her.

The last forty-eight hours were mostly a blank for her. She only remembered bits and pieces since Malachi's knife had sliced into her neck. She remembered being scared senseless when she started to have contractions over a month early. She remembered the ambulance's sirens and flashing lights; she remembered voices jabbering senselessly above her, and she remembered her husband's hovering face and soothing voice.

Laura didn't like that she had been sedated. She was pregnant. Any medications she was given could affect her baby. And she had already had contractions.

Seemingly reading her mind, Jack said, "The doctors didn't have a choice, Laura. You know that. He cut you. You were losing blood, and you were hysterical. Neither of those were good for the baby. They had to get you stable. They've been giving the baby medication to help mature its lungs in case you go into labor. I know you're scared. I'm scared too. But we just have to have faith."

Allowing Jack's calm blue eyes to soothe her, she whispered, "Okay."

He leaned in close, resting his forehead against hers. His blond hair tickled the skin on her temples, his warm breath whooshed gently across her lips, and the top of his nose brushed the tip of hers. Laura loved the intimacy of having him so close to her. She loved Jack so much.

Holding her face in his hands, he kissed her lightly, then sat back and ran a hand through her long black hair. "I'll bring Zach in to see you later today. He misses you. I told him you were sick and sleeping, but he can't wait to see you."

"I can't wait to see him either. I want you to go back to work. I'm fine; you don't have to stay by my side." Laura half meant the words. She knew Xavier would be working on his own, and she was reasonably sure that she could hold it together without her husband sticking to her like glue. She'd suffered a lot worse on her own. A four-day long hell of an ordeal when she was twenty. If she could make it through that, then she could spend a few hours in a hospital room without her husband at her side.

"I don't know, Laura. I'd rather stay here with you. You were having panic attacks and nightmares even before Malachi took you hostage. So far, they've been sedating you. How are you going to cope if you fall asleep and have nightmares?"

Laura didn't want to think about nightmares. Or panic attacks. Or her agoraphobia. She had developed agoraphobia after her abduction fifteen years ago. It had improved after Jack came back into her life, but she still found it immensely difficult to be around large groups of people.

"I'll be okay in here. It's quiet, and you can come back at night." Too late, she realized she'd already told him off for not going home to bed last night. Now he knew that she wanted—or maybe even needed—him here with her. Laura hoped he wouldn't notice her slip.

Of course, he did. Jack grinned, making his dimples show. "I knew you needed me here."

"Maybe just at night," Laura admitted. "But you should go back to work. My parents are still here, right?" She hadn't been close with her parents since before her kidnapping. She wanted to fix that, but she didn't know how to start. After the trial that had sent her attackers to prison, she'd disappeared and stayed gone for ten years, until Jack found her. She didn't know how her family could forgive her for that.

Arching his blond brows, Jack opened his mouth to say something when the door to her hospital room opened. Both of them turned to see who it was, and Laura was surprised to find Annabelle Englewood standing there. She and Annabelle were friends, although not close, as the other woman found forming close bonds difficult. They worked together at the Matilda Rose Women and Children's Center, named after her college friend Matilda who had been murdered by the man who abducted her, and Jack's former partner Rose who'd been murdered by the man who wanted Laura dead. The center was for women and children who'd been victims of violence. Annabelle ran the children's programs, and Laura was a counselor.

"Hi, Annabelle." Laura smiled at her.

"Hi, Laura, Jack." She gave a tight smile. "I'm sorry, this is a bad time."

"No, Annabelle, it's fine, did you want to talk?"

"I shouldn't bother you while you're in the hospital," was Annabelle's response.

"Really, it's okay," Laura assured her.

"I'll go see if Xavier needs help with this presumed kidnapping case, but I'll be back," Jack promised. Gently, he cupped her face in his hands and pressed a soft kiss to her lips. "Promise me you'll call me if you need me."

She knew Jack wouldn't leave unless she promised, and since she knew he wouldn't be able to focus on anything else if he was worried, she acquiesced so he would hopefully be safe at work, despite how dangerous his job was. "Okay, I promise. I love you, Jack."

"Love you too, angel." He kissed her again. "I'll be back soon. Bye, Annabelle."

"Yeah, bye, Jack," Annabelle replied distractedly.

"Come, sit." Laura gestured at the chair beside her bed that Jack had just vacated.

Annabelle complied, taking the seat and twirling her shoulder length brown hair between her fingers. "Is everything okay with the baby?" she finally asked.

"They gave me something that's supposed to help mature the baby's lungs in case my water breaks. But thankfully, so far, they seem to have been able to stop the contractions. Tomorrow I'll be thirty-four weeks. I doubt I'll make it to my due date, but every day that passes, the baby gets stronger. What do you need to talk about?"

Annabelle avoided eye contact for several seconds, when at last she looked at her, her unusual, near-white eyes were wet with unshed tears. "I'm ruining things with Xavier, but I don't know how to stop. I keep pushing him away even though I don't want to."

Laura knew the feeling. If Jack hadn't been so obstinate, she would have pushed him away when he'd come back into her life. Her family and Jack's had lived across the street from each other when they were kids; they'd known each other their entire lives. They'd dated in high school until Jack cheated on her. Devastated, she'd broken up with him when he'd told her, even though she still loved him.

"Do you know why you keep pushing him away?"

"No." Annabelle sighed.

"Yes, you do," Laura pushed.

Annabelle shrugged. "I think I want him to prove that he'll never walk away from me. Which isn't fair since he's never walked out on me in the five years we've known each other."

"Except that one time," Laura countered gently. She hadn't known either Annabelle or Xavier back then, but she'd heard the story. A neighbor and friend of Annabelle's had embarked on a killing spree, murdered her entire family, parents, two brothers and a sister, but left her alive. The police had initially believed it was a murder suicide until the evidence proved otherwise. The killer had then waited until Annabelle was alone, then abducted her and used her as a distraction to escape. Annabelle had been alone because she and Xavier had had an argument, and he'd walked out.

"That was my fault because I wouldn't believe him," Annabelle protested quietly.

"No, it wasn't. You had a valid concern about Xavier's commitments to his ex-wife. You expressed that. Xavier didn't have to leave, or he could have made sure that someone else was watching you. It's okay to be angry that he walked out and you got hurt. Have you told him that you still think about that?" Laura was sure Annabelle hadn't but asked anyway.

She shook her head. "He already blames himself. It'll be worse if he thinks that I blame him too."

"But you *do* blame him. You blame him, but it doesn't change how you feel about him because realistically you know that Ricky

Preston was coming after you anyway, and if he hadn't used that opportunity, he would have simply waited for another to present itself. Why haven't you talked to him about it?"

"I don't want to hurt him."

"But you already are," Laura reminded her. "You're hurting him by keeping your feelings bottled up and pushing him away."

"I don't want to push him away anymore, but I don't know how to stop. I want to trust him. Completely. Yet there are all these doubts in my head."

"What kind of doubts?"

"Doubts about how he could love me. How *anyone* could love me," Annabelle added softly.

"Because of what happened when you were a kid and how your parents changed afterward?"

"Yes." Annabelle's voice wobbled but she held back her tears. "I feel like there's something broken inside me and I don't know how to go about fixing it. Or even if it *can* be fixed."

"Yeah, I know the feeling." Laura could completely commiserate.

"But you have Jack and you let him help you." Annabelle was staring at her intently as though Laura held the key to all the answers she sought.

"Yeah, but things with my family are still messed up. I want them to get better, but I don't know how to make them better. I feel like they should be angry with me for running away and hiding, and it doesn't matter how many times they tell me that they aren't, I can't believe it," Laura admitted.

"It's like that with Xavier and me. It doesn't matter how many times he tells me he loves me and isn't going anywhere, I still just can't make myself believe it, no matter how hard I try. The scars don't help. Every time I see them I think about how I got them. They completely represent how I feel on the inside."

"Mine do too." Laura hated her scars. They covered virtually every inch of her body except her face. The men who had abducted her had been sociopaths. They had enjoyed inflicting pain on her simply for fun.

"Sometimes I wish that I'd died then, rather than living all this time suffering." Annabelle looked at her anxiously.

"Sometimes I feel like it should have been me who died instead of Rose. I was the target, not her. It doesn't seem fair that she died just so he could get to me." Laura's guilt over the death of Jack's partner hadn't diminished in the last four years. "But I can't change what happened. And I have to live for the future. If I'd died, I would've never had the chance to reconnect with Jack and marry him and have kids with him. Jack and our son and this baby are my reason for getting up every morning. If it wasn't for Jack, I'd still be hiding out in my old apartment. It's the little things he does for me that are so important. Like making sure someone put this long-sleeved T-shirt on for me under the hospital gown because he knew I'd freak out if I woke up and had to face the scars I can't even face when I'm calm." Laura had noted immediately upon waking that she was wearing a long-sleeved T-shirt beneath her hospital gown, and she had known immediately that it was Jack's doing.

"Xavier stopped wearing his hazel contact lens for me because he knows I'm sensitive about my eyes." Annabelle smiled.

"Then focus on those things every time you have doubts. It's not an easy road ahead of you, Annabelle, but you can make it if you really want to. It starts with being honest with Xavier. If you can't trust him enough to handle your feelings and help you deal with them, then you're not going to be able to make things work. You need to do some serious thinking. You need to decide whether or not you're committed to working on yourself because, until you decide that you're worthy of Xavier's love, it's never going to work between you two."

* * * * *

12:06 P.M.

Xavier was hoping this didn't turn out to be a bust.

There were no guarantees that the other missing women all attended this support group even if they had all been through a traumatic experience.

But they had to start somewhere. Faith Smith had been missing for almost forty-eight hours, and this was the only viable lead they had.

"So, we don't know if any of the other women reported missing the same night as Faith Smith attend this support group?" Jack asked. Laura was doing better, so his partner was back. For the time being, at least.

"Right. All we know is that Faith attends this victim support group; we got the address and time of the meeting from her phone. Of the other four women reported missing that night, I know at least one of them has been through a traumatic experience. Twenty-two-year-old Vanessa Adams was one of Ricky Preston's victims. I'm hoping we can at least confirm that they all attend the group, then we can get DNA samples and Stephanie can compare them to the ones she collected from Faith's house. Once we confirm they're all victims of the same abductor, it'll hopefully lead us to who this guy is," Xavier explained.

"Do they know we're coming?"

"No. I don't even know if anyone will be here. None of Faith's family or friends knew anything about her group. They all said she wanted to keep that separate from the rest of her life. For all I know, the other women *do* attend the group, but it's only the five of them, so no one else will be here today."

"Except for the one empty place at the table," Jack added. "If the connection is the support group, then that implies there is at least one other person involved."

Xavier nodded his agreement as they entered the church hall.

Faith's victim support group met once every two weeks at lunchtime in a local church hall. There were no signs up advertising the meeting, so it obviously wasn't an open invitation group. Xavier wondered who organized it and how people were referred.

Inside the large, virtually empty space sat four young men. They were down the other end, near the kitchen, all seated at a round table and munching on sandwiches. All four looked up as he and Jack entered, and identical wary and yet curious frowns creased their brows.

"Who're you?" a brown-haired, brown-eyed man asked.

"Is this the victim support group?" Xavier asked instead.

"Did Dr. Fitzgerald send you?" a tall, skinny, redhead asked.

"Is Dr. Fitzgerald the one who runs the group?"

"He's the one who organized them, but he doesn't run them. We run them ourselves," the first man replied.

"Who are you?" an Asian man demanded, his expression gone from wary to downright suspicious.

"Detective Montague, and this is Detective Xander."

Confused, the Asian man asked, "Did something happen to Dr. Fitzgerald? Is that why you're here?"

"No. As far as we know, he's fine. Does anyone else attend your group?"

"No." The redhead stood. "We're not answering anymore questions until you tell us what you're doing here."

"We're investigating the disappearance of Faith Smith," Xavier told them.

"Faith is missing?"

"Since when?"

"What happened to her?"

"She's been missing since the evening of the third. We don't know what happened to her. We were hoping you might be able to shed some light on it."

"Us? Why us?" the brunette demanded.

"Because Faith had some friends over either right before or at the time she went missing. Her boyfriend didn't know of any plans she had, but he thought she might have made last-minute plans with some of the people from her support group. Did any of you plan to visit with her that night?"

Four heads shook in the negative.

"Vanessa did," a voice spoke behind them. "Hello, Detective Montague."

"Hello, Vincent." Twenty-four-year-old Vincent Abrams was Vanessa Adams' boyfriend. Five years ago, Vanessa's parents were convinced that Vincent was only interested in their daughter for sex. And yet here they were still together, despite the fact that Vincent had been badly injured and nearly killed by Ricky Preston simply for being in the wrong place at the wrong time. Sometimes young love really was the real thing.

"Vanessa's missing." Vincent's blue eyes were scared. "Since the third. Faith called, asked her to come over, but she never arrived home. I called the police right away, but they didn't care. They said Vanessa is twenty-two, and she can come and go as she pleases without having to tell anyone. But she wouldn't just disappear. She wouldn't. You know her, Detective Montague. You know she wouldn't do that. She wouldn't do it to her dad, and she wouldn't do it to me," he finished defiantly.

"Other than the five of you, and Faith and Vanessa, who else attends this group?" Jack asked.

"There are three others. Ava Burns, Mackenzie Willows and Ruby McBrady," Vincent replied.

The three other missing women on his list. He exchanged a glance with Jack; that confirmed a link. All five were missing. All five attended this group. Five people had been eating ice cream in Faith's house right before they all disappeared without a trace. Wherever these women were, they were together.

"You know something." Vincent's eyes brightened in hope.

"Nothing good, Vince," Xavier said gently. He liked the young couple. They had weathered a lot; they deserved their happy ending. "When Faith went missing, we searched her house. Her table was set for six. Five spots had been occupied. There were half finished drinks and ice cream residue in the bowls. One person never turned up. I looked into other missing young women. Ava, Mackenzie, and Ruby, as well as Vanessa were all reported missing that same night."

"Someone abducted them?" the redhead asked incredulously.

"At the moment, that's our theory," Jack confirmed.

"Are we in danger?" the Asian man looked panicked.

"We don't know," Xavier replied. It was possible that someone was after this group of people in particular; Or they only wanted the women, or it was possible that they had just been after one of the women and taken the others because they hadn't had a choice. "We need your names and what led you to the group."

"Why is what happened to bring us here important?" the brunette asked.

"Because we don't know if one of the perpetrators in the crimes you were all victims of is after one of you," Jack said.

"I'm Troy Tranchina, I'm twenty-two, and I was injured in a carjacking four months ago," the brunette told them.

"David Murfet," the Asian introduced himself. "I'm twenty-four. Eleven months ago, I was badly beaten when I stepped in and tried to help a woman who was being attacked."

"My name is Roman Tallow," the redhead said. "I'm twenty-five, and my sister was murdered by her boyfriend. I was the one who found her body."

"And you are?" Xavier addressed the only young man who had remained silent since they arrived.

"I'm Miles Lanyon," the black man replied. "My fiancée and I was killed in a hit and run. I was in the car, injured but not seriously. They never found the driver."

"Ricky Preston is dead. Troy, David, Roman, what about your cases? Were they solved?" Jack asked.

Roman nodded, his green eyes hard. "My sister's boyfriend is in prison serving a life sentence."

"The carjacker's in prison," Troy confirmed.

"The man who beat me up ran off when the police showed up. The woman was still there, but she wouldn't give him up. The police thought it was her ex-husband, but they couldn't prove it," David explained.

"What about the girls?" Xavier asked. "We know about Faith and Vanessa, but what happened to the others?"

"Ava was raped by a teacher at her school when she was fifteen. She wound up pregnant. I think the guy's in jail. Mackenzie was in bed asleep one night while her husband was working late at their nightclub when someone broke in. They tied her up, terrorized her, then robbed them. There were three guys. I don't think they were caught—at least, not all of them. And Ruby was married to an alcoholic who beat her when he was drunk. She put up with it for a while, then after he beat her so badly she had to have surgery to release the pressure on her brain, she finally wised up and left him. He committed suicide shortly after their divorce was final," Vincent summarized.

"You really think they were all abducted?" Troy looked like he couldn't believe any of this was happening.

"Ava's car was found outside Faith's house," Jack informed them. "And they're all missing. We'll be talking with their families and collecting DNA samples to compare with the ones our CSU team collected from Faith's house, but at the moment, yes, we believe that they were all abducted by the same perpetrator."

"You keep saying 'at the moment,' but what else could have happened to them?" Vincent began to pace, running his hands through his reddish-brown hair.

"None of you know who this mystery visitor who never showed up could be?" Xavier found that hard to believe. If this was a meeting of the victim support group, then it would make sense that the sixth person was also either a member of or associated with the group.

All five of them shook their heads.

"We're going to need to talk to you again at some point, but here's a card." Xavier set one down on the table. "Please call us if you think of anything you think might be relevant."

Vincent was the only one who followed them out. "You're going to find Vanessa, right?" he asked them anxiously.

Xavier sincerely wished he could guarantee that. "We're going to do everything we can, Vince."

"Vanessa is pregnant. Four months. I was going to propose. You have to get her back," Vincent pleaded.

"Keep faith, Vince," Xavier encouraged. He'd said the same thing to Bobby Kirk and to the friends and family members of more victims than he could count.

"Yeah, okay, thanks, Detective Montague." Vincent turned and headed back inside the church hall.

"We need to know who the other person in that house that night was," Jack said as the climbed back into the car. "Even if they weren't involved, they might have been there, and they might have seen something."

"Maybe one of the guys was there, but turned up late, saw something, and is afraid to tell us," Xavier suggested.

"Once we confirm that all of the missing women were in Faith's house that night we should get prints from the guys in the group and see if their prints match any Stephanie collected. I'm going to head back to the hospital and check on Laura," Jack announced.

"No more contractions?" Xavier really hoped that nothing went wrong with their pregnancy. Laura didn't deserve any more heartache.

"So far, so good," Jack replied.

"Does Laura know about Paige?"

"No. I don't want her worrying any more than she already is. Besides, there isn't anything she could do for Paige at the moment. Mark is taking care of Paige's medical needs, and Ryan is making sure the stalker doesn't get to her again. Right now, Paige just needs to rest, and we need to catch the stalker, so she stays safe."

"I'm going to go with you to the hospital, try and convince Ryan to go home and rest, that I'll stay with Paige."

"You should go home, get some proper sleep. You've spent the last three nights at the hospital. I'll be there all night with Laura anyway; I can watch over Paige," Jack offered.

"Thanks, but Laura needs you, and with Annabelle moved out, there's nothing at home for me. I'd rather be at the hospital doing something than at home on my own with nothing to think about other than my failed relationships."

"Annabelle came to see Laura," Jack informed him.

"Really?" He was surprised. "She said that she was going to go back to therapy. She apologized for her part in the problems between us, said she wanted to change. I didn't believe her. I walked away because I was hurt and angry, but maybe she was serious."

He had told Annabelle that maybe things between them were too broken to fix, but maybe they weren't. Maybe it wasn't too late for them.

* * * * *

4:18 P.M.

Paige felt like she was stuck between being asleep and being awake.

It was because Mark kept giving her sedatives. She knew he wanted to keep her here in the hospital where she was, at least theoretically, relatively safe, for as long as possible. The fact that she had already woken up screaming and in a complete panic twice, believing that she was still trapped inside her sinking car probably played quite heavily into that decision.

Plus, her body was completely exhausted. She still hadn't recovered from her near drowning and hypothermia. Mark had already warned her several times that he was going to be keeping her in the hospital for several days, at least.

Elias had brought the girls in to see her earlier; she had been so tired she could hardly keep her eyes open, but there was no way she was sending those children away. No matter how bad she felt. And she was feeling pretty bad. Her head ached constantly, despite the painkillers Mark kept giving her. Her stomach swirled with nausea; the drugs Mark had given her to counteract that weren't helping. She was still wrapped in warmed blankets, but she was still chilled. The cold seemed to have seeped into her bones and she presumed it was going to take a while before she felt truly warm again.

Despite all of that, she felt almost giddy with joy.

How had she managed to get so lucky?

After everything she'd been through, she'd ended up with the two most beautiful little girls in the world. Hayley was already very attached to her and seemed to be bonding with Elias as well, and Arianna was a sweet and happy little baby.

As happy as she was she couldn't let go of the niggling doubt that kept trying to crawl inside her mind. Things seemed too good to be true. She couldn't quite believe that something wouldn't go wrong. She couldn't help feeling that Eliza would decide that she wanted to keep her daughter after all, or that Hayley's grandmother would decide that she couldn't give up her only grandchild.

Overwhelming fatigue washed over her, and she felt herself edging closer toward sleep.

The quiet whoosh of her door opening announced the arrival of someone. Probably one of the two nurses Mark had trusted enough to allow near her. Or perhaps it was his friend, Dr. Eric Abbott, who had been treating her the few times Mark had left her side.

She ignored whoever it was; they always came in quietly, not wanting to disturb her. Mark kept reiterating to her how it important it was that she rest, so she let sleep begin to claim her. She felt someone fiddling with her IV. Mark had told her no when she'd asked him to take it out, telling her that she still needed fluids and that having it in made it easier to administer any other medications that she required.

She was just drifting off to sleep when a hand clamped down on her mouth and a voice whispered close to her ear, "Wakey, wakey, Paige."

Her eyes popped open as panic swamped her.

She recognized that voice.

She had heard it before.

It belonged to the man who had tried to beat her to death almost five years ago.

This was her stalker.

He was standing right beside her bed. His hand on her mouth, his face close to hers, his blue eyes dark with uncontrolled rage.

Instinctively, she tried to fight him off but almost immediately she realized something was wrong.

Her body wasn't working properly, over and above the trauma it had been through the last few days.

The sound of chuckling chilled her. "You can fight all you want. It won't do you any good," the stalker whispered.

Vainly she tried to control her fear, but she was fighting a losing battle. She was utterly terrified. Something was wrong with her. She couldn't draw a proper breath, and her limbs were beginning to tingle. He had been fiddling with her IV. He'd injected her with something. She feared it was already killing her.

As if reading her mind, he spoke, "You're not going to die; not yet, anyway. Not until I'm ready. I gave you Pavulon. It's a muscle relaxant used for anesthetic. You won't be able to move. It'll paralyze your vocal cords and your diaphragm so you can't breathe."

He said it so matter-of-factly that it chilled her even more than the river's icy water.

Paige desperately wanted to believe that he was lying.

But she knew he wasn't.

Already, she was struggling to breathe.

Apparently confident that the drug had incapacitated her, the stalker released his grip on her. She immediately tried to scream for help, but she couldn't produce even a squawk. She tried to throw herself off the bed, but she was completely numb. She couldn't so much as twitch her little finger.

She was trapped.

Again.

She had been trapped in her car as it slowly filled with freezing water, and now she was trapped inside her own body.

Suddenly, the man beside her removed the pillow from behind her head, laid her down flat against the mattress and slid a tube down her throat.

It took her terrified brain a moment to process what he was doing.

When her lungs suddenly began to inflate with ease she realized he had hooked her back up to the ventilator that Mark had her on earlier. Clearly, he had something he wanted to do before he let her die.

And let her die he would.

Paige was under no illusion that she was leaving this room alive.

She'd been lucky all three times he'd tried to kill her. Lucky that Ryan had stumbled upon them before the stalker could deliver enough blows to her body to kill her. Lucky that Ryan had pushed her out of the way before the car had run her down. Lucky that Ryan and Jack had found her before she drowned in the river.

Her luck had to run out eventually.

Tonight, it seemed.

She couldn't talk her way out of this; she couldn't fight her way out of this. Even if he hadn't drugged her, she had been so weak she wouldn't have stood a chance at fighting him off.

"You're a bad person, Paige." The stalker was back in front of her. "You want to hurt Sofia, and I can't let that happen."

Even if she could talk, she knew it would do no good. He was insane. He would never understand that Sofia was her friend, and that all that was between her and Ryan was friendship. She loved her husband and their new family. She didn't want Ryan.

"And now you're after other men as well. As if hurting Sofia wasn't enough, you also want to hurt Laura."

Hurt Laura?

Did he think she was after Jack now?

Why would he think that?

Then it clicked. At the hospital, before the stalker had tried to run her down with a car, she and Jack had been looking for Malachi's kidnap victims. They'd been talking about Rose, Jack's ex-partner and her best friend, who'd been killed four years ago. They both missed her. They'd both been upset, and when Paige cried, Jack had held her.

It meant nothing.

Jack loved his wife, and she loved her husband. She already had the man she wanted. Why did the stalker not see that? She loved Elias—he was hers, and she was his. And now she had the chance to have the family that this man had viciously ripped away from her once already. He had nearly killed her, caused her to miscarry a baby she hadn't even known she'd been carrying. He had taken away her chance to have children of her own. And now, miraculously, she had the children she'd thought she'd never have, and she was going to lose them. She already loved Hayley and Arianna. She wanted to be their mother. She wanted a family with the man she loved. And she was going to lose it all.

"It's over, Paige. No one is going to rescue you this time.

You're like a cat with nine lives, but you've used them all up. I'm going to teach you a lesson, and then I'm going to unhook that ventilator and watch you die."

Whatever lesson he wanted to teach her terrified her as much as the thought of death. Made her almost wish that Ryan and Jack had been five minutes later pulling her out of the river. Then their attempts at CPR would have failed and she would have remained dead—if she was going to die anyway. At least that way, she wouldn't have had to suffer all over again.

Slowly he pulled the blankets off her and threw them to the floor. "You used sex to lure men into your trap. Sex is supposed to be something special between a man and a woman who love each other and yet you used it as a weapon. Well, I'm going to use it as a weapon against you."

He pushed up her hospital gown—she was naked beneath it. He unzipped his pants. If she could, she'd have gone ballistic. Shrieking and scratching and biting and kicking and doing whatever she had to in order to get away from him.

But she couldn't.

She was completely powerless and at his mercy.

And this man would show her no mercy.

Of that, she was certain.

He climbed on the bed, straddling her, and she attempted to ready herself for what was to come.

Then the door to her room suddenly burst open.

She would have turned her head toward it if she wasn't paralyzed.

"Get away from her."

It was Mark.

It seemed her luck hadn't quite run out just yet.

Mark launched himself at the stalker, but the other man reacted quickly. Swinging his fist, it connected with the side of Mark's head, temporarily stunning him. Mark stumbled and nearly fell. The stalker jumped off the bed and grabbed Mark's shoulders, throwing him toward the wall.

"I'm sorry, Mark. I don't want to hurt you, but I can't let you stop me. She deserves what she's getting." With that, the stalker slammed Mark into the wall once, twice, and Mark went completely still.

The hope that had been swelling inside her when Mark had busted into the room burst like a balloon popping when poked it with a pin.

Dropping her friend to the floor, the stalker returned to the bed. "I told you your luck had run out." Yanking his pants down, he resumed his position on top of her. "I don't want to do this. You're vile and despicable, but you deserve to be taught a lesson."

That was a lie. He was already erect, his blue eyes dark with lust, his breathing heavy with hungry anticipation. He wanted to rape her.

Even though she knew it was pointless, she tried to scream. The sound echoed inside her head but never reached her ears. Desperately, she tried to force her body to move. The harder she tried, the more her panic grew. It grew and grew until it consumed her.

Paige couldn't accept that she was trapped.

But she was.

She might not be able to move, but she could still feel everything he did. She felt him spread her legs. She felt him force himself inside her. It was rough and violent and over in less than a minute. She couldn't see, but she knew the assault had left her bleeding.

"And now, the finale."

The stalker climbed off her, zipped himself back up, and disconnected the ventilator.

Without the aid of the machine, she was immediately in distress.

Her lungs couldn't inflate.

Mark was unconscious.

No one else was coming.

She was going to die.

She didn't want her last thoughts to be of this vile man. So instead, she focused on her family and friends. Mentally she said goodbye to each, apologizing for leaving them even though she didn't want to.

It didn't take long. Her body was already weak. A rushing sound filled her ears and her vision dimmed and then went black. And then she was gone.

* * * * *

4:52 P.M.

He felt groggy.

Groggy and odd. Off somehow. His head pounded, and his stomach churned.

For a long moment, Mark didn't remember where he was or what had happened.

Then it began to filter back.

He was at the hospital. In Paige's room. When he'd walked in the room, the stalker had been there, on the bed, about to rape her. He'd fought the stalker but was knocked out.

Paige.

Ignoring dizziness and a pounding headache behind his eyes, he jumped up and ran to the bed. His hand went straight to her neck. He had to move his fingers several times and press deeply before he detected a pulse—extremely weak—but there. Moving his hand to her chest, he could feel her heart beating faintly, but she wasn't breathing.

Quickly, he hooked her back up to the ventilator and then ripped the IV from her arm. He knew something was wrong. Paige hadn't moved when he'd entered the room earlier. She had been weak from her near drowning and hypothermia, but she would have fought for her life as hard as she could. She wasn't restrained which meant she had to have been given something. Probably something to paralyze her. Since they were in a hospital and Paige was already attached to an IV, that would have been the most convenient method of administration.

"Come on, Paige, fight," he urged then rushed to the door, flinging it open. "I need help in here. Now."

Not waiting for anyone to reply, he returned to the bed, reattaching wires so he could monitor Paige's vitals on the screen behind her bed.

"What happened?" Ryan demanded. Both his brothers and Xavier Montague ran into the room.

"She was given something—I think a muscle relaxant—she wasn't breathing. The stalker is Bruce Daniels. He knocked me out. You need to do a rape kit on her," he rattled off.

"She was raped?" Ryan's eyes went to the blood on the bed between Paige's legs.

Covering Paige's lower body with a sheet, Mark didn't have time to explain because his friend and colleague, Dr. Eric Abbott, came running in. "What happened to her?"

"The stalker is Bruce Daniels. I think he gave her something to paralyze her. Can you start a new IV? The other one is contaminated, and it's evidence now. We need to run blood and urine tests, but I think we should give her edrophonium right away." Edrophonium could reverse the effects of non-depolarizing neuromuscular blocking drugs. Mark would bet anything it's what Bruce Daniels had given Paige.

Eric's brown eyes grew wide as he learned they'd been working with a vicious would-be killer, but he quickly took Paige's arm and set up a new IV, then a catheter, and then he collected blood and urine samples.

Bruce Daniels had come dangerously close to succeeding in killing Paige this time. If he hadn't regained consciousness when he had, she wouldn't have survived. She still might not.

This was all his fault.

Seemingly sensing this, Ryan glared at him. "What happened to the guard on Paige's door?"

Before he could answer, Paige's eyes fluttered open—full of fear and panic. Aware that she couldn't move, Mark took hold of her shoulders and leaned right over her. "Paige, its Mark. Look at me." He waited until he could see her eyes were focused on him. "I know you're scared, but you're going to be fine," he said gently. "He gave you a drug to paralyze you, but it will work itself out of your system, and I'm going to give you something that should reverse the drug's effects. I'm going to sedate you. When you wake up, you should be able to move again." Mark paused, knowing he should sedate Paige immediately, but there was something else he needed to tell her. "I'm so sorry, Paige. This is all my fault."

"Your fault?" Ryan whirled on him. "What did you do, Mark? Where was the guard on her door? Why was she alone?"

Slowly, he turned to meet Ryan's angry gaze, and Jack and Xavier's confused ones.

Understanding dawned on Ryan's face. "You agreed to help her play bait," he accused.

"It was her idea," he said quietly. But he knew he should never have agreed to go along with it. He hadn't expected the stalker to be so quick. He'd thought once confronted, the stalker would realize it was over, and Mark would be able to call in someone to arrest him. Instead, the stalker had knocked him out and then continued with his plan.

"Her idea?" Ryan raged. "He tried to kill her two days ago! She almost died, she was in *no* condition to be making decisions like that! You should have told her no."

"Your boss knew, she okayed it," Mark informed them, although what Ryan said was true. He was Paige's doctor, and he was responsible for keeping her safe; instead, she'd been raped and almost killed.

"I don't care!" Ryan growled. "You knew she wasn't up to this. You're not a cop, Mark. If you wanted to go through with this idiotic plan, then why didn't you bring Jack or Xavier or me in on it? We could have watched over her, protected her. Instead, you got knocked out and she stopped breathing. What if he'd killed you too?"

Mark had never even considered his own safety. This had been all about making sure Paige stayed safe. Bruce Daniels was relentless. He wasn't going to stop until she was dead. But he'd messed up. Ryan was right. He wasn't a cop, and he had never wanted to be one. He'd had no right being any part of this, but Paige had begged him to help her. She'd been worried that Ryan, Jack, and Xavier would have tried to stop her from doing it if they'd known, and she was desperate for this to be over. He was the weak link because he wasn't a cop, so he hadn't realized just how risky this was. What if he'd been killed? Then his wife would have been left raising their four kids all on her own.

But he hadn't been killed. Just gotten a bump on the head. And thankfully, Paige was alive. And now they knew who the stalker was, they'd be able to find and arrest him. Bruce Daniels thought he'd won but he hadn't.

Behind them, machines began to beep.

He returned his attention to Paige. The arguing was adding to her stress levels, and she was quickly becoming agitated.

"I can't believe you did that, Mark. What were you thinking?" Ryan glowered.

"Stop it!" He whirled on his brother. "Can't you see you're upsetting her? Shh, it's okay, Paige." He forced his tone to be calm and soothing. "It's going to be okay. Try to calm down. I can't even imagine how scared you must feel right now, but I promise you that you're going to be fine." His assurances must have helped to calm her because her heart rate slowed a little. "There you go; good girl. I'm going to sedate you now."

While Mark prepared the syringe, Ryan leaned over her. "Hey,

Paige, now we know who he is, we can arrest him. Then you'll be safe permanently," he tried to reassure her. Gently, he tucked Paige's curly brown hair behind her ears. "I'm so sorry, Paige. I shouldn't have left you alone."

"Okay, Paige, I'm going to give you something to make you sleep. I'm going to stay right here with you. When you wake up, I'll be here." Mark injected the sedative and Paige passed out almost immediately. "It wasn't your fault, Ryan."

Some of the anger was gone from his face. "Yeah, it was," Ryan contradicted softly.

"She's stable, Mark. Let me check you out now," Eric said.

"I'm fine," he replied distractedly.

"You passed out, right? You could have a concussion." Eric shone a light in his eyes.

"I wasn't out for more than a couple of minutes at the most," he countered. His head hurt, but the dizziness and nausea were gone. He didn't think he had a concussion.

"Go home, Mark," Ryan ordered.

He hadn't let his older brothers boss him around since he was six. "I'm staying here with Paige."

"Go home to your family," Ryan repeated.

"*You* go home to your family," he snarked back. Mark didn't want to bicker with his brother, but he wasn't leaving this hospital until Paige was okay.

"I am not leaving this room until Bruce Daniels is in custody."

Mark softened; he knew how close Ryan and Paige were and how scared his brother must be over his partner right now. "She's going to sleep for the next few hours. The guard will be back on her door. She's going to be okay, Ryan. You haven't slept in days because you've stayed here. Go home, grab some sleep, come back in the morning. I'll watch over her."

The distrust in his brother's blue eyes hurt him. "I'm staying," Ryan insisted stubbornly.

"You left her alone, too, Ryan."

"I left her at an active crime scene surrounded by dozens of cops with instructions not to leave until Xavier or I came and picked her up. You left her alone—weak and vulnerable—in a hospital bed."

"Go home, Ryan," Mark repeated, cutting his brother some slack since he knew Ryan hadn't slept in seventy-two hours.

"Go home, Ryan," Jack added before Ryan could protest. "You're no good to Paige right now. You're too tired. Go home and spend a few hours with Sofia and the kids, sleep, and then come back refreshed tomorrow morning."

"I can't believe you're taking Mark's side after that stunt he pulled," Ryan whined, sounding more like his five-year-old daughter than a thirty-five-year-old man.

"I'm getting tired of your attitude, Ryan," Jack snapped. "Stop acting like you're the only person who cares about her. I met Paige first. We dated, I've slept with her, she's my friend too. And Mark's friend and Xavier's and Sofia's and Laura's. She has her parents and brothers and sister, nieces and nephews, a husband who loves her and two little girls who are counting on her. I'm not going to remind you of that again. Now go home and get some sleep," Jack ordered in the tone that had sealed his reputation with everyone who knew him as bossy.

Ryan glared at them all and then stalked from the room. Mark shot his oldest brother a grateful smile. Jack had stepped in before Mark said something he'd regret.

"I'll be right outside all night," Xavier assured him, taking Paige's limp hand and squeezing before leaving.

"I'll go check on Laura, and then Xavier and I will take turns at Paige's door," Jack informed him. He, too, went to Paige, pressing a kiss to her forehead then following his partner from the room.

"If I can't convince you to go and get a brain scan, then I'm, at least, going to be checking on you at regular intervals over the next several hours. Checking on both of you," Eric added with a glance at Paige.

Once he was alone, Mark checked all of Paige's vitals to make sure she was still stable and then sank into a chair at her bedside. He wasn't going to make the same mistake and leave her alone again.

The rhythmic hiss of the ventilator lulled him to sleep.

Hours later, he awakened to a sharp intake of air.

Momentarily disoriented, it didn't take long for everything to come flooding back. Glancing at his watch, he saw it was close to midnight. Last time Eric had woken him up to check on him, they had decided it was time to take Paige off the ventilator. Her vitals had remained stable and the drug should be mostly out of her system by now.

Standing by her bed, he reached for her hand. "It's okay, Paige … you're okay," he soothed.

Her eyes struggled open. Tentatively, she turned her head toward him, then wiggled her fingers and toes, and let out a relieved breath.

"I told you it would pass." He smiled at her.

She returned his smile with a weak one of her own. "Thank you," she murmured. Her voice was hoarse and faint, but Mark had thought he'd blown it and he'd never hear her talk again.

He shook his head at her. He didn't deserve her thanks. Because of him she'd been raped and almost killed. "I'm so sorry, Paige."

She shook her head right back at him. "You saved my life," she croaked.

That Paige could be so forgiving after everything she'd been through was amazing. Mark grabbed a cup of water from the bedside table and held the straw to her lips. "Drink this."

She took a couple of sips. "Sorry you got hurt." Paige's eyes were filled with guilt.

"Oh, honey, that is not your fault. I am so sorry I didn't get here sooner, that I let him knock me out, that you got hurt," he finished softly. A rape kit had been done on Paige while she'd been unconscious. They had also transferred her to another bed and another room when CSU had arrived to process the crime scene. They had the evidence they needed to arrest Dr. Bruce Daniels. Now they just needed to find him.

Paige's eyes closed, and tears rolled down her cheeks. "He got away again, didn't he?"

"I'm so sorry, honey, but Ryan and Jack and Xavier will get him. I promise you."

Her eyes opened, and she searched his face, as if trying to gauge the truthfulness of his words. Some of the fear left her face and Mark guessed she believed him. "What happened tonight wasn't your fault, Mark. It was my plan. I knew the risks. I decided to do it anyway. You saved my life. You can call me Paigey whenever you want." She gave him a small smile.

He smiled back at her. Paige hated it when he called her Paigey, and since they were close like siblings he often did it to bother her. Mark was pleased that she was able to make jokes. It reassured him that she was hanging in there emotionally, and she was going to need that strength to get through this. "You should be resting," he told her.

Fresh tears filled her eyes. "I thought everything was going to get better, but now everything is ruined. Now I won't be able to have Hayley and Arianna. Having them near me is too risky. Eliza loves them. She'll want them someplace safe."

"No, Paige, Eliza didn't change her mind. She still wants you and Elias to have the girls. He's with them right now. That's the only reason he isn't here in your room."

Cautious hope lit her eyes. "Are you sure?"

"Of course, I'm sure. You have the family you deserve. You need to take some time off work, Paige. You need to recover from everything that's happened. Emotionally and psychologically as well as physically. I won't be clearing you for work any time soon. Take time to heal, focus on your new family. Ryan's vacation idea was a good one."

"Maybe you're right. I'm so tired," she murmured, her eyes fluttering closed.

"You're still very weak, Paige. You need to rest." She still hadn't recovered from the hypothermia. Her body temperature was still too low and they had rewrapped her in warmed blankets.

Her eyes remained closed and Mark thought she had drifted back off to sleep, but then she spoke. "I was so scared. I couldn't move. I couldn't stop him. I couldn't protect myself." She began to cry softly. "I felt everything, but I was powerless to do anything about it."

Anger coursed through him. Mark hoped Bruce Daniels resisted arrest. Resisted so the use of deadly force was necessitated. Instead, he kept his voice gentle. "You know my friend, Eric Abbott? Well, he has a brother who's a really great psychiatrist. I'm going to give you Charlie's number. I think you should talk to him. Right now, though, you need rest, honey."

Paige nodded, but her haunted eyes opened to stare beseechingly at him. She wanted him to take away her fear, but he couldn't. Suspecting what was scaring her most at the moment was nightmares, there might be something he could do about that.

"Want me to give you something to help you sleep?" he offered.

Her watery eyes confirmed that she did. He gave her another sedative then took her hand. "Sleep now, Paige. I'm not going anywhere. You're not alone."

NOVEMBER 7TH

8:00 A.M.

"Okay, let's start with an update on Paige because I doubt anyone will be concentrating if we don't," Lieutenant Belinda Jersey announced.

"Jack and I saw her before we came here. She's conscious but extremely weak," Xavier told the others. When he and Jack had gone in to tell Mark they were leaving and that Ryan was back at Paige's door, she'd been asleep. She'd woken at the sound of their hushed voices. Even though she'd barely been able to keep her eyes open she'd thanked them several times for saving her life and watching over her.

"Is she improving?" Stephanie Cantini asked.

"Mark hasn't left her side. He said her temperature is still too low, and she's having some trouble keeping food down, but the drug she was given is out of her system. Mark said she's stable, but it will take time for her to recover and regain her strength. Ryan went home for a couple of hours last night, but he's back at the hospital with her. The stalker is Dr. Bruce Daniels. There's an APB out on him," Xavier explained.

Both Ryan and Jack had wanted to track the doctor down themselves, but that was out of the question. For him too. They were Paige's friends, and they were too close to this. They couldn't be objective or even rationally calm when it came to Bruce Daniels. Xavier had to talk the brothers out of it. He only managed to convince them by pointing out what could happen if they messed up the case and Dr. Daniels walked. There was zero chance he would leave Paige alone. The only way to keep her safe was to send the doctor to prison.

Last night when they'd answered Mark's calls for help and gone running into her room, he had been sure that Paige was dead.

Somehow, she had managed to survive.

Again.

She'd been lucky. Extremely lucky.

Paige had fought for her life because she had a lot to live for. She was going to need that strength to make it through the next several days, weeks, and months.

"She's a fighter," Jack assured the others. "She'll make it through this. She has a lot of people here to help her."

"How's Laura?" Stephanie asked.

"Right now, she's doing okay. We just have to pray her water doesn't break. Still, even if it does, at thirty-four weeks, the baby has a good chance at making it."

"Okay, both of them are in our prayers. Let's get this meeting over quickly so we can make some progress on this case. Stephanie, you start with forensics," Belinda ordered.

"Yesterday I collected DNA and fingerprint samples from the houses of the other women from the support group who went missing the same night as Faith. I compared them to the samples from the bowls, glasses, and cutlery on Faith's table. According to her boyfriend, Vanessa Adams was at Faith's house that night. I was able to confirm that. I was also able to confirm that the others were there too. Ava Burns, Mackenzie Willows, Ruby McBrady, Vanessa Adams, and Faith Smith were all in that house, and now they're all missing."

It was what they'd already believed but Xavier was pleased to have confirmation. "Are there any unknown prints that you processed?"

"We collected a *lot* of prints," Stephanie explained. "We'll work through them, but it'll take a while, and we have a ton of open cases. I got samples from Faith's boyfriend and family members, so we can exclude those prints, and if you can get prints from the other members of the group, I'll see if any match, but I doubt they're going to lead you anywhere. Even if I match prints, any one of them could claim they were friends with Faith and had been to her house before."

"Did you find any drugs in the drinks?" Jack asked the crime scene tech.

Stephanie nodded. "Tranquilizers in the soda."

"Given that this was a support group for victims of violent crimes, do we think maybe they had some sort of group suicide pact?" Belinda asked.

Xavier couldn't deny that could be a possibility. He didn't think it was likely though. "Bobby Kirk denies that Faith was suicidal. He said she was finally happy with the direction her life was going. She had dropped out of college when she was twenty because she didn't know what she wanted to do with her life. She'd worked at a jeweler and then at the bank, but now she wants to work with kids. And she and Bobby had talked about marriage and a future. I don't think she would hurt herself."

"And Vincent Abrams said that Vanessa Adams was pregnant. I don't think she'd kill herself and her baby," Jack added.

"We'll talk to the other families, but I don't think any of the women had suicide on their minds. They were all seeking help, reaching out, still connected with family, still working or attending school. Vince said that Faith called Vanessa and asked her to come over for ice cream and to talk. If it were a prearranged suicide pact, I think they would have organized it in advance. Besides, none of the guys from the group were there. And Vanessa wouldn't have left Vincent, not after everything they've been through," Xavier said with certainty.

"Talking of the other members of the group, do we like any of them for this?" Belinda asked. "It wouldn't be hard to set it up. If one of them called and asked the others to meet, said they needed to talk, I'm sure everyone would drop what they were doing. I mean, that was the point of the group, right?"

"Possible." Jack nodded. "We'll definitely be looking into them. And it would explain why there was an extra place set at the table. One of the guys could have set things up, drugged the food or drink, then waited for everyone to pass out and take them all."

"Or it could be one of the people responsible for the original crimes. Some of them were never caught," Xavier added.

"What about relatives of the women?" Belinda continued.

"I know Vincent Adams. He wouldn't hurt Vanessa. Her only other family is her father. He wouldn't hurt her either. Faith's family has also been counted out. Ava is a single mother who spends all her time with her kid and at school. The only other family she has are her parents. Ruby has an ex-husband who beat her, but he committed suicide. She started dating someone new recently—he's the one who reported her missing. We'll look into him. And Mackenzie is married, and her husband reported her missing. He was at their nightclub when the women disappeared, but we'll check him out, just in case."

"All right, at the moment let's look into the four other men from the support group and Ruby's boyfriend. Right now they seem like the most likely potential suspects. If, indeed, these women were kidnapped," Belinda added. "At the moment, we don't have any definitive proof that these adults didn't just walk away of their own free will."

* * * * *

9:11 A.M.

Laura woke with a start.

Heart thumping wildly, she could feel the metal of Malachi's knife against her throat as though he were still holding it there.

She knew it was just a dream, but it still terrified her.

She hated nightmares. She had suffered from them ever since

her abduction. They'd finally started to fade, and now in one night, she was right back to where she'd been before. Malachi had ruined everything, and his actions could still end up costing her her baby.

Part of her knew that the return of the nightmares wasn't all Malachi's fault.

It was also hers.

She had been pushing herself too hard. Forcing herself to come to the hospital with Sofia because she had wanted to prove that she was conquering her agoraphobia. But she wasn't. She'd been having panic attacks and nightmares before Malachi had grabbed her.

If the baby didn't survive, she would blame herself.

And what would that do to her marriage?

Jack would be insistent that it wasn't her fault, but she wouldn't believe him. That would be sure to drive a wedge between them.

Laura knew she was working herself up over nothing. Her baby would be fine. She just needed more sleep. She was exhausted. She'd been physically and emotionally exhausted even before Malachi held her hostage.

Using techniques she usually recommended to her patients, Laura attempted to calm herself down.

They weren't working.

They never worked.

Laura wondered whether they worked for anyone and why she bothered teaching them.

She forced herself to take long deep breaths, clear her mind, and let sleep trickle in.

But with sleep came more bad dreams.

Horrors from the past mixed with horrors from the present.

Snippets of images. Blood. A knife. Hands on her throat, squeezing so tight she couldn't breathe. Water. Burning. Begging. Screaming.

Laura jolted awake with a strangled scream.

Hands immediately gripped her shoulders. "It's all right, Laura. You're okay. It was just a dream."

She expected it to be Jack in her room, but the voice wasn't her husband's. It was her sister's.

"It's okay," her sister repeated.

She drew in several shuddering breaths before she felt steady enough to pry her eyes open. Her older sister, Mary, was sitting on the edge of her bed. Mary was three years older than her, married with two kids whom Laura had only met a handful of times. As kids they'd been close, spending most of their time playing with the Xander brothers and other neighborhood kids. But ever since Laura had reunited with her family four years ago she just couldn't connect with them. She wanted to—she really did—but like she'd told Annabelle earlier, she just didn't know how to make it happen.

"Do you need me to go and get a doctor?"

Not quite ready to speak, Laura just shook her head.

"Are you all right?" Mary was studying her with concerned blue eyes.

Slowly, Laura nodded. She wasn't really. She wasn't sure she'd been all right in fifteen years and she wasn't sure she'd ever be all right again, but she didn't know how to talk to her sister about that.

Mary sighed, frustration and disappointment clouding her face. "I wish you'd talk to me, Laura. Like you used to. I wish you wouldn't shut me out. I'm right here. I was *always* right here, but you won't open up to me."

"I'm sorry," she whispered, tears welling up in her eyes. Laura knew she'd been a terrible sister and a terrible daughter after her abduction.

Sad now, Mary stood and paced the room. "Don't be sorry. Now I feel like the bad guy making you cry after everything you've been through the last couple of days."

This was exactly why she couldn't fix things with her family. She couldn't deal with her own emotions about what had happened to her, let alone theirs. That was why she'd left. That was why she'd stayed away.

"I shouldn't have come." Mary stopped pacing but kept her back to Laura. "I'll call Jack and ask him to come back here to be with you. I don't think you should be alone right now."

Watching her sister walk to the door, Laura knew that if she let Mary walk away, nothing was ever going to change. In the last four years, Mary was the one who had made all the attempts at reclaiming the closeness they'd shared as children. Laura had resisted because it was easier. Easier to spend her time with Jack and his family because she was more comfortable with them. But she didn't want to lose her sister. "Mary, wait."

Mary paused, hand on the door handle, but she didn't say anything.

"I don't want you to go."

"You could have fooled me," Mary said softly.

"I'm sorry. I want to be close like we used to be, but I don't know how to make it happen."

Mary slowly turned around to face her. "Why?"

She studied her sister's face, searching for what, she wasn't quite sure. Maybe affirmation that Mary still saw her as her sister and not just a victim. "Because what happened to me changed me."

"Of course, it did. I understood that, Laura."

"I know. That was the problem."

"What?"

"Come and sit," Laura implored. She had the feeling that it was now or never if she wanted to get her sister back. When Mary complied, she tried to think of how to explain so that her sister understood. "You and Mom and Dad always saw me as a victim. You stayed beside me all the time; you and Mom even started sleeping in my room."

"You were terrified when you were alone, and you had nightmares," Mary protested.

"I know. But it was a vicious cycle. The more you all hovered around me, the more I doubted that I could cope on my own. You all did everything for me. You cooked and did my laundry and never made me lift a finger. You never yelled at me or disagreed with me. You were all scared of me. Scared that I would fall apart, so you stopped treating me like a real person and just treated me like a victim. And that made me feel like a victim."

"I'm sorry." Mary's blue eyes were pained.

"I don't want you to be sorry." Laura shook her head. "I know everything you did was because you loved me and wanted me to get better. Only I didn't know how to get better, and I felt like I was letting you all down. Every time I looked in your eyes I saw such pain, and I knew it was my fault it was there. I was so overwhelmed that I didn't know how to get better or if I even could. And then you all treated me so carefully, it made me feel like you all thought I wasn't strong enough to make it."

"I didn't realize we made you feel so bad. It was hell when you were missing, Laura. We knew that if you were still alive that you were suffering, and we were powerless to do anything about it. We all felt guilty … we should have protected you … only we didn't, and you got hurt so badly. When you came back, we wanted to make it up to you. We wanted to make everything better, and it killed us that we couldn't."

"Mary, I know I made a mistake running away. I'm sorry," Laura implored.

Her sister gently grasped her hands. "I don't want you to ever apologize to me for that again," Mary told her seriously. "We all understand that you were overwhelmed and traumatized. I wish you hadn't done it. I wish you'd stayed, but I'm not angry with you about that. I wish you could believe me."

"Sometimes I feel like a burden," Laura admitted. "I felt like one back then. I mean, Mom and Dad took time off work and you postponed your studies to take care of me. And I feel like a burden now, to Jack. He's already helped me so much, and now after what happened with Malachi, I'm scared that he's going to have to do it all over again."

"He loves you. He *wants* to be there for you, just like we did. Sometimes I get jealous of Jack, because you're so comfortable with him and his family."

"Because I didn't let them down. I know, I know, you're going to tell me I didn't let you down, but I feel like I did. I'm trying hard to get over it. I'm going to go back to seeing my therapist."

"I think that's great." Mary beamed at her. "Laura, we might have inadvertently treated you like a victim, but we were all so proud of you. More like in awe of you. I don't know how you survived that. I don't think I could have. No, I know I couldn't have survived that horror. I remember seeing you in the hospital just after you were brought in. You were still unconscious. You had bandages everywhere … all over your body. I had nightmares that night. I had a lot of nightmares after you were found. And then when you left, we were scared. Dad was worried that you had hurt yourself, but Mom and I weren't. We knew you wouldn't. You're a survivor."

"I'm not," Laura murmured, embarrassed.

"Yes, you are," Mary contradicted fiercely. "You're a survivor. So, you suffer from agoraphobia, so what? You have a successful marriage with a great guy who is totally in love with you. You have a sweet, adorable little boy and another baby on the way. You have an important job that you're amazing at. I'm so proud of you, Laura."

"I wish we'd talked properly before now." Laura wished she'd learned her lesson with Jack and reached out to her family immediately.

"Me too, but Jack says you're doing great. He's so proud of you too. He says you don't have nightmares much anymore, the last few days notwithstanding, and that your panic attacks are also mostly gone. What happened with Malachi might set you back a bit, but you're strong. You can get through it."

Her sister's confidence in her made her feel stronger. "You talk to Jack about me?" Laura hadn't known that.

She shrugged. "Or Ryan or Mark or sometimes Paige."

"You and Paige are friends? I didn't know you two knew each other."

"Yeah, we met one day at the hospital after Zach was born. We talked; I like her. I like all your friends. I want to be a part of your life again. I mean, we both have our own lives, but I want those lives to intersect more. I want to hang out with you and your friends sometimes."

"I'd like that." Laura smiled at her big sister. Maybe it *was* possible for them to get back the closeness they'd had when they were kids. Thinking of Paige reminded her that she hadn't told Jack yet that Paige wanted to use herself as bait to catch the stalker.

Laura was about to say something to her sister about it when she felt a rush of liquid between her legs.

Her water had just broken.

She was going into labor.

Panic seized her.

Noticing, Mary frowned in concern. "Laura, is everything okay?"

"The baby's coming," she whispered. It was too soon. What if the baby didn't make it? It would be all her fault. She'd been off on her own when Malachi had grabbed her. If she hadn't been abducted she never would have started having contractions over a month early.

"All right, I'll go get a doctor and then call Jack. You need a cesarean, right? Because of your scars, you'll have panic attacks with people seeing them. Hey." Mary paused by the bed. "Everything's going to be okay."

Mary's calm and in control tone helped to calm her a little. She was thirty-four weeks as of today, and the baby had a great chance of making it. She wanted Jack here with her, but she was glad her sister was by her side. She grabbed Mary's hand. "Stay with me, please."

"Always, Laura."

As Mary went to get a doctor, Laura took deep cleansing breaths. She could do this. She had family and friends who loved and supported her. Everything was going to be okay.

* * * * *

11:06 A.M.

Something was still wrong.

It had been nearly four days since he took Faith and the others. The police should have done something about it by now.

The Protector was starting to get angry.

He was trying to help.

Didn't they get that he wanted to protect the women of the city? He was just trying to make things right. No one had done that for him. No one had helped when it was important, and now it was too late. Just like it was too late for Faith and Ava, Vanessa, Ruby, and Mackenzie.

The police had failed him before and now they were failing him all over again.

It wasn't fair.

He was trying to do something good.

They weren't smart enough on their own to fix their failings. They had *needed* him to prompt them. Remind them of why they joined the police force to begin with.

He really and truly did want to help them, but they were making everything so difficult.

Five women, all friends, all previous victims of crime, all disappeared on the same night, and yet there was nothing on the news about it at all. And as he knew, unless the media picked up on a crime, then the police couldn't care less about it.

Well, that was going to stop.

Now.

He'd had enough.

Changes needed to be made, and if the police hadn't realized that yet, then he would simply step things up a notch.

He already knew how.

Stowing his phone in the glove compartment of his truck, he climbed out and headed for his specially constructed underground bunker. He had built it himself. He'd been planning this for a long time.

He couldn't wait to see Faith again.

He had tried talking to her earlier but that hadn't gone well. The women had yelled at him, cried at him, begged him to let them go. He had told them that he didn't intend to hurt them, and it hurt him that they didn't believe him.

They would learn.

Soon, they would understand.

Soon, *everyone* would understand.

Sliding on his mask, he unlocked the door, and set the keys on the small platform at the top of the stairs. He couldn't risk bringing the keychain downstairs with him where the women might get the idea of hurting him, grabbing the keys, and letting themselves go. He'd explained that to them, reminding them that if they hurt or killed him, then they would all die down there. He would let them go—just not yet. He still needed them.

So, with the keys safely out of reach, he descended into the dark space. Rigging electricity had been impossible, so he had hung battery powered lamps from the ceiling. His five girls were illuminated in the gloom.

It was Vanessa he was worried about.

She sat slumped against the wall, her chained hands hung by her shoulders. He had deliberately put the chains at waist height if the women were standing; he had thought that would be for the best because then they could sit or stand freely. Chaining them above their heads or to the floor wouldn't have afforded them that luxury. He truly didn't want to cause them harm.

"Please, let us go," Ava Burns whimpered. "I want to see my son."

"Who are you? Why are you doing this?" Faith asked.

"Let us go." Mackenzie Willows kicked her legs and tried to swing her chained arms at him.

"We all have families," Ruby McBrady pled. "I have a boyfriend, Mackenzie is married, Ava has a little boy, Faith is practically engaged, Vanessa is pregnant. We all want to go home."

Vanessa pregnant? He hadn't known. He would *never* have drugged her if he'd known she was pregnant. Had he harmed her unborn baby? He would never forgive himself if he'd caused her to miscarry.

Kneeling beside Vanessa, he patted gently at her cheek. "Vanessa?"

The woman's brown eyes slowly blinked open. "I don't feel so good," she murmured.

She didn't look so good either. Her skin was pale, but her cheeks were flushed bright pink, sweat beaded her forehead. Something was wrong with her.

"Let her go, please," Faith implored. "She needs a doctor. She's pregnant, you drugged us, something could be wrong with her baby."

Anger flashed through him. How dare Faith imply it was his fault.

Without thinking, he backhanded her across the face.

Faith yelped in shock and shrank away from him.

"What's wrong with you?" Mackenzie screamed. "You said you wouldn't hurt us. Why did you hit her?"

It was Faith's tear-filled brown eyes rather than Mackenzie's

107

yelling that tugged at his heart, swamping it in guilt. The red mark his hand had left on her beautiful face was like a flaming arrow through his chest.

Moving quickly toward her, she flinched and pressed herself into the wall to get as far away from him as possible. The raw fear in her eyes ate away at more of his heart.

He held his hands up, palms out, hoping to indicate to her that he wasn't a threat. "I'm sorry," he implored. "I shouldn't have hit you. I didn't mean to … it just happened. I don't want to hurt you."

He was going to have to work on that. He didn't want to hurt these women, but he didn't know how to make them understand this. Maybe he should let them know who he really was. That should calm them down. So far, he'd kept his mask on whenever he was with them and kept his voice low and deep so they wouldn't figure out who he was. He had decided to hide his identity because he wanted the girls to feel like they were a part of this plan. He didn't want all the glory. He'd been going to reveal his true identity when this was all over, but maybe …

No, he told himself. He was already changing one part of his plan. That was enough for now.

"You keep saying that," Faith rebuked. "But you *are* hurting us. Please, at least let Vanessa go."

He wavered. Vanessa looked in bad shape. Maybe he should take her to a hospital. She hadn't eaten much of the food he'd been bringing to them over the last four days. She hadn't drunk much of the water either. But he was apprehensive about making any more changes.

"I'm sorry," he said again. "She'll be okay for a little longer. Hopefully it won't take much longer for them to pay attention and fix things, and then you can all go home."

"Who?" Mackenzie demanded. "For who to pay attention?"

"All in good time," he assured her. "I'm sorry, Faith."

"Sorry for what?" Her brown eyes were wary as she again

attempted to shrink away from him.

He pulled out a syringe; he didn't want to knock her out, but he didn't have a choice. She didn't understand yet. She would fight him as he moved her to the other location. He couldn't have that. He couldn't let anything mess this up. Not when he had worked so hard on this. Not when he was so close to getting what he wanted.

"Don't, please," Faith begged.

"Leave her alone," Mackenzie screeched, thrashing wildly against the chains.

Faith began to move, darting back and forth, moving as far as her chains would allow. Trying to be gentle, he grabbed hold of her and pressed her against the wall, doing his best to block out her pleas and the other women's screams, as he held her in place with his body and pressed the needle into her arm.

The drug took effect quickly and Faith slumped silently against the ground. He ran up the steps and collected one key from the chain. "This key only undoes Faith's padlocks," he warned the other women as he descended.

"You monster," Mackenzie yelled at him.

Monster.

Someone had called him that before.

It wasn't true.

He was *not* a monster.

He was on top of Mackenzie Willows before he even realized it. His hands around her neck, squeezing.

Her body bucked beneath him.

Ruby and Ava were screaming at him that he was killing her.

Eventually, common sense kicked back in, and he released her.

She wasn't moving.

"You killed her. You said you wouldn't hurt us!" Ruby was sobbing.

Had he killed her?

Pressing his fingers to her neck, he felt her pulse thumping strongly. She had only passed out. He'd been lucky, but next time he might not be. He was going to have to get better control of his emotions.

"She's alive," he assured her friends.

Returning to Faith, he picked her up and started up the stairs.

"What are you going to do with her? You're going to kill her, aren't you? Oh my gosh, you're going to kill us all," Ava gasped.

"I said I wouldn't," he reminded her patiently.

"You also said you wouldn't hurt us, but you won't help Vanessa even though she's clearly sick. You hit Faith and then gave her drugs to knock her unconscious, and you strangled Mackenzie." Ava's voice had reached a high-pitched squeak as panic and terror overwhelmed her.

The Protector didn't have time to explain. He needed to get Faith safely to the next destination before she woke up. Closing and relocking the door behind him, once again ignoring the women's petrified screams for help, he hurried to his truck. Securing Faith in the back, he climbed into the driver's seat. This was going to work. It had to. He was going to show the police first-hand what their negligence was doing to the victims of this city.

And he knew just who to send his message to.

The lead detective handling Faith's missing persons case.

Detective Xavier Montague.

* * * * *

2:51 P.M.

"News?" Xavier asked as Laura's sister approached them.

"It's a girl." The proud new aunt beamed.

He let out a relieved breath, and beside him Ryan did the same thing. Laura's water had broken a few hours ago while he and Jack had been interviewing Mackenzie Willows' husband. Jack had left for the hospital immediately. Xavier had wrapped up the interview and then headed here too.

"How's the baby?" Ryan asked.

"She's doing great. She's five pounds five ounces. She's in the neonatal intensive care unit. She's probably going to need some respiratory support and feeding support for a while, and she still has a long road ahead of her, but so far, things look really good," Mary explained.

"Did they name her yet?" Ryan was smiling, the first smile Xavier had seen on him in days.

"Jack said they had chosen boy and girl names, since they were waiting for the baby to be born to find out the gender, but he won't tell us until Laura is awake."

"How is Laura?"

"She's still out but she should wake up soon. Jack's with the baby, and my parents are with Laura." Mary's blue eyes moved to the door behind them. "How's Paige?"

"Mark's in with her. He's going to want to hear about the baby, so let's go in and tell him and he can update us on Paige's condition." When they'd arrived at the hospital, over an hour ago, and gone into her room, she'd been asleep. Mark had also been asleep in the chair beside her bed.

Mark woke at the sound of the door opening, his eyes blinking sleepily open but then sharpening in apprehension when he saw Mary. "How are Laura and the baby?"

"They're both good," Mary assured him. "Baby is a girl and they're getting her settled in NICU. Jack's with her. Laura hasn't woken up yet, but she's stable and our parents are with her. How's Paige? Is she doing better?"

Scrubbing his hands over his face, Mark looked exhausted. He hadn't left Paige in the four days she'd been in the hospital. "She's stable, her temperature is back up to normal, but she's still not eating and she's very weak. She can hardly stay awake for more than ten to fifteen minutes at a time."

"You're worried about her?" Ryan phrased it as a question, but they could all see the concern on Mark's face.

"Yes. She's been through a lot in the last few days, both good and bad. She needs to know the stalker is caught. She needs to know that she and the girls are safe. She needs him caught soon or I don't think she's going to make it. The stress is already affecting her physically, and I don't think she's going to get better until this is over. Do you have any leads on where Bruce Daniels is hiding out?"

"None," Xavier replied quietly. It was like the man had simply disappeared. "Has she been having nightmares?"

"Oh yeah," Ryan replied with a shudder. Xavier had seen enough of Annabelle's nightmares to know what is was like watching someone you cared about reliving something horrific and suffering all over again. "After the last one, Mark had to sedate her to calm her down."

"I can't keep giving her sedatives indefinitely," Mark added. "But I'm not sure she can handle the stress right now. She keeps getting claustrophobic, but she's so weak, I haven't been able to get her up yet."

"Have you set her up with a counselor?" Xavier asked. Paige was high risk for developing post-traumatic stress disorder, she needed a good therapist.

"Charlie Abbott," Mark replied.

"Eric's brother?" Ryan asked.

"Yes, he's the best. He's going to come and see her as soon as she's strong enough. Hey, sleepyhead." Mark leaned his forearms on the bed's guardrail as Paige's eyes slowly opened, all traces of anxiety wiped from his face and voice.

"Hey, Mark," Paige returned, her voice a faint whisper. Her face was paper pale, and dark circles marred the skin under her eyes, which seemed way too big for her thin face. There were a few bruises and scratches on her face and arms from the car accident, which reminded him he needed to file an insurance claim, so he could buy a new car. The one Paige had been driving when the stalker forced her off the road and into the river was destroyed. "Hey, Ryan, Xavier." Paige's brown eyes grew concerned when she spotted Laura's sister. "Mary, is something wrong with Laura and the baby?"

"Laura had the baby, a little girl, the baby is in the NICU but she's doing really great," Mary assured her. "I wanted to come and check on you, see how you were doing."

"I'm fine," Paige said without conviction.

"You should be resting," Mark told her.

"*You* should be resting," Paige shot back. "You haven't gone home in days. You don't have to stay with me."

"Shh, I'm not going anywhere," Mark informed her, affectionately brushing at her brown curls.

"When can I go home?" Paige asked.

"When you start eating, and you're strong enough to get up and about," Mark replied. "Going home now isn't just you and Elias. You'll have two little girls to care for."

"I heard about that." Mary grinned at Paige. "Congratulations! I'm *so* happy for you, and I can't wait to meet Hayley and Arianna."

Paige smiled back, but Xavier could tell she was already fading. He was about to say something when his phone buzzed in his pocket. When he pulled it out, he knew immediately that something was wrong. The email was from someone he didn't know and addressed to Detective Xavier Montague, the subject line read, "You are failing the people of this city."

Catching him staring at his phone, Paige asked, "Xavier? Is something wrong?"

"No, honey." He certainly didn't want to worry Paige given her current condition. "Absolutely nothing is wrong, but Mark is right, you should be resting." Stowing his phone in his pocket, he pressed a kiss to Paige's forehead. "I'll be back to check on you soon." Catching Ryan's eye, he nodded toward the door.

Taking his partner's hand, Ryan squeezed it tightly. "Get some more sleep, Paige. I'll be right outside your door so there's absolutely nothing to worry about." Ryan kissed her cheek.

"Okay, bye guys." Paige's eyes were already falling closed.

Mark shot them a curious glance but didn't comment. "I'll let you know if there are any changes with her."

"Thanks, Mark." Ryan hustled Mary toward the door.

"Bye, Paige," Mary called over her shoulder. "I'll go see how Laura's doing," Mary said when they were back in the hall and headed off toward the maternity ward.

Once they were alone, Ryan turned to him. "You got some sort of message on your phone; what was it? I'm guessing nothing good since you didn't want to worry Paige with it."

Retrieving his phone, he held it out so both he and Ryan could see it. "I think this email is from whoever abducted Faith Smith and her friends from the support group. It says it's from The Protector. The subject line says that we're failing the people of the city."

"What does it say in the email?" Ryan glanced at the phone over his shoulder.

Opening it up, there was a single line of text: "Meet you here soon." And a link. Xavier glanced at Ryan.

"Click on it."

Xavier did. Immediately, a room appeared on the screen. The walls were concrete, the room was well lit, a single table sat in the middle. The table was huge and appeared to be made of metal.

A sinking feeling began in the pit of his stomach. "Are you thinking what I'm thinking?" One look at Ryan confirmed he was. "He's going to kill them there. He wants us to watch."

"He wants *you* to watch," Ryan corrected. "He could have sent this to the department, but he sent it to you personally. He's someone who knows that you're the lead detective on this case. It's probably someone you interviewed already."

"We need to see if we can track his location from the feed. I'm guessing it's streaming live if he wants us to watch. I don't see the women though. There are no doors that we can see from the angle he's set up the camera, but he has to be holding them somewhere close by." Xavier felt like he was babbling a little, but he was unnerved that the killer had reached out to him personally. He had a bad feeling about it. Right now, though, he shoved those concerns aside and continued. "If we see him on camera, we may get enough to ID him even if he keeps his face covered. Which, if he's even somewhat smart, he'll do."

"Xavier, I don't like that this guy singled you out. Call me paranoid but with the stalker making three attempts on Paige's life in four days, and Laura being held hostage …" He broke off and took a steadying breath. "I just don't want anyone else I care about to get hurt. Be careful."

Before he could assure Ryan that he would, movement on his phone caught his attention. "Ryan, look."

On the screen two people came into view. A man, dressed in jeans and a black hoodie with a black balaclava and sunglasses, was carrying a woman. The woman was Faith Smith and she appeared to be unconscious.

"Is that one of your missing women?" Ryan asked.

He nodded. "Faith Smith." Part of him wanted to watch every second so they could identify this man. And part of him wanted to shut his phone down so he didn't have to see what was going to happen next. Xavier didn't know exactly what the kidnapper intended to do to Faith, but he could make a pretty good guess. Given the level of confidence he had displayed so far, abducting five young healthy women simultaneously, and his level of planning, bringing the drugs with him, having a place prepared to stash them, having this room ready to go and the camera already set up, he wasn't letting any of these women go alive. He was going to kill Faith and then the others and he wanted them to watch.

As they watched, they saw the man lay Faith's limp body down on the table then set about restraining her. Faith was small and the table was large. Even when the man stretched out her arms on either side of her body, they didn't quite reach the edge. He handcuffed her wrists and ankles, securing her firmly to the table.

Faith wasn't wearing the clothes they thought she'd been wearing when she was abducted. What she wore now didn't seem to fit her well. The sleeves of the sweatshirt hung over her hands, and the sweatpants had been rolled up a few times. She also looked clean and her hair shiny. Both her hands were bandaged and there was a red mark on one cheek.

Xavier attempted to look beyond Faith, to focus on the man. He appeared to be of average height and weight, and with his body completely covered it was impossible to see skin, hair, and eye color.

He barely resisted the urge to toss the phone to the floor. A combination of frustration that the video wasn't giving them anything useful, and the helplessness that came with knowing this man was about to kill Faith Smith, and there was nothing he could do to stop it.

"I just spoke to the forensics unit. I told them to access your email and start a trace to see where the video is being streamed from," Ryan announced.

Barely hearing him, Xavier's gaze was riveted on the phone. "Look, Faith is waking up." The young woman was beginning to move on the table, her movements slow and sluggish as she awoke from what he assumed was a drug-induced sleep.

Suddenly the kidnapper's masked face appeared right in front of the camera, blocking their view of Faith. Xavier tried vainly to search for anything that would identify the man, but there was nothing.

"This is your fault," a low, gravelly voice spoke through the phone. "I don't want to hurt them, I only want to help. You should be protecting them. It's your job and you're failing."

"Do you recognize the voice?" Ryan asked quietly.

He shook his head. His eyes and ears were straining, desperate to find something, anything that pointed them in the right direction. His pulse was pounding, the sound throbbing in his ears almost drowning out the kidnapper's voice. They were about to watch Faith Smith die. He knew it. And there wasn't a single thing he could do to stop it. Pictures of Faith's parents and Bobby Kirk were swirling in his head—already thinking of the notifications he was going to have to make.

"Don't worry, it won't hurt her. I'll make sure of that." The kidnapper sounded sincere.

What was he going to do to her? Shoot her? Stab her? Strangle her? The best Faith could hope for was something quick.

* * * * *

3:34 P.M.

Faith was fighting the grogginess that swamped her.

She could hear a voice speaking softly in the background, but she couldn't make out the words.

It took a moment for her to put the pieces together of what had happened before she passed out.

Getting free, finding the locked door and then her friends. Being knocked out, then coming around to find herself and the others chained up in the middle room. Being brought food and water by her captor, the keys always left out of reach. Then being hit in the face and knocked out once again.

Now it didn't feel like she was in the same place.

This place smelled different. Gone was the scent of dirt and human waste. This room smelled of metal. She smelled different too. Clean. Her hair smelled of shampoo, only not the kind she usually used. Her clothes had been changed. They were no longer wet and stiff from soiling herself. She was no longer on a dirt floor or a bed. Now she was lying on something hard and cold.

Experimentally, she tried to move her limbs and was not surprised when she found that she couldn't. Of course, he had restrained her. She expected nothing else by now.

It didn't feel like he had blindfolded or gagged her this time around. Was that a good or a bad thing?

She had her answer when she opened her eyes.

She was in a big concrete room. Lying on a metal table. Her wrists and ankles were cuffed. On the walls hung several tools. Saws and blades and other horrifying looking things. Was that how he was going to kill her?

His behavior had been erratic.

Every time he had spoken to them or fed them, he'd been calm and gentle.

Until last time.

Her pointing out to him that he was hurting them had set him off. He had lashed out. Hit her. Her cheek still throbbed from the blow.

But that was the least of her problems.

He was going to kill her.

She knew it.

Despite the many times he'd said he would let them go and that he had no interest in hurting them, she knew it wasn't true.

He stood in front of her. Down by the wall a couple of feet from the end of the table she was bound to. He was talking to someone, only she couldn't see anyone else in the room with them.

"Wh ... who are you talking to?" she asked shakily.

The man—he called himself The Protector—turned to her. She couldn't see his face. He still wore the mask and sunglasses, but his demeanor was calm again. He was back in control.

"I didn't want it to have to come to this." His tone was imploring as he walked toward her. "I thought just taking you would be enough for them to realize that they failed you. That they failed me. That they failed and continue to fail all of us."

"Who failed us?" If she could get him to open up to her then maybe she still stood a shot at talking her way out of this.

But the man wasn't to be drawn into a conversation. His warped mind was stuck on its own thing. "Don't be scared. You'll be going to a better place. Here, everything is so messed up, but there, everything will be better. So much better." He ran a gloved hand gently through her tangled hair and then cupped her face.

Fighting her instincts to squirm away from this horrible man, she kept as still as she could. If she let him know that he repulsed her then the slim chance she could connect with him would evaporate. He seemed to like her. Earlier he had been asking her questions about what she looked for in a man. "Please," she begged, "I want to stay here."

"Shh." He trailed his fingers down her cheeks. "You're scared. That's understandable, but you don't have to be. It won't hurt. I promise you that."

Tears were streaming down her cheeks. She didn't want to die. But she knew no one was coming for her. No one even knew where she was. Maybe no one was even looking for her. No, someone knew about her because he'd been talking to someone.

Scanning the far wall, she saw a computer and a camera. Someone must be on the other end. The man had moved off, over to the wall, surveying the tools.

Her heart began to race. She didn't have long left.

He wasn't going to be persuaded to let her go. He was crazy. She had nothing left to lose.

She looked straight at the computer. "If anyone is there, please, I need help. My name is Faith Smith. This man kidnapped me. Me and four other women. One of them is sick. They need help, we all do. Please…" The last was a desperate sob.

The man came calmly back to the table, unperturbed by her outburst. "Shh, Faith, I told you you didn't have to worry. It won't hurt a bit."

Faith didn't hear his words. Her eyes were locked on the saw in his hand. "No. Please."

"My sweet Faith. I envy you. Soon, you will be in a place free from pain and fear and worry." He held the saw in one hand; his other he pressed on her chest. "I take your pain, Faith. I take it in my hand. I take it from you and throw it away." He lifted his hand and mimed throwing something away.

This man was a lunatic. If he intended to hack her to death with a saw, it was most certainly going to hurt. A lot.

And then any shred of sanity that she had been clinging to in the deluded hope that she might make it home alive burned up.

Faith completely lost it. She thrashed wildly, yanking on the cuffs at her wrists and ankles, screaming and crying and pleading for her life.

The first blow hit her like a ton of bricks.

Pain rocketed up and down her body relentlessly.

It was so bad she threw up.

The man didn't notice.

Blood was flowing from her body, seeping underneath her, soaking through her clothes. Ironically, the blood warmed her as her body grew cold.

Very cold.

Deathly cold.

She was quickly dying from blood loss and the blows kept coming. She lost count. The pain all melded into one gigantic throbbing mess.

Her heart was hammering in her chest.

Her vision was growing cloudy.

Her mind had all but stopped working. It could think of only one thing. The life she had almost had that had been cruelly ripped away from her.

"I love you, Bobby," she whispered.

* * * * *

10:48 P.M.

"Are you ready?" Jack asked his wife.

Slowly, Laura's violet eyes moved from the phone she held clutched in her hand to him. "She's so beautiful. She's going to make it, right?"

Gently, Jack kissed her lips. "She's a fighter, angel, just like her mommy. She's going to make it. She's already doing great. How are you doing?"

"You've asked me a million times already," she murmured sleepily.

"Then consider this one million and one." Jack had made it to the hospital before Laura was put under general anesthetic to undergo an emergency cesarean section. He'd been in the room with her the whole time and witnessed his daughter's birth, but he hadn't been able to hold her. The baby had been whisked away quickly to be monitored and he had gone with her to the neonatal intensive care unit.

"I'm okay, just tired," Laura told him.

"You're not in too much pain?" he asked although it was her mental well-being he was more concerned about. She needed to deal with being held hostage and not get distracted by the baby; otherwise, it was just going to catch up with her later on.

"No, I'm really okay. I just want to go and see her." Laura's voice took on a pleading note.

"Your doctor said you can go in the morning. Until then, this will have to do." Jack pointed at the phone. He'd explained to the staff in the NICU about the events leading up to Laura going into premature labor and they had agreed to let him set up a small camera in the baby's incubator so Laura could see her.

"Thank you for doing this." Laura's eyes were watery, and she smiled at him before returning her gaze to the baby. "She's so little, and there are so many machines."

It had been overwhelming seeing so many machines and tubes

121

attached to his tiny baby girl, but the doctors had assured him several times that she was doing great. "The continuous positive airway pressure machine, which they call a CPAP, helps to keep her lungs open in between breaths, but she's breathing on her own. They're feeding her intravenously at the moment, but they're hoping to get her on a feeding tube and try her on formula or breast milk tomorrow. The incubator helps to keep her warm, so she doesn't get hypothermic. They let me touch her for a moment and she held on to my finger, just like Zach did when he was born. They're hoping to move her to the special care nursery maybe tomorrow or the next day if she keeps doing this well." Jack had already told Laura this several times, but he would keep reminding her as many times as it took to calm her fears—which, he suspected, wouldn't happen until they brought the baby home.

"I can't wait to hold her." Laura traced a finger over the baby's image on her phone.

"Knock, knock." The door to Laura's hospital room opened and Ryan stuck his head in. "Ready for us?"

Jack's parents and Laura's parents had already seen the baby via the video. He didn't want anyone else meeting her in person until Laura did, so he'd invited the rest of the family to come and see the baby this way too.

"Yes," Laura replied, wiping at her wet cheeks.

"Congratulations." Ryan carried in armfuls of flowers, all different types, all pink.

"This was the biggest teddy bear we could find and still carry in here." Sofia followed Ryan into the room. The teddy bear she carried was almost the same size as her.

"I love it." Laura smiled as she tried to drag herself into more of a sitting position.

"Stop moving," he rebuked gently, holding her in place and picking up the bed's controls, elevating it slightly.

"I'm dying to know what you named her." Mark's wife Daisy paused at the door holding it open.

"Me too," Mark agreed, pushing a wheelchair into the room.

"Paige," Jack exclaimed, surprised to see her up out of bed. Last time he'd seen her, she hadn't looked like she was doing very well. She still didn't. "I didn't know you were up and about yet." He cast a glance at Mark whose concerned eyes watched Paige carefully. Jack hadn't told Laura yet what had been going on with Paige, but he would have if he'd known she would be here.

"She keeps pestering me to let her out of bed. This is her first time up, so she won't be staying long." Mark explained.

"What happened to her?" Laura's eyes were scanning the group, searching for answers, aware they had all kept this from her.

"I'm fine," Paige spoke up. "We're not here to talk about me. We're here to meet your beautiful new baby."

"The stalker came after her again." Laura answered her own question. "How badly was she hurt, Mark?"

"I'm fine," Paige repeated.

Laura rolled her eyes at that. Paige couldn't have looked less fine if she tried. However, the look Laura shot Paige went deeper than simple concern, and Jack wondered if Laura had known that Paige intended to try and make herself bait. "Mark?" Laura asked.

"You don't need to worry about her. I'm taking good care of her," Mark assured Laura.

"Do you at least know who the stalker is?" Laura asked.

"Yes, and we'll find him," Jack told his wife. "Until then, we're watching over her. Now, let's tell them about the baby."

Laura nodded slowly, but the glance she shot him indicated she expected the details later. Then she turned to their friends and family. "We named her Rose."

They had chosen the name when they'd been pregnant the last time around. If they had a girl they both wanted to name her after Jack's partner who had died saving Laura's life.

"Oh," Paige gasped, tears welling up in her eyes and trickling down her pale cheeks. "That's so sweet."

Rose Lace had been Paige's best friend as well as his partner. Neither of them was over her death. Laura smiled at Paige. "If it hadn't been for Rose, I wouldn't be here, and Jack and I would never have gotten married and we wouldn't have Rosie."

"Do you have pictures?" Xavier asked.

"We have better than that. Jack set up a camera in Rosie's incubator, so I could see her since I can't go up to the NICU until tomorrow." Laura held up the phone.

As Sofia, Daisy, Paige, and Mark pored over the images of the baby, Jack noticed the look that passed between Xavier and Ryan. Something was up, and Jack wondered if it had something to do with the missing women case.

Right now, though, he wasn't going to worry about work. He was just going to enjoy the day of his daughter's birth. Perching on the edge of Laura's bed, he eased his wife gently into his arms and stared adoringly at his brand new baby girl.

NOVEMBER 8TH

10:11 A.M.

Xavier had actually slept well last night. Again, he'd spent the night at the hospital, taking turns with Ryan keeping watch at Paige's door. He'd felt stressed and wired until the second his head hit the pillow, then exhaustion had taken hold and he'd slept like a rock. Paige, too, had slept well. The excursion to Laura's room had completely worn her out, and she'd still been asleep when he'd left.

Once Mark released her from the hospital, Ryan had already arranged a safe place to take her and Elias and their new daughters. Sofia had thought the vacation idea was a good one, so she and Sophie and Ned would be going too. Mark also thought it was a good idea, so he and his wife and their four kids were in. Whether Jack and Laura were in depended on how long Rosie needed to stay in the hospital, which could be months or just a week or two depending on how quickly the baby grew and began eating and breathing independently.

He, however, wasn't so sure he wanted to be in on this big family vacation. His friends were like family to him; he was closer to them than his own family. Xavier had been the product of a one-night stand. Both his parents had remained with their respective partners, and he'd grown up being bounced from his mom's house to his dad's house. He knew his parents, stepparents, and half-siblings loved him, but they'd never been close.

As much as he loved his friends and he'd enjoyed sitting and chatting with them last night, going away with all the kids, who he also loved dearly and was Uncle Xavier to, was another story.

Xavier was thrilled that Rosie was doing so well, and all his prayers were going toward her staying healthy and growing stronger quickly, but seeing the baby reminded him of his own daughter. His little girl would have been eight by now. He still thought of her often, imagining what she would have been like and what she would have looked like, but up until a few weeks ago he honestly thought that kids with Annabelle were in the cards. Then after Annabelle moved out, he's thought it was never going to happen. Only ever since Jack had told him that Annabelle had reached out to Laura he's been having more doubts.

He really needed to try and make time to talk to Annabelle. He needed to know where her head was.

Standing, he paced around the large office. He was waiting for Dr. Fitzgerald. Hank Fitzgerald was the forty-four-year-old psychiatrist who was behind the support group Faith and the others attended. The doctor had been married for the last decade, had no children, and no criminal record whatsoever. Not even a parking ticket.

While Dr. Fitzgerald ran Faith Smith's support group as well as several others across the city, he wasn't the treating physician of any of the participants of any of the groups.

Sighing, he continued to pace irritably. Dr. Fitzgerald was nearly twenty minutes late now, and Xavier had the feeling he was late on purpose.

To pass away the time, he examined the space. The furnishings looked expensive; the suite was huge and broken into three distinct areas. There was a desk at one end with several bookshelves grouped around it and a door that Xavier guessed led to a bathroom was in the wall behind the desk. The middle part of the room had a table and twelve matching chairs and a small kitchenette. And then on the other end was a couch and two armchairs separated by a coffee table that contained only a box of tissues.

The walls were filled with framed copies of his degrees and every paper or article he'd ever written. Apparently, Dr. Fitzgerald was an expert in the field of post-traumatic stress disorder and associated conditions in victims of trauma.

The building was a nice one in an expensive part of the city. The practice he co-owned with four other psychiatrists, all specialists in various areas, occupied one whole floor. Obviously, Dr. Fitzgerald was doing quite well for himself.

"Detective Montague." The doctor suddenly burst through the door, his arms full of books and papers. "So sorry I'm late. I was held up I'm afraid."

The man didn't sound sorry in the least. Still, Xavier kept his voice pleasant. "That's okay, Dr. Fitzgerald, but do bear in mind that time is of the essence if we want to find these women alive."

Unfazed by the rebuke, the doctor dropped his armload of papers on the table and went to the kitchenette, busying himself making coffee. "May I offer you anything, Detective?"

"No, thank you." Xavier didn't want to waste time on pleasantries. Images of Faith being hacked to death with a saw were seared into his mind's eye. He had attempted to block them out, if he allowed himself to take on Faith's terror in her final minutes, he wouldn't be able to function. Faith Smith might be dead but Ava Burns, Mackenzie Willows, Ruby McBrady, and Vanessa Adams weren't and they needed him one hundred percent focused.

"Let's sit." With coffee cup in hand, Dr. Fitzgerald gestured at the sofa and armchairs and took a seat at one end of the couch. Turning long-lashed brown eyes on him, the doctor asked, "What do you need from me?"

Despite the fact the man looked like a model, and Xavier suspected he had a constant stream of women throwing themselves at his feet, he wasn't getting a good vibe from this man. Hank Fitzgerald felt fake, insincere. He was a psychiatrist. It would seem that he would want to help those in his care, and yet he seemed completely disinterested in the disappearance of five of his patients. Maybe he'd talk to Mark's friend's brother, Charlie Abbott, and see if he knew anything about Hank Fitzgerald. "I understand you run the victim's support group that our missing women all attend."

Dr. Fitzgerald nodded. "That's correct."

"But you aren't the treating doctor for any of them."

"Correct." He nodded again.

"So, how did you meet them?"

"I advertise—well, no, advertise isn't really the right word. I make other doctors aware of my support groups and invite them to refer to me anyone they think might benefit from them," Dr. Fitzgerald explained.

"How many groups do you run?"

"Quite a few. I try to match the participants of each group according to age so they have more in common. I have groups with children, teenagers, young adults, middle-aged and the elderly. I try to have equal numbers of men and women wherever possible. I wanted to make every participant feel as comfortable as possible. I mean, that's the point. Lots of victims don't talk to their families and friends, or even therapists, because they think that the person doesn't truly understand, but the group provides them an outlet to talk about what they're feeling with someone who's been through something similar." The doctor's eyes were sparkling with excitement as he spoke about his work. He was obviously passionate about it. More passionate than he seemed about the abducted women.

"How well do you know the participants in the groups?"

"The groups run themselves," Dr. Fitzgerald told him. "I have an initial consultation with everyone here." He gestured at the large central table. "And then they run themselves autonomously. They decide where, when, and how often to meet up. I have their contact information and I do the occasional follow up, and make it clear I'm always available to talk with them. Depending on their preference, they continue to see, or not see, their own therapists."

"That wasn't an answer," Xavier pointed out, wondering whether it was possible the doctor was the kidnapper. He was tall and obviously spent hours working out, so he was physically able to carry five unconscious women around. He also wouldn't have been seen as a threat to the women, so if he'd asked them to come to a group meeting at Faith's house they would all have readily agreed.

Shooting him a smile Xavier assumed he thought was a winning one, the doctor elaborated. "I've only ever met them all once. I have their files, so I know what they all went through, and they all signed a release for me to speak with their therapists, so I get the occasional update on how they're progressing."

"Based on what you know, do you believe that there is any chance that any of the women in that group would harm themselves?" Given that he'd seen Faith Smith viciously murdered, the possibility of some sort of suicide pact was clearly out, but he wanted the doctor's take on the women involved.

"You mean do I think they'd kill themselves?" Dr. Fitzgerald's eyes widened in surprise. "No, I didn't get the feeling that any of them were suicidal. Nor did anything I read in the reports from their counselors indicate it. They all seem to be fairly strong individuals. All have remained connected with families and friends. All have continued to work or study. They've forged new relationships, jobs, and studies. All of them are doing well. I like to think that the support group had something to do with that."

"So, I guess you also don't think the women would just leave, start new lives someplace else?"

"Definitely not," Dr. Fitzgerald stated firmly. "Vanessa Adams is very close with her boyfriend and father. Ava Burns has a three-year-old son who is the product of being raped by a high school teacher, but she is extremely devoted to him. Mackenzie Willows and her husband have a very successful business and are very committed to each other. Ruby McBrady is close to finishing her degree in advertising and has embarked on a new relationship. And Faith Smith is making great progress in deciding what she wants to do with her life, mostly due to her new boyfriend. All of these women had lives they were happy with and a lot to live for."

"What can you tell me about the men in the group?"

"You think one of them may have kidnapped the women?" The doctor appeared intrigued by the prospect.

"What can you tell me about them?" Xavier repeated.

"Well, there's Troy Tranchina. He's smart and confident, he works construction, and he was nearly killed in a carjacking. Miles Lanyon is quiet and withdrawn, losing his fiancée in the hit-and-run really hit him hard. Of all of them in the group, he's having the hardest time moving on. Roman Tallow is a tax accountant. He and his sister were close, and he was the one to find her body. She had filed nearly forty complaints against her boyfriend, and he'd been arrested for domestic violence eight times before he killed her. David Murfet doesn't take anything from anyone. He has a temper—more so since his attack. He has a strong sense of justice and hates to see anyone taken advantage of. And Vincent Abrams is a sweet guy. His whole focus in life is Vanessa. It hurt him that her parents thought he was only after her for sex, but he's close with her dad since the murders. So, do you really think one of them could be involved in abducting those women?"

"Abduction and murder," Xavier informed the doctor, watching the man closely.

Running his hands through his thick, wavy brown hair, for the first time Hank Fitzgerald seemed genuinely distressed. "Murder? One of the women was murdered?"

"Faith Smith. Last night." Xavier worked hard to block the memories of her voice, her eyes, her panicked thrashing as the killer held a saw above her body. "Where were you on the night of the fourth?"

"Me? You think *I* did this?" The man looked incredulous.

"The women all agreed to meet at Faith's house that night. There was meant to be a sixth person who seemingly never showed up. They would have met up if you asked them to."

"I never meet with any clients anywhere but here." The doctor looked offended now.

"Where were you, Dr. Fitzgerald?"

"At home, with my wife." Dr. Fitzgerald rolled his eyes and Xavier wondered about the state of his marriage.

"And last night?"

"I was with a client." He sounded sulky now, almost like a petulant child.

"We'll need that client's name and contact information," Xavier informed him. "Remain available, Dr. Fitzgerald." Xavier stood and left the room feeling a little satisfied to leave the doctor sputtering in his wake.

* * * * *

12:17 P.M.

Why was she nervous?

She was only going to talk to Xavier. There was nothing scary about that. And yet she *was* scared.

Annabelle was determined to fix things with him but that didn't mean she wasn't a little anxious. The last time they'd talked they hadn't left things on a very good note. She had told him that she wanted to change, to stop shutting him out, but he hadn't believed her. Then she had asked him if it was too late for them. He'd told her he didn't know. She had declared that she would prove him wrong, prove she could change and that they could fix things between them. And then she'd walked away. Part of her had hoped, believed even, that he would come running after her. But he hadn't. And it had hurt.

Like the coward she often was, she had run, thinking it was

more important to sort things out in her head first rather than just go to Xavier and let him help her. Talking with Laura had changed her mind. Laura was right; she had to talk to Xavier, be honest with him, trust him with everything that she was thinking and feeling.

Approaching his desk, she felt her heart flutter in her chest. She was completely in love with Xavier. She wanted a future with him. She had to let go of this notion that she didn't deserve him. She felt inadequate around him, like she wasn't good enough.

They loved each other. That was what was important.

She had messed things up, but she didn't believe they were beyond repair.

A sandwich sat, virtually untouched, on his desk beside him, and Xavier was completely engrossed in whatever he was reading. She had aimed to catch him on his lunch break, because otherwise he would have told her he was too busy to talk.

"Hey," she said quietly, coming up beside him.

He jumped at the sound of her voice. "Oh, Annabelle, hey. What are you doing here?"

He wasn't exactly screaming excited to see her, but at least he hadn't told her to leave. "I was wondering if we could talk. Just for a few minutes … I can see you're busy," she added.

He studied her with an expression she couldn't read for almost a minute, before he nodded slowly. "Just for a few minutes," he agreed.

Annabelle waited until he'd led her into a nearby interview room, then met his gaze squarely, willing herself to sound strong and sure of herself. "I talked to Laura the other day. Some of the things she said got me thinking, made me reconsider some stuff."

Raising an eyebrow was as much of a response as she got from Xavier. Obviously, he wasn't going to make this easy for her, but then again, she had never made things easy for him. She has made him prove himself to her over and over again. It only seemed fair that he make her prove herself this time around.

Plowing on, she said, "I want to come home. Moving out was a mistake."

Xavier didn't look surprised. In fact, he didn't look much of anything. His face remained a blank mask. "I don't think that's a good idea," he said at last.

Her stomach dropped. "Wh...what?" Annabelle stammered. She had not expected that reaction.

"Look, Annabelle, I really hope you're serious about working through things, and I'm not saying that things between us are over. I'm glad you talked to Laura and I hope you were serious about going back to therapy—"

"I was. I am," she interrupted.

"Great. I'm glad, and I hope it helps you. I just don't want to get burned again. When I said I didn't know if we could fix things between us, I meant it. You don't trust me and that's a pretty big issue to overcome."

Xavier needed for her to prove to him that she trusted him. The only way she could do that was to be honest. "I trust you, Xavier, and I know you wouldn't intentionally walk away from me." She took a deep breath. "Only you did that one time."

He paled, no doubt remembering returning to her motel room to find her gone, then being forced to let a vicious killer walk free in order to save her life. "I've apologized for that," he said quietly.

She nodded. "I know, and I'm not angry, it's just that sometimes it makes me doubt you. I'm sorry. I don't want it to. I can't help it." Anxiously she watched him, awaiting his response. She wasn't good at talking to people about what was going on inside her head. More so than ever since Ricky Preston had used everything she'd told him against her.

His eyes softened a fraction. "I'm glad you told me," he said. "I know that isn't easy for you. And I'm glad that you know what you need to work on in therapy."

"But you still don't want me to come home." Annabelle fought to hold in the tears burning her eyes.

He sighed deeply. "It's not that I don't want you to. It's just that you're not the only one who's scared of getting hurt again. I'm going to be busy watching over Paige until the stalker is caught, and I have a pile of open cases I'm working right now. Maybe we should take a break. Let things calm down. You can work on things with your therapist and then, maybe, we can try and work things out between us. For now, I think it's best if we just put some space between us."

Xavier reached out a hand, then froze, his palm just an inch from her face. Taking the initiative, she tilted her head until her cheek was cupped in his hand. Ever so slowly, he brushed his fingertips across her temple. Then his hand dropped, and he left the room.

Annabelle stood there for a long time after Xavier had gone—feeling both disappointed and encouraged by their talk. She wished that Xavier had accepted her moving back into their home, but she had seen in his eyes that he was proud of her when she had admitted one of her fears to him.

She could do this. Maybe she was stronger than she gave herself credit for. She had survived the deaths of her parents and three siblings. She had survived being abducted and raped. She had survived killing two people. If she could survive all of that, then surely, she could survive something as safe and simple as reaching out to people for help.

She could definitely do this.

* * * * *

12:59 P.M.

"So, have we narrowed down the suspect list?" Belinda Jersey asked.

"I think we can rule out Mackenzie Willows' husband," Xavier replied. "He was at work—several dozen people confirm it—at the time the women were abducted. Nothing funny in his financials, no family or friends of the couple indicated any marital problems, or that he had ever been violent with her. Also, nothing suspicious on Ruby McBrady's boyfriend. They're both out as suspects."

"What did you think of the psychiatrist who runs the support group?" his boss asked.

"I didn't like him."

Chuckling softly, Belinda gave a wry smile. "Good to know. But do you think he's a viable suspect?"

"Maybe." Xavier considered this, attempting to set aside his dislike for the man and think about it logically. "He was physically capable. He had the women's trust, so he could easily have set up the meeting and all of them would have willingly come."

"But ..." Belinda prompted.

"But, I don't know. He was much more interested in his work than the missing women. I'm not sure he would have done it unless he thought it would get publicity for himself."

"So, he's not in or out at the moment," Belinda summarized.

"I guess," Xavier agreed.

"And the men from the group?"

"Vincent Abrams is out. I know him; he wouldn't do this." Of that, Xavier was positive. "Of the remaining four men, all had the women's trust. The point of the group was to support one another. If one of them called and asked to meet, they all would have done it if at all possible. All could be physically capable. Troy is a builder, so he'd have access to all the tools that were in the room; then again, all were readily available in any number of stores. Miles is the quiet one and apparently the one finding moving past what happened the hardest. He lost a loved one which could be a trigger. Roman also lost his sister and was hospitalized for a short time after it happened. And David is the one with a temper. I don't think we can discount any of them at the moment."

"Any alibis?"

"Nothing definitive at the moment. Troy, Miles, and Roman all live alone. David claims he was at his girlfriend's house, but so far, we haven't been able to contact her. She's apparently out of town, but she hasn't returned any of the messages I've left her."

"The video didn't give you any hints or at least something to count one of them out?"

Focusing on the image of the man in the video, Xavier detached his emotions, so he could mentally compare each of their suspects. The man had been wearing baggy clothing, so it was difficult to get a sense of his build. And gauging height was difficult because there was nothing to compare him to. There had been no way to determine skin color, eye color, or hair color. The man had even disguised his voice. "Nothing yet, but I am assuming he's going to continue to send us feeds of his kills, so hopefully, he'll become complacent and sloppy as time goes on." Knowing they had to wait for the killer to make another move to get enough information to identify him was torture.

"What about anything he said, did that point to any of the men, in particular?"

"He said it was our fault. By 'our,' we're assuming he means the police. He said that we failed Faith and him, that we were meant to protect people and we didn't. He said he'd thought taking Faith and the others would be enough, but it wasn't. Then he told her she was going to a better place and said some gibberish which he believed would take away her pain as he killed her."

Faith's screams and pleas continued to echo inside his head. Xavier doubted he'd ever forget.

Even worse was knowing that the killer wanted him to watch Ruby, Mackenzie, Ava, and Vanessa murdered as well.

In his mind, Xavier saw Annabelle, virtually naked, tied up and bleeding, in her father's airtight wine cellar. He could so easily have lost her that night. Her life or death had come down to mere minutes.

He'd made the right decision with Annabelle today, right?

He'd wanted to take her back, have her move back into their home, have things go back to the way they'd been. Only he didn't really want things to be the way they'd been before. He wanted them to be better. If Annabelle couldn't trust him, then they couldn't be a couple. It wasn't fair to him, and it wasn't fair to Annabelle either. He hadn't wanted to hurt her, but he had to be honest with her. Maybe after some time away from each other, they'd both be able to think more clearly about what they really wanted.

Xavier knew he couldn't commit to Annabelle until he knew that she could stand on her own two feet. That she was making these changes for herself and not just to pacify him. Otherwise every time they had difficulties, and that was inevitable because every couple had problems from time to time, he would be worrying that she would bail on them. He didn't care how long it took her to work through everything Ricky Preston had done to her. He wanted to be by her side helping her every step of the way, but he had to know that she trusted him to be there to help her.

She had taken the first step though. She'd reached out to Laura and taken on board what they'd talked about. She had admitted to him that her fear of him leaving her stemmed from that night he'd left her alone at the motel. He still felt guilty about his decisions that night because not only he had to live with the consequences, but Annabelle did too.

"Xavier?"

Blinking slowly, he'd forgotten he was at work—in a meeting. Belinda was looking at him expectantly. She'd obviously asked him something, but what, he had no idea.

"You didn't hear a word I said, did you?" Belinda asked, her dark eyes full of understanding. "Things improving between you and Annabelle?"

Xavier liked his boss, but he wasn't comfortable discussing the details of his personal life with her. "Maybe."

A hint of something, perhaps disappointment, flashed across Belinda's face, but it was quickly covered by her usual unflappable calm. "I was saying that all four of the men in the support group could have cause to be angry with the police since all are victims of crime. But the doctor probably wouldn't."

"I agree. I think the doctor is probably out, but I'll do a little more looking into him. I think we need to start pulling them all in for interviews, push them hard, hope whoever's guilty cracks."

"We don't have enough for a warrant on any of them," Belinda reminded him.

"I know, but I'm hoping they'll all come in voluntarily if they think we just want their help. If they've got nothing to hide, then they should agree, and if one doesn't, that'll be our guy."

"Okay, make times to bring them in, make it seem like we just have follow-up questions."

"We need to try and locate where the women are being held. It has to be someplace large enough for him to keep five women restrained. The women had the majority. They probably could have overpowered him, and he would have needed to keep them tied up. It also has to be somewhere that no one would hear them call for help. There has to be at least two rooms because there were no signs of the other women. And Faith was clean in the video, so this place also has to have facilities for him to wash them. That would have been risky. She could have run while he had her unrestrained."

"Or he cleaned her while she was unconscious. We know he drugged them to abduct them, and she was drugged when he took her into the room where he killed her. Could be he's using two separate locations," Belinda suggested. "One where he keeps them and one where he kills them."

He nodded slowly; that was a definite possibility. If he had Faith and the other women right next door to the killing room, then he wouldn't have had to drug her. Whereas, if he had to transport her, then drugging her was definitely the safest way to do so. "Faith's body hasn't turned up yet. Could be he's buried her on his property."

"Maybe," Belinda agreed.

The killer had hacked Faith Smith's body into six pieces. Head, torso, arms, and legs. So far none of the pieces had turned up anywhere. "He kept them for almost four days before he killed Faith, but there are no guarantees he'll wait again. He could kill another woman at any time."

"They might already be dead," Belinda inserted.

"No, if they were dead we would know. It's *us* he's angry with, not them. He seemed to honestly believe that he was helping Faith and that when he killed her she would feel no pain."

"He's delusional. Shouldn't his therapist know that?"

"I don't think he's delusional, not in the completely crazy lunatic sense. He knows how to hold it together, but he seems to be unraveling quickly. He told Faith that he had thought just abducting the women was enough—that he'd never planned on killing them, yet he had the room set up and ready to go. He *did* plan on killing them. Everything he's done so far has been methodical, perfectly planned and executed. At the same time, he seems to be reacting to his interpretation of our apparent lack of interest in the abductions. Unless we find them first, he will kill all four of the women."

And Xavier knew the killer would make sure that he would see every horrible second.

* * * * *

3:41 P.M.

"Where's Faith? What did you do to her?" Mackenzie screamed at the man as the door opened.

Ruby blinked her eyes open at the sound of her friend's hoarse voice. The man hadn't been back since he'd drugged and taken Faith. He hadn't brought them any more food or water and Ruby guessed it had been over twenty-four hours since Faith had been gone, and another five or six before that since he'd last fed them. Her whole body was crying out for water. She was so dehydrated, she could think of nothing else. Except her terror.

"Shh, Kenz," she whispered to her friend. Mackenzie was going to get herself killed. It had taken her ages to regain consciousness after that man had strangled her. And her voice was still hoarse. Not that it was stopping her from yelling.

Ignoring her, Mackenzie continued to rant. "Did you kill her? You said you weren't going to hurt us, but you killed her, didn't you?" Mackenzie demanded, yanking on her chains.

The man didn't respond. Instead, he carried down four bottles of water and four sandwiches, setting one of each down in front of them.

"Answer me." Mackenzie would have been screaming at top volume if her larynx hadn't been damaged. "Did you kill Faith? Are you going to kill us too?"

"Mackenzie, shh," Ruby begged. She just wanted to go home. Hadn't she been through enough? Hadn't all of them already been through enough? She was finally moving on with her life.

She had stupidly married her high school boyfriend right after graduation. At only eighteen neither of them had been ready for marriage. The stress had gotten to both of them, but while she'd buried herself in her studies, her husband had turned to alcohol. She'd known she should leave the first time he hit her. But she hadn't. She'd been too embarrassed to let her parents know that they'd been right, and she was too young to be married. So, she'd stayed and he had continued to beat her. Until the time he'd almost killed her. Then she had finally wised up and left. Filed for divorce. Moved on with her life.

And now, she was happy. For the first time in her life she was truly happy. She had a boyfriend she loved. She had almost finished her studies and was looking forward to working in a field she loved, and she was closer with her family than she had been since she was in elementary school.

Her life had been good. And now, it was ruined. Now she was chained to a wall, dressed in clothes stained with her own waste, desperately fighting the knowledge that her life was soon going to be over.

The man knelt in front Mackenzie, and her friend fell silent, shrinking away from him, fear filling her blue eyes, her matted red hair framing her pale face.

"Please don't hurt her," Ruby implored. "She'll keep her mouth shut; she won't say anything else."

Now the man turned to look at her, and Ruby wished he would take off the glasses and mask, so she could see his face. It was so hard to read him and thus know how best to act and respond when she couldn't see him. "I don't want to hurt anyone," he said quietly.

"Did you kill Faith?" Mackenzie demanded.

"Kenzie," she admonished desperately.

The man turned back to Mackenzie. "Yes. I killed her."

"You monster." Rage and hatred flushed across Mackenzie's pale face, turning it bright red as she apparently forgot how the man had reacted last time she had called him a monster.

The reaction from their abductor was the same this time.

Launching himself at Mackenzie, the man straddled her, his fists swinging wildly, connecting time and time again with her face.

"Stop! Stop, you're killing her!" Ruby realized as she said this that the man wouldn't care about that. He had killed Faith and he no doubt intended to kill the rest of them too.

Even Ava, who had done nothing but cry since Faith was taken, roused. "Please, stop!" she shrieked.

Their screaming had Vanessa stirring, staring at the man's

violent attack through sunken, dazed eyes.

It wasn't until Mackenzie's cries of pain ceased that the man paused.

"Is she dead?" Ruby asked shakily. Mackenzie's face was a bloody mess and she wasn't moving.

The man felt Mackenzie's neck and then sunk down to the floor. "She's alive. I ... I ... I didn't mean ... I don't like to be called ... it wasn't my fault," he stammered.

"Just let us go home," Ava wailed. "I want to see my little boy."

"Why did you kill Faith?" Ruby asked.

"I had to. They didn't do anything. They keep failing everyone. They don't do their job. I just wanted to make them understand that wasn't acceptable. I didn't want to have to kill Faith. I loved her. But I needed to push them further. Don't worry. It didn't hurt her, I made sure of that, she didn't suffer." The man's voice had gone imploring.

"Who? Who are you talking about?" If she could get him to start opening up, then maybe there was a way to get out of here alive.

Shaking himself as though to clear his head, the man pulled another syringe from his pocket. "It's time, Ruby."

"No," she protested. She didn't want to die. So many times when she'd been married she had prayed her husband's blows would end her life and the misery she was stuck in. Until that day she had awakened in the hospital and learned how close she had come to death had she realized how much she wanted to live.

"It won't hurt," he said softly, reaching for her arm to inject her.

"No!" she screamed more earnestly this time. "No, get away from me! Let me go home. Please. Let all of us go. We won't tell anyone what you did. We don't even know who you are. Vanessa and Mackenzie need a doctor. Please."

Her pleas fells on deaf ears as the man shoved her up against the wall and tried to hold her arm still so he could stick the needle in it.

Ruby fought with every ounce of strength she possessed—thrashing and kicking and clawing and swinging her arms. Remembering her self-defense training, she tried to aim her hits for his groin, eyes, and throat. She wasn't sure she was achieving much, but she felt one hit connect with something, heard his grunt of pain. It didn't slow him down.

She yelped, in terror more than pain, as the needle pierced her skin. Whatever drug he'd injected her with took effect almost immediately.

The world began to swirl around her, the colors becoming one mass of gray.

She heard Ava scream her name.

And then nothing …

Ever so slowly she became aware of her surroundings.

The air smelled coppery. She could even taste it.

Where was she?

What was the last thing she remembered?

The dirt room.

The man had been beating Mackenzie for calling him a monster.

Then he had told her it was time and he'd come at her with a syringe.

He had given her something to knock her out.

And now she was waking up.

But where?

Ruby tried to open her eyes, but they were too heavy.

Instead she tried to figure out where she might be.

She wasn't in the dirt room. It not only smelled different, it felt different too. She was lying on something cold and hard, nothing like the bed she had first awakened to find herself on.

Tentatively, Ruby tried to move but found she couldn't.

She was tied up.

She couldn't take this anymore.

Ignoring her pounding head and the nausea that relentlessly wracked her stomach, Ruby began to scream. Scream and yank violently on the cuffs that bound her.

Then abruptly, she went still.

Voices.

She could hear voices.

Maybe she was in a hospital. Maybe someone had found them. Maybe she had been rescued.

That notion died quickly. If she were in a hospital, then doctors and nurses would have come running at the sound of her screams.

She was still trapped.

Then who was the man talking to?

This time she focused all her energy on just opening her eyes.

When she finally managed to do it, she screamed.

Screamed until her throat was raw.

The ceiling above her, the table she was tied to, the walls, they were all streaked in dried blood.

Faith's blood.

She was lying in Faith's blood.

This was the room where the man had brought her friend to kill her.

This was the room where he was going to kill her too.

Hysteria was overwhelming her.

She couldn't concentrate, couldn't think, could barely even breathe.

In front of her stood the man. He was talking to someone, only no one else was in the room with them. He was probably talking to someone on the phone. Did he have a partner? She hadn't seen one but that didn't mean he didn't.

Ruby blinked and the next thing she knew the man was standing over her.

A hatchet in his hand.

He rested his other hand on her chest and began to mumble something she was way too far gone to understand.

A white haze descended on her.

She was going into shock.

Maybe that was for the best.

Her overwrought mind transported her away from the here and now, depositing her back in time to her childhood. Playing on soft, sandy, white beaches. Swimming and tumbling in the surf. Building snowmen and throwing snowballs in a forest that looked like something from a Christmas card. Jumping in piles of crunchy autumn leaves. Gathering flowers from the neighbor's gardens to bring home to her mother. Christmases, birthdays, barbeques, parties ...

Ruby never even felt the first blow, nor the second or third. She never noticed her blood flowing freely from her wounds and mingling with her friend's.

She simply slipped quietly away.

* * * * *

7:19 P.M.

The Protector was tired.

And not just from the physical toll of disposing of Faith Smith and Ruby McBrady's bodies.

He was emotionally tired. Drained.

He had been for a long time now.

It didn't matter how hard he tried to make things better, it could never overwrite what had happened.

Nothing could.

The events of that night were forever seared into his mind. No, deeper than that. They were seared into his soul.

He had been changed forever.

That's why he had to do this.

He couldn't let others go through what he had.

That was the only reason he was doing this.

It had broken his heart to have to kill Faith. If he hadn't known he was sending her to a better place, a peaceful place, he wouldn't have done it. Now she could be happy. She was without pain, without heartache, without failure. A place of eternal happiness. She deserved that.

Killing Ruby hadn't been as hard. He hadn't wanted to kill her, had even regretted it, but it wasn't quite the same as the loss he'd felt when Faith moved on.

Ruby was his friend. He liked her. He wished there had been another way. A way to have kept Faith and Ruby alive. A way to spare Ava, Mackenzie, and Vanessa.

But there wasn't.

He had to follow through.

He had to push harder.

It still wasn't enough.

Even killing two women hadn't changed the police.

He had watched the news today. Robberies, rapes, murders, more of the same.

He had to make it stop.

If he couldn't, he would never be free of the horror that tortured him.

He needed to do more.

And The Protector knew just what that more should be.

The police needed to know that horror could touch their lives too. That they weren't immune to the evil that stalked humanity. No one was exempt from that.

So, his next step was to remind them of that.

He had done a little research.

Found what he needed.

A detective whose wife had been touched by evil.

She was the perfect one. He would take her. Bring her to the others. He would set her free too.

If that didn't motivate the police of the city to start doing their job, then nothing would.

NOVEMBER 9TH

8:22 A.M.

"Hey," Sofia whispered quietly as she stepped into the room.

Ryan and Mark stopped their hushed conversation and turned to her. Her husband smiled and came to give her a quick kiss. "I've missed you," he murmured into her hair, holding on to her tightly.

She had missed him too. Not that she minded Ryan staying at the hospital to keep Paige safe. If the stalker killed Paige, then Sofia would never forgive herself.

This man, whoever he was, had been stalking her for seven years now. It had started with flowers and letters and phone calls. Then he'd started to break into her home to leave her gifts. Then he'd gone quiet for a while. She had thought he was gone, moved on to an obsession with another woman, or maybe even been arrested on other charges.

But then he'd come back.

Breaking into her and Ryan's house several times when she was home alone. She had even shot at him one night.

Then the stalker had fixated on Paige. Convinced himself that Paige was having an affair with Ryan and that the only way to end it was to end Paige's life.

Sofia had tried so hard to figure out who this man was. And now that she knew it was Dr. Bruce Daniels, she had tried, unsuccessfully, to figure out why he would have cause to stalk her. To the best of her knowledge the first time she had met Dr. Daniels was in the hospital after an encounter with two vicious killers, one of whom was her own sister, had resulted in her being stabbed. But that was after the stalker had already been fixated on her for several years and after he had made an attempt on Paige's life.

And now, because of her, because she hadn't been able to identify the man stalking her, Paige had almost lost her life two more times, and she'd been raped.

A shudder rippled through her as she pictured how terrified Paige must have been, trapped inside her car as it slowly filled with icy water. If Ryan and Jack had been just a couple of minutes later, then their attempts at resuscitation would have failed. She couldn't even think about how Paige must have felt trapped inside her own body. It was simply too horrific.

Noticing her shudder, Ryan pulled her against his chest, cradling her head in his hand, his fingers massaging the base of her skull. "It's not your fault," he said firmly.

His words didn't ease her guilt. Of course, it was her fault. If this man hadn't been stalking her, if she hadn't become friends with Paige, then none of this would have happened. Her friend wouldn't be lying in a hospital bed right now.

"How's she doing?" she asked Mark.

"The same," her brother-in-law replied. "She wears herself out every time Elias brings Hayley and Arianna to visit. She slept for twelve hours straight after visiting Laura the other night." Mark ran his hands through his short blond hair, making it stand straight up. "I don't know what to do for her. Charlie Abbott is coming later today. I wanted to wait until she was stronger because I didn't think she could handle talking about what happened, but she's not getting any stronger. Maybe Charlie can help her."

"She looks so fragile." Sofia couldn't take her eyes off Paige's pale face.

"Hey." Ryan hooked a finger under her chin and tilted her face so she had to look at him and not at Paige. "She is not fragile. You know that. She's tough. She's been through a lot and she always comes out on the other side. She will make it through this. She has a lot of support, and she has the best motivation in the world to get better—Hayley and Arianna."

"Yeah, you're right," she agreed. Paige had the family she had always wanted, and she would do whatever she had to, to work through what had happened to her. "And speaking of the girls, Elias and I are going to go shopping, pick out furniture, clothes, and toys for them. I'm supposed to meet him at nine, but I just wanted to come and see Paige first."

"Paige will get better once we catch the stalker," Ryan assured her.

She wanted to believe that, but Paige had stopped breathing twice in as many days. What if she'd suffered permanent damage? What if she never got better? She looked to Mark for his opinion.

"Her brain scan is clear. She should make a full recovery," Mark said.

Mark's words didn't really provide much comfort since he was clearly extremely concerned about Paige. "I better go, but I'm going to come back later and spend some time with her and Laura. Ryan, maybe you could have dinner with us tonight? Sophie and Ned miss you."

Her husband pulled her back into his arms. "How about dinner at home. Then I'll drop you and the kids back at my parents' place when I come back here. I'm sure Xavier will stay with Paige."

Ryan had insisted that she and their kids stay with his parents, so they weren't home alone. The stalker was escalating, and her father-in-law was a retired cop. If the stalker changed track and came after her, then she would be safe with her in-laws. "The kids will be thrilled." She stood on tiptoes and tugged on Ryan's shoulders, so he leaned down and kissed her.

"Okay, bye guys. Mark, call me if anything changes with her."

"Of course."

With a last look at Paige, she headed for the hospital's parking garage. Sofia didn't think she was ever going to stop feeling guilty for what her friend had gone through. Even if Paige fully recovered, she was always going to bear the psychological scars.

In her mind Sofia tried to work out what she could have done differently. Surely there had to have been a way to figure out that Dr. Daniels was her stalker. Ryan had asked her if she thought it could have been him when she was in the hospital almost a week ago.

She had said no.

Only she hadn't been positive. The doctor had creeped her out since the first time she'd met him, but she hadn't thought that was reason enough to believe that he'd been stalking her.

Within hours the stalker had tried to run Paige down with a car and then run her car off the road and into the river.

She could have stopped it from happening.

If she'd said it was a viable possibility when Ryan asked her and she'd asked him to look into it, then he would have put someone on Dr. Daniels and Paige wouldn't have nearly died.

Movement in her peripheral vision caught her attention.

She turned just as a man emerged from between two cars and tried to grab her.

The fact that she was turning saved her from having the syringe he clutched in his hands plunge into her arm.

But it didn't buy her much time.

He was big, and he moved quickly, grabbing hold of her wrist and yanking her up against his rock-hard body.

Paige had drilled her in self-defense for years, and Sofia knew that screaming for help was the number one thing she could do right now. Many women who ended up hurt or raped or dead could have potentially been saved had they simply screamed.

Opening her mouth, she let out an ear-piercing scream.

That caught her attacker by surprise, and she took advantage of his loosening grip on her arm to do the second thing Paige had taught her.

Pivoting, she rammed one knee up and into his groin.

Grunting in pain, the man let her go and doubled over.

Spinning around, Sofia attempted to run. However, the man wasn't out yet. A hand wrapped around her ankle and tugged, causing her to fall to the ground. Pain shot up her arms, but she didn't have time to think about it.

Clawing with her hands, she tried to drag herself away from the hand clutching her.

Why wasn't anyone coming? The hospital parking lot was always busy. How had she managed to get attacked the one time it was quiet?

The man hauled her closer, and Sofia kicked out with her other leg, failing to connect with anything. He climbed on her back and pinned her to the ground, Sofia knew she was in the most vulnerable position possible. On her stomach she couldn't properly use either her hands or her legs to fight back.

That didn't stop her from doing everything she could to get free. There was no way she was letting this man get her in a car. If she did, she would probably never be found alive. And Sofia had no doubt that he intended to abduct her. If all he wanted was to rob her, he'd have done it already.

The man wrapped her long wavy red hair around his fist and slammed her head into the concrete. Once, twice, three times.

The blows to her head didn't knock her unconscious but everything began to swirl around her. It was like a fog descended over her.

Vaguely, she felt the man climb off her.

Then he was reaching for her, flipping her over and hooking his arms under her shoulders and knees, preparing to lift her.

He was going to take her.

All of a sudden, a blur came rushing toward them.

Or maybe she imagined it.

No. It was definitely something.

Another man.

For a second, she thought there were two of them. She didn't stand a chance against two men. Although with head injuries, she didn't even stand a chance against one.

The second man attacked the first, knocking him off her and throwing him to the ground.

Maybe the second man was a Good Samaritan, answering her screams for help.

Sofia knew she had to move, only she didn't think she was capable of walking right now. Her head was throbbing. If she stood, she was probably going to pass out. Instead she rolled back onto her stomach. The movement sent spasms of pain through her skull and she threw up.

Still, she tried to move, attempting to crawl on all fours. Sick to her stomach and her entire body shaking, she didn't make it more than a yard before she sank down to rest against the concrete. Her eyes fell closed. She could feel unconsciousness tugging at her mind, but she fought it with every bit of strength she still possessed because once she was unconscious she was completely vulnerable.

"Police!" a voice yelled, the sound echoing inside her pounding head.

A third man came running up.

Forcing her eyes open, she saw blond hair and a familiar face. It was Ryan.

Relief overwhelmed her, and she sank down, allowing herself to let go a little and rest. Ryan wouldn't let anything happen to her.

Ignoring the scuffle going on behind her, she just laid there, trying to breathe slowly through her nose to still the churning in her stomach.

Someone knelt beside her, and fingers pressed into her neck.

"Mark, get Jack to stay with Paige and get down to the parking garage now. Sofia was just attacked."

Not wanting her husband to worry, Sofia pushed herself up on her elbows. "I'm okay, Ryan."

She felt him relax at the sound of her voice. "Lay back down, sweetheart, your head's bleeding," he ordered gently.

Ignoring him, she continued to struggle to get up. Now that it was over, the fear she hadn't allowed herself to feel before came rushing in. She needed to be in her husband's arms. "Hold me, please," she whimpered.

Gathering her into his arms, Ryan sat, leaning back against the closest car and cradled her in his lap, rocking her back and forth. "I thought you were dead," he whispered into her hair, reflexively clutching her tighter.

"He was waiting for me. He had a syringe, but he didn't get a chance to inject me. I got away for a moment, but he grabbed me. I fell, then he slammed my head into the ground," she explained haltingly. The nausea had receded, and her head didn't hurt so badly anymore, but her terror was rising.

Ryan continued to rock her. "Shh, honey, you're safe now. You're safe," he repeated, as much for his benefit as hers, she suspected.

Snuggling deeper into Ryan's arms, Sofia pressed her face against his neck, and twisted her hands into his sweater, clinging to him.

She'd been lucky.

Very lucky.

If she hadn't seen him coming a split second before he grabbed her, then the man would have injected her with whatever he had in the syringe and he would have had her out of the parking garage before anyone even knew she was gone.

The fragile barrier holding back her tears gave way and she began to sob.

* * * * *

9:46 A.M.

Ryan's heart rate still hadn't slowed.

When he'd come down to the parking garage hoping to catch Sofia before she left only to find her lying unmoving and bleeding on the ground and two men fighting beside her, he thought he'd lost her.

For one horrifying, earth-stopping second, he had truly believed that his wife was dead.

Two men had been scuffling nearby, but when he'd yelled out that he was the police, one of them had taken off running. He hadn't known if both men were involved in whatever had happened to Sofia or if one was a Good Samaritan who had stepped in to help, but he couldn't risk leaving one of them with Sofia while he chased after the man who'd run. So, he'd let him go and focused on the man left behind.

Ryan couldn't have been more shocked to see who it was.

Stepping inside the interview room, the other man's gaze snapped up immediately, blue eyes widening in fear. "Is that her blood?"

Glancing down, Ryan saw that Sofia's blood smeared the front of his sweater. He had to take a moment to remind himself that she was fine. Mark had put a couple of stitches in the cut on her head and sent her off for an X-ray of her wrist, which she had hurt when she'd fallen.

"Is she okay?" Panic made the other man's voice rise an octave. "I tried to stop him, but he had already hurt her before I got there."

Staring at the man, mixed emotions battled inside him. Ryan had no doubt that he had saved Sofia's life and yet that didn't undo every despicable thing he'd done.

"Is she okay?" Dr. Bruce Daniels demanded. "Is Sofia okay?"

Bruce Daniels had dyed his naturally reddish blond hair that was speckled with gray completely gray, and wore a pair of wire-rimmed glasses, hoping the disguise would throw off the police he knew were hunting for him. The doctor had obviously been hanging around the hospital, hoping that another opportunity to get at Paige would present itself. Instead, he'd stumbled upon Sofia's attempted kidnapping.

"Answer me."

"Yes," Ryan answered at last. "Sofia is fine. You saved her life. But she will still never forgive you for what you did to Paige."

Arching a brow, the doctor smirked. "I don't know what you're talking about."

"Give it a break, we know it's you. My brother saw you in Paige's room right before you attacked him. You didn't use a condom when you raped Paige, so we have your DNA." Ryan had to take a minute to stow his anger. This man had single-handedly nearly destroyed Paige's life. To say he hated Bruce Daniels was a gross understatement.

The doctor continued to stare at him, his face an infuriatingly blank mask.

Taking a deep, calming breath before he did something he'd regret, Ryan heard Xavier's warnings echo in his head. He didn't want to do anything that would give the doctor cause to get off. Prison was the only thing that was going to stop Bruce Daniels from coming after Paige again. "Look, I'm not going to tell you again that Paige and I are not now nor have we ever been having an affair because I'd be wasting my breath. At the very least, you're going to be charged with four counts of attempted murder of a police officer, sexual assault, and assault. If you don't want to hurt Sofia more than you already have by targeting her friend and making her feel responsible for your behavior, then I suggest you plead guilty and don't inflict further trauma on Paige by making her go through a trial."

Bruce looked offended. "I would never do anything to hurt Sofia."

Ryan shook his head. His loathing of this man grew exponentially every time he pictured Paige's haunted brown eyes or Sofia's guilty silver ones. "You don't get it. Sofia and Paige are friends—good friends. I am in love with my wife. Paige is in love with her husband. There was no affair. Your targeting Paige and nearly killing her several times hurt everyone who cares about Paige, including Sofia."

Doubt crept slowly into Bruce's eyes. "There was no affair?"

"No. You almost killed Paige for nothing. You took away her ability to get pregnant. You raped her. She's lying in a hospital bed right now because she's so traumatized she can barely function. Do you have any idea what it would have done to Sofia if Paige had died? She would never have stopped blaming herself."

Stricken, Bruce asked, "Sofia would have blamed herself?"

"I guess you don't know her as well as you think you do," Ryan informed him. "Sofia is the kindest, sweetest, most generous person. She lives for her family and friends. When you called her right before you ran Paige off the road, she begged you not to do it. You ignored her. She hates you."

Dr. Daniels flinched. "She hates me?"

"You've terrorized her for seven years. You've terrorized one of her best friends because of her. Of course, she hates you. But there's something you can do for her. You can give her closure by telling me why you're obsessed with her, then you can plead guilty and spare Paige more pain."

Considering this, the doctor nodded slowly. "Okay. I'll plead guilty. I'll apologize to your partner ..."

"You stay away from Paige," Ryan interrupted. Paige didn't need an apology from this man. She just needed to know she was safe. "You go near her again and I will kill you. And enjoy it. Now, how did you meet Sofia?"

The man hesitated, opened his mouth as though to reply and then snapped it closed again.

Ryan didn't have time for this. He wanted to know how Bruce Daniels had first come into contact with Sofia but not enough to waste time with him. He wanted to get back to the hospital and give Paige the good news. "Fine, whatever." He turned on his heel and headed for the door.

"Wait."

He stopped but didn't turn around, not wanting to play into the doctor's games. "Don't waste my time. Either tell me why you're obsessed with Sofia or I'm leaving."

"She's my sister," Bruce Daniels murmured.

Ryan was shocked, to say the least. That was not the answer Ryan had been expecting. Sofia's father, who growing up was actually the man she thought was her oldest brother, had only been fourteen when she was born. Dr. Daniels was fifty, which would have made him just three years older than Sofia's father, had her father still been alive. Sofia's mother, whom she had grown up thinking was her stepmother, had only one other biological child, a little boy who had died when he was just two years old.

"Yes," Bruce Daniels confirmed when Ryan turned back around, apparently correctly interpreting the question in his eyes.

"You're Logan Everette III. Gloria's son with the doctor she met in the hospital after she attempted suicide."

"I didn't die as a toddler," the doctor explained. "My mother found out about what the judge was planning, so she got the maid to help fake my death and sent me to be raised by my father. I didn't even know about the Everettes until my father's death. I couldn't go to my mother because the judge was still alive. He was still a threat to me. So, I kept tabs on Sofia. She was all the family I had left. And then when all the rest of them were dead, I was scared. I didn't want to lose her too. So, I kept my distance, but I wanted to be a part of her life, in whatever way I could. She's my sister. I didn't want to see her hurt. That's why I went after your partner. I just didn't want anyone to mess with Sofia's happiness."

Ryan shook his head in disbelief. He'd always assumed Sofia's stalker was a guy she'd crossed paths with somewhere along the way who'd developed a secret crush on her. That Gloria's dead son was actually not dead had never occurred to him. This whole thing was so unbelievable he didn't know what to say.

"Do you think Sofia would come and see me? Just once?" Bruce Daniels asked, looking almost childishly hopeful.

"No way," Ryan answered firmly. "I don't want you near Sofia. I don't want you near Paige. I don't want you near anybody I care about." Ryan wanted to leave. He'd had enough of being in this despicable man's presence, but he needed to know if the man had seen anything useful in Sofia's attempted abduction. "What did you see in the parking garage?"

Hurt and disappointment clouded Dr. Daniels' face and he didn't reply.

"Hey." He thumped a fist on the table and the doctor jumped. "You can help Sofia one last time. Tell me everything you saw this morning. Someone tried to abduct her. They could come back. I need to know everything I can, so I can protect her. So tell me everything that you saw."

"I didn't see much. I was in the parking garage. I just needed one more go at your friend to finally kill her. Sorry," he added when Ryan flinched.

He forced his anger down. Paige was safe, and he just needed to hear this and then he never had to see this man again. "Just keep going."

"I saw Sofia go into the garage. I didn't follow her right away. I had to debate whether trying to get into the hospital was worth the risk or whether I should go after Sofia, just watch her for a while. I decided to go after Sofia. When I came around a corner, I saw her on the ground. A man was on top of her. He climbed off and was picking her up, so I ran over. I knocked him down and we fought, then you came. I got distracted when you yelled out, and he got a hit in to my stomach. I let go of him, he ran, you cuffed me."

"What did the man look like?"

"He was dressed all in black. Jeans, hoodie, gloves, sunglasses,"

Dr. Daniels elaborated.

"Did you get a look at his skin color?" This guy was sounding suspiciously like the man in Xavier's case who had abducted Faith Smith, Ruby McBrady, and the other women from their support group. Especially given the fact that Sofia had been a victim of a violent crime.

"I don't know. White I think, but I'm really not sure."

"He wasn't wearing a balaclava?" The man in the videos of Faith and Ruby's murders had worn one.

"I don't think so."

"Did he say anything?"

"Nope, not a word. We were probably fighting for less than a minute when you turned up. Enough time to get in a couple of blows each but that was it."

"Did you see what he was driving?"

"No, he was with Sofia when I got there, and then he ran off when you arrived. I don't know anything else. I'm sorry. If I did, I'd tell you. I'd do anything to protect Sofia."

Ryan believed that. In his own warped, depraved, twisted mind, Dr. Bruce Daniels had believed he was helping Sofia. Not that that excused his behavior. It would take Paige years to work through everything this man had done to her. She would never fully recover—she would always bear the psychological scars. And Sofia would likely never stop blaming herself for Paige's suffering. Ryan hoped the doctor rotted in hell.

"You'll tell her that, won't you?" Dr. Daniels implored. "You'll tell Sofia that I love her, that I only want the best for her, that I never meant to cause her a second of pain? You'll tell her? Please?"

Bruce Daniels was still yelling at him as he left the room.

* * * * *

11:04 A.M.

Lifting open her heavy eyes, Paige was surprised to find herself alone in the hospital room.

When she'd woken earlier, Jack had been here. She had asked where Mark was and if something had happened to Laura, but he'd told her there was nothing to worry about and to go back to sleep. She had obeyed, not because she made a conscious decision to but because she hadn't possessed enough strength to hold her eyes open.

Paige was tired. So tired she could barely think of anything else. Every time Elias brought the girls around, she had to force every cell in her body to function. Once they left, she usually passed out into an exhausted slumber.

She knew Mark was worried about her. She could see it in the way he looked at her. She wasn't getting better, and he couldn't find a medical explanation for it. He wanted to fix her, but she was starting to wonder if that was even possible.

She couldn't live any longer with the stress of knowing that her stalker and would-be murderer was still out there.

"Hey, you're awake."

The door to her room opened and Sofia pushed a wheelchair with Laura in it inside.

"Where is everyone?" she asked, hating how faint her voice was these days.

"Jack and Mark are just outside your room. Do you need Mark?" Sofia asked.

"No," Paige replied. There wasn't anything he could do for her anyway. "Is everything okay with Rosie?" she asked Laura. Then her eyes narrowed on Sofia's face. Her friend had a bandage taped across her forehead. "What happened to you? Are you okay?"

"Rosie is fine," Laura assured her. "She's doing great. Breathing on her own, and they're feeding her breast milk with a feeding tube. They're going to be moving her out of NICU to the special care nursery this afternoon. The doctors sent me away to get some rest."

"Then why aren't you?"

Laura smiled at her. "Because I wanted to come and see how you're doing."

Paige offered up a weak smile back. "What about you?" she asked Sofia. Paige attempted to pull herself into a sitting position, but her cracked ribs protested at the movement and she winced.

"Are you all right?" Laura asked.

"Just my chest. Some ribs got cracked when Jack and Ryan were doing CPR." She attempted to breathe through the pain, which didn't work too well given that breathing aggravated the damaged bones. She was getting the feeling that her friends were trying to keep something from her. Something related to whatever had left Sofia with a head injury. "What happened to you?" she repeated.

"I came to visit you earlier," Sofia somewhat reluctantly began. "Then I was supposed to meet Elias to go shopping for the things you guys need for the girls, but I was attacked in the parking garage."

"What?" Paige bolted upright, wincing against the pain in her chest.

"Careful," Sofia murmured, easing her back down against the mattress. "I'm okay. No concussion, just a couple of stitches to close a small gash on my head and a sprained wrist."

She searched Sofia's silvery gray eyes to see if she was telling the truth. When she decided she was, Paige asked, "How did you get away?"

"Someone knocked the guy off me and then Ryan turned up. I'm really okay, Paige. There's nothing for you to worry about."

She let her eyes fall closed because it took too much effort to hold them open. "You should be resting. Both of you should," she added.

"Do you need to sleep? Do you want us to go?" Laura asked.

Paige forced her eyes back open. She would much rather spend some time with her friends than go back to sleep, even if her exhausted body disagreed. "No, if you guys are up to it, the company is nice."

"We're more worried about whether you're up to it," Sofia said, perching on the side of the bed.

"I'm just tired," she murmured.

Laura took hold of her hand. "Paige, I'm so sorry. I knew you wanted to use yourself as bait. I should have stopped you. I'm sorry," she repeated, her violet eyes shimmering with tears.

"It's not your fault. I asked you not to tell anyone," she reminded her friend.

"I know, but I was going to tell Jack anyway because I knew it was a bad idea. Only then Malachi grabbed me, and then they had me sedated for a while, and then I was going to tell Jack, but I went into labor, and by then it was too late."

Shaking her head, Paige ignored the headache that hadn't left her since she'd woken up in the hospital after nearly drowning. "Laura, none of those things are your fault. And even if you'd told Jack, I still would have found a way to try and lure him. It's not your fault. Nor is it yours." She turned to find Sofia's guilty eyes watching her.

"I don't happen to agree," Sofia replied.

"You didn't even know who he was. How could you have done anything to stop him?"

"If it wasn't for me, he would never have come after you." Sofia looked on the verge of tears. "Then you wouldn't have been almost killed, and you wouldn't have been raped."

She flinched at the word. Paige couldn't deal with that right now.

"Are you okay?" Laura was watching her, concerned. "I know what you're going through. I know what it's like to be completely helpless, trapped, alone. I know what it's like to be violated. If you want to talk, I'm here."

Paige shook her head. She couldn't talk about what had

happened. Not yet. Maybe not ever.

"Honey, you can't just pretend it never happened," Laura said gently. "Believe me, I know. I tried that; it doesn't work. I'm worried about you."

"I don't want anyone worrying about me. You have enough going on right now after what Malachi did, and with the baby," she said to Laura. "And you were nearly abducted and injured," she told Sofia. "Neither of you should be worrying about me."

"Well, we are. You've been through a lot the last few years, especially in the last few days." Sofia took her hand and squeezed.

"And all of it is on me." Paige pressed her eyes closed. She was so tired of everyone feeling guilty over her attacks. Everything that had happened to her had been her own fault. No one else's.

A wave of claustrophobia so intense that she couldn't move smashed into her. She could practically feel Bruce Daniels hands on her as he spread her legs, the feel of him forcing himself inside her as real as though he were still in the room. Her lungs wouldn't inflate properly just like they hadn't when he'd paralyzed her. Her breath came in small pants. The walls were closing in on her. She wanted to move. She needed space, but there wasn't any. A moan of terror escaped her lips.

"Paige, look at me."

Laura's voice was close, right beside her. Paige attempted to hold on to it, but it swirled out of reach.

"Paige, it's going to be okay. You're having a panic attack but you're okay. You're safe."

The soothing tone calmed her enough so she could turn her head to meet Laura's serene eyes.

"Just breathe with me, okay?"

Fighting her panic, she allowed Laura's voice to lead her through some breathing exercises. A couple of minutes later, her panic eased enough that she could breathe again. The sense of claustrophobia didn't leave her, but it dropped to a more manageable level. "Thank you," she whispered to Laura.

"You're welcome." Laura patted her hand comfortingly.

Then Paige could feel her face crumple and her tears came in a rush. Sofia's arms were immediately enveloping her in a firm hug. "It's my fault," she cried into her friend's shoulder. "All of it. I was stubborn. I wanted to believe that I could take care of myself, that I didn't need help. Every time he attacked me it was because of me. I was distracted the first time, and then I ignored Ryan when he told me to stay at the cemetery and went off on my own, and then I played bait even though I knew it was dangerous. It's all my fault." Her guilt was crushing her as much as her fear that Bruce Daniels would come back and he'd succeed in killing her the next time.

"Shh, honey, it's okay," Sofia soothed, her hand smoothing Paige's hair. "It's not your fault, Paige, you have to believe that."

But she didn't.

It was her fault.

And now she had to find a way to make peace with it because Hayley and Arianna were counting on her. Those two little girls needed her. She couldn't fall apart. She wouldn't.

"Knock, knock."

Paige lifted her head from Sofia's shoulder as Ryan entered the room. She was too tired to bother hiding her tears, and she could never fool Ryan anyway. He always knew what she was feeling.

"Hey, guys, can I have a moment alone with Paige? Laura, I think Jack intends for you to go and rest, like your doctor told you to." His tone was mildly rebuking.

"Okay." Laura nodded distractedly. "Paige, I'm here anytime you need to talk. And Jack said that Mark organized for Charlie Abbott to come and see you. He's really good; he'll be able to help you."

"I have a friend who's a patient of Charlie's. She thinks he's great, he's helped her a lot," Sofia agreed.

"Come here." Ryan tugged on Sofia's arms, pulling her to him. "How are you doing?"

Sofia rested her head against her husband's chest. "I'm fine."

Ryan pressed his lips to her temple. "You should go back to my parents' house, lie down for a while and try to rest. I'll come pick you and the kids up later for dinner."

Sofia looked like she was going to argue, then gave in with a sigh. "Yeah, okay, I probably won't sleep if I go home alone, and I do have a small headache. Paige, call me if you need anything."

Sinking back against the mattress, Paige watched as Ryan pushed Laura's wheelchair to the door. Given everything that had happened in the last few days, she didn't have high hopes that whatever Ryan wanted to tell her would be good.

"Relax." Ryan smiled at her as he came to sit on the edge of her bed. "It's good news."

Paige did relax at her partner's words. Raising a tired eyebrow, she asked, "Good news?"

His grin widened, making his dimples show, and he said the words she thought she'd never hear. "Bruce Daniels is in custody. You're safe. It's over."

She gasped and then fainted.

"Mark, I need you in here."

The words hovered above her as she slowly swam back to consciousness.

"What happened?"

She felt her wrist being lifted and tried to open her eyes, but they wouldn't cooperate.

"I told her that the stalker is in custody and she just fainted. I was totally not prepared for that reaction. Is she okay?"

"Yeah, she's fine. Paige, its Mark, can you hear me? I need you to open your eyes for me."

Summoning every ounce of strength she had left, Paige managed to open her eyes. Mark and Ryan were perched on either side of her.

Ryan had said that the stalker was caught. Hadn't he?

"Was I dreaming?" Hesitantly she looked into his eyes, seeking confirmation.

"No, you weren't. Bruce Daniels is at the station right now. He's writing out his statement. He's going to plead guilty to all the charges. It's over, Paige. It's really over. You're safe now. That man can never hurt you again."

Relief washed over her, and her tears came in a flood. She threw her arms around Ryan's neck, clinging to him as she cried.

* * * * *

2:31 P.M.

"I heard." Xavier jogged over to Ryan's car as it pulled up at the curb. "I bet Paige was so excited when you told her."

"She fainted," Ryan explained as he climbed out, yanking out his coat and slipping into it.

His brow furrowed in concern. "Fainted? Is she okay?"

"She's fine, was only out for thirty seconds or so, gave me a fright though. I wasn't expecting her to pass out when we finally caught the stalker. Then she cried in my arms for a solid ten minutes. And then she fell asleep."

"Hopefully now that the stress of having Bruce Daniels out there isn't hanging over her, she should start regaining her strength. And we can finally relax and know she's safe. I'm going to go see her when we finish up here. All good with Laura and the baby?"

"They're getting Rosie ready to move her to the special care nursery. She's doing amazingly well. She's a little miracle, and she definitely has her namesake's strength."

Xavier hadn't known Rose Lace for very long, only a few months before she died, but what he'd known, he'd liked. Rose had been strong and confident and smart, a loyal and caring friend, and a great cop. "I hope she keeps doing so well. Laura doesn't deserve anymore trauma."

"No, she doesn't," Ryan agreed. "She's been through enough."

Thinking of people who had been through a lot, Xavier asked, "How's Sofia holding up?"

Ryan's face paled as he was reminded of his wife's near-abduction. He drew in a shaky breath. "She's doing okay. I just keep seeing her lying unmoving on the ground when I came running up. If Bruce Daniels hadn't interrupted the abduction ..."

Ryan trailed off, but he didn't have to continue. They both knew what would have happened if Dr. Daniels hadn't shown up when he did—they'd be investigating Sofia's abduction right now. Her would-be attacker had already incapacitated her, and he'd have easily been able to throw her in a car and drive off. Thankfully, the abduction had been foiled and Sofia had received only minor injuries. "She's safe now, Ryan," Xavier reminded him.

"I know." Ryan shuddered, his blue eyes bleak. "At least for now."

"You think he'll come back for her?"

"Depends on whether she was targeted or if it was opportunistic."

"You really think this could be related to the support group women case?" Xavier had been intrigued by the possibility when Ryan had first floated the idea.

"At thirty-three, Sofia's a little older than the other victims, but the man who attacked her was dressed the same as the killer in the video, and Sofia is a victim of crime. Your guy blames cops for failing victims, and he's escalating; he could have deliberately targeted a cop who had a wife or girlfriend who'd gone through something traumatic. I mean, what better way to get his point across? He wants the police to stop crime, and in his mind, that would be great motivation."

"It definitely bears looking into," Xavier agreed.

"Has he started streaming again after Ruby McBrady's murder?"

Xavier forced images of the second bloody murder from his mind. Ruby's final moments had been different from Faith's. The man had killed them in the same manner, hacking their bodies into six pieces. However, while Faith had begged and pleaded for her life, attempting to free herself from her bonds and screamed as the blade connected with her flesh, Ruby had screamed and thrashed once when she first awakened and again when she opened her eyes to see the blood, but then she seemed to descend into a shock-induced haze. She hadn't made a sound, hadn't moved, hadn't done anything—not even when the first blow struck her shoulder.

"Xavier?"

He blinked, clearing his mind. "Yeah?"

"I asked whether he's started streaming something else?"

"No. Nothing since it went dark after he murdered Ruby."

"Bruce Daniels thinks the man who attacked Sofia was white. If it *is* the same guy, that should help us narrow down suspects."

"Us?"

"Jack is still at the hospital with Laura and Rosie. Paige is out of work for a while. I'm yours unless you'd rather work alone." Ryan shot him a grin.

"I think I can tolerate working with you for a while. Barely," he added with a grin of his own. He didn't have to catch Ryan up on the case because they'd talked about it after the killer sent him the link to watch Faith Smith's murder, which was convenient and a time save, but he also enjoyed working with his friend.

"So, we're interviewing the psychiatrist who runs the support group but isn't treating any of your victims or suspects?" Ryan confirmed.

"Right."

"Do we think he did it?"

"No, I'm pretty sure he didn't. No motive, and he had an alibi for the night of the abductions, home with his wife. And the night of Faith's murder, he was with a client. We checked with the client and she confirmed it. I want to get an idea from him which of the guys from the group he thinks might be most likely to do something like this. Since he's not actually their doctor, we don't have to go through the whole doctor-patient confidentiality thing."

"He could still claim it though," Ryan argued. "He may not technically be their doctor, but he ran a session with them, right? He could say that it put him in a position of a therapist."

"Maybe, but he's not technically their doctor and we won't ask him about anything that he discussed with them in that session. We'll just focus on who, in his professional opinion, is most likely to be the man we're looking for. I think he'll do anything he thinks may further his career. If he views this whole situation as something he can use to do that, then I think he'll talk."

"I hope you're right because not only does he have three more victims holed up somewhere, but if he *is* the one who tried to abduct Sofia this morning, then he has no intention of stopping. There are thousands of women in the city who are victims of a crime, including my wife, my sister-in-law, and my partner. He could go after any one of them. Xavier, Annabelle is a victim too. That puts her at risk, especially since he's already latched on to you."

Unfortunately, he'd already thought of that. He'd made the mistake once before of not making sure Annabelle was safe and she'd been kidnapped—something she still hadn't completely forgiven him for. He wouldn't do it again.

"I increased patrols on her street and I'll call her later, tell her to be extra careful."

"Maybe you should get her to move back to your house," Ryan suggested hesitantly. "I know things are strained between you two right now, but we all know you're going to work things out. With Bruce Daniels in custody, Paige is safe now, and Mark wants to stay with her until she's strong enough to be released, so she's not going to be alone. You should go home and take Annabelle with you, and then you know she'll be safe."

"Yeah, maybe." He would consider it, but he wasn't sure that bringing Annabelle home just yet was the right thing to do. He needed to know that she was serious about getting help before he could take her back. He would make sure she was protected, though.

When they entered the doctor's waiting room, there was a woman flicking through a magazine in the corner. Xavier recognized her as the woman who had been Hank Fitzgerald's alibi the night Faith was killed. There was also a couple sitting at either end of a couch, both on their respective phones. And a woman with a little boy of about three were over in a corner. She had him on her lap and was busy reading to him.

Bypassing the reception desk, Xavier walked right to Dr. Fitzgerald's office door, knocking briskly.

"Excuse me, but Dr. Fitzgerald is in with a patient." The receptionist rose from her desk and glared disapprovingly at him.

"We're investigating a murder, ma'am," Xavier rebuked her and rapped on the heavy wooden door again.

Refusing to budge, the woman repeated, "You'll have to talk to him later. He's in with a client."

Ignoring the woman, Xavier turned the door handle, half expecting it to be locked, and entered the room.

"You can't go in there," the receptionist yelled at them as he and Ryan stepped into the suite.

It was immediately apparent why the receptionist had been so adamant they not enter the room.

Hank Fitzgerald was half naked on the sofa.

A woman's dress lay on the floor.

The two were so engrossed in each other, they didn't hear the door open.

Rolling his eyes, Xavier was not surprised to find the doctor bedding a patient.

"Put your clothes on, Dr. Fitzgerald, and send your patient

outside," he commanded. "We need to talk."

Hank's face turned bright red at the sound of his voice and he froze.

"Come on, we don't have all day," Xavier prompted, annoyed. There were three abducted women who might have only hours left to live if they weren't found. They didn't have time for the doctor's embarrassment at getting caught with his pants down.

As he walked closer, catching a glimpse of the face of the woman on the couch, Xavier realized why Hank Fitzgerald looked so stricken.

His patient was a teenager.

The girl looked no older than fourteen, her skin flushed, her eyes bright, her brown hair tangled.

He pulled out cuffs. "Hank Fitzgerald, you're under arrest for statutory rape."

"What? No!" the teenager protested, jumping to her feet. "He didn't rape me. I wanted to have sex with him. He didn't take advantage of me. We're not in love. He's married, and I have a boyfriend. It was just sex. Consensual sex."

The face and the voice clicked, and Xavier realized where he'd seen the girl before. She was the daughter of the woman who was Dr. Fitzgerald's alibi for Faith's murder. He'd seen the girl when he went to her house to confirm that the woman had been with her psychiatrist that night. The teenager was the spitting image of her mother. They were both tall and lean, both had amazingly bright green eyes and long brown hair. Xavier wondered whether the doctor was also sleeping with the mother.

"What are you, about fourteen?" Ryan asked the girl. Sullenly, she nodded back. "Then the law says you can't give consent."

"What's going on in here? Tracy?" The girl's mother appeared in the doorway. When she saw both her fourteen-year-old daughter and her psychiatrist half naked, she paled so dramatically that Xavier grabbed hold of her elbow in case she fainted.

"Get a grip, Mom," Tracy groaned. "You were sleeping with

him too. You wanted me to come see him to learn and grow and get over what your loser ex did to me. Well, guess what? I did. Dr. Fitzgerald has taught me a lot. This is so lame." The teenager shot them all an icy glare, then snatched up her dress, threw it back on and stalked from the room.

"How could you?" Tracy's mother turned eyes as icy as her daughter's on the doctor. "She's *fourteen* and you're supposed to be a doctor."

Surprising them all, the woman launched herself at Hank Fitzgerald, slapping him across the face then storming from the room, calling after her daughter.

Brown eyes devastated, Hank Fitzgerald looked around the room. "My career, it's over."

That five of the women he'd vowed to help had been abducted, two of them murdered, didn't seem to enter his mind. Xavier couldn't wait to get him back to the precinct and grill him hard.

* * * * *

10:54 P.M.

Annabelle was on edge.

She was tired. She wanted to sleep, but every time she closed her eyes her mind spun off in a million different directions at once.

Maybe it was because she just wasn't comfortable here in her new apartment. It didn't feel like home. The only place she had ever lived in that had truly felt like a home was Xavier's house. And she had foolishly thrown that away.

She shouldn't have left. Xavier had begged her to stay and she should have listened to him. Now she couldn't even remember why it had felt so important to have her own place and spend some time on her own.

She had never lived on her own before. She had lived in her parents' home until she was twenty-three. When her parents, her two younger brothers, and seven-year-old sister had been murdered in their beds while they slept and their killer was still on the loose, Xavier had invited her to move in with him.

They had lived together ever since.

Until a couple of weeks ago when she had decided she needed time on her own.

Well, now she had it and she didn't want it.

She would give anything to be curled up in Xavier's bed right now, her head on his shoulder, his arms wrapped around her.

Annabelle knew she would get him back. She wouldn't rest until she did. She would do whatever was necessary to make it happen.

Throwing back the covers, she climbed out of bed. She wasn't going to sleep, so lying there was pretty pointless.

She weighed her options: she could make some tea, put on a movie, and try to fall asleep. However, she didn't feel like just sitting still. She needed to move. Maybe a jog would help to clear her mind. Annabelle had never jogged in her life until she'd met Xavier. He was a workout addict and he'd convinced her to go jogging with him one day. She'd enjoyed it and started running every day—with or without him.

Throwing on some sweats, she grabbed a bottle of water, and as she opened the front door and was about to step through it, she was yanked violently back inside her apartment.

For a moment Annabelle was too stunned to do anything.

Someone was in her apartment.

She'd been home for a few hours and not seen anyone.

She hadn't heard anyone break in either.

And when she'd arrived home, all her windows had been locked. She was obsessive about checking them.

How had he gotten in?

More importantly, who was he?

A horrible thought occurred to her.

Xavier had left her a voicemail earlier telling her that someone had attempted to abduct Sofia earlier this morning, and he was concerned that it may be related to a case he was working. He had told her that he had increased patrols on her street and told her to be careful.

Was that who was in her apartment right now?

While all of these thoughts had been spinning through her mind, the man had maneuvered her away from the door, clamped a hand over her mouth, and was pushing her toward the bedroom.

Annabelle had no intention of letting this man abduct her.

At least, she was going to do everything she could do stop him.

She had been there and done that. And she was *not* going through it again.

So far, she hadn't fought back, and the man had loosened his grip on her a little. He was fumbling for something in his pocket.

Taking advantage of his distraction, Annabelle stomped her heel as hard as she could on the intruder's food.

Startled, he yelped and further loosened his grip.

Once again taking advantage, she rammed her elbow back into his stomach and then up into his jaw.

Grunting in pain, the man released her.

Knowing she didn't have a second to spare and that she may not get another chance, she sprinted for the front door.

The man recovered and charged after her, blocking her path.

Diverting at the last moment, Annabelle ran for the kitchen, grabbing a knife from the counter. She knew that a knife could end up being used against her. Xavier had told her that several times, but she didn't have a lot of other options. For the first time, she was wishing she had allowed Xavier to teach her to shoot. She had always refused when he'd offered. She didn't like guns, but now she wished she had one to protect herself.

She couldn't take her eyes off the kitchen door, waiting for the man to come.

Only he didn't.

Maybe she had surprised him by fighting back and he had given up and left?

Could she really be that lucky?

Slowly, she edged toward the door.

Her heart was beating so loudly she couldn't hear anything else.

Reaching the door, she eased it open just enough to peek through.

Her front door was open.

Had the man really left or was he just trying to trick her?

She caught sight of her cell on the desk, it was just a couple of feet from the kitchen door.

Should she risk making a run for it?

Her mind was already formulating a plan: grab the phone then run out the door, hammer on a neighbor's door or run outside and see if a cop car was around or even just scream for help.

Which reminded her that she hadn't screamed for help.

Annabelle was just opening her mouth to yell when the door slammed into her, sending the knife clattering to the floor.

Before she could react, a needle was jammed into her arm.

Just like last time.

Wobbling, her knees went weak, and she grabbed hold of the back of one of the chairs at her table for support and tried to remain standing. The man just watched. He was dressed all in black, including a balaclava and sunglasses.

Her arms grew as wobbly as her knees and they could no longer keep her upright. Losing her grip on the chair, she slumped to the floor, the chair toppling down beside her.

Her eyes wanted to close but she was fighting it. Once she passed out she was all his.

Despite her efforts to fight the drug's effects, she couldn't.

It did its job and seconds later she was falling into

unconsciousness.

NOVEMBER 10TH

10:33 A.M.

"Okay, Dr. Fitzgerald, you've wasted enough of our time. Time that Mackenzie Willows, Ava Burns, and Vanessa Adams don't have. Now you'll answer our questions."

Ryan was tired and grumpy this morning. Despite the fact that he'd been in his own home in his own bed with his wife in his arms, he hadn't been able to sleep. Every time he closed his eyes, he saw Sofia lying unmoving on the ground in the hospital's parking garage. Every time he'd drifted off to sleep, he had dreamed of Sofia being abducted.

He was tired of living scared that the people he loved and cared about were in danger. With someone now targeting victims, he was once again worried about the safety of his family and friends. He wanted answers. And at the moment, Hank Fitzgerald was their best chance of getting them.

"I didn't have anything to do with the disappearance of the women from one of my support groups," Dr. Fitzgerald repeated for what seemed like the hundredth time. He had refused to talk to them yesterday, requesting his lawyer to shut them down. They had to wait for him to be processed and booked, but he'd finally agreed to sit down with them, Ryan suspected in the hopes of trying to wager a deal.

"We're not saying you did," Xavier replied.

Although, Ryan wasn't completely convinced. The psychiatrist was obviously sleazy. He'd been sleeping with twenty-eight-year-old Hannah DeMoise, a woman who had been through multiple bad relationships, and her fourteen-year-old daughter, Tracy.

Hannah had gotten pregnant at fourteen after a drunken one-night stand at a party. She'd been kicked out by her parents and lived on the streets with her newborn before being taken in by an uncle. The uncle had abused her, and she had married the first guy who came along to get away from him. That man, too, had turned out to be abusive, as had her second husband. When the second husband had started abusing her daughter, she had finally left him. Only, he had tracked them down and attempted to abduct them and wound up being shot and killed by the police, in front of Hannah and her then twelve-year-old daughter. Returning to her parents' home, Hannah had decided to fix up her life. She'd returned to school, gotten a job, and gotten psychiatric help for herself and her daughter. Dr. Fitzgerald had played on and exploited her vulnerabilities and began a sexual relationship with her. And then with her daughter.

If Hank Fitzgerald had slept with the DeMoises, then who knew how many of his other patients he was also sexually involved with. Maybe he had tried something with the women in the group only to be rejected and so he had taken out his anger on them and abducted them.

"*He's* not saying you did," Ryan added. "I'm still not convinced."

"I have an alibi," the doctor reminded him as though he were an idiot.

Ryan shrugged indifferently. "So?"

"So? Well, how could I have done it if you know I was somewhere else when they were abducted and when Faith was killed?" Dr. Fitzgerald spluttered.

"Maybe you hired someone, maybe you have a partner. All I know is you're a psychiatrist, a doctor, and you're supposed to help people. I'd say you failed in that with the DeMoises. How many other patients are you sleeping with?"

Cheeks turning bright red, the doctor refused to answer that. "I had nothing to do with what happened to those women, and you already have me on statutory rape since you found me with Tracy, but if I tell you whatever I know about the men in the group, will it help when I go before the judge?"

"We're not in a position to make deals," Ryan informed him. He didn't want to see this man make any sort of deal. Over the years, Dr. Fitzgerald had no doubt had a sexual relationship with dozens of patients—most likely a lot of them underage.

The doctor turned disappointed brown eyes to Xavier, hoping he would have a more positive answer.

"I would think, given that you're in the business of helping people, that you would want to tell us anything that could be helpful in finding those women regardless of whether it positively impacts you or not," Xavier told him.

Hank sighed like they were being deliberately difficult. "What do you want to know?"

"Everything you know about Troy Tranchina, David Murfet, Roman Tallow, and Miles Lanyon."

"What about Vincent Abrams?"

"I know him. He was a victim in a case I worked a few years ago, and he's not a suspect," Xavier told him.

"I already told you about them the other day," Dr. Fitzgerald whined. "I don't really know them. I'm not their doctor. I just organize the groups. You should really speak with their family and friends, or their doctors."

"Doctor patient confidentiality," Ryan reminded him. "Technically, you are not their doctor, so the rules don't apply to you. I think you're a sleazebag, but that doesn't necessarily mean you aren't good at reading people. We're hoping you can give us insight that friends and family would be too emotionally invested to see."

"You said that David Murfet has a temper," Xavier said. "Do you think it's possible he could have done this? The killer has told us that he thinks we, the police, are responsible for the women he abducted—victims of crime. You also said that David has a strong sense of justice. Should we be looking at him as a viable suspect?"

Considering this, the doctor spoke slowly. "David has a temper, but I've never seen him hurt anyone or be violent at all. You know the reason he got beaten so badly was that he tried not to hurt the wife beater. He attempted to simply hold him down until help arrived. He didn't want to actually hurt the guy. David couldn't keep him contained; the guy broke free and slammed David repeatedly into the ground."

"What do you know about David's relationship with his girlfriend?"

"Not a lot. I've never met her, and he didn't talk about her in the one session I had with them. I think she was there the day of his attack and called the cops. From what I gathered from reading between the lines, it became a bit of a stumbling block for them as a couple. David was self-conscious that his girlfriend saw him get beaten nearly to death, and she felt guilty for not doing more to stop it from happening. I can't see David doing this, but if he did, I feel it would be more likely he would have abducted his girlfriend and not the women from the support group."

Ryan glanced at Xavier and saw that they both agreed. They had spoken with David's girlfriend and confirmed his alibi for the night the women were abducted. David Murfet was basically out as a suspect.

"What about the others?" Ryan asked. "Do you think any of them are capable of doing this?"

Dr. Fitzgerald hesitated, his brown eyes darting back and forth between them.

"Dr. Fitzgerald?" Xavier prompted.

"What if I'm wrong and I needlessly implicate someone who's innocent?" For the first time the psychiatrist looked nervous.

"Then when we further investigate we'll find them to be innocent. We're not going to lock whoever you implicate up in prison and throw away the key. We just want a direction to look in," Ryan assured him.

"Which one do you think could have done it?"

"Any one of them."

"They've all displayed violent tendencies?" Ryan asked, surprised.

"No, but Miles, he's so quiet and doesn't talk much at the group sessions."

"How do you know that?" Xavier raised a suspicious brow.

His cheeks turned an even brighter shade of red than earlier. The doctor stuttered, "S-sometimes I'd bug the church hall with microphones. I just wanted to see how the groups were going, whether they were working, whether they were all opening up to one another, trusting one another," Dr. Fitzgerald explained in a rush.

Not caring about that right now, Ryan pressed on. "Miles wasn't moving on from the death of his fiancée?"

"He was still grieving," Hank Fitzgerald agreed.

"And that the cops never found the driver would be plenty reason to blame us and try to teach us a lesson," Ryan said.

"People sometimes do crazy things in their grief," Dr. Fitzgerald said quietly, and Ryan wondered if the doctor was talking from personal experience.

"You said all three might have done this. Why do you think Roman or Troy would have cause to do this?" Xavier asked.

"Troy seems to be very tightly wound up. He's edgy and jumpy and overly sensitive. He tries to cover it with confidence, but ..."

"But you think he could explode at any second," Ryan finished for him and the psychiatrist nodded.

"And Roman?" Xavier asked.

"I understand Roman was very close to his sister. They were all each other had. Parents died in a car crash when they were kids. Roman was twelve, his sister eighteen. She raised him, worked several jobs while in school so they could stay together. Roman tried to help her leave her abusive boyfriend. The guy got obsessed with her, refused to believe she wasn't coming back to him. Roman was apparently a mess after he found her body, had to be hospitalized. He's had a hard time finding that sense of family that he craves and lost, first with his parents and then with his sister. So, I was thinking that since he couldn't save his sister, maybe he would feel compelled to help these women who are victims of crime just like his sister was. And since his sister filed over forty complaints, and her ex was arrested eight times, he would certainly have cause to hate cops."

They'd lowered their number of suspects from four to three. The talk with Hank Fitzgerald had been worth it.

Beside him, Xavier pulled out his phone, his expression going stark.

* * * * *

11:26 A.M.

"Did you just get what I think you did?" Ryan asked him as they left Dr. Fitzgerald in the interview room.

"Another email," he confirmed grimly. Which of the remaining women was about to die? The killer only activated the stream when he was ready to commit another kill. Once he was done hacking the body into six pieces, the link went dead. The forensic unit was still working frantically to attempt to pinpoint the location the videos were live-streaming from, but so far, had come up empty.

"Who?"

"I don't know. He started streaming again but he's not there yet."

"He held them for four days before killing Faith, but waited only a day before he killed Ruby, but it's been two days since then. Why slow down? When we interview Troy, Miles, and Roman, we should see whether any of them were occupied yesterday afternoon. It just doesn't make sense that he'd escalate to less time between kills and then go backward. Typically, these kinds of killers continue to escalate. I'd be expecting him to kill more regularly and more elaborately," Ryan mused.

"And what he does to the bodies after they're dead. That has to have some meaning," Xavier added.

"You mean cutting them into six pieces?" Ryan looked as repulsed as Xavier felt. Ryan had seen Faith's murder but had been at the hospital with Paige when Ruby was killed.

"Yes, they were already dead before he did it—it wasn't necessary. He has to be doing it because it means something to him," Xavier added.

"Six pieces. He could easily have done more or less, and yet he chose the number six. Both times. We should see whether the number six is significant to any of them," Ryan agreed.

Xavier hadn't taken his eyes off his phone since he'd received the email, waiting to see which of the remaining women was going to be next.

Part of him hoped it wouldn't be Vanessa Adams. Not that he wanted to see any of the women killed, but he knew Vanessa. He'd saved her life once before. He'd visited her in the hospital, kept in contact with her and Vincent, and Vanessa's father.

Vanessa had suffered a lot in those first months. They had all been worried about her. But she was strong, and she had survived. Xavier just hoped she could survive this.

According to Vincent, her pregnancy so far hadn't been a smooth one. She was four months along and had already experienced two scares. Xavier wasn't holding out a lot of hope that if Vanessa somehow managed to survive that her baby would too. They already knew that this guy had drugged them. That couldn't be good for Vanessa and her unborn child.

"Xavier, the door just opened."

Ryan's voice snapped his attention back to the phone.

The man in black, The Protector as he called himself, carried a woman into the room. One of her arms was slung across the man's shoulders, her head hung back exposing her white throat, long red hair reaching halfway to the ground.

"Mackenzie," Ryan said quietly.

Xavier nodded. It was Mackenzie Willows. Already he was dreading having to notify her husband.

"Did she just move?" Ryan was pointing at Mackenzie's arm.

Looking closely, Xavier saw her move it off the man's shoulder. Her legs too began to move restlessly as though she was trying to get away from the man carrying her. "He didn't drug her. She's conscious." He was wondering why when it suddenly became apparent.

As the man turned to carry Mackenzie toward the table, they caught sight of her face. One of her eyes appeared to be swollen shut. A mottled mix of black, blue, and purple bruises covered almost every inch of her face. Dried blood covered a cut on her lower lip. Unlike Faith and Ruby, it didn't look like the man had bathed her before bringing her to his kill room. Her clothes were the ones her husband had said she was wearing when she disappeared, and they were smeared with dirt and blood and grime.

"He beat her," Ryan murmured.

"Badly," Xavier added. Mackenzie's face was a mess. "He didn't beat either Faith or Ruby. Either he's devolving or she did something to make him angry."

"Angry enough to do that?" Ryan gestured at the phone, where Mackenzie's injuries became even more evident as the man laid her down on the table.

As her abductor went about restraining her, Mackenzie made a feeble attempt at fighting him off. Her movements were clumsy and uncoordinated. Xavier suspected she may be suffering from a concussion.

"You won't get away with this," Mackenzie's weak voice told the man.

He stopped what he was doing and looked at her. Even though

the killer's face was covered, they could sense his puzzlement. "I don't want to hurt you. I just want to help you, Mackenzie."

"Help me?" Mackenzie's eyes fell closed. "You beat me up while I was chained to a wall. You killed Faith and Ruby. You have Ava and Vanessa and some other woman chained up in your little homemade dungeon."

Eyes wide, Ryan looked at him. "Another woman?"

"We'll have to go through missing persons reports, look for any previous victim of crime who's been reported missing in the last twenty-four hours." This was the last thing they needed.

"Because he didn't get Sofia," Ryan said, stark relief on his face. "He's a threat to every woman who has ever been a victim. I'm going to call Jack later and have him keep a close eye on Laura and Paige. I don't think this guy would be stupid enough to try and abduct them from the hospital, but I don't want to take any chances. And I'm going to tell Sofia to stay at my parents' house during the day."

"You mean *ask* her," Xavier said with a small smile, attempting to distract himself from what was about to happen to Mackenzie.

"Sure," Ryan returned with an equally small smile.

"You're insane!" Mackenzie's shrill voice returned their attention to his phone. "You're not helping us. If you wanted to help us, you'd let us go. Vanessa is sick, she needs a doctor. Ava wants to go home to her little boy. You're hurting us on purpose. You're a monster!"

The reaction was instantaneous.

As soon as Mackenzie said the word "monster," he slammed his fist into the side of her head. Knocking her out with one blow.

"Did you see that?" Xavier asked Ryan.

"He lost it when she called him a monster. It's a trigger. He didn't flinch when she called him insane or said he was hurting them. Another thing to bring up when we interview our suspects."

Unknowingly, Mackenzie had provided them with a lot of

information they hadn't had. They now knew that the killer had the skills to build his own dungeon somewhere. They knew that he was abducting more victims. They knew that the word "monster" set him off; it was probably how Mackenzie had gotten the bruises on her face.

However, the thing that he was most thankful for at the moment was that Mackenzie was already unconscious and wouldn't have to suffer any more as this man killed her.

✳ ✳ ✳ ✳ ✳

3:49 P.M.

"Would someone please wake up now? I'm going crazy here."

Annabelle heard the words but didn't know who spoke them or why.

The voice didn't sound familiar.

And whatever she was lying on didn't feel familiar either.

A horrible stench hit her nose and she gasped in a breath.

"Hello? Are you okay?" The same voice spoke.

Memories smashed into her. She'd been at home about to go for a jog when someone had grabbed her. She'd been injected with something and passed out, and now she was waking up.

But waking up where?

"Are you awake?"

This time at the sound of the voice, Annabelle pried open her sticky eyes.

At first her vision was cloudy and she couldn't really see where she was. But slowly it returned. She was in a room made of dirt, approximately eight feet by eight feet. There were three doors and a rickety looking staircase that led to a fourth door.

Her wrists were shackled to a set of chains embedded in the thick wall. There were another five sets of chains. Two of which were attached to people.

The smell in the room was so overpowering that Annabelle gagged. Sweat, blood, and human waste. She attempted to breathe through her mouth. It didn't do any good. A waft of the vile odor hit her like a ton of bricks. It was so strong that her stomach churned, and she threw up.

"He left you water," a timid voice informed her.

Groping around, her trembling hands found a bottle. Clutching at it, she twisted off the lid, poured a little into her mouth and used it to rinse, then spat it out beside her. Then she took a long drink, the warm liquid doing little to ease her dry, sore throat.

"I'm Ava," a young black woman with scared dark eyes and a tearstained face sniffed. "Who are you?"

"A ... An ... Annabelle," she croaked. She coughed to clear her phlegmy throat. "Where are we? Who are you? Who brought me here? What's he going to do to me? Why is he doing this? Who is that?" She peppered questions at Ava and finished by pointing to a skinny blonde woman who was lying, unmoving, chained to the adjacent wall.

Ava began to cry. "I don't know where we are, and I don't know who brought us here. But he knows us, so maybe you know him too. He says he doesn't want to hurt us but he killed Faith and Ruby. Mackenzie too after he beat her," the young woman sobbed. "That's Vanessa, she's pregnant. She's been sick since we got here."

"How long have you been here?" Annabelle was clinging to sanity by attempting to pacify her mind with facts.

"I don't know, maybe a week, I can't keep track of the time," Ava cried.

"The other women ... did you know them?" She was wondering if these were the women from Xavier's case who had been abducted—the case he had called to warn her about.

"Yes. We were all friends. We were together when he took us, but he always wears a mask, so I don't know who he is. I just want to go home," the young woman finished with a hiccupping gulp.

"You said he killed them. Did you see him do it?" Annabelle had been forced to kill two people before to save her own and Sofia's lives. She didn't want to have to do that again, but she would if she had to. Nor did she want to witness the death of either of these young women.

"No." Ava brushed at her wet cheeks.

"Then how do you know he killed them?"

"He told us he did. We begged him to let us go but he wouldn't. I don't know why he's doing this. I told him I have a little boy at home, but he didn't care. Why would he do this to us?" The last was a whispered plea.

"Because we're all victims of crime," she murmured. That was what Xavier had said in his message. That someone was after women who'd been involved in a violent crime because he wanted to prove a point to the police.

Annabelle could feel her grip on calm beginning to slip.

She had been through this before.

Twice.

She didn't want to do it again.

Especially not like this. She was finally ready to work on getting her life together. She was going to get help, work on herself, find her self-confidence, let go of her fears, make sure that she could give Xavier the life that he deserved.

And now in an instant it was over.

Ava and Vanessa had been here for a week already. The police hadn't found them, and the three other women who'd been taken with them were now dead. How long before he killed them? How long before he killed her?

As far as she could see, there was no viable method of escape. She was chained to a wall; she couldn't get out of the chains. She could try and talk her way out but that hadn't worked last time.

This wasn't fair.

Hadn't she been through enough?

Didn't she deserve her happy ending?

That she didn't have one was her own fault. She had been the one to mess up their relationship, not Xavier. If she hadn't been such an idiot she would have been at Xavier's house, safe with him, not alone in an apartment, vulnerable to a killer.

Her tears burst out in a noisy rush.

She didn't bother to try and hold them back.

She could very well die here, alone, away from Xavier, with him disappointed in her and not trusting her.

Allowing herself only a couple of minutes to wallow, she sobbed, screamed, yanked on the metal chains until her wrists ached, and then she fell silent.

She had to make a decision.

There was a very real possibility that no one would be looking for her. She and Xavier weren't talking, and she didn't have the kind of relationship with her friends where they talked on the phone every day. The best she could hope for was that someone would realize she didn't turn up at work.

Whether she survived this was up to her.

She could give up, as she had done so many times before in her life. Giving up had become a habit—so much so that often she didn't even try something because she didn't think it was going to work out.

She'd told Xavier she wanted to change. That she was serious about personal growth.

Now was the time to take the first step.

She wasn't going to die here.

She couldn't give up now.

If she could work to change a lifetime of negative thinking and self-image, then she could do this. Surely, she could find a way to get back to the man she loved.

Annabelle was wearing her mother's engagement ring. She had worn it ever since her mother's death, as a kind of link to the woman she'd loved but had never been sure loved her back.

The ring had a large diamond.

Maybe she could use that to dig away at the dirt around where the chains were embedded. The chances she could get free weren't very high, but it was worth a shot. She had nothing to lose, after all.

* * * * *

4:18 P.M.

"Miles Lanyon is up first." Ryan came up behind him.

"Yeah, okay," Xavier replied a little distractedly, staring at the phone in his hands.

"Something wrong? Did he send another link?"

"No, he didn't send another link," he assured Ryan. "And nothing is wrong—I was just trying to call Annabelle to make sure she was being careful, and she didn't answer." Deliberately, he brushed away his concerns. "I'm sure she's just busy at work. I'll try again later. Okay, let's go and do these interviews. Hopefully we can narrow things down from three to our guy."

Scared dark eyes darted up at them as they entered the interview room. "Do you really think I abducted Faith, Ava, Ruby, Vanessa, and Mackenzie?"

"We think it's a possibility," Xavier replied, taking a seat at the table.

Miles sighed deeply and informed them, "I have an alibi for the night of the kidnappings."

Ryan raised a doubtful brow. "Then why didn't you tell us this when we first asked you?" he asked.

"Because I was scared," Miles answered in a small voice.

"Were you doing something illegal?" Xavier prodded.

His eyes widened. "No, nothing like that. I was with a woman. Not ... not ... like a ... a prostitute or anything. I met someone.

Only no one knows about us. It's only been eleven months since Theresa was killed. I know it's too soon to move on. I met Grace in a support group for widows and widowers. Not that I'm really a widower since Theresa and I were never married. But she lost her husband just two months before the hit-and-run. They'd only been married six months. At first, we just talked, but then ... I think I've fallen in love with her. We haven't told anyone. It's too soon. I still love Theresa, but she's gone—I can't get her back. It's too soon," Miles moaned miserably and dropped his head into his hands.

It was apparent to both him and Ryan that Miles Lanyon was not the killer. He was swamped with guilt over falling in love so soon after his fiancée's death. He wasn't interested in abducting women to prove some sort of point to the police that they should do more to stop crime.

"We're going to need to speak with her," Xavier told Miles gently.

The man nodded but wouldn't lift his head. "We knew you'd need to confirm that we were together the night the girls were abducted, so she came here with me. She's outside in her car. We decided we didn't want to hide anymore. We're going to tell our families and friends that we're dating."

"You haven't done anything wrong, Miles," Xavier said gently. "If you love Grace, then it's not too soon. Theresa would have wanted you to be happy, wouldn't she? If things had been the other way around, if you'd been killed and Theresa had survived, wouldn't you want her to try to find happiness again?"

Reluctantly, Miles looked up at him, his dark brown eyes twin pools of pain. "Theresa didn't want to be out that night. I pushed her into going out for dinner. If we'd been at home—like Theresa wanted—she'd still be alive. I don't deserve a second chance, yet life has given me one. I don't deserve Grace. Here's her number. She'll come right up and answer whatever questions you have for her and then I assume we're free to go?"

"Yes," Ryan confirmed. "Go easy on yourself. I know what it's like to lose the woman you love and blame yourself for it. I was lucky too. I met an amazing woman who is now my wife and the mother of my kids. You love Theresa and she knows that. She would want you to be happy."

Xavier often forgot that Ryan had been engaged years before he met Sofia. His fiancée had committed suicide and Ryan had blamed himself for it for a long time.

Miles studied Ryan for a long moment, then nodded. "If Theresa had lived and I hadn't, then I'd want her to be happy. I suppose she would want the same for me."

As they left the man alone in the room, Xavier wondered how long it would take before he actually came to believe that.

It didn't take long to confirm with Grace Ellis that she and Miles had been together the night the women were abducted, and that they spent most nights together, alternating between her house and his. She echoed Miles' feelings of betraying her deceased husband by moving on at a pace she believed to be too soon after his death. Xavier hoped the couple were able to let go of their guilt and make it work.

With Miles Lanyon ruled out, he and Ryan turned their attention to Roman Tallow, the twenty-five-year-old tax accountant.

Calm green eyes watched them as they took a seat at the interview table. Immediately, Xavier noticed the bruises on the knuckles of Roman's left hand. The killer had beaten Mackenzie. The bruises could have come from his knuckles connecting with her bones.

"What happened to your hand, Roman?" he asked.

He glanced down, his pale cheeks turning red. "I lost my temper earlier today. Accidentally dropped my phone in the kitchen sink while I was doing dishes and paused to reply to an email. Took my anger out on the kitchen wall. Now I have a hole in the wall, a broken phone, and a really sore hand."

The story was potentially plausible. Since they didn't have enough to get warrants for anything related to either Roman or Troy, they wanted to gauge their reactions to the word "monster" and see if the number six meant anything to them. They'd also need to find out where they were yesterday morning when the abduction attempt was made on Sofia. And if they have anything going on yesterday afternoon that prevented them from committing another kill? Plus, they needed to know if Roman had building skills, since they already knew Troy did.

Hopefully, once they had narrowed it down to one man, they would be able to get enough to make a case to a judge. Search houses, properties, phones, computers, etc., and hopefully get enough for an arrest warrant.

"What were you doing yesterday?" Xavier asked.

"Why? What happened yesterday?" Roman asked.

"Where were you, Roman?" Xavier repeated.

"Nowhere in the morning. I'm an accountant and I didn't have any appointments until lunchtime. I worked through till around nine, then went home. Where I was alone," he added. "Why? You think one of the guys from the support group did this, don't you—me or Miles or Troy? I saw them here too. I didn't do it. We were friends. I liked all of them. I wouldn't hurt them."

Roman's face was the picture of earnestness, but Xavier was never fooled by appearances. This tall, skinny redhead didn't look like someone who would brutally slaughter three women, yet that didn't mean he hadn't. "What kind of monster do you think did take your friends?"

The man tensed at the word "monster," but his face remained gravely calm. "I don't know. Maybe the men who terrorized Mackenzie in the home invasion. They were never caught," Roman suggested.

That was a possibility but not a very likely one. Given the emphasis on victims and blaming the police, Xavier was confident it was one of the men in the support group, and they were down to Roman or Troy.

"Roman, we understand you lost your parents when you were twelve. That must have been hard. Do you remember the date of the accident?"

"Of course. I'll never forget that day—every single thing that happened is seared into my mind. It was December sixth. They were out buying a Christmas tree. I wanted to go, but I was sick. If I'd been there, I would have been killed too." Little emotion brimmed in his green eyes as he spoke of the day his parents died. Xavier didn't like that.

"And then losing your sister. That must have been terrible. I understand you two were close," Ryan continued.

"Yeah. So?" Roman was suspicious now.

"What was the date of your sister's murder?"

"It was the seventh. Why are you asking me all of this? I thought you were looking for the girls? What do the dates of my family losses have to do with that?"

Ignoring his questions, Xavier asked, "Did you blame the police for what happened to your sister?"

"No, of course not," Roman replied a little too quickly.

"She filed over forty complaints. Her ex had been arrested eight times and kept getting let out," Xavier pointed out. "You didn't blame the police even a little bit?"

Roman shrugged. "I guess a little. But mostly I blamed that monster who killed her." Roman spat out the word "monster" as though it were poison on his tongue.

"One last question," Ryan told him. "You ever build anything?"

"Build anything?" Roman echoed.

"You know, bricks and mortar, wood and nails, building things," Ryan elaborated.

"My dad was a builder," Roman replied. "Before he died we often spent our summers building things. Forts and tree houses and things like that."

So far Roman fit everything they were looking for. He had no alibi for the night of the kidnapping or murders. He had no alibi for Sofia's attempted abduction. He clearly blamed the police for his sister's death. His parents had been killed on the sixth and his sister the seventh. He reacted to the word "monster," and he knew how to build.

"Thank you for your time. We'll be in touch." Xavier stood, dismissing the young man and he strode for the door.

"What? You brought me all the way down here for a few minutes? What a waste of my time." Roman said the words but there was no heat in his tone. It was almost like he was saying it because he thought it was the appropriate thing to do.

Leaving Roman Tallow, they headed straight for the adjoining room where Troy Tranchina was awaiting them.

Unlike Roman, Troy wasn't sitting in a chair. He was pacing the small room, a tightly coiled rage clearly visible inside him. "What took you so long?" he demanded angrily when they opened the door. "This is a joke. Why would you think that I'd kidnap my friends? *Kill* my friends? Just because I knew them doesn't mean I was involved," Troy raged.

"Take a seat, Troy," Xavier commanded quietly, gesturing to the chairs at the table.

For a moment it looked like Troy was going to refuse, then he sighed loudly and slid into the nearest seat, perching on the edge and tapping his foot.

"The date of your carjacking was the sixth of July, correct?" Ryan asked, even though they knew it was.

"So, what?" Troy's brown eyes were staring at them suspiciously.

"Just confirming. What were you doing yesterday?"

"Why?"

"Please answer the question, Troy," Xavier reprimanded.

"It was my day off," Troy sulked. "I slept late and then took my mom to a doctor's appointment in the afternoon. She's got cancer."

"We're trying to find the man who abducted your friends, who's killed three of them already. Who, no doubt, intends to kill the other two. And who's started abducting more innocent women. Do you know how he kills them, Troy?" Xavier paused to study the man watching him with sullen brown eyes. "He hacks them to death, cutting them into six pieces, while they're still alive. I'd say we're looking for a monster, wouldn't you?"

"Are you calling me a monster?" Troy exploded, bounding up from the table so quickly his chair clattered to the floor. "You think I'm a suspect. That means you think I'm a monster."

"Sit down, Troy. Now," Xavier ordered.

Groaning loudly, the man complied. "I am *not* a monster," he insisted. "And I don't appreciate being called one."

"That's a nasty looking bruise on your chin," Xavier commented, gesturing at the large black and blue mark that covered most of his lower jaw.

The sudden change in topic momentarily confused him. Then his eyes darted away, refusing to meet theirs. "It was an accident at work," Troy muttered.

Just like Roman, Troy also fit every aspect they were looking for in the killer. Unfortunately, the interviews hadn't helped them narrow things down to just one man. And even more unfortunately, Xavier knew what they really needed to get more information was another video. But another video meant another woman had to die.

NOVEMBER 11TH

9:34 A.M.

Sofia checked in on the kids. Besides her own two—her and Ryan's son Ned and adopted daughter Sophie—she was looking after her nephew Zach, to give her in-laws a break, as well as Hayley and Arianna. Laura and Mark had said that Paige needed some one-on-one time with Elias, so she had volunteered to babysit. Paige was an important part of her life and she was excited to get to know her new daughters.

Elias had dropped them off about twenty minutes ago and Sophie had insisted that she show her new friend this month's favorite TV show. The kids were in the playroom they had watched Peppa Pig, a British show for preschoolers about a rambunctious four-year-old pig named Peppa and her family and friends. Now, the girls had quickly lost interest in the TV and were busy with the huge dollhouse that Ryan, Jack, and Mark had built for Sophie's fifth birthday. Zach and Ned were building with blocks and giggling, as only toddlers could, as they knocked down their towers.

Closing the child gate, Sofia left the kids for the moment and went to prepare some fruit for a morning snack. Two-month-old Arianna was in her bassinette and Sofia ran a hand over the baby's soft little head. She missed having a little baby around. Ned was no longer a baby. He had moved firmly into the toddler category, and they'd even started toilet training last month. But now with Paige and Laura's babies, she'd get to have all the fun of babysitting a little one and then get to hand them back and not have to worry about all the things that came with very young babies.

She was glad the kids were playing happily. She'd known they would, but Elias had been concerned about how Hayley would cope interacting with a child her age given her history. But Sophie was a bubbly, confident little girl who was great at making friends and had instantly put Hayley at ease. Sofia wasn't anticipating any problems, so she turned her attention to her friend Annabelle.

Annabelle had been struggling for a while and Sofia tried to check in with her regularly. But the last couple of weeks had been busy. Sofia had been sick with the flu, then ended up in the hospital when she got dehydrated, then Laura had been held hostage and had the baby prematurely, and Paige had been almost killed, and she hadn't checked in with Annabelle in almost a month.

And now she was getting worried.

Her friend hadn't turned up to work yesterday and she hadn't called to say she wasn't coming in. They worked together at the women's and children's center she'd started with the money she inherited from her family. It wasn't uncommon for her or Laura or Annabelle to take a day off to take care of personal business, but they usually let someone know so their duties could be covered for the day.

Not only had Annabelle skipped work and not let anyone know, but she hadn't answered any of the phone calls or texts that Sofia had sent her yesterday or today.

She was starting to get a bad feeling about it.

Maybe it was just because of what had happened the other morning. Her near abduction had really shaken her—a fact she was attempting to keep from Ryan but that he probably already knew. She'd had nightmares last night and the night before. She'd awakened drenched in a cold sweat, her body shaking violently.

Ryan had been exhausted from almost a week's worth of sleepless nights spent at the hospital and hadn't awakened. So, she had crept from their bed, gone into Ned's room and carefully pulled him from his bed, holding his sleeping little body in her arms to calm herself.

"Mommy, we're hungry," Sophie's voice called from the playroom.

"Coming, honey." Sofia gathered up the fruit platters in one arm and the bassinette in the other and spent the next twenty minutes hanging with the kids while they ate their snack.

Once they were done, Sophie took Hayley upstairs to her room and the boys got out their trains. Sofia gave the baby a bottle, put her back to sleep, and then tried calling Annabelle again. Again, there was no answer.

More than concerned now, she dialed Xavier's number.

"Sofia? Is something wrong?" his voice came on the line almost immediately.

"No, everything is fine," she assured him.

"Ask her if my parents are there yet," Ryan's voice floated in the background.

"Did you hear that?" Xavier asked her.

"Yes, and no they're not. They got held up, but they'll be here soon. Tell Ryan not to worry. We're all fine here." Sofia knew that Ryan was worried that her would-be abductor would come back. Yesterday he had informed her that his parents would be coming over to spend the day with her. She didn't like Ryan ordering her around, but she'd gone along with him this time because he'd been so stressed lately, and she didn't want to add to that. Besides, she was still too shaken up and having Ryan's parents here with her made her feel better, especially since her father-in-law was a retired cop.

Xavier relayed that to Ryan and then asked, "What's up?"

"I'm worried about Annabelle. She didn't come to work yesterday and she hasn't replied to any of my messages. Have you heard from her?"

"No, but I'm sure she's fine," Xavier replied.

"I have a bad feeling about her." She'd had a bad feeling the night Laura had been attacked by Malachi and Paige had been run off the road into the river too. She'd been right then, and she was scared she was right now.

"Honey, I'm sure she's fine," Xavier soothed in a patronizing tone that irritated her.

"Don't placate me, Xavier," she snapped.

"I'm sorry, I didn't mean to. I just don't want you to worry unnecessarily. We've all had enough to worry about the last few days without creating drama where there isn't any. Annabelle wants to take time to sort some things out. The last time we spoke, she asked to move back in with me. I said no because I had to be sure that the changes she wants to make she's making for the right reasons. Maybe she just decided to go away for a while, clear her head, find her focus."

Sofia knew Annabelle wouldn't do that. "She would have called. At least to let me know we needed someone to cover for her at the center," she protested.

"I'm sure she's fine," Xavier repeated firmly.

"What about this case you and Ryan are working? He said that this guy is going after victims of crimes. Annabelle is a victim of crime. Ryan said that you think it was this guy who tried to abduct me in the hospital's parking garage. What if he went after Annabelle next? Ryan said that he's been sending you videos." Her husband didn't usually talk in much detail about his cases, but he had wanted to imprint on her why he felt it was so important for her not to be alone.

"I have patrols increased in her area. No one has reported seeing anything suspicious. I'm really sure she's fine. The chances of this guy going after her aren't high."

"Couldn't you go and check on her? Please?" she implored. She wanted to put her mind at ease and it wouldn't be until she spoke to Annabelle. "I'd go myself, but I have all the kids."

"Sure, Ryan and I will pop by her apartment as soon as we get a chance and I'll have her call you," Xavier promised.

"Thanks. One more question—"

"Yes," Xavier interrupted to answer.

"I haven't even asked yet."

"You were going to ask if Ryan and I made sure Jack is keeping an eye on Laura and Paige, and yes, he is. I know as a group of friends we have a bad track record of terrible things happening, but I'm sure Annabelle is fine. Try not to worry."

"Okay," she agreed, although it was easier said than done. Xavier was right about them—they'd had an awful track record lately. "Tell Ryan I love him and you two be careful, please. I can't take any more stress right now."

"We'll be careful," Xavier promised. "Say hi to the kids from me. I'll call you later, tell you what we find at Annabelle's apartment."

Sofia hoped they checked on Annabelle soon. She was tired of worrying about something terrible happening to the people she loved.

Maybe she'd take the kids outside in the backyard where they had swings and a slide and a trampoline. The kids would have fun and playing with them would be the perfect distraction.

* * * * *

11:22 A.M.

Xavier was almost positive that nothing was wrong with Annabelle, but to put Sofia's mind at ease, he didn't mind driving to her apartment to check on her.

If he were completely honest, it probably wasn't just to put Sofia's mind at ease that he had so readily agreed to check up on Annabelle. He wanted to see her too. He wanted to assure himself that she wasn't too angry with him for saying no when she'd asked to move back in. He wanted things to work out between Annabelle and him. He just didn't want to wind up in another

Julia situation.

His marriage to Julia had ended in disaster.

She had been raped one night while he'd been at work but kept it a secret. When she had announced she was pregnant, he'd been thrilled. She, on the other hand, had been afraid she was pregnant with her rapist's baby.

Maybe if she had confessed to him that she'd been assaulted, then what happened next could have been avoided.

Unfortunately, their baby had been stillborn and Julia had blamed herself and gone to drastic measures to procure another baby for them. What she had done had landed her in prison.

That she hadn't told him about the rape still hurt. Hurt because he had loved Julia and she had shut him out at the time when she needed him the most. If he'd known about Julia's assault, he would have done whatever was needed to help her through it.

Xavier was determined not to go through that again. If he and Annabelle were going to move forward, then it was with the understanding that they shared everything, they worked on every problem together, they supported and trusted one another implicitly. He truly couldn't cope with another disaster like the way things had turned out with Julia.

He wanted to believe so badly that Annabelle was serious about overcoming her fears. He knew that what had happened to her as a child and the impact it had on her relationship with her parents had scarred her. Scarred her more deeply than the physical scars she bore. He wanted to believe her, but he was cautious of believing without proof.

Last time they'd talked, something had felt different. There had been a change in Annabelle's white eyes. A spark of strength and independence that hadn't been there before.

Maybe he'd been wrong.

Maybe she *could* change.

He loved Annabelle, and he owed it to her to let her prove to him that this time was different. This time *she* wanted to be different.

"We're here," he informed Ryan, pulling to a stop in front of a large apartment building. "Her apartment is 6L."

"I texted Sofia. My parents are there and they're having a blast with the kids. Hayley is doing really well, coming out of her shell already," Ryan told him.

"That's great. I bet knowing that will help put Paige's mind at ease."

"Yeah, she was looking a lot more relaxed when I visited her on the way home last night. Mark says she's doing better. She's eating a little and able to get up and walk around a bit, and even take a shower. Apparently, she's even been sleeping really well—made it through the last two nights without nightmares."

"Has she seen Charlie Abbott?"

"Yes. She told me she really likes him. She and Elias are going to have him work with Hayley too."

"I'm really happy for her." Paige had finally gotten her happy ending. Maybe he and Annabelle would get theirs too. "You better knock," he told Ryan as they reached her front door. "If I upset her the other day then she might not open up for me."

Ryan rapped on the door. "Annabelle? It's Ryan. I need to talk to you for a moment, can you open up?"

No response.

"Try again." Xavier felt the first niggling feelings of doubt. Could Sofia have been right? Had something happened to Annabelle?

"Annabelle, it's really important that I talk to you, now. Please open up," Ryan called out.

Still no response.

Without thinking, his hand moved to the handle. "Ryan, the door's unlocked."

"I don't like that." Ryan snapped immediately into cop mode.

Xavier didn't like it either. After being nearly killed in her bed while she slept and then abducted twice, Annabelle was extremely diligent when it came to security. Doors and windows were always locked, and she checked them with a near obsessive-compulsive addiction.

Ryan raised an eyebrow at him. Xavier nodded that he was ready and they both pulled out their guns.

"Annabelle? It's Xavier, can you please open the door?"

When they once more got no reply, Xavier slowly edged it open. The living room was empty. A sense of déjà vu descended on him. Annabelle's phone was on her desk, her handbag hanging on a hook by the front door. The scene reminded him of Faith Smith's house where everything appeared to be in order and all personal effects left behind but their owner nowhere to be seen.

Without pausing, they continued to the kitchen. Ryan nudged the door open and Xavier's stomach dropped.

A knife lay on the floor next to a toppled chair.

The ability to function—let alone do his job—vanished.

Annabelle was gone. Of that, there was no doubt. He also had no doubt that whoever had abducted Annabelle from her home was the same man who had taken Faith, Ruby, Mackenzie, Vanessa, and Ava—as well as attempted to kidnap Sofia.

Ryan left the room, returning a minute later. "Bathroom and bedroom are clear. She's not here. We'll get CSU over here immediately, then we'll start canvassing her neighbors. When was the last time someone saw or spoke to her? We need to know the window of time where she may have been taken."

Xavier heard the words, but they were nothing more than gibberish. Annabelle had asked to come home and he'd said no. He'd said no and now she was gone.

"Xavier?" Ryan gently prompted. "Try to focus. When was the last time you spoke to her?

He forced himself to take a deep, cleansing breath and focus. "A couple of days, the eighth I think. But I think she was at work on the ninth. Sofia said she never turned up yesterday."

"Okay, the ninth makes sense because that was the day he tried to grab Sofia. That didn't work out, so he went after her instead." Ryan was already pulling out his phone and walking from the room.

Xavier couldn't take his eyes off the knife and chair.

It was clear there had been a struggle.

For some reason, that thought comforted him a little. It meant that Annabelle wasn't giving up. She had fought to get away. He just had to believe that she would continue to keep fighting until he found her.

* * * * *

4:34 P.M.

Annabelle had been working at systematically digging in the dirt around where her chains were embedded in the wall for hours. Her hands were cramping and her eyes were stinging. She was hot and tired and scared, but she wouldn't stop. Not for anything.

She wasn't going to die here.

She had too much to live for.

Too much she still wanted to do.

"Ava, are you making any progress?" Annabelle paused to give her aching hands a quick break. She couldn't afford long, but a minute or so was permissible.

"Not really," the younger woman cried.

Ava had done pretty much nothing but cry since Annabelle had woken up in this horrible hot little dungeon. She was doing her best to calm the younger woman, but most of her energy was going into trying to get herself free. In truth, the only thing that was going to calm Ava down was getting out of here alive, so it wasn't Annabelle's priority. "Keep trying ... we have to get free."

"It won't help," the girl sniffed. "He keeps the door locked.

Even if we get free, we won't be able to get out of here."

"I know." Ava had told her that several times already. "But if at least one of us gets free, we could surprise him as he comes in the door, maybe knock him down the stairs. Then we can make a run for it."

"What if only one of us gets free?" Ava asked.

"Let's cross that bridge if and when we come to it," she soothed. Annabelle wasn't used to being the calm, cool, in-control one, unless she was teaching, of course. She had been a preschool teacher before her family's murders, then taken time off from work as she recovered. Now she ran the children's programs and day care at the women's center.

"I just want to go home," Ava cried, fresh tears filling her eyes.

Annabelle felt for her. She really did. Ava was terrified, and after over a week of being held captive here, had lost her physical and emotional strength. Annabelle was just as scared, but she had to keep it together. If she didn't, she would never make it back to Xavier.

She turned her attention to the other young woman. It was Vanessa Adams. She and Vanessa had both been victims of the same madman. She had lost everyone; Vanessa and her father had both survived the killing spree. If Annabelle had woken up just a little sooner and told Xavier that another family was going to die, then all of Vanessa's family might have been spared.

"Vanessa?" she called out. "Are you with us?"

"Mmm?" came the faint reply.

"Try to hang in there, okay?"

"Yeah," Vanessa sleepily agreed.

Returning to her task—her hands had had enough rest—she continued to dig away at the wall. Progress was slow but little bit by little bit, Annabelle was getting closer to her goal.

* * * * *

SIX

4:51 P.M.

The Protector was in a good mood today.

Things were finally looking up.

At last the police were starting to get it. They weren't where he wanted them to be just yet, but they were definitely making progress.

Taking one of their women had been the key.

He hadn't expected the redhead at the hospital to fight back. She'd almost gotten away, but he'd taken back control. Until that other man had shown up. He had still believed he could take the man down and get the girl, only then the woman's cop husband had arrived. The whole thing had turned into a veritable disaster.

So, next time, he'd played it smarter.

This time he'd gone after Detective Montague's girlfriend. He would have picked her first only he hadn't realized the man was seeing someone. When he'd broken into his house, he hadn't seen any signs that a woman lived there. On closer investigation, he had learned the detective was dating someone, but the couple were having difficulties.

Targeting Detective Montague's girlfriend was a much better option, and he was glad he'd done it. He had hidden in her apartment for hours, intending to wait until she'd fallen asleep, but then she'd thrown on some clothes and been about to leave. Unable to risk letting her go, since he didn't know if she was planning on returning, he had been forced to grab her.

Everything was going smoothly but then she'd fought back.

It had seemed his day was going to end the same way it had started.

This time, however, no one had come running to her rescue. The woman had made a break for it, which he had nixed, and she had fled to the kitchen. Assuming she had armed herself with a knife, he had waited until he thought she was distracted and then pounced. Catching her unawares, he had managed to pierce her with the syringe and send her floating into unconsciousness.

Now he had Annabelle Englewood tucked away in his special little room.

Confident and happy in the fact that finally the police were moving forward, he had one more little surprise for them.

A video.

This time, the video would star someone the detectives knew. This video would be personal.

Parking his car, he got out and headed to the secret entrance to the underground room.

As soon as he opened the door, he smiled. Annabelle and Ava were digging away at the dirt around where their chains were embedded in the wall. Neither were making much progress, but that they had enough spirit left, even though he knew they were scared, was a testament to their strength.

The police needed to see that. They needed to know that even though they failed these women, the women prevailed. The policed owed it to them to do better.

Both Annabelle and Ava stopped as soon as they registered his presence. Their hands dropped as though they were children caught stealing cookies from the cookie jar.

Ava burst into a fit of noisy tears. He was getting sick of hearing her cry. He attempted to block her out as he descended the stairs.

Annabelle, however, was eyeing him defiantly from eyes that were so intriguing that if they'd met under different circumstances, he would have been compelled to get to know her better. "Why did you bring me here? Are you the man that Xavier is looking for?" Her voice was strong, despite her obvious fear. He respected that.

"I am," he acknowledged. Feeling her strength under pressure, he owed her the truth. "I met him ... several times. If he weren't a cop, I might have liked him."

"You don't like cops? Why?"

He smiled. He liked this woman, could even have seen they might have been friends if he didn't have to do what he did. "A story for another time. Right now, I need you for something. Please don't fight me. I don't want to hurt you, but I will if you give me no choice." He sincerely meant that. He didn't want to hurt Annabelle, but he absolutely would if he had to.

Indecision battled in her white eyes, but she nodded.

"I'm going to put this chain around your neck. Only so you don't run," he added. "I really don't want to hurt you."

Gingerly, he took a step toward her, anticipating her making a move to attack him when he got within reach. But she didn't. Annabelle remained perfectly still as he clamped the metal ring around her neck and padlocked it closed. Attaching a long chain to one end, he took it through to the bedroom Faith had occupied when he'd first brought her here and fastened it to a ring above the bed.

Returning, he pulled out a key and undid Annabelle's manacles. "These don't undo yours, Ava," he reminded the still quietly crying woman. "Stand up, Annabelle."

The woman complied, but too long spent sitting on the ground with her arms in an awkward position had left her weak and shaky. She stumbled, and he grabbed her elbow meaning to steady her, but she snatched it back and leaned against the wall for support. "Please don't touch me," she whispered.

He was offended. He didn't want these women to be scared of him. He was doing this to help people. He wished they understood that. Still, he honored her wishes and kept his hands to himself. He gave her time to regain her footing, then tugged on her chain to regain her attention and led her into the bedroom.

"Go sit on the bed," he ordered gently.

For a moment it looked like she was going to refuse, but she sighed and went to sit on the bed.

"Okay, now we're going to make a little video. You say exactly what I tell you to."

* * * * *

5:32 P.M.

"Anything?" Ryan asked Jack as he entered the room.

"Nothing yet," Jack replied.

Xavier felt like he was stuck in one of those dreams where you couldn't move or talk. He fought through the feeling since it wasn't going to be productive. "What are you doing here?" he asked his partner.

Jack just looked at him like he was an idiot.

"You should be at the hospital with Laura and Rosie," he protested.

"They're both fine. Laura is most likely going to be released tomorrow, and her parents are there with her. And Rosie is a miracle baby, she's doing amazing. She has no breathing issues and she's feeding on her own. If she keeps doing this well, she may make it home in a week or so. Annabelle is missing. Where else would I be? Laura knows, she practically shoved me out of the room as soon as she heard. If it were Laura, you'd be right here. When it *has* been Laura, you've dropped everything to be there. This is where I want to be and where Laura wants me to be."

"Thanks, Jack," he murmured quietly. He was glad his partner and Ryan were here. He was having trouble coping with just the basics right now. Breathing without hyperventilating, focusing on anything other than his fear. He hadn't eaten since breakfast, hadn't had any water either. He knew his body and mind needed fuel to function, yet he couldn't summon enough energy to care.

As if reading his mind, Ryan set a sandwich and bottle of water down in front of him. "You have to eat," Ryan said gently. "Believe me, I know what you're going through. I've been there with Sofia. Jack has been there with Laura. *You've* been there before with Annabelle. You have to try and keep faith, as hard as it is, you can't give up, Annabelle is counting on you."

Keep faith. He'd said the same thing to Bobby Kirk when Faith Smith had first gone missing. And now Faith was dead, and Bobby couldn't even have a proper funeral because they didn't know where the killer had buried Faith's body.

Was Annabelle next?

He'd seen in horrifyingly graphic detail just how this killer slaughtered his victims. It would kill him to have to watch Annabelle tied to a table, scared and begging for her life, awake and aware of what was happening as the man hacked at her over and over again until she died from blood loss.

And yet, watch it, he would—because he wouldn't stop until this man was dead.

Not arrested and in prison.

Dead.

And if watching the video was the only way to get enough information on this man to identify and find him, then he would watch it.

Ryan nudged him. "Xavier, eat," he commanded.

With a stomach that felt like it was full of lead balloons, he obediently ate the sandwich and drank three quarters of the water. He felt a tiny bit clearer headed when he did. "We have to follow Troy and Roman. It's one of them. If we follow them for long enough, they'll lead us to Annabelle and the others."

Exchanging glances with Ryan, Jack cleared his throat. "I already tried that, both of them have disappeared."

"Disappeared?" He exploded, bounding to his feet because he needed to move. "How could they have disappeared? They are both our prime suspects in three murders. Why weren't we already keeping an eye on them?"

Nobody bothered to remind him that they didn't have the resources to follow every suspect. They had nothing concrete on either man, which meant there was a limit to what they could do.

"Annabelle's building is still being canvassed. Hopefully someone saw something," Jack assured him.

Before Xavier could respond, his phone vibrated on the table.

It was another email.

He didn't even have to look at it to know it was from the killer. Annabelle was about to die.

It wasn't fair. He hadn't given them enough time to find her. He still had Ava and Vanessa. Why had he taken Annabelle too?

Xavier knew the answer. It was because he wanted to teach them a lesson and he thought making things personal would be added motivation.

"It's from him," Jack said gently. "You want me to open it?"

"Yes." He had thought he could watch but it turned out he couldn't stomach seeing what he knew was about to happen to Annabelle. Fear was eating away at him, like a flesh-eating bacteria, devouring him molecule by molecule, and he was afraid that if he didn't get Annabelle back alive, he was going to be eaten down to nothingness.

"Xavier, he's not going to kill her."

He snapped his head up at Ryan's words. "How do you know that?"

"Because he's not live streaming. This is a video he filmed and sent to you. She's not in his killing room. She's someplace else," Ryan explained.

A tiny glimmer of hope lighted inside him. Maybe there was still time to find Annabelle before this man killed her. With a shaking hand, he took the phone from Jack. The video hadn't started yet, but he could see Annabelle. She was sitting on a bed, a metal ring around her neck, secured by a chain to the wall.

Anger burned inside him.

How dare this man abduct Annabelle from her home, take her against her will to his dungeon, and chain her up like she was an animal.

Hesitantly, he pressed play. This might not be a kill video, but he still wasn't sure he wanted to see it. Annabelle sprung to life when he touched the screen. Fear coated her face, yet her eyes remained defiant, and he let out an inward sigh of relief. She hadn't given up yet. He couldn't give up either.

Pushing himself to look beyond Annabelle's obvious terror, he tried to focus on the details. She didn't appear to be injured, her hands were dusty and a little swollen, her face and clothes were also dirty but the fact that she was wearing her clothes was a huge relief. They didn't yet know if the killer sexually assaulted his victims before killing them since they didn't have any bodies.

Annabelle was looking off to the side of the camera, and when she spoke she sounded as though she were reciting lines she had been taught. "The Protector is sorry that he had to kill Faith, Ruby, and Mackenzie, but you didn't leave him any choice. He doesn't want to have to kill Ava and Vanessa too. He thinks you're doing better, but you need to stop crime if you want to get me back alive."

"Stop crime?" Xavier repeated incredulously. "How on earth does he think we can do that?"

Ryan and Jack didn't offer an answer to his rhetorical question.

Something was mumbled quietly from the person holding the camera.

Annabelle shook her head, fire shooting out of her eyes. "No. Xavier isn't a failure. He'd do whatever he could to help anyone who needed it."

The man must have set the phone down because he lost sight of Annabelle and instead got a shot of a dirt ceiling.

"Say it," the man's gravelly voice insisted.

"No," Annabelle's voice was strong, confident.

The unmistakable sound of a hand slapping flesh came through his phone.

Xavier very nearly threw it across the room.

Apparently aware of that, Jack tugged it from his hand.

"Say it," the voice repeated.

"I'm not going to say it. I won't. You can't make me."

Sounds of a struggle followed and then the video ended.

Leaving him with no idea of Annabelle's fate.

* * * * *

8:48 P.M.

"You didn't have to drive me. I could have taken a cab," Paige told Mark.

"Or you could have gone home like I told you to," he muttered back. "I thought you wanted to go home. You've been begging me for days to discharge you."

"I do want to go home." She wanted it more than anything. She wanted to move forward. To forget the last four years had ever happened. Forget that she had been nearly killed and forget she had been raped.

She wanted to focus on the future.

And her future looked bright. Brighter than she had dared to hope it could be after such a dark time in her life. She had her husband and she had two beautiful little girls. That was her focus.

But this was something she had to do, something she couldn't ignore. "Annabelle is missing. How can I go home? Xavier is going to be out of his mind."

"How much help do you think you're going to be?" Mark pulled the car to a stop outside the precinct. "I discharged you only because Charlie said you'd recover better at home, not because I thought you were well enough to go home."

She knew she liked Charlie for a reason. He was calm and smart and a little charming. If she wasn't married and he wasn't married, she would probably have found herself attracted to him. He was definitely someone she'd have as a friend. As it was, she was glad he was her therapist. He had a knack of making people feel comfortable. She felt comfortable enough with him after just a couple of sessions to ask him to work with Hayley too.

Xavier had done so much for her. It was because of him that she had the children she'd always dreamed of. She couldn't not be here now. "I had to come," she whispered.

Mark's face softened as he understood why she needed to be here for her friend. "Okay, but you only stay a little while. I know you don't want to hear it, Paige, but you're still weak. You're going to need a lot of rest if you want to get better. You can't push yourself."

He was right, she didn't want to hear it. But she knew she had to listen. She would never do anything to put Hayley and Arianna at risk.

Opening the car door for her, Mark took her arm, helped her stand, then kept hold of her until she felt steady enough to keep her balance. She was dressed in a ridiculous amount of clothing, leggings under her sweatpants, two sweaters, coat, gloves, and scarf, and still she shivered as the night air hit her.

"Hey, Mark?" Paige asked, trying not to let her teeth chatter with the cold or Mark was likely to bundle her straight back into the car and take her home no matter how much she wanted to be here.

He looked down at her. "Yeah?"

"I really appreciate everything you've done for me this last week. And I don't just mean saving my life. That you gave up time with Daisy and the kids so you could stay with me the whole time really means a lot to me. Knowing that you were there and that I wasn't alone is all that kept me from falling apart. You're a really good friend."

"You're more than welcome. Not that you have to thank me. We've been friends for a long time. I wanted to be there with you." He stooped and kissed her forehead.

Despite her best efforts at holding them back, tears rolled down her cheeks anyway. Quickly, she brushed them away.

"It's okay to be emotional, Paige. After everything you've been through, it's completely natural. Don't try to fight it."

"You sound like Charlie." She attempted a smile.

"You're strong. Don't forget that."

Paige didn't feel strong. She felt weak and drained and empty. If she didn't have Elias and the girls waiting at home for her she didn't think she could make it through this.

"Why are you here?" Ryan rolled his eyes at her as she and Mark entered the conference room where they had set up all their files.

"Because Annabelle is missing," she replied even though she knew he hadn't wanted an answer. "Where else would I be?"

"Oh, I don't know, at home in bed, maybe. Because you look like a toddler could take you out right now. At least sit down," Ryan snapped.

Jack was closest to her and scooped her off her feet. Startled, she automatically curled an arm around his neck even as frustration set in. Deposited in a chair, Paige realized a little dismally that she was too tired to complain to Jack about just picking her up and carting her around like she was some helpless child. Instead, she propped her elbow on the arm of the chair and rested her head in her hand.

As soon as she was back to normal, she was putting an end to this over-protectiveness that had developed between her and her friends since the stalker first tried to kill her. Bruce Daniels was in prison now. He was no longer a threat. They didn't need to worry over her anymore.

"Really, Mark? Why did you bring her here? Why is she even out of the hospital? She still looks terrible." Ryan was ranting at his brother.

"Charlie said she'd get better quicker at home. And she insisted on coming here. She said she'd take a cab if I didn't drive her, so I thought it was best I came with her," Mark explained.

Paige lifted her head, which was pounding with a headache. She really needed to lie down, but how could she while Annabelle was in the hands of some lunatic killer? "Ryan, don't yell at Mark. I told him I was coming with or without him. How could I not have come?" She turned her watery eyes to Xavier.

Her friend looked pale and drawn. Fear radiated off him in waves and Paige could only imagine what he was feeling right now. She had never had to worry about her husband being in danger like that. Elias was a firefighter and she worried about him constantly. He'd been injured on the job a couple of times, but nothing too serious. Ever since the stalker, Elias had been the one who'd had to deal with her in danger. It was one thing to worry about your own safety but another to worry about the people you loved. Paige didn't think she could cope if Elias, Hayley, or Arianna were ever taken from her.

"I'm so sorry about Annabelle," she told Xavier. "I want to help."

Xavier crossed the room and crouched in front of her, taking her hands. "That's sweet, Paige. And I appreciate it. I can't tell you how much it means to me that you came here straight from the hospital when I know how much you want to go home. But you should go home. You're still not strong enough to be here. You should go home, rest, spend time with Elias and the girls. We have a lot of people looking for Annabelle. We're going to find her," he finished firmly.

She wavered; she wanted to stay and yet at the same time she knew the boys were right. As strong as her desire to help was, her body was letting her down. It just couldn't physically cope with much at the moment. Already she was so tired that staying awake required effort, and she had been asleep just an hour ago when Mark came to tell her she could go home. Still, she couldn't accept that there wasn't something she could do to help, even just for a little while.

"I can at least read some files or something," she offered. She stood, intending to collect some from the table. Unfortunately, she swayed, and all four guys reached for her. She shrugged them all off. "Stop, stop, stop!" she protested. "I'm fine, a little wobbly, that's it. I can't live like this. Bruce Daniels is going to prison. I *am* going to be okay. You all have to stop worrying about me, no more over-protectiveness. I can't take it anymore."

Determinedly, she walked to the table, collected some files, and then returned to her chair. Sure, she had to will her legs to move, but she uttered only a small sigh of relief as she sank back down into the chair.

"Do you have any leads?" she asked Xavier. She only knew bits and pieces about the case from Mark, Sofia, and Laura.

"We have two suspects," Xavier replied. "We're trying to narrow it down so we can get warrants to search their homes, phones, computers, et cetera. And also warrants for the patient files from their therapists."

"Right now, we're going through background information on both of them," Jack added. "Hoping we find something that might point us in the direction of where he's keeping the women. We've checked out both Troy and Roman's homes and neither have the facilities to build an underground dungeon."

"Underground?" she repeated, unable to stop a sudden onslaught of claustrophobia at the thought. She was going to have to get used to that. Obviously, she now suffered from the phobia. Fighting down the terror that threatened to swamp her, she tried to take long, controlled breaths. Ryan noticed her distress and put a hand on her shoulder. His touch calmed her a little. She was going to have to learn how to manage the sensation or she wasn't going to be able to function.

"In the video of Annabelle, we saw the walls and ceiling were made of dirt, so we're assuming he's holding them underground someplace," Jack explained, distracting her.

Opening the top file, she began to flip through it. It was the file on the death of Roman Tallow's sister, Raina, and as she read, a small frown creased her forehead.

"What's up?" Jack asked.

"A neighbor said he saw a red-headed man at Raina's house around the time she was murdered, but her ex is Latina. Roman has red hair though. And the ex said he was home, drunk and passed out that night."

"You don't think he killed her?" Ryan asked.

"Given the history of abuse, the investigating detectives wouldn't have looked at anyone else," Paige noted, fighting back a yawn.

"We assumed that Troy's carjacking or Roman losing his sister was a trigger, but that's not necessarily the case," Ryan perked up.

Paige, however, was too tired to be perky about anything. She'd been fighting sleep, keeping her eyes open by sheer force of will, but she couldn't keep it up much longer.

"Why would he kill his sister?" Xavier asked.

"She was planning on moving away, right? Because we couldn't stop her ex from harassing her. Roman had already lost his parents. His sister was all he had. Maybe he panicked, asked her to stay, she said no—she had to get away from her ex and start a new life, Roman lashes out, temporarily loses control and hurts her. Then he's remorseful after and decides to blame it on the ex-boyfriend as there's history there anyway and we probably would have looked at him even if Roman hadn't immediately blamed him," Ryan hypothesized.

"It could be another reason why he blames the cops," Xavier continued. "If only we had been able to stop Raina's ex from harassing her, then his sister wouldn't have decided to leave him, and he wouldn't have killed her."

The guys' voices bumbled about her, but she wasn't really hearing them. Paige's eyes fell closed against her will. And before she knew it, she was asleep.

* * * * *

9:32 P.M.

"Is she out?" Xavier gestured at Paige, whose eyes had fallen closed.

"Yeah, I think so. I knew she wouldn't last long." Mark reached out a hand and gently grasped Paige's shoulder. She didn't respond. "I'll take her home."

"I can take her, if you want," Ryan offered, "so you can go home."

"Thanks, but I'll do it. I want to talk to Elias, make sure he knows a few things about her follow-up care and to call me if Paige needs anything."

"I'm probably going to be texting Elias several times tonight to check on her," Ryan said.

"Me too." Mark grinned. "Between the baby, Paige, and both of us texting him, I don't think Elias will be getting much sleep." Then he sobered. "You don't think this guy is going to go after someone else, do you?"

"He knows we're on to him, and he seems happy to have Annabelle. Sorry, Xavier." Jack cast him an apologetic glance. "I don't think he'd go after anyone else. At least, not right now."

"Are you sure? Because you said he doesn't like cops and Paige is a cop and a victim. I don't want him coming after her. And he already went after Sofia once. What if he tries again?"

"Mom and Dad are spending the night with Sofia and the kids. Zach is still there too," Ryan reassured him. "And I asked a friend of ours to watch Paige's house just to be safe. I really don't think he's going after her, but better safe than sorry. Just don't tell Paige that if she wakes up because she'll most likely flip out and insist she doesn't need anyone watching over her."

"Okay, that's good, because I was tempted to spend the night just in case." Mark stood and scooped up Paige, who stirred a little but didn't wake. "Good luck, guys. Xavier, I'm praying for Annabelle."

"Thanks, Mark," Xavier said as Mark carried Paige from the

room.

He still felt like he was walking around in a trance. Annabelle had been missing for around forty-eight hours now. What was worse was that for most of those hours, he hadn't even known she was gone.

How could he have let things get that bad between him and Annabelle?

So she had issues with trust, so what? Could he blame her? She had been abducted as a young child, an event she didn't even remember except for a couple of random snippets. When she'd been rescued and returned to her family, her parents had treated her differently—not as lovingly as they had before. Annabelle believed it was because of the scars she had gotten while she was missing. He didn't believe that, but he did believe there was a reason for the change in her parents' behavior. It was too bad Annabelle's parents were dead and they could never find out what it was.

It was killing him that he'd broken his promise to her. He had promised Annabelle that he would never leave her and yet he'd walked away because she'd hurt his feelings by insisting on moving out. He should have said yes when she asked to move back in with him. He should have trusted her when she said she wanted to make some changes and not been so scared of getting hurt again. In his attempts to avoid it, he had hurt her instead. Annabelle wasn't Julia and it wasn't fair to compare her to his ex-wife.

"Xavier, what do you think?" Jack asked. "Is Roman capable of killing his sister?"

"Yes," he replied without hesitation, focusing himself back on the task at hand. If he didn't shove down his near overwhelming fear, then he could lose Annabelle forever. Her life literally depended on him holding it together. "He's more calculating than Troy and this involved a lot of planning and forethought."

"I agree." Ryan nodded. "If Troy had done something, it

would have been bigger, more explosive, not long and drawn out like this."

"We got a description of the man who took Annabelle." The door suddenly burst open and Belinda rushed in.

"Roman or Troy?" Xavier couldn't help but bound to his feet, ready to go running straight to the home of whomever it was.

"A neighbor in Annabelle's apartment building remembered seeing a tall, brown-haired man he hadn't seen before hanging around Annabelle's door a couple of days ago. He asked the man what he was doing, and he said he was a locksmith and that the resident had lost their keys and he was there installing a new lock. The guy had no reason to doubt that. Apparently he was wearing a jacket with a company logo and had several tools. He thought no more about it until the police showed up at his door asking questions," Belinda explained.

"Why are we just hearing about this now?" Xavier asked, frustrated. If the guy had told them this earlier, then they could have rescued Annabelle already.

"Guy was out when we first started canvassing. The officer who interviewed him called it in immediately. The neighbor had no reason to doubt the guy was there legitimately just doing his job," Belinda reminded him.

Xavier knew that and yet still, he wished they'd known earlier.

"So brown hair, that means it's Troy," Jack stated.

That was what the evidence seemed to be saying but for some reason, his gut was telling him the opposite. "That feels wrong. I don't think it's Troy; I think it's Roman."

"You think he was wearing a disguise?" Ryan asked.

"He made the effort to wear clothes that backed up his story of being a locksmith in the event that someone saw him, so it makes sense that he would try to alter his appearance."

"Maybe," Ryan agreed somewhat doubtfully.

"Before Belinda came in, you agreed with me that it was more likely Roman than Troy," Xavier pointed out.

"The witness ID changed my mind," Ryan explained. "Are we going to see if the neighbor can pick Troy out of a lineup?" He directed his question to their boss.

Belinda nodded.

"I just don't think it's Troy," Xavier insisted.

"You said you thought that Troy would be more likely to do something big," Jack started slowly. "Well, kidnapping five women simultaneously, knowing we're going to link them together quickly ... then killing them and sending you live-streamed footage of it is pretty big."

Xavier couldn't deny that, but it still felt wrong. "But Troy was carjacked. That's not personal. This feels personal. Roman's sister was beaten several times by her boyfriend. She reports it, files complaints, has him arrested, gets a restraining order which he violates several times. He continues to harass her until she feels like her only option is to leave town. This is personal to Roman."

"If it were Roman, wouldn't he be more likely to go after victims of domestic violence specifically?" Belinda asked.

"Ruby *was* a victim of domestic violence. Mackenzie's home was broken into while she was there alone. Ava was raped by a teacher. Vanessa witnessed her family's murders and was almost killed herself. All of these women were hurt by someone who either specifically targeted them or their family or were hurt in their home—a place where they were supposed to be safe," Xavier explained.

"Don't forget about Troy's childhood," Jack reminded him. "He definitely has cause to hate cops if he chose."

Again, Xavier couldn't deny that. Troy had started fighting with other kids around fourth grade. In an attempt to find out the reason why, he'd been sent to a therapist and had confessed that his dad beat him. His mother hadn't known. Her husband had never laid a hand on her, but upon finding out, she'd immediately filed for divorce. Troy's father had been a cop.

"Maybe the carjacking set him off. Triggered unresolved issues he had about his dad and he decided to do something about it," Ryan suggested. "In the video he's not specific about any type of crime. He just wants us to stop crime altogether. So, it doesn't really matter what happened to the women, or to him, he just doesn't want it to happen to anyone else."

"Troy was a kid when his dad beat him. If he were going to make some sort of statement about that he'd go after kids, claim he was protecting them, not adult women," Xavier protested. "It's Roman. I'm sure it is."

"Well, we'll know soon enough. Warrants are on the way. When Troy is found, he'll be arrested. If we don't turn up any evidence that he did it, then he'll be released, and we'll know for sure that it's Roman Tallow," Belinda said.

That was true, but it would take time. Time to prove that he was right and Roman—not Troy—was the killer. Time that Annabelle didn't have.

NOVEMBER 12TH

12:01 A.M.

He was *so* excited.

Everything was going so perfectly. He couldn't have planned it better if he'd tried. Except he *had* planned it this perfectly. He chuckled to himself.

The Protector knew that he was standing at the dawn of a new age. An age where people could walk the streets of their city no longer afraid of being attacked or robbed or beaten. Where children could play in the streets and the parks without their parents being scared that someone would take them. Where women no longer had to be fearful of being raped or abused simply because they were physically smaller and thus more vulnerable. Where storing valuables in a safe was no longer needed, where locks on doors became obsolete, where house and car alarms could be a thing of the past.

And it was all because of him.

He was a hero.

For so long, he had dreamed of a better world. Of one without pain and suffering and fear, and now it was almost here. The police finally understood. They knew they needed to do better. They *would* do better. They would make things right.

He had been intending to sacrifice Annabelle just like he had been forced to sacrifice the others, but he was rethinking that. Perhaps it would be best to keep her alive. In case he needed her in the future. There was always the chance that the police would improve only temporarily. That after time they would sink back into their patterns of laziness that had created this problem in the first place. Annabelle could be his leverage to stop that from happening.

He wouldn't keep her here, of course. He would find a nicer place for her. She was a nice woman, after all, and he wanted her to be comfortable. Maybe something would even develop between them. She was beautiful and unattached. She was scared now, but once she understood why he'd done this she would respect him, possibly even come to love him.

He entered the middle room. He'd left Annabelle on Faith's bed and put Vanessa on one of the others, which only left Ava in here. Her tearstained face looked up at him as he opened the door and she whimpered pitifully. Of all the women he'd had to sacrifice, he was feeling the least remorseful about Ava. He was sick and tired of her crying.

"It's time, Ava." He started toward the woman.

She shrunk away from him. "No, no, no, no," she pleaded. "Don't you care that I have a little boy at home? How can you kill me knowing you're going to make an innocent child grow up without his mother?"

"You should be proud," he told her. "Proud that you are going to be instrumental in making the world a better place for your son. One day he'll come to understand the important role you played in creating this new world. He'll be proud of you. He'll know that your death wasn't in vain."

It was late. He didn't typically move the women at this time of night, but since he couldn't go to work with the police onto him, he'd decided to mix things up a little. Given the late hour, he wasn't going to bother drugging Ava. The chances of anyone seeing anything untoward were pretty slim.

Instead, he pulled out some plastic ties. "Don't make me regret not tranquilizing you, because I assure you that if you do, I will knock you out, painfully," he told her as he unlocked the cuffs and secured her hands with the plastic ties. He pulled them a little tighter than necessary because he was annoyed with her and her constant whining.

Ava whimpered again but made no attempt to fight back as he secured her ankles and then hoisted her into his arms. Carrying her from the room, he locked the door behind him and then popped the trunk of his car, tossing Ava inside.

The Protector was in such a good mood that he turned the radio way up high and sang along as he drove the short distance to his specially-designed killing room. When he'd built the room, he hadn't really intended to ever use it. But now he was glad he'd gone the extra yard and been so prepared. It made everything that much easier.

He wasn't surprised to find Ava crying again when he went to retrieve her from the trunk. "What is wrong with you?" he snapped, irritated. "Why are you always crying?"

"Because you kidnapped me and my friends. You killed them and now you're about to kill me."

He wasn't going to bother explaining once again why he was doing this. If Ava was too stupid to get it, then that was her problem.

Carrying her indoors and then down to the basement, he was once again thankful that he had taken the time to soundproof the basement. It wasn't a large space, just two rooms, but plenty big enough to serve its purpose.

The smell hit him as soon as he opened the door that led down there. Maybe he shouldn't have left Faith, Ruby, and Mackenzie's bodies here, but he just hadn't been able to part with them.

He wasn't the only one who noticed the smell. Ava stiffened in his arms, her head twisting about as she sought the source of the smell.

The second he crossed the smaller room and opened the door to the larger one, Ava realized what she was smelling. Her body began to jerk and twist violently in his arms, seeking an escape he knew she was aware didn't exist.

"Don't worry, Ava, it won't hurt," he assured her. He may be annoyed with the girl, but he would *never* cause anyone pain. He just wasn't that kind of man.

Plopping her down on the table, he had to keep a firm grip on Ava because she tried to roll away. He handcuffed one wrist before he cut the ties, not wanting to risk her getting away. Not that he really thought she'd get far.

With Faith and Ruby, he'd bathed them in the upstairs bathroom. Dressing them in some clothes that had been lying about, before bringing them here. He hadn't bothered doing that with Mackenzie. She hadn't deserved it after calling him a monster.

He had been called that before. It hadn't been true then and it wasn't true now.

Ava also didn't deserve to be cleaned. She could die in the filthy clothes she'd had on since he'd taken her and her friends over a week ago.

As he went to choose a tool, he had to block out Ava's wailing screams for help and pleas for mercy. She was so annoying. She sounded like a screeching cat. He found he was actually looking forward to killing her.

Choosing his tool, he was about to go and activate the webcam when an alarm sounded.

That couldn't be good.

The house was wired with a top-of-the-line security system, and it alerted him when anyone stepped foot on the property.

He was about to have visitors.

* * * * *

1:26 A.M.

They were standing outside Troy Tranchina's house, ready to go in. Xavier had decided not to come with them, and Ryan was glad. He was too emotionally involved.

It hadn't escaped him how easily their positions could have been reversed. The killer had gone after Sofia first. If it hadn't been for Bruce Daniels, she would have been abducted. Having seen firsthand what this man did to his victims, Sofia had been extremely lucky to escape alive and with just minor injuries.

Xavier was still convinced that they were wrong and that Roman was the killer. Ryan wasn't sure either way, but they were about to find out. As Belinda had said, they would either prove or disprove his guilt. If it wasn't Troy, then they'd know it was Roman. Xavier was just worried that it would waste time going after Troy—time that Annabelle may not have. But they couldn't do nothing. Troy could be the killer, and if they didn't jump on this and spent more time trying to figure out who it was while he had Annabelle, Vanessa, and Ava stashed away, it could cost them their lives.

Jack nodded at him and they and several cops got ready to enter the house. The building they stood in front of looked newly renovated. It was a weatherboard, freshly painted, bright white with green trim. It was by far the nicest house in the neighborhood and Ryan assumed that being a builder, Troy had made the improvements himself. It looked like he was in the process of adding a deck, and there was a small fenced area that enclosed a vegetable garden.

If Troy was the killer, then he wasn't keeping his victims here at his house. He lived in the middle of a busy neighborhood. Lots of the houses had kids' toys in the yards, and even at one in the morning, there were people out walking their dogs and jogging. They were going to need to find out if he owned or rented any other properties.

He and Jack rounded the house to the back door, the others would enter at the front. As soon as they opened the door, a large dog came bounding toward them. Ryan aimed his gun at it. He absolutely did not want to shoot the animal, but he would if it tried to attack them. However, it quickly became evident the dog was not a guard dog. It wagged its tail at them and licked his hand when he held it out to grab hold of it. Jack quickly cleared the kitchen and the adjoining laundry room, and he dragged the dog to stow it in there while they searched the rest of the house.

The rest of the downstairs, a living room, dining room, den and study were all cleared, and they headed upstairs. Up here there were five doors going off the central hallway, three were open and two were closed.

Jack took the closest of the closed doors and Ryan moved farther down the hall to the other one.

He slowly edged the door open.

It was a bedroom and the bed was mussed.

Mussed, but empty.

His eyes scanned the room, and he took a small step inside when something suddenly slammed into his back.

Hands clawed at him, and a fist swung, connecting with his jaw hard enough that he knew it would leave a bruise, but not hard enough to do any real damage. Ryan spun around and was fairly easily able to push the other man off him. Shoving him up against the wall, Ryan pinned him in place and twisted one arm up behind his back.

"You're under arrest, Troy," he informed him as he snapped on handcuffs. "He's in here," he yelled to the others.

"What were you thinking, Troy?"

"I didn't know it was cops. I just heard people sneaking around out there and had to protect myself. For all I knew, you were breaking in here. I've been attacked before, and I wasn't going to be again," the man explained in a rush.

Jack flipped the light on as he entered the room. "You got him under control?"

"Yep, he attacked me though." Ryan was still trying to catch his breath from the surge of adrenalin that had spiked his blood pressure.

"You okay?" Jack's gaze searched him from head to toe.

"Fine." His jaw hurt a little, but it was no big deal.

"If you want to make it a little easier on yourself, you should tell us where you're keeping the women," Jack told Troy.

"I can't believe this is happening." Troy's brown eyes were wide in shock. "You really think I did this. Before, I thought you were just kind of going through the motions, but you *really* think I did this."

"You're under arrest for the crimes." Ryan led him downstairs. "A witness saw you pretending to be a locksmith while you broke into Annabelle Englewood's apartment."

"I don't have a clue what you're talking about." Troy stared at them blankly.

Sitting him down on a couch in the living room, Ryan continued. "We *are* taking you down to the station. You *have* been arrested. You *were* seen at the scene of one of the abductions. You have a motive." Ryan stood in front of him, looking down at him and trying to decide if Troy was guilty or not. Xavier was right. Until they'd gotten the ID from Annabelle's neighbor, he'd thought the killer was Roman. Now he wanted to be sure one way or the other.

"Motive?" Troy repeated incredulously. "What motive? Because I was carjacked? So, what? Look, that night was terrifying. More so than I've ever admitted to anyone, but the guy who stole my car and shot me is in prison, and I've recovered. It's done and finished, I'm over it. The support group really helped. I didn't want to go at first. I didn't think I needed help, but my mom saw I was struggling, and she pushed me to get help and now I'm glad I did. Well, I was until you accused me of killing my friends," he amended. "I liked all of the girls in our group. I wouldn't hurt them. Or anyone. I know I have a temper, but I'm not violent. I've never hurt anyone in my life. Just because I know them doesn't mean that I abducted them."

"You have reason to hate cops though, don't you?" Jack asked.

Understanding dawned. "That's why you think I did this?

Because of my father? Because he was a cop and he hit me when I was a kid?"

"Certainly adds to the motive," Ryan said. "Some of his friends knew, and they didn't do anything to stop him. I could see how you could blame cops for not doing more to protect the public."

He shook his head emphatically. "My dad was a loser, but I wasn't bitter about it. My mom remarried when I was twelve, my stepdad was a great guy. I loved him. My parents made sure I had therapy, worked through things, and I was fine. Once my dad was in prison, my life was so much better. For the first time, I was happy. I didn't blame the cops—just my dad, and he got his punishment."

Jack raised a skeptical brow. "Maybe what you did had nothing to do with your dad or the carjacking. Maybe you're just evil or crazy or thought it would be fun—I don't know. But you were identified as the man who was breaking into Annabelle's house. That means you're the killer."

"Your witness got it wrong," Troy stated through clenched teeth. "What do I say or do to convince you? Whatever you need, I'll do. You can see no one's here. You can check my car, you can check my mom's house, you can go through my computer, phone, bank accounts. You can talk to my shrink, if you want. I'll give him permission to share what we talked about. I'll take a polygraph. Seriously, whatever you want, I'll do." He looked at them earnestly.

He exchanged a glance with his brother, Jack's face clearly saying he no longer believed that Troy Tranchina was the killer. "We'll take you up on all of those," Ryan said.

Troy relaxed. "Of course. Does that mean that the killer is Roman?"

"What do you think?" Ryan was interested to get the man's opinion.

"He had a crush on Faith. He thought no one knew, but I could tell. He wouldn't do anything about it though because she was involved with someone. I think he called her the day the girls disappeared."

"Why do you think that?"

"Sometimes Roman and I would catch up for lunch. We had lunch that day. I heard him on the phone making plans to catch up with someone that evening. He didn't know I was listening. I'd gone to the bathroom and as I was coming back to the table, he was telling someone he really needed to talk and asked them to call the others."

"Did you ask him about it?" Jack asked.

"No, I didn't really think about it until I realized you were seriously looking at us just because we were in the support group," Troy replied.

"Why didn't you tell us this?" Ryan had to force himself not to snap. He wasn't close with Annabelle, not that he disliked her in any way, it was just that she had trouble getting close to people, and Xavier was a close friend and he hated to see him suffering. And whether he was close with Annabelle or not, he wouldn't wish what Roman Tallow had in store for her on anyone.

He shrugged apologetically. "I don't know for sure that Roman was talking to Faith on the phone and asking her to gather the girls to talk that night. And besides, you clearly had decided that I was the killer, so would you have believed me or thought I was trying to take the heat off myself?"

Troy may well be right about that. "Do you think Roman is capable of doing this?"

"I liked him, we got along well, I can't see him doing this."

Sensing a but coming. "But ..." Ryan prompted when Troy didn't continue.

"But I saw something creepy in his house one day," Troy began nervously. "It was a couple of weeks ago. We were all having dinner at his house. I needed the bathroom, but someone was in the downstairs one already, I can't remember who, so Roman said to use the upstairs one. I found something in his cabinet. I wasn't snooping. I was just looking for the soap, there wasn't any out."

"What did you find, Troy?"

"Hair."

"Hair?" Jack repeated.

"Human hair. Long brown human hair. Roman has red hair. It obviously wasn't his."

Ryan knew exactly who in Roman's life had had long brown hair. Roman's sister Raina. Paige had been right. Roman and not Raina's ex had murdered her. And then he'd killed Faith, Ruby, and Mackenzie. That still left Ava, Vanessa, and Annabelle. Ryan prayed they found them before they met the same fate as the others.

* * * * *

1:58 A.M.

"Text me the location right now," Xavier demanded. Not bothering to listen for a reply, he hung up. His phone beeped a moment later with an incoming text message that contained the location of where the video of Annabelle had been filmed. Someone from the forensic unit had contacted him with the news he'd been waiting for. Their guy had gotten sloppy. He had forgotten to be careful when filming the video, and as such, had left behind information in the video file that had allowed them to trace the location.

Glancing at his phone as he drove, Xavier let out a sigh of relief. The location was only about a ten-minute drive from where he was right now. From what he could gather, it was in the woods just outside the city, close to where Roman's parents had died in the car accident.

He altered the direction he was driving and sped up. One handed, he dialed Jack's number. "They have a location of where the video was shot," he announced without preamble. "I'm heading there right now. I'm texting you the location as soon as we get off the phone."

"Xavier, wait for us," Jack protested. "We're thirty, forty minutes tops, away. Troy isn't the killer, it's Roman, and I think Paige was right and he killed his sister. Apparently, he has her hair in his bathroom cabinet. This guy is dangerous and unpredictable."

No way was he waiting. "Annabelle is there. I'm going in as soon as I get there. I'm not risking her life by waiting."

Jack muttered something unintelligible. "I think you should wait, but I get why you don't want to. If it were Laura, I'd do the same thing. Just be careful."

Sending the text, Xavier knew he would be as careful as it was humanely possible to be. He wouldn't do anything to put Annabelle further at risk.

A couple of minutes later he was pulling his car to the side of the road close to the coordinates. He ditched the car so as not to announce his arrival, and it would be easier looking for the underground room on foot.

It wasn't difficult to locate the right place.

He had travelled maybe a half mile into the woods when he found a narrow track. The track had been used recently as tire tracks were visible in the dirt. Following the tire marks, he quickly located the spot where the car had been parked. The ground was disturbed, and when he looked closer, he spotted what was most likely blood.

Xavier tried not to let his imagination run away from him. There was no reason to believe that it was Annabelle's blood. She hadn't looked injured on the video, but it was clear that Roman Tallow had attacked her when she refused to comply with his orders that she say that he was a failure. That she had stood up for him even when Roman was hurting her made Xavier feel that much worse for the way he'd treated her the last few weeks.

Supposing Annabelle, Vanessa, and Ava were still alive, he had to get them out of here. Since there was no evidence to the contrary, he refused to believe they were anything but alive.

He'd made good time—the others wouldn't arrive for at least half an hour. Waiting was not an option. Just because he didn't see a car didn't mean one wasn't hidden around here somewhere. No one knew where Roman was, and he could turn up here at any second.

He began searching the area for signs of an entry. Finding what looked like a trail, he followed it through the brush until he found it. It was hidden beneath a pile of leaves that stood out because they were the only large pile around.

Reaching out a hand, he pulled on the handle, fully expecting the trapdoor to be locked, but instead, it lifted. He was immediately hit by a hideous odor—blood, vomit, sweat, and human waste all mixed together with an overlying smell of fear.

Breathing through his nose, Xavier dropped down onto a small platform at the top of a set of unsteady looking wooden steps. The room beneath him had dirt walls, just like the room in the video of Annabelle. Five sets of chains were embedded in the solid dirt wall but none of the women were there. There was also no bed, but he saw three doors and assumed that Annabelle, Vanessa, and Ava were in another room.

Bounding down the steps, he went with the door straight ahead, throwing it open to reveal Annabelle chained to the wall. She was propped up in an awkward position against the head of the bed. The chain had been shortened so that her movement was severely limited. She couldn't lie down or stand up but was forced to remain sitting in one position.

Dried blood stained her left cheek and her bottom lip was swollen and split. His blood boiled at the sight of her bruised and swollen face. How dare Roman lay his hands on Annabelle.

She didn't look up as he entered the room and Xavier hoped she was merely asleep and not unconscious.

"Annabelle?" he called softly as he crossed to her, gently cupping her uninjured cheek in his hand.

At his touch and the sound of his voice, her head lifted, and her eyes opened slowly—disoriented for a moment—then they flashed with fear.

Startled, he released her. "Annabelle, it's me, Xavier. I'm here. You're safe now."

She reached out a trembling hand and traced her fingertips down his cheek. "Am I imagining you?"

He understood her fear. She didn't want to believe that she was rescued in case she was hallucinating. "You're not imagining things. I'm right here. I love you, Belle." Gently, he held her face, being careful not to hurt her, and pressed his lips against hers.

"I love you too, Xavier," she murmured against him.

As soon as he released her, she burst into a fit of noisy tears. She would have flung herself into his arms, but she couldn't move enough to do so. Instead, he moved closer, drawing her against his chest, stroking her hair with one hand. He rubbed her back with his other hand, whispering what he hoped were soothing consolations in her ear.

"I'm so sorry," he said when at last her tears had dried up, leaning his forehead against hers.

"Not your fault." Her arms wrapped around his neck and she clung tightly. "I just want to go home."

Xavier didn't agree that this wasn't his fault but now wasn't the time to argue about it. Annabelle needed to be checked out by a doctor. Vanessa and Ava may still be here. Both women were probably also in need of medical attention. And they still had no idea where Roman Tallow was. Gently, he took hold of Annabelle's wrists and untangled her arms from around his neck. "I'll be right back," he promised

"You're leaving? Where are you going?" Panic poured out of Annabelle.

"Just back to my car. I need to get something to get you free."

She burrowed her face against his neck. "Don't leave me," she begged.

"I'm not, honey. But I can't leave you like this. I need to get you free, get you out of here."

Steeling herself, Annabelle sat back up. "Okay," she whispered.

Xavier had never run so fast in his life. He was up the stairs, across the half mile to the car, then back down in Annabelle's room in less than five minutes.

"Drink this." He handed her a bottle of water and unscrewed the lid for her when her trembling hands struggled to perform the task.

Once she'd had a couple of mouthfuls, he snapped the chain as close to her as he could. There was nothing he could do about removing the metal ring around her neck at the moment. As soon as he had her free, Xavier sat back down on the bed and drew her onto his lap. Annabelle rested heavily against him, her hands curled into his shirt.

After holding her for a few minutes, he tilted her head back so he could see her better and brushed his fingers lightly over her bloody cheek and lip. "Sweetheart, are you hurt anyplace else?" he asked her.

"He hit me in the stomach," Annabelle replied. Her white eyes brimmed with more tears.

Sliding her off his lap, he helped support her weight with one arm behind her shoulders, while he eased up her sweatshirt to reveal a large purple and black bruise on her abdomen. When he was gently probing the area, Annabelle flinched. He thought it was just bruised and nothing too serious. At the moment, he was more concerned about her going into shock. Her eyes had lost their fight, and she was trembling in his arms despite the near stifling heat of the small room. Shrugging out of his jacket, he put it on her, then wrapped her back up in his arms.

Annabelle lifted one hand and tugged at the metal around her neck. "Can't you take this off?" she pleaded.

He took her hands in his, taking note of her red and scratched fingers and torn fingernails, probably from pulling pointlessly at the chains that bound her. He brought one of her hands to his mouth, kissing her palm. "I'm sorry, Belle, I can't take it off. Help will be here soon though. Honey, I need to know if anyone else is still here."

"I think he took Ava, but Vanessa is here somewhere." Annabelle's voice was alarmingly quiet.

"I need to go and check on her. Do you want me to leave you here so you can rest?"

"No," Annabelle protested immediately, scrambling to get closer to him. "Don't leave me."

"Shh." He kissed her temple, then her mouth. He kissed her hungrily as though he were dying, and she alone could sustain him. Annabelle kissed him back just as hungrily. "I'm never leaving you again, Belle. Ever."

She smiled at him, kissed his cheek, and he scooped her up and into his arms. Leaving Annabelle's room, he picked the door on the left and opened it. Inside was another bed with Vanessa lying on it. Like Annabelle, she didn't stir as they entered the room.

"Can you stand?" he asked Annabelle as he stood beside the bed. He couldn't juggle her in his arms and free Vanessa from her bonds at the same time, but he wasn't sure Annabelle had enough strength left to remain on her feet.

"Yeah," she replied, but her voice was shaky, and her arm lingered on his shoulders as he let her feet slide down to the ground. Still, she didn't collapse when he tentatively released her, and he turned his attention to the bed.

"Vanessa?" He patted gently but firmly at her cheek. "Vanessa, it's Detective Montague, can you hear me?"

Moaning, Vanessa's eyes opened heavily and blinked in surprise when she saw him beside her. "Detective Montague?"

"I'm right here. Just hold on and I'll get you out of here." Already he was reaching for the bolt cutters but paused when he saw Annabelle sway and lean against the wall for support. "Are you okay?"

She nodded. "Let's just get Vanessa and go. Are the others coming?"

"They're on their way," he promised. "Sit before you fall down."

Xavier broke the chain binding Vanessa. "Are you hurt anywhere?" he asked her.

"No, but I don't feel so good."

She didn't look so good either. Her complexion was a sickly shade of gray, and her skin was hot and damp—clearly running a fever. He wasn't sure what was wrong with her, but she looked very ill.

"Annabelle, can you make it on your own?" He was hoping she was at least strong enough to get up and out of the underground dungeon. He wasn't sure if she could make it all the way to the car, but Vanessa definitely couldn't, and he couldn't carry them both. Hopefully Jack and Ryan and the others would be here soon. He wanted both Annabelle and Vanessa checked out by paramedics and then he wanted to focus on finding Roman Tallow.

"I can make it," Annabelle replied determinedly.

"That's my girl." He grinned at her and bent to pick up Vanessa. "Okay, girls, let's get out of here."

"Sorry, Detective Montague, I can't let that happen."

* * * * *

2:41 A.M.

Detective Montague moved so that his body was between the women and him. Roman wasn't offended. He was pleased that at last the detective seemed to be taking his job seriously.

"You don't have to keep doing this, Roman." Detective

Montague's voice and face were calm, but Roman could sense his underlying tension. "You got what you wanted. You got our attention."

"It's not enough," Roman whispered, keeping his gun trained on the detective. He was starting to wonder if anything could ever be enough to undo what had happened.

"We can't stop crime, Roman, you know that. I know you do," Detective Montague told him.

Maybe that was true. Maybe he was naïve to think that he could. And yet he couldn't give up now. Maybe it *was* possible. He'd never know if he didn't keep trying. He had worked so hard, made so much progress, but he wasn't stopping now. He'd rather die first.

"Roman, let Annabelle and Vanessa go. They need to be checked out by a doctor. Then you and I can sit down and talk."

His gaze drifted toward the women. Vanessa lay listlessly on the bed. Annabelle was leaning against the wall for support.

The blood on Annabelle's face hit him hard. He shouldn't have taken out his frustration on her. Only he hadn't been able to help himself. That had always been a problem for him. Uncontrollable rages. But he wasn't a monster. He wasn't.

"You said you want to help them. Well, here's your chance … let them go."

He hesitated. Should he, or shouldn't he?

If Detective Montague had found this place, then his friends knew about it too. He may have come alone but the others couldn't be far behind him. He didn't have much time left. He had to make them understand.

"Annabelle, grab Vanessa and leave. Wait outside for Jack and Ryan," Detective Montague ordered.

"No, Annabelle, don't do that." Roman swung his gun in her direction. Detective Montague moved, angling his body so that once again he was in between Roman and the girls. He really wanted to do the right thing, but at the moment, he thought it was better to keep everyone together in one room.

"We know what happened, Roman—with your sister," Detective Montague informed him.

Roman was so shocked to hear that, he almost dropped his gun. They knew? How? How could they possibly know? No one knew. That wasn't possible. He was bluffing. He had to be. Cautiously, he raised his gaze to meet the detective's.

"I'm not bluffing, Roman." Detective Montague seemingly read his mind. "We know you killed Raina. Troy found her hair in your bathroom. What happened?" he asked almost gently.

"She was going to leave me," he said softly, the pain in his heart as strong as it had been that night. How could Raina even think of leaving? After all they'd been through together. His sister was all he had, he couldn't let her go. He had tried to convince her of that, but she had been determined.

"You didn't mean for it to happen, did you?"

Roman shook his head emphatically. "It was an accident. I begged her to stay, but she wouldn't. She said Dylan was never going to let her go. She said she couldn't live like that anymore. I asked her about me … how she could leave me. I reminded her that we were all each other had … but she said she was sorry, this was something she had to do. I didn't want to hurt her."

"Did she call you a monster, Roman?"

Fury flashed through him.

He *wasn't* a monster.

He wasn't.

He wasn't.

Why would Raina have called him one? She was his sister. She'd raised him after their parents died. She knew him. She knew he wasn't a monster, but she'd told him he was. He'd been begging her not to leave him, begging her to let him come too, and she had told him that she was going, and he couldn't follow. When he'd told her he wouldn't allow her to leave, she'd called him controlling and no better than her monster ex-boyfriend

Dylan.

Upon hearing the word, he had just snapped.

They'd been in the kitchen, he'd been making dinner, he'd held a knife in his hand, and he'd pierced her heart even before he knew what he was doing.

Afterward had been horrendous.

The guilt, the sorrow, the gut-wrenching pain.

He had killed the sister he loved—the only family he had left—and there was nothing he could do to bring her back.

It wasn't his fault though. The police were to blame. They should have protected Raina. They should have kept Dylan away from her. If they had, Raina would still be alive. If they'd done their job, his sister would've never been killed. It was as if *they* had held the knife and plunged it into Raina's chest.

"Why does the word upset you? Don't bother denying that it does. We saw what you did to Mackenzie when she called you a monster."

Roman growled angrily. He didn't want to tell Detective Montague. It wasn't any of his business. It wasn't *anyone's* business.

"Roman?" Detective Montague prompted.

Against his will, his mind flitted back in time. His voice spoke almost without his knowledge, saying the words he hadn't confessed to another living soul. "My parents were coming to get me that night ... When I was a kid, I got in trouble a lot ... Fighting and graffiti and vandalism ... I was away at a school camp ... A friend and I were spray painting the sides of the cabins ... We got caught ... They called our parents to come get us ... Mine died in a car accident on the way ... After, I went to live with my grandparents for a bit ... They blamed me ... They knew why my parents were in the car ... They said I killed them ... That it was my fault ... They called me a monster ... I lost it ... Tore up their house ... They kicked me out, and that's when I went to live with Raina ... After that, I straightened out, stopped getting into trouble—my sister was everything to me."

"I'm sorry, Roman. I'm sorry about your parents and what your grandparents did to you. I'm sorry that you blame yourself for your parents' deaths because it was not your fault. And I'm sorry about your sister. But what you're doing is wrong. I understand what you want to happen, and it's a noble ambition to make the lives of others better but kidnapping and killing isn't the way to achieve that. You *know* that even as cops we can't stop crime. You're not a monster, but killing your sister and framing Dylan, abducting and killing your friends ... that was terrible; it was exactly what you've been trying to stop."

"I just wanted to fix things, so no one else would ever be hurt the way Raina was," he whispered. "Six, it's always six." He spoke more to himself than the detective. "My parents' death ... the day my grandparents kicked me out ... Raina's death ... I had to break the curse."

"That's why you cut their bodies into six pieces?"

Slowly, he nodded. Roman hated that number. It had been the source of all his pain.

"This is over, Roman. You will be arrested. You just have to decide how you want this to end. You can let Annabelle and Vanessa go. You can tell us where Ava is; I know you haven't killed her yet. And then you can agree to come with me, let me arrest you. You need help, Roman; let me get you the help you need."

Detective Montague sounded so reasonable. And what he said made sense. Maybe he had made his point. Maybe things would get better from now on. Maybe he had atoned himself for Raina's death. Maybe he did need help.

There were too many maybes.

His head hurt.

Roman wanted to put his gun down, lie down, and sleep—just sleep. He didn't think he'd had a good night's sleep since his parents' deaths.

His mouth opened to agree with Detective Montague when a

voice spoke in his head. Roman tried to tune it out but he couldn't. It was too insistent.

"I can't. I'm sorry," he murmured. "I can't let anyone leave alive. He said I couldn't."

A little distracted, he was raising the gun and readying it to fire at the detective when he was suddenly knocked to the ground. His head thumped painfully into the dirt floor and the gun went flying across the room.

* * * * *

3:16 A.M.

"Annabelle, run," Xavier screamed at her as he launched himself at Roman.

She hadn't seen Roman's face before. Her captor had always kept himself hidden behind a balaclava. He looked so innocuous. Tall, skinny, a little geeky looking with red hair and green eyes— she would've never guessed he was a vicious killer.

"Annabelle, grab Vanessa and get out of here," Xavier repeated.

She was conflicted. She wanted to do what he said, but she also wanted to help him get Roman under control. The two men were wrestling, and despite the size discrepancy between Xavier and Roman, the smaller man was surprisingly strong, and Xavier was having trouble restraining him.

She couldn't go. Xavier needed her. She didn't want anything to happen to him. Things between them were going to work out. She'd known that as soon as she'd woken up to see him sitting beside her. If anything happened to him, she didn't know how she would survive.

There were two guns involved. At *least* two, she corrected herself since she didn't know if Xavier had a backup on him. Roman's gun had slid out of sight somewhere, but Xavier still had his—he just couldn't get to it. What if Roman managed to get his hands on it?

Roman's had to be around here somewhere. Tentatively, she pushed away from the wall that she'd been using as support to keep herself upright. Battling light-headedness, she began to scan the room. When she spotted the gun in a corner, she darted for it and gripped it in both hands.

She pointed the gun at the men. "Roman, stop," she commanded in a shaky voice.

"Annabelle, what are you doing? Just go," Xavier ordered.

She didn't know what to do. With Xavier and Roman wrestling, she couldn't get off a good shot. And she had never shot a gun before, hadn't even held one, she was scared if she tried to shoot Roman she would end up getting Xavier by mistake.

"Annabelle, now. I'll be fine, just go. Go get help," Xavier's roar finally prompted her into action.

Maybe he was right. She didn't think she would be able to fire the gun and hit her target. Perhaps the best thing she could do to help Xavier was go and find the others. She grabbed hold of Vanessa, who was basically a dead weight and started to pull her toward the door.

"No," Roman protested, managing to shove Xavier off and lunge at them, wrapping a hand around her ankle. "You can't leave. He'll be angry."

Roman yanked and she came down hard on her bottom, and pain shot up her spine. She lost her grip on the gun and it slid off somewhere. She kicked out with her free foot and managed to connect with Roman's mouth, causing him to release his grip on her.

Xavier stood over Roman, a gun in his hand. There was blood on his face and his shirt was torn. "Don't move, Roman," he ordered.

Annabelle slumped in relief. Xavier had everything under

control. Jack and Ryan and whoever else was coming would be here soon. She could go home, her real home—Xavier's home. She hated her apartment and never wanted to set foot in it again. But now she didn't have to. She had her life back.

All of that flew through her mind in the split second between Xavier pulling out his gun and Roman launching himself at Xavier, who fired but the shot went wide. Xavier's head hit the floor with a sickening thump, and Annabelle prayed he wasn't badly hurt.

Fighting her instincts, which were to stay and help Xavier however she could, Annabelle forced herself back to her feet, and began to half drag and half carry Vanessa toward the stairs.

By the time they'd reached the top, they were so breathless they could hardly move. Annabelle knew that she couldn't carry Vanessa any farther. She wasn't even sure she could move herself. But she couldn't stop. Xavier needed help and since she wasn't strong enough to help him, the best she could do was make sure the others found them quickly.

"I can't go any farther," Vanessa panted. She was lying on her stomach on the small platform at the top of the steps.

"I know." Annabelle could hear the sounds of the struggle in the other room and was desperate to keep moving and find the others. Surely, they weren't far away. "Help should be here soon," she assured Vanessa.

Then she climbed up through the trapdoor and into the dark night. It was cold, and she was dressed only in sweats, but she didn't have time to worry about that. Instead, she surveyed the area, trying to decide which way to run. An SUV was parked close by on a small trail. That seemed like the best option, so she started running.

Annabelle ran along the trail until her chest was tight and her stomach burned. She was weak. She hadn't had anything to eat since she was brought here, and Roman hadn't given her much water to drink. She hadn't slept—only dozed when her body became so exhausted it passed out.

Exhaustion wasn't going to stop her though.

When she thought she heard a noise, Annabelle paused.

Breathing hard, she looked around, hoping it was reinforcements.

She was just determining it was nothing and was about to start running again when something slammed into the side of her head.

Stunned, she stumbled, and her legs gave away and she fell to the ground.

Someone stood above her.

It took her swirling mind a moment to process what had happened. She had just been attacked. Had Roman hurt, or worse, killed Xavier and come after her?

Footsteps and voices sounded in the distance.

Maybe this was just some sort of accident.

Maybe whoever hit her had done so by accident.

Unable to stand, she tried to drag herself in the direction of the voices.

A hand roughly grabbed her wrist and began to pull her in the opposite direction.

She struggled against it.

This was all so wrong.

It wasn't an accident.

Someone had hurt her on purpose and they were now intentionally dragging her away from help.

Annabelle was opening her mouth to scream when something slammed into her head again.

This time the blow knocked her unconscious.

* * * * *

3:34 A.M.

Another kick to his kidneys virtually incapacitated him. The only thing keeping him going, keeping him conscious, was the knowledge that he had to buy enough time for Annabelle to get someplace safe.

Xavier knew that Jack and Ryan and backup would be here any moment now. Perhaps they already were. Annabelle could already be safe.

Vision cloudy, Xavier attempted to struggle to his feet. When Roman had been distracted, trying to stop Annabelle and Vanessa from leaving, he had managed to pull out his gun. His mistake had been assuming that Roman was sane enough to comply because of the threat of being shot. Instead of worrying about being hit by a bullet, Roman had thrown himself at him, knocking the gun from his hand and sending his head thumping into the hard ground. The blow had knocked him around enough that he was struggling to get Roman under control. He didn't really care how badly he was injured as long as he had enough strength to keep Roman occupied.

Not that he had any intention of letting this man kill him. He had too much to live for. He and Annabelle still had issues they needed to work through. Only now, they were going to face them together. He was going to take her home and there was not a doubt in his soul that this time when he proposed, Annabelle was going to say yes and then they could officially begin their lives together.

Unable to make it to his feet, he staggered to his knees. Roman planted a foot in the middle of his back and shoved him back down. Roman was stronger than he looked, and the blow to his head had nearly incapacitated him immediately. By the time the world had stopped spinning mercilessly around him, the other man had already gotten in several blows.

"I'm sorry, Detective Montague. I don't want to kill you. I didn't want to kill anyone, but He'll be angry if I let you go." Roman sounded truly repentant.

Who was the "He" that Roman kept referring to? He'd said

that earlier too, when Annabelle and Vanessa had been trying to leave. Roman had said they couldn't go because "He" would be angry. Was this "He" a real person or was it just a figment of Roman's clearly crazy imagination?

Roman pressed down on his back and Xavier struggled to draw a proper breath. He couldn't hold on much longer. He prayed that Annabelle was safe now. Even with her injuries, she should have had time to get away.

"Don't worry, when the time comes, I'll make sure Annabelle doesn't feel any pain."

Anger flashed through him, and with it a surge of adrenalin. Xavier would kill this man before he let him lay a hand on Annabelle. Flipping to his stomach, he shoved at Roman's leg and the man lost his balance, stumbling backward.

Recovering quickly, Roman resumed his position standing over him, a foot on either side of his hips, gun held in a two-handed grip, aimed directly at his head. "It'll be quick," Roman assured him.

He pushed up onto his elbows, unable to give up and simply let this man kill him. Roman, the walls, the ceiling all began to spin in a series of slow revolutions. The sensation was so sickening, Xavier had to fall back against the floor in an attempt to stop himself from throwing up. Lying down didn't help much. The world still seemed to swirl around him.

Just as he was about to black out, he heard footsteps.

"Roman, freeze."

The room suddenly filled with people.

Roman turned his head but didn't lower the gun.

"Drop your weapon, Roman."

A loud bang echoed through the small space.

For a moment, Xavier thought Roman had fired at him. As he waited for the pain to hit him, all the things he was never going to get a chance to do flashed through his mind.

He blinked at movement above him. Roman had disappeared.

Jack was now kneeling down at his side. At least, he thought it was his partner, but both Jack and Ryan looked similar with their dimples, blond hair, and blue eyes, and his vision was blurry.

"We need medics here," the person beside him yelled. It was Jack's voice. His partner was crouched beside him.

Relaxing in relief, no new burst of pain had shot through him, Roman's bullet must have missed. Roman was nowhere in sight, but he would be arrested and taken away to prison. Annabelle, Vanessa, and hopefully, Ava too, were now safe. Thankfulness had him nearly passing out. Jack's face above him blurred even more and the voices in the room dimmed until they were the merest hint of a whisper.

"Xavier. Hey, man, come on, snap out of it."

Jack's voice penetrated the hazy fog that had descended on him, and he blinked once, a slow blink that cleared his vision, and he focused on his partner's face.

Seemingly sensing the change in his mental state, Jack's brows snapped together in a small concerned frown. "Are you with me?"

"Yeah," he managed to croak.

"Medics are coming. How badly are you hurt?"

Taking stock, his head and face ached, his right shoulder burned, his chest and abdomen were hurting, but he didn't think anything was overly serious. "I'm all right."

Jack huffed a mirthless chuckle. "Yeah, right. What hurts? I see multiple head injuries, your left eye is swollen closed, your shoulder looks dislocated. What else?"

"Ribs and stomach," he replied tightly, trying to ready himself to sit up. "Where's Roman?"

Glancing off to the side, Jack replied, "He wouldn't put the gun down. He was going to shoot you, Ryan shot him in the shoulder. He's bleeding, but he'll be fine. Right now, I'm more worried about you."

"I'm really okay," Xavier assured his partner and was reasonably sure that was true. Tired of being stuck on his back, he slowly got his hands beneath him, and eased up so he was sitting.

Putting hands on his good shoulder, Jack tried to press him back down. "You shouldn't move until the medics check you out."

"I need to get up."

Jack sighed and moved his hand so it was under his elbow and helped to pull him up so he was standing. His stomach rebelled at the sudden change in position and Xavier had to fight the urge to be sick. Breathing through it, he was pleased that his head was barely swirling now.

"At least sit on the bed." Jack guided him to it and helped him sit.

Now that he was off the ground he could see Roman lying a few feet away. Ryan was crouched at his side, pressing a towel to Roman's shoulder to stem the flow of blood. Xavier wasn't sorry that Roman had been shot for refusing to comply with directives to put down his weapon. The man had hurt Annabelle, and he deserved a whole lot worse than a hole in his shoulder.

Xavier was about to ask Jack to go bring Annabelle down when several paramedics suddenly bundled into the room. Two of them went to kneel beside Roman and two came toward him. Reluctantly he sat still while they checked him out, politely declining their insistence that he go to the hospital.

"You really should get your ribs x-rayed," the younger paramedic, a pretty woman who looked about the same age as Annabelle, informed him.

"They're not broken," he assured her. "Trust me, I've broken ribs before. These are just bruised."

"You took several blows to the abdomen, you could be bleeding internally," the other medic, an older man who looked to be in his late forties, objected.

"I'm not," he protested. "I'm okay. Just sore and bruised."

"You probably have a concussion," the female EMT muttered under her breath.

"And your shoulder is dislocated. You'll need to go to the hospital to have it put back in." The male medic looked frustrated by his repeated refusals to comply with their suggestions.

"Can't you do it here?"

"It should be done in the hospital. Ligaments, tendons, muscles, nerves, can all be potentially damaged by a dislocated joint. It really should be x-rayed before it gets put back in."

"Is that a yes or a no?" Xavier was already wondering if he could do it himself. He was not going to the hospital. They still needed to get Roman to tell them where Ava was. He was sure that the woman was still alive, but if they didn't find where Roman had stashed her, then she could still die.

"It's going to hurt."

He gave a one shoulder shrug. He was already in pain, a little more wasn't going to make that much difference.

"You should go to the hospital," Jack objected. "We can handle things here."

"No," he told his partner, then to the medics, "do it."

All but rolling their eyes at him, they relocated his shoulder. The resulting stab of pain as the joint went back into place went barely noticed as he replayed Roman's words in his head, trying to figure out whether the "He" the other man kept referring to was a real person or not.

"All right, if you won't go to the hospital, we've done all we can," the male medic informed him as he adjusted the sling they'd put on to ease the tension on his injured shoulder.

"Yeah, thanks." He nodded distractedly.

"You really should go get checked out later," the woman all but ordered.

"I will," he promised. Later, once everyone was home safely and he and Annabelle had had time to talk.

"We need to get Roman to tell us where he put Ava," he said to Jack as they both watched Roman being loaded onto a stretcher and taken from the room.

"We will," Jack assured him.

"And he was talking about some guy, only I don't know if it's a real person or not," he continued.

"We'll find out," Jack promised.

"Did the medics check out Annabelle and Vanessa before they came down here?"

"Annabelle?" Jack's eyes grew wide with concern. "We only found Vanessa up there."

"What?" he asked, sure his injuries had caused him to mishear.

"We haven't seen Annabelle," Jack repeated.

"Why didn't you say something sooner?" Xavier demanded. As his heart rate and pulse both jumped, he did too, staggering as he stood, not quite properly balanced yet.

Jack grabbed hold of him to steady him. "Because you were out of it when we first got here, and we just assumed that Annabelle was down here somewhere."

"Well, she isn't. I told her to run, to go get help." He started walking toward the middle room as Jack kept his grip on his arm. "She knew you guys were coming, she probably tried to find you."

"How badly was she hurt?"

"He'd hit her but not too badly. She was weak from being restrained for so long and dehydrated. I was concerned she was going into shock," he summarized.

"Okay, then if she was running through the woods looking for us, it's possible she may have collapsed and is lying somewhere passed out." Jack nodded slowly.

"What's up?" Ryan asked as he met them at the top of the stairs. "You okay?"

Xavier waved off his concerns; he didn't care about himself right now. "Annabelle is missing."

"She's not here?" Ryan looked surprised. "We just assumed she was down here someplace."

His battered body protested as he tried to drag himself up through the trapdoor. With the use of only one hand, he had no choice but to let Jack and Ryan help him up. Much to his frustration, Xavier had to sink down to the ground to rest once he reached the top.

"I knew you should have gone to the hospital," Jack muttered. "Are you all right?"

Taking a few deep breaths, he willed his body to cooperate. He probably should have agreed to go to the hospital, but now that he knew Annabelle was out there somewhere—possibly hurt or unconscious—he knew he'd made the right decision. Squinting as he looked up, even the thin moonlight seemed too bright for his one good eye. "We have to find her. She has to be around here somewhere."

"We'll call in a search and rescue team." Ryan was already pulling out his phone.

"We can find her ourselves," he objected. "She can't have gotten far."

"You said she wasn't badly injured, she might have made it farther than we think. And if she ran the wrong way, it could take her hours to find her way out of the woods. It's cold and she's hurt and not dressed to be outdoors—she may have fallen or passed out. I know you don't want to hear this, but depending on how far she got, it could take us hours to find her," Jack finished gently.

Jack was right. He didn't want to hear that. He didn't want to think of Annabelle still suffering. Unfortunately, his partner was right. Search and rescue would be able to find Annabelle quicker than they could. Still, he couldn't just sit here while the woman he loved could be lying somewhere in the woods. He had to be out there looking for her. Determinedly, he pushed to his feet, ignoring light-headedness that he feared would soon have him out of commission.

"Where do you think you're going?" Jack demanded, grabbing his arm and holding him in place.

"To look for Annabelle."

"You are not going anywhere. I get that you don't want to go to the hospital, especially with Annabelle still out there, but you cannot go looking for her. Not in your condition. You can go sit in the back of my car and wait for news." Jack's tone had changed to full-on bossy.

Reluctantly, he nodded, allowing Jack to guide him to the car and help him in. Ryan followed, and he and Jack began to talk in earnest. For the life of him, Xavier couldn't distinguish a single word they were saying.

The next thing he registered was light.

When he opened his eyes, he saw that the sun had risen. He must have fallen asleep in Jack's car. He was lying on his back. Someone had covered him with a blanket, and another blanket had been wadded up and slipped under his head as a makeshift pillow.

A million new aches and pains had developed while he'd been sleeping. Ignoring them all, he sat up. Jack and Ryan were right outside the car, so he opened the door. "Any news?" he asked.

Both of them turned to face him. "Nothing yet. CSU is here. They're going through everything," Jack replied.

"They should have found her by now." Needing the cold air to refresh him, he forced his body—which had stiffened during his nap—to stand. His head and stomach had settled enough that neither bothered him anymore. "She was too weak; she couldn't have gotten far." Of that he was positive.

"We'll find her," Ryan assured him.

"Any updates on Roman?"

"He was in surgery last we checked. We won't be able to talk to him until at least tonight, most likely tomorrow," Ryan replied.

Jack pulled his phone from his pocket when it began to ring and glanced at Ryan. "Have you been ignoring calls from Paige?"

"I didn't want to have to tell her about Annabelle, so I was avoiding her."

"Well, now she's calling me. Xavier, your call, do you want me to tell her what's going on?"

"No." He knew Paige too well. If she found out what had happened she would come straight here, whether she was up to it or not, and she most definitely was not up to it. "If she knows, she'll head down here, and she's not strong enough."

"I'm going to have to tell her something," Jack said. "If we all keep ignoring her, she's going to know something is up, and I don't want to stress her out any more right now."

"Be vague with her," Xavier suggested. "Just tell her that we found where Roman was holding the women but don't give her any details."

"She's going to be mad when she finds out we all lied to her," Ryan murmured.

"Would you rather tell her the truth and have her come down here?" Xavier asked.

"She's calling back," Jack informed them. "Hey, Paige, how're you doing?" He paused as he listened to her response. "You sound tired. Did you sleep?" Another pause. "Did you have nightmares?" he asked gently. "I don't have a lot to tell you, we don't really know much, but we did find where Roman Tallow was holding his victims, CSU is …" Jack broke off and paused for a moment. "Okay, I'll talk to you later. You take care of yourself. I mean it, Paige. You're still recovering, you need to be taking it easy. All right, bye." Hanging up, he said to them, "Mark just arrived to check on her, so we got lucky she didn't get a chance to drill me for information."

"Did she have more nightmares?" Ryan asked. "Last time I checked in with Elias, he said she'd had trouble falling asleep. He had to give her sleeping pills. She'd only slept a couple of hours before she woke up in a panic thinking she was still trapped inside that car."

"She said she had dreams about Bruce Daniels in her room at the hospital," Jack replied.

"When is she seeing Charlie Abbott again?" Xavier asked.

"This afternoon," Jack answered.

"I'll give Mark thirty minutes, then I'll text him and ask how she's doing physically," Ryan said.

"You should get more sleep," Jack told him.

"I feel better," he protested. How could he sleep, warm and reasonably comfortable, while Annabelle was out there somewhere alone, cold, and hurt?

"Because you slept," Jack reminded him. "The same advice we just gave Paige applies to you as well."

He had no comeback for that because he knew his partner was right.

"We'll wake you if any news comes in," Jack continued. "If you don't sleep, you're going to end up passing out, then what good will you be to Annabelle?"

Jack's guilt-trip worked, and Xavier climbed back into the car and promptly fell asleep. He hadn't expected to sleep again. His concern for Annabelle would have had him personally searching every inch of the woods if he'd been physically capable. But the combination of fear, his injuries, lack of sleep since Annabelle's abduction and the drugs the paramedics had given him to manage his pain had his mind crashing, taking his body along with it.

Awakening around lunch time, he ate a little, and talked with the head of the search and rescue team that were combing the woods looking for Annabelle. After the sleep he'd gotten and with something in his stomach, he felt well enough rested and sufficiently recovered to help with the search. Before he could, Jack approached.

"They found something," his partner informed him grimly.

His heart plummeted, taking his stomach along with it. Was Annabelle dead? He didn't believe her injuries were serious enough to kill her, but she could easily have fallen out there somewhere and hurt herself more or hypothermia could have claimed her, or he could have been wrong about her injuries and they were worse than he'd thought.

"They found blood," Jack told him. "Blood, but no sign of Annabelle."

If she'd been hurt, she couldn't have just disappeared. And yet it seemed she had. Search and rescue had been looking for twelve hours and hadn't found her.

Xavier hadn't wanted to believe it. Because believing it meant that there was a chance that this wasn't over. But now it looked like he had to admit that it was true.

The "He" Roman had been talking about.

Roman Tallow had a partner.

And that partner had Annabelle.

NOVEMBER 13TH

4:35 A.M.

Still half out of it, Annabelle rolled onto her side and threw up. It had been the vague knowledge that she was about to vomit that had ripped her from unconsciousness. Even now as she was sick over and over again until her already mostly empty stomach was emptied further, her mind wanted to slide back into the blissful nothingness.

Annabelle fought with every bit of strength she possessed to stay awake.

Part of her numb brain knew she was in trouble.

At the moment she just couldn't quite recall how or why.

Breathing slowly through her mouth, she willed her mind to kick back into gear. She had a feeling that time was not on her side.

First things first, she took stock of her body. Both her head and her face hurt, her stomach too. The pounding in her head led her to believe she probably had a concussion, and from the floaty feeling she was experiencing, she had almost definitely been drugged.

Hospital would have been her first thought, only she could tell she wasn't lying on a bed. Instead, she was on something cold and scratchy. It occurred to her that she shouldn't know that. Last she remembered she had been fully dressed, now she feared she was naked.

That horrifying thought was enough to pop her eyes open.

The resulting stab of pain from the brightly lit room made her moan, and her eyes slid closed again.

Once the pain had passed, Annabelle tried again, this time cracking her eyes open only a tiny bit. It still hurt but this time she was able to keep them open and survey her surroundings. She was in a small room made of concrete, there were two chairs and a table, a bed, a toilet, and a sink.

A terrible thought occurred to her. This room looked like it had been built for someone to live in. Did whoever put her in here intend to keep her here indefinitely?

She fought down panic, only because she had to focus on what she remembered. She'd been kidnapped and taken from her apartment by someone named Roman. She'd been held in a dungeon, chained to the wall, forced to make a video for Xavier, blaming him for crime. She had refused, and Roman had gotten angry and beaten her. Then Xavier had turned up. He'd gotten her free, and she'd thought it was all over, but then Roman had come back. Xavier had fought him, and she and Vanessa Adams had run for freedom. Vanessa had been unable to move, so she'd left her and gone looking for help, which Xavier had said was on the way.

But someone had hit her.

Then they'd dragged her away from the help she'd heard coming and hit her again.

Annabelle didn't think it had been Roman.

That meant someone else had been out there.

Did Roman have a partner?

Was that who had her now?

And why? Why take her? Roman had clearly been insane, believing the police were to blame for crime and that if he could only motivate them to work harder they could eliminate crime. Was his partner equally as unbalanced?

What if it wasn't Roman's partner? He could have been working alone, but then what were the chances that someone else was hanging around in the woods looking to abduct someone?

Struggling into a sitting position, she was surprised to find that she hadn't been restrained. Her wrists, bruised from the manacles that had fastened her to the wall in the dungeon, were bare. Upon learning that, her hands moved straight to her neck, and she was even more surprised to find that the metal chain that had been there had been removed.

That seemed to cement the fact that whoever had brought her here had been working with Roman.

Looking down at her body also cemented the fact that she was indeed naked. Roman hadn't laid a hand on her, but it appeared his partner had other ideas.

Trying to stand, Annabelle found her body wouldn't quite cooperate yet. Knifing pain in her head assaulted her so badly she moaned and pressed her hands to her temples as though she could force the pain to leave her. She tried to breathe through it, but that didn't work, and she leaned sideways as she threw up again.

She eyed the bed. She needed to lie down, rest, get stronger so she could try to figure out a way to save herself. Unable to stand, she crawled on her hands and knees across the room. When she reached the bed, she had to drag herself up onto it as her legs still refused to support her.

The pain in her head eased as she lay it down on the pillow. Since she was shivering, she tugged the blanket over her and curled herself into a little ball.

Tears were pricking her eyes and she desperately held them back. She didn't want to cry. She hadn't cried in the dungeon, not until she had been safely wrapped up in Xavier's arms. And she wasn't going to cry here, not until Xavier was here and she was once again safe in his arms.

Annabelle couldn't even allow herself to think that Roman had killed Xavier. If she thought she didn't have Xavier to go home to then she had no reason to care whether she got out of this alive or not.

She was just drifting off to sleep when she heard voices.

They sounded like they were coming from just outside her room.

Then someone screamed.

Annabelle gasped.

All of a sudden, she realized why she was experiencing a strong sense of déjà vu. At first, she'd put it down to simply being held once again in a small, enclosed space.

But now she knew she'd been wrong.

Her sense of déjà vu was because she'd been here before.

Here in this exact room.

She remembered it.

This was where she'd been kept when she was abducted as a young child.

* * * * *

5:01 A.M.

Ava screamed as the man stepped toward her.

He was different, not the man who'd kept them in the dungeon, who had brought her here, chained her to the table and then left. This man was bigger, taller, more muscled. This man was scarier.

The other man had been Roman. She'd never seen his face. He'd kept it disguised along with his voice, but when he'd brought her here, she had recognized his car. She'd been in it before. Sometimes he picked her up and drove her to their support group meetings.

If only she'd known at the time just how insane he was, then maybe all of this could have been avoided.

She knew she was going to die. Then after her, Vanessa and Annabelle. And then who knew how many other women until Roman and this man were caught.

When Roman had first brought her down into the adjoining

room, she had smelled death. Her brain had tried desperately to convince her she was wrong, but she had known she wasn't.

While Ava had known this was the room where her friends had been killed, she hadn't seen the bodies until after Roman left. She'd been crying again. Then she had turned her head away from the door Roman had left through.

Her friends had been lying on the floor beside the table she was tied to.

Only they weren't her friends anymore.

Their bodies had been cut into pieces.

Her once vibrant, caring friends now lay in a pile of arms and legs and torsos. Their heads were there too, sightless eyes staring back at her.

Ava had screamed so loudly and so long that she had actually ended up passing out.

Being left in the room alone with the bodies for hours on end with no food and no water, and nothing but her imagination for company had left her so strung out she could no longer function.

Although she had little voice left, she still screamed as loudly as she could at the man who stood beside her. She no longer screamed for help. She had accepted her fate, She knew no one was coming, and now she just screamed from pure fear.

Sure, she was about to die, but die how? Had Faith, Ruby, and Mackenzie been alive when Roman had cut them into pieces? If not, how had he killed them? Had they been conscious up until the moment of death or had they passed out? Maybe this man and not Roman had killed them. If Roman had been the one to cut her friends into pieces, then what did this man intend to do to her?

Under the circumstances, it didn't seem unreasonable for her to yell and cry no matter how much Roman had kept telling her otherwise.

"Roman said you were annoying and was he ever right." The man stood over her.

Her gaze darted beyond him to the array of tools on the wall. Roman had been about to choose one when he'd suddenly disappeared. Now she wondered which one this man was going to use to kill her.

Following her gaze, he smiled at her. It wasn't a pleasant smile. She had no idea who this man was. She'd never seen him before in her life, but she knew without a doubt that he was pure evil.

"I don't kill with other people's tools. I have my own." He held up his hands and wiggled his fingers.

"Why are you doing this?" she whispered, her voice hoarse and croaky from so much screaming. For some reason she needed to know why she was about to die. Why her son was about to be left a virtual orphan. Her little boy would have had enough to deal with once he got older and learned that he had been conceived when she had been raped by one of her high school teachers. Now he was going to have to deal with her being abducted and murdered as well.

At least she knew that her parents would look after her precious little boy. Despite how he'd been conceived, Ava loved her son more than anything in the universe. Throughout her pregnancy she'd been unsure if she would be able to raise the child or whether she'd have to give him up for adoption if all she saw when she looked at him was her rapist. But the second the doctors had placed the baby in her arms, she'd known that she loved him, known that she could set aside how he'd been conceived and focus on her child. And she had dedicated every second of the last three years to being the best mother she could be.

The man didn't bother to provide her with an answer. He simply shot her another one of his horribly creepy smiles and wrapped his hands around her neck.

With her wrists and ankles bound, she couldn't put up much of a fight.

Not that it took long.

With the blood supply to her brain cut off by his squeezing hands, the world began to recede around her.

Seconds later, she was unconscious.

A minute after that, she was dead.

* * * * *

7:31 A.M.

"Hey." A voice at the door yanked his mind back from the edge of darkness that it was precariously teetering on.

Surprised when he saw was who was standing there, Xavier stood and crossed to kiss his old partner on the cheek. "Kate, what are you doing here?" Kate had decided not to return to work after the birth of her son five years ago. Now she worked for a private security firm. They were still friends and kept in contact often.

"I came to help." Her dark blue eyes looked a little offended that he would even have to ask. Then she turned serious. "Are you sure you should be here? And I don't mean just because of the obvious." She gestured at him.

Xavier knew his bruises had darkened to a bluey black, and he hurt every time he moved. Even the waistband of his jeans was pressing on his bruised stomach and causing him pain even when he wasn't moving. He didn't care about his injuries. All that mattered was getting Annabelle home safely. However, he knew it wasn't really his physical state Kate was concerned about. When Annabelle had been abducted by Ricky Preston the first time, he'd ended up taking himself off the case because he'd recognized that he was falling apart. This time he was determined to follow things through till the end. If Annabelle could hold it together, then he could too.

"I'm fine," he assured Kate firmly.

She studied him for a moment longer, then spoke. "Ryan and

Jack filled me in on Roman Tallow. They're going through all his family and friends, looking for anyone he was connected to who might be involved, or anyone with a connection to Annabelle. Including relooking at the other members of the support group who were already cleared since the new dynamic of a partnership changed things. I thought since we worked Annabelle's family's case I'd be most useful working with you at trying to find someone with a grudge against her."

He deliberately pushed thoughts of Annabelle from his mind. If he thought about what was happening to her right, now he couldn't function. And he had to be able to function. He knew Annabelle better than anyone else. Right now, he had to focus on doing his job and trust Annabelle to take care of herself until he found her.

That she had held it together so well while being held in Roman's dungeon reassured him. He'd seen the dirt embedded in her ring. She had used it to try and dig free the chains that bound her out of the wall. She had stood up to Roman. She'd tried to help him, and she'd helped Vanessa escape and then gone to find help. She was a lot stronger than she gave herself credit for, probably a lot stronger than he ever gave her credit for.

If he was honest, he sometimes tended to treat her like she was a helpless child who wasn't capable of taking care of herself. He didn't mean to do it, and it wasn't that he believed she was weak or incapable, he just loved her so much and hated to see her in any sort of pain that he sometimes tried to preempt it, stop something from hurting her before she had a chance to deal with it herself.

Maybe that was part of the reason why she'd felt she had to move into her own apartment to prove to him that she could survive on her own. When he got Annabelle back, he was going to make sure he never made that mistake again. He was going to treat her like the strong, competent, caring, compassionate woman that he believed her to be.

When he got her back, because to think it was a possibility that he might not would render him useless.

"I shouldn't have told her to go," he said, aware that he was promptly sinking into a pit of self-pity and self-recrimination but seemingly unable to stop it. "She would have been safer with me."

"There was no reason to think she wouldn't be safer on her own away from Roman. You had no indications that Roman was working with a partner," Kate reminded him.

"We never saw anyone else on the video. Roman never mentioned a partner and neither did Annabelle in the short time I was with her." Xavier had believed that it would be over once he'd found Annabelle. Now it'd started up all over again.

"The partner is the dominate one," Kate said. "Roman is unbalanced. He seems to truly believe he's some sort of hero saving the city from crime. I don't think he could have engineered this alone. Someone found him and thought they could use him for their own purposes. We need to find out who it is."

"I don't know where we should start," he murmured aloud. They needed a direction to move in, only he couldn't come up with a single one. Too bad they couldn't just ask Roman who his partner was. Roman had lost a lot of blood from the wound to his shoulder, and he'd lapsed into a coma. His doctors didn't know when or even if he'd wake up, or what condition he would be in if he did. That meant they were walking blind, stuck trying to figure out who this mystery partner was on their own.

"Can you think of anyone who would want to hurt Annabelle?" Kate asked.

"We can't be positive that he took Annabelle for a specific reason," Xavier countered. "If he were working with Roman, he could have just taken her because he had the opportunity to. She, Vanessa, and Ava were the only ones left. They already had Ava. Vanessa was harder to get to, but Annabelle was all alone in the woods. Reclaiming her would have been fairly easy. We thought he only took Annabelle because his attempt at Sofia got interrupted. We should also be looking at anyone with a grudge against Sofia. Or it's just a crazy friend of Roman's who doesn't want to stop until their plan is finished." Xavier didn't know if he hoped Annabelle was specifically targeted or not. Both brought with them their own pros and cons.

"Valid point," Kate acknowledged. "It could have been random, but Roman targeted the women in his support group specifically, so we can't discount that he wanted Annabelle in particular. And we can't assume that Roman and his partner were both in this for the same reasons. We should also consider that he was targeting you since he did send all those links to you specifically."

Xavier frowned; he hadn't thought of that. "We assumed that was just because I was the lead detective on the case. Which I guess could also be a reason why he took her to begin with."

"I still think we should go through your old case files and check to see if Roman's partner could be connected to any of them. Does anyone stand out from any recent cases?"

"No, I can't think of anything."

"Okay, for now let's look at Annabelle as the primary target. Where do *you* think we should begin?"

"I don't know. We couldn't find anyone with a grudge against her last time. Why should we find anything this time around?"

"Last time we found the link," Kate reminded him. "You just have to keep believing we will this time around too. What about a friend?"

"Annabelle doesn't have a lot of friends. Sofia, Laura, Paige—you know all of them. None of them did this. Besides, they all have pretty good alibis for the last couple of weeks."

"Yeah, they sure do. How are Laura and the baby?"

"They're both doing well, really well. So well they're hoping the baby can go home soon. You know they named her after Rose?"

"Yeah, I can't wait to go and meet her. I saw Paige earlier. I see you guys finally told her what was going on."

Xavier hadn't wanted Paige to know about Annabelle, but Ryan and Jack had made the call yesterday while he'd still been asleep to update Paige. Since she'd kept calling them, they'd decided continually putting her off was only going to increase her suspicions, so they told her everything. "I think Elias, Mark, and Charlie Abbott all refused to drive her, and she's too weak to drive herself, otherwise she'd be here."

Kate chuckled. "Elias took her purse, so she doesn't have any cash or cards to take a cab. She's pretty mad you guys kept it from her, so she started calling me to be kept in the loop."

He understood Paige's frustrations at being unable to help. They were a close group of friends, and if he was prevented from helping any one of them, he'd be feeling just as annoyed as Paige was. Still, right now, she was where she needed to be, and that was for the best. "Other than that, Annabelle doesn't really have any friends. Even before what Ricky Preston did to her, she wasn't comfortable letting people get too close. His taking things she told him in confidence and using it against her has only reinforced that and made her warier."

"What about her work? Any chance of someone developing a grudge against her there?"

"There have been a couple of incidences where she's reported families to social services. But she works at a center for women and children in trouble. Most of the kids she looks after have been victims of abuse, or their mothers have." Something tickled his brain as he spoke. "There was one case, a couple of months ago. The little girl, a four-hear-old, had been sexually abused by her father. The father beat his wife, and the mother finally took the kid and left—they were staying at the center. A couple of weeks had gone by, but Annabelle saw bruises on the child. The mother explained them away, said the little girl fell, but Annabelle wasn't buying it. She kept watch and when the kid kept turning up to day care with bruises, she reported it, the mom had been beating the little girl. The kid went into the care of an uncle and the mom went to jail. The little girl kept attending day care and Annabelle kept having problems with her. The girl lost weight, always came in dirty, and child protective services got involved again, said the uncle was neglecting the girl and she was put in foster care. The uncle threw a fit, said he was doing the best he could and had to work three jobs to support his niece."

"Okay, we'll look into that, it's a viable possibility. Is she still seeing a therapist? Roman Tallow targeted women because they were victims of crime, and he believed he could abolish crime. This guy might too; it could be what bonded them."

"She quit about two years ago. She told me just before she disappeared that she was thinking of going back. She told me that she wanted to make changes in her life and I didn't believe her. I was scared about getting hurt again so I wouldn't let her move back home until she proved to me that she was serious. If she'd been home with me, Roman wouldn't have been able to get his hands on her." He dropped his head into his hands, ignoring the pain as his bruised eye and cheek pressed against his hand.

"Don't blame yourself, Xavier. You couldn't have known this would happen. And it's totally reasonable that you were concerned about getting hurt again after Julia and everything you've already been through with Annabelle. Right now, though, you have to focus on getting her back."

Resolutely, he lifted his head. Kate was right. Guilt wasn't going to help Annabelle. Only getting answers was. And he had a meeting in thirty minutes with someone who could hopefully give him some.

* * * * *

8:49 A.M.

Sleepily, Vanessa opened her eyes to find her hospital room full of people. All she'd done since she was brought to the hospital yesterday morning was sleep and cry in her boyfriend's or her father's arms.

So far, she hadn't been interviewed by the police, which had been a relief. She wasn't ready to process everything yet. Now it seemed the time had come.

"Hey, Vanessa, how're you feeling?" Detective Montague smiled at her. Well, he sort of smiled at her. Half his face was swollen and bruised.

"What happened to you?" she asked, reaching for the controls to elevate her bed so she was no longer lying down.

"It's nothing," he assured her.

"It's not nothing," she contradicted. "You got hurt. Did that man do that to you? It was Roman, wasn't it?" Vanessa still couldn't believe it. How had sweet, geeky Roman been so unbalanced and none of them even noticed it?

"It was Roman," Detective Montague confirmed. "He's in custody now; he can't hurt you again, Vanessa."

She nodded slowly, very glad of that. She knew what it was like to live with the fear that the person who'd hurt you was still out there. The man who had murdered her mother, brother, and grandparents right in front of her, then used her as a human shield to attempt to escape, slitting her throat and almost killing her in the process, had been on the run for months before he was finally killed. Vanessa didn't think she could live through something like that again.

That time in her life had been dark. So dark she hadn't been sure that she'd be able to make her way through it. If she hadn't had her dad and Vince she knew she wouldn't. Now, the thought of having to go through it all over again was petrifying. What if this time she wasn't strong enough to make it?

"Vanessa?" Vince sat on the edge of her bed and rested a hand on her shoulder. "You okay?"

Shakily, she nodded, leaning into him, attempting to absorb his strength. Vince was the best thing that had ever happened to her.

She'd known she was in love from the moment she laid eyes on him. If only she hadn't been so stupid and stubborn back when they first met. She'd let Vince come between her and her parents, and while she didn't regret standing up for her love for Vince, she wished she had been smarter about showing her parents just what a great guy he was. Instead she'd let the last days she'd spent with her mother be ruined.

"We need to ask you some questions," Detective Montague told her. "I wish that we could wait until you're stronger but we can't. Annabelle is still missing."

She scrunched her brow in confusion and asked, "Missing? But we left together, she ran off to find you guys." She gestured at the Xander brothers.

"She never turned up," Detective Montague said softly.

"You mean she's lost in the woods somewhere?"

"Search and rescue looked everywhere. She's not in the woods," the detective replied, fear evident in his voice.

"We think that Roman was working with a partner," Jack Xander explained. "Do you think that's possible?"

"I know you were out of it most of the time you were there, but we're hoping you saw or heard something," Detective Montague added.

Dipping embarrassed eyes, Vanessa began to fiddle with the hem of the blanket.

"Vanessa?" Detective Montague prodded.

Hesitantly, she looked up at him. "I wasn't out of it the whole time," she admitted.

"What do you mean? Mackenzie said you were sick, and when I found you, you could hardly move."

"Mackenzie? You spoke to her? I thought Roman killed her."

"He did. He made a video." Xavier didn't elaborate, and Vanessa got the feeling she didn't want to know the specifics of the fate of her friends.

"I was sick, really sick when I first woke up, but when I

realized that Roman basically left me alone once he realized I was pregnant and unwell, I kind of played it up a little." Tears were pricking her eyes and she held them back. Guilt was stabbing at her. If she hadn't, some of her friends might still be alive. On the flip side, she may be dead. She'd been left behind once before. What about her was so special that she kept surviving when everyone around her didn't?

"You did the right thing," Detective Montague told her gently.

"I was scared, and when I realized that being sick was working to my advantage, I just went with it," she continued, feeling the need to further explain, perhaps to attempt to assuage her own guilty conscience. "Faith was trying to reason with him, Ava couldn't stop crying, Mackenzie kept making him angry, Ruby kept pleading with him; nothing they were doing was working."

"Don't feel guilty, honey." Vince's arm slid around her shoulders and drew her close. "You did what you had to do to survive. I couldn't have survived losing you." Vanessa felt his shudder as he wrapped both arms around her and hugged her fiercely, before kissing the top of her head and slightly loosening his grip.

"Vince is right, Vanessa," Detective Montague assured her. "You didn't do anything wrong. You kept yourself alive. And to be honest, you weren't completely faking when Annabelle and I found you. You couldn't even stand up."

Not really believing them, Vanessa nodded, then asked, "What about Ava? I know he killed the others, did he kill her too?"

"We don't think so," Detective Montague replied. "He didn't send us a video, so we're hoping she's still alive someplace. Roman's partner might have killed her, but we have no idea who he could be. Did you see or hear anything that might help us identify him? We think he may have Annabelle. We found blood in the woods … it was Annabelle's blood. I need your help to find her, Vanessa."

She forced her mind to travel back to the dungeon. Detective

Montague had saved her life twice now, as well as being amazingly supportive as she struggled to deal with what had happened. Annabelle had saved her life too by telling the cops that the killer had another family left on his list. "There was another man," she said slowly. "He was there right before you came."

A shiver rocketed through her at the memory. She had been lying in the bed, no longer really faking or even exaggerating how badly she was feeling. Her head had felt stuffy, like someone had filled it with cotton wool—she'd been nauseous and very sleepy. She'd been drifting off when she heard voices. Both were male and the sound of them had snapped her fully awake. When they entered the room, she had concentrated on remaining completely still, and on keeping her breathing calm and even. Wondering whether help had arrived, she had cracked her eyes open and caught a glimpse of the two men. What she had seen chilled her. Seeing Roman had been a shock, but the other man had seeped evilness.

"Did you see him, Vanessa?" Detective Montague asked hopefully.

Tugging the blankets closer around her, she edged closer to Vince. "Yes," she whispered. "Roman was insane, but this man … he was evil."

"Can you describe him for us?" Ryan Xander asked.

"He was tall, really tall, maybe close to seven feet. He was big too. He obviously worked out a lot." She didn't realize she was crying until Vince brushed away the tears that were slowly winding their way down her cheeks. How had she managed to survive? She should be dead. If Detective Montague hadn't managed to find her, she *would* be dead now. There was a chance with her being pregnant that Roman would have spared her, but the other man wouldn't have. He killed for fun. She knew that as certainly as she knew she was sitting in this room right now.

"You're doing great, Vanessa," Detective Montague assured her. "Did you see his face?"

Absently, she moved a hand to her stomach. Thanks to Detective Montague, her baby had survived too. Although now her pregnancy was considered high risk, there were no guarantees she would carry to term, and if she did, her baby could have suffered permanent damage from the drugs Roman had given her. She owed the detective so much. She had to remember enough about the other man for them to ID him—Annabelle's life depended on it. "He had brown hair, cut really short." She squeezed her eyes shut as she willed herself to remember more. She'd seen this man for no more than a second or two.

"Maybe that's enough for now," Vince told the detectives. "I know you hope that identifying this guy will help you find Annabelle, but there are no guarantees it will, and Vanessa is still recovering from being that madman's prisoner."

"Do you want us to stop, Vanessa?" Detective Montague asked.

Ignoring both of them, she concentrated really hard. She was on the verge of remembering something important, she was sure of it. Deliberately, she put herself back in the dungeon. Focused on his face. She'd been distracted by the sheer size of the man, and he had been facing away from her most of the time. But for a split second he had turned toward her. She remembered because she had been afraid he would realize she was awake and looking at him and had snapped her eyes quickly closed.

Now her eyes popped open. "It was his eyes," she told them. "I'd seen them before. Not on him, on someone else. They were pale blue, so pale blue they looked like they were white. His eyes were Annabelle's eyes."

* * * * *

10:31 A.M.

Who could it be?

Xavier had been asking himself the same question since Vanessa Adams' revelation that the mystery man involved in her abduction had the same eyes as Annabelle.

It could be a coincidence. But Annabelle's eyes were extremely unusual. What were the chances that she was abducted by someone with whom she shared an unusual trait and he wasn't somehow related to her?

Virtually zero, he answered himself.

That her disappearance was mere chance or happenstance was no longer a question. Roman was obsessed with the number six. There had always been six intended victims. The five girls from the support group plus Annabelle. Roman's friends had probably been his part in the deal between him and his partner. That meant Annabelle had been meant for the mystery man.

But who could it be?

Her parents, brothers and sister were all dead, as were her grandparents. Her father had had two sisters, but neither were close with their brother or his family, and as far as he knew Annabelle hadn't seen them since the funerals. There were four cousins—three girls and one boy—but the only male was a skinny kid of fifteen, definitely not the man Vanessa described.

There had to be a relative they didn't know about. Xavier was positive that Annabelle would have mentioned another family member if she'd known about one.

"It's a relative. Vanessa Adams said the other man had extremely pale blue eyes just like Annabelle."

Kate nodded thoughtfully, and said, "Someone from her mother's side. We spoke with basically everyone from her father's side of the family when we were investigating who would have cause to kill them and frame Annabelle," Kate added when he shot her a confused glance.

John Englewood's family had been easier to locate so they had spoken to all of them. Unfortunately, they hadn't been able to locate Kathy Englewood's family. Then they'd stopped trying.

Another family had been slaughtered in identical circumstances and it no longer looked like it was someone targeting the Englewood family, so they had moved on to looking for connections between the families. Now they needed to track down any relatives of Annabelle they could find.

"Has Annabelle mentioned her mother's family?"

"She doesn't know a lot about them. They weren't around when she was growing up. All she knows is that her grandparents were both drug addicts who didn't really look after their kids."

"Kids? So, Kathy has siblings?"

"Annabelle thinks so, but she doesn't really know. She says her mom didn't like talking about her childhood. Apparently, Kathy didn't have it easy. Her parents didn't have jobs, so they usually went without food. Sometimes they were homeless, lived on the streets. There are no photos of Kathy as a kid. Annabelle thought she vaguely remembered an uncle coming by the house when she was very small, but to be honest we never really talked much about her parents, either their childhoods or Annabelle's, because it was too painful for her."

"We can easily find out if Kathy had siblings, and if she does, then we have some suspects." Kate sat at the table and fired up her laptop. "Do you know if Annabelle's grandparents are still alive?"

"She's never met them. Doesn't even know their names."

"We'll look into them as well. Once we get names we can start tracking them down."

"Even if we find them, why would they want to abduct Annabelle?" Xavier couldn't think of a single reason why Annabelle's long-lost family would have any cause to hurt her.

"I don't know, Xaiv. I know you're scared for her, and I know you want answers, but right now the why is not the most important thing. It's the who."

"Kathy's parents and siblings might not even know about Annabelle." He was barely listening to his friend. "They never came to the funerals, and if Kathy didn't talk about them, then it makes sense that she was no longer talking *to* them."

Kate didn't reply. He was about to start up again, mostly just to fill the silence, which kept leading his imagination down a dark path, when Kate finally spoke. "Got them. Kathy's mother died fourteen years ago. Her father has dementia. He lives in a nursing home, and he's dying. That counts him out. But Kathy has two brothers: Jeremy and Luke. Jeremy is two years older than Kathy. They would have grown up together. But Luke is a lot younger, only a couple of years older than Annabelle."

"I've never heard Annabelle mention the names Luke or Jeremy. If she knows about them, she never said anything to me." He couldn't think of a feasible reason for either of Annabelle's uncles to go after her, but at least it was a direction to move in. "Do either match the description Vanessa gave us?"

"Both," Kate nodded. "According to their driver's licenses, both have brown hair and blue eyes. Looking at the pictures, both seem to have the same pale eyes as Annabelle."

"We'll show the pictures to Vanessa, see if she can identify which man it is. What are the addresses? Let's go pick them up."

"Can't." Kate stopped him before he could bound to his feet. "It looks like both are in the wind."

* * * * *

2:43 P.M.

Who could it be?

Why had he taken her?

Why hadn't she seen him in Roman's dungeon?

It was driving Annabelle crazy that she had no answers to the questions that filled her head.

Whoever this man was, he had taken her for a reason. She had been targeted. Otherwise, she wouldn't currently be curled up in the bed of a room she had been in nearly twenty-five years ago. It couldn't be a coincidence that the person who'd held her prisoner as a child was now holding her prisoner again.

Annabelle knew the man had killed someone earlier. She hadn't been able to really decipher the words he was saying, but she'd heard the woman's screams. They would forever be etched into her mind.

She felt a connection to the woman. She may not even know her, but they had a lot in common. They shared the same fate. Unless someone found her, Annabelle knew she was going to die in this room.

And she also knew that the chances of anyone finding her were not good. Wherever she was, her captor was confident that no one would hear her screams for help, otherwise he would have bound and gagged her.

All her hopes rested on the cops figuring out that Roman had a partner.

Surely, they would.

Xavier had sent her to find help. He knew she'd been in the dungeon. He would have told the others and when she never turned up, they would have to realize something had happened to her. Wouldn't they?

One horrible little thought continued to niggle at her.

What if Xavier had been so badly hurt that he hadn't been able to tell the others that she'd been there?

They might not even know.

They might think Roman had taken her somewhere else, that she'd never been in the dungeon.

Maybe they didn't even know she was missing.

No, Annabelle reminded herself. They knew she was missing. Xavier had come looking for her. And Roman had made her film the video. Surely someone other than Xavier had seen that. She was just being paranoid.

They were looking for her.

Of course, they were.

She just had to hold it together a little longer.

She could do that. Whoever had locked her up in here had left food and water. After sleeping for a while, she'd had some, and already she could feel her strength returning. She could keep her wits about her until Xavier found her again.

Her resolve wavered as the door handle jiggled. A moment later the door swung open.

A man stepped through.

He was tall, gigantically tall. And as big and solid as a mountain. Annabelle knew she wouldn't stand a chance at out muscling him.

The man was familiar. She'd seen him before. Since she remembered this room from when she was a child, she supposed the man was the one who had kept her locked up in here before.

If only she could remember more about that time besides screaming, dark, and a man with a scary face.

This man.

Annabelle didn't have to see his face to know that it was scary. Menace seemed to roll off him in waves. He was dangerous, and she was all alone with nothing at her disposal to use against him.

Alarmingly conscious of the fact that she was naked, Annabelle tugged the covers right up to her chin and held them there.

The man noticed and chuckled. "Don't worry, I couldn't be less interested in having sex with you if I tried."

Instead of reassuring her, his words only heightened her fears. This man was beyond creepy. There was something so cold about him. Without needing to be told, Annabelle knew he inflicted pain simply because he enjoyed it. He reminded her of the man who'd killed her family. She had shot and killed that man, and if she were able to get her hands on a gun, she would shoot this man too.

"You don't know who I am, do you?"

"You took me when I was a child. You kept me in this room while you killed women in there." She lifted a trembling hand and pointed at the door through which he had just entered. She didn't remember what was on the other side of the door, but she assumed at least one other room, possibly the same as the one she was currently trapped in.

"But you knew me before that." He took a step closer and she got her first proper look at him. Her gaze was immediately drawn to his eyes. Her eyes. Like her own, they were such a pale shade of blue that they appeared to be white.

"We're related," she whispered.

"Mmhmm," he nodded.

She scrunched her eyes as she thought. The voice, the eyes, she'd heard and seen them somewhere before. One night when she was very small, maybe three years old, she'd had a bad dream. It had been late. Very late. She'd crawled out of her bed and scampered to her mom's room. Only her mom wasn't in bed. There had been a light on downstairs and voices whispering quietly. She had crept down the stairs, hiding in the shadows, somehow knowing without needing to be told that this was not a conversation she wanted to interrupt.

Then suddenly, a man had been there.

This man.

Her mother had quickly hustled him out the door, and her back to bed. But not before she had told her who the man was.

"You're Uncle Jeremy." She looked at him for confirmation. When he nodded, she continued. "I don't understand why you took me when I was little. You kept me here in this room. You hurt me. I have scars all over my back and arms."

"You wouldn't stop crying," he said and shrugged. "I was trying to teach you a lesson. I whipped you. I wanted to train you to behave yourself."

There was no time to dwell on that right now. "But why did you care? I don't understand why you took me at all? Why would you do that to my mom, your sister? And why did you come back for me? You didn't come back for the funerals. I never saw you again after I was rescued from here. What is so important that you'd team up with crazy Roman just so you could lock me back up in here?"

NOVEMBER 14TH

7:48 A.M.

"This is where we put all the stuff from Annabelle's parents' house when we sold it." Xavier led Kate into his attic. They'd sold the furniture as well as the house, but every other item that had been in there had been boxed up by a team of movers. Those fifty or so boxes had sat in his attic for the last five years. "I don't know that we're going to find anything useful in here though."

He was running on fumes and he knew it. It had been a little over forty-eight hours since Annabelle disappeared for the second time, and so far, they weren't any closer to finding her. They had been unable to locate either of her uncles, nor did they even know which one had taken her, or if it was some other relative they knew nothing about.

Jack, Ryan, and Kate had all ganged up on him last night and insisted he go home and get some rest. Reluctantly he had, even going so far as to eat some dinner and then climb into bed. Xavier hadn't expected to actually sleep, and yet his drained body and mind had crashed the second he slid under the covers.

Thankfully, he had slept a dreamless sleep and woken up this morning feeling better—physically, at least. While Jack and Ryan worked on locating Jeremy and Luke, he and Kate were going to go through Annabelle's mother's things and see if they could find anything about her brothers that might help them figure out which one might have cause to go after Annabelle and where he might currently be keeping her.

That Annabelle was already dead was a thought that Xavier could simply not entertain at the moment. He was proceeding

287

under the determination that Annabelle was alive and waiting for them to find her.

"At this point, it can't hurt." Kate was already using a pair of scissors to cut open the tape on the closest box.

"True," he acknowledged as he opened another box.

For the next couple of hours, they worked in silence. Going through box after box, looking for anything that may give them even the slightest of clues.

Xavier steadfastly avoided any of the boxes that contained Annabelle's personal things.

When she had first moved in with him, Annabelle had been hesitant to unpack anything. She had been scared that what they shared wasn't real. That he was simply physically attracted to her, despite her doubts it was possible for any man to view her as attractive, and that she simply saw him as her savior and protector. She had believed that in time their mutual attraction would wear off and they would part ways, never to speak again.

It had been several months before she removed a few of the items that had been packed from her house and moved to his. A couple of family pictures, a few stuffed animals from her childhood, and some recipes that had been her mom's favorites were the only things besides clothes that she had added to the house.

Despite the fact that he didn't want to look at Annabelle's things and be further reminded of how much he missed her and how scared for her he was, he also knew he wouldn't find the answers he needed in those boxes.

He hesitated as his hand held the scissors over a box labeled family photos. He was unsure if he wanted to look through them. No, actually he was positive that he didn't. Annabelle's childhood and adolescence hadn't been happy ones.

After the couple of days she'd been missing as a small child, her whole life had changed. According to Annabelle, after returning home, her parents had been cold and distant, no longer the loving mother and father she was used to. Over time Annabelle grew to become self-conscious about her scars, which she believed were the cause of her parents' sudden disinterest in her. This in turn led to her becoming extremely self-conscious about herself and thus left her feeling unworthy of love.

Xavier didn't agree with Annabelle. He didn't think her parents' abrupt change had anything to do with her scars, but since they weren't alive he couldn't ask them and prove it to Annabelle. Seeking some sort of affirmation that he was right, and that Annabelle's parents had still loved her, he somewhat reluctantly cut the tape and began pulling framed photos from the box.

These were the pictures that had been displayed in the Englewood family home. There were some of Annabelle's father, John, as a child. None of her mother. A few of John and Kathy's wedding. Lots of Annabelle, Paul, Julian, and Katherine as they grew up.

Suddenly, he froze.

Something had been bothering him about the photos and it had just occurred to him what.

"Kate, how many pictures do you and David have of the day Tate was born?"

"I don't know. A lot. Why?" she asked, her dark blue eyes curious.

"John and Kathy Englewood don't have a single photo of the day Annabelle was born." Xavier had gone through the entire box, maybe a hundred pictures and hadn't come across a single one from Annabelle's birth.

"Maybe they didn't like that kind of thing," Kate suggested.

"They have pictures of Paul, Julian, and Katherine."

"Maybe they didn't put one up of Annabelle."

"But why? Why would they put up pictures of themselves with their newborns, in the hospital, right after they were born, but only of three of their four kids?" This was somehow important;

he could feel it.

"You think this is significant?" Kate asked.

"Yes, but I'm not sure how yet."

Xavier picked up the photo of newborn oldest son Paul and realized that the photo frame felt wrong. Thicker than it should considering it only contained a single photograph. Turning the frame over, he popped open the back and was surprised to find several sheets of paper hidden inside.

"What are those?" Kate asked, watching him.

Unfolding the stack of papers, which were filled with messy, scrawled writing, his brow furrowed. "It looks like diary entries. From Kathy."

"What do they say?" Kate set down what she was holding and sat cross-legged on the floor beside him.

He skimmed the first page. "They're from when she was a kid. Thirteen, to be exact. About what she and Jeremy used to do. Their parents were always high, all their money went on drugs, Jeremy and Kathy never had enough to eat so they used to scam people for money. Jeremy was good at pickpocketing, but now that they were teenagers it was getting harder and harder to find ploys that worked. Shoplifting was getting harder too. People weren't suspicious of a little kid, but a teenager is a completely different story. Jeremy wanted Kathy to sell her body. He'd said their mother did, so what was the harm in her doing it, but she refused. Said she didn't want the kind of life they had, she wanted more—an education, a real job, a real marriage, a real family."

"How did Jeremy react to that?"

He turned to the next page. "This one is from two years later. Kathy says she started spending all her time in the library studying, then would stop by a local church on her way home because the pastor would always leave her a bag with some sandwiches and fruit. It says one night she got home early. Both her parents were passed out on the couch in the living room. Her brother was in her bedroom with a woman. They were in bed together. It says Jeremy told her the woman was a hitchhiker and was there voluntarily, but Kathy doubted him. Something in the young woman's eyes told her that she was scared of Jeremy."

"What happened next?" Kate asked, intrigued.

He continued to read. "Kathy came home early again the next night and found her brother in bed again with a different woman this time. She confronted him and asked if this was another of his scams. Jeremy confessed that it was. Said he was picking up hitchhikers, then bringing them back to the house, forcing them to have sex with him, then making them give him all their money in exchange for their freedom. Kathy was upset, outraged, threatened to turn him into the cops if he didn't stop. Jeremy said he'd stop if she went back to helping him steal."

"Did she?"

"She did. She didn't want to and was upset about it, but she didn't want to turn her brother into the cops and be left all alone with their parents. And she didn't want him to keep abducting and raping young women. So, she went along with it."

"I'm sensing an *until* coming."

He shot Kate a quick smile. "Until," he nodded, "about a year later she stayed at the library late one night, studying for a test. When she got home, she found her brother throwing something into the trunk of his car. It was a woman's body."

Xavier had read enough to know that Jeremy had Annabelle. Why, he didn't know yet. But there was no doubt about it. Jeremy had progressed from petty theft and scams to kidnapping, rape and murder all before his eighteenth birthday.

"Is there more?" Kate asked.

He shook his head. "That's it."

"Check the next photo," Kate suggested.

"What?"

"That was behind Paul's picture, right? There could be more behind Julian's."

He should have thought of that. Picking up the photo of Julian and his parents on the day he was born, he removed the back of the frame. "There's more," he told Kate, as he pulled out several more sheets of paper.

"What does it say next?"

He skimmed the scrawled writing, pieces of the puzzle finally falling into place. He wasn't sure whether this revelation made Annabelle's current situation better or worse.

"What? You just went white as a ghost."

"After Kathy found her brother with a dead body, she ran. Left home, lived on the streets, finished school, got married. Then one day Jeremy turned up on her doorstep."

"And?"

He swallowed hard, not wanting to say it aloud as though that might make it true. But it was already true, and if she survived, Annabelle was going to have to deal with it. "And he wasn't alone. Jeremy turned up on her doorstep with Annabelle."

"With Annabelle?" Kate echoed.

"With newborn Annabelle," he elaborated. "That's why there is no picture of her with her parents in the hospital—because John and Kathy Englewood are not Annabelle's parents. Jeremy is her father. Who knows who her mother is. Kathy didn't. Kathy took the baby, said if Jeremy didn't give her Annabelle, then she'd turn him into the police. Said she had proof. Jeremy gave her the baby and disappeared again. Until Annabelle was four."

"He's the one who kidnapped her when she was a little girl." Kate's eyes were wide as she took it all in.

Which meant that Jeremy had hurt Annabelle. Left her with scars all over her back and arms. "He kept killing. Annabelle remembers screams from during that time she was missing. He probably had another victim with him while he had his four-year-old daughter there."

"How did the police find him the first time around?"

"Kathy turned him in to get Annabelle back. She took the proof to the police and they were able to find him at a house that their mother had owned. We have to check that out—now. That could be where he took Annabelle again."

"I'll call it in." Kate stood, grabbed her phone from her bag and headed downstairs.

Xavier was slower at standing. He kept hold of the entries from Kathy Englewood's diaries. Annabelle needed to read them. She needed to understand once and for all that the distance between her and her parents hadn't come because her body was physically scarred, but because Kathy's guilt at not protecting her niece had been greater than she could overcome.

Knowing that, maybe Annabelle could finally accept that she was worthy of being loved.

Unless the knowledge that her biological father was a murderer was too great for her to overcome.

* * * * *

11:22 P.M.

This man was her father.

Her whole life had been a lie.

Everything.

Her parents, who weren't her parents at all, had been lying to her from the moment she was born.

Annabelle had never felt more alone in her life than she felt right now, curled up in a little ball under the blanket on the bed. She felt like she'd lost everything. John and Kathy Englewood were not her parents. Which meant that Paul, Julian, and Katherine weren't her siblings. Her father was some sort of psychotic murderer who had kidnapped her once already and had now kidnapped her again.

Her father.

She was still in shock about the fact that Jeremy was her father.

Why hadn't her parents said anything?

Her mom had never talked about her family or her life before she married.

Was this why?

Because she knew that Jeremy was insane?

Or was it because she didn't want Annabelle to figure out her true parentage?

Not that she would have. Annabelle had had no reason to believe she was adopted. She looked enough like the people she believed were her parents to easily pass as their daughter. They all had fair skin, brown hair, and blue eyes. She'd been the only one with the really pale blue eyes, but she'd always believed that was just a fluke.

But it wasn't.

She obviously had her father's eyes.

And who was her mother?

Jeremy had refused to answer when she'd asked him that earlier. After dropping the bomb of her paternity, he'd simply left her some more food, told her he had business to take care of and left.

Coping with the revelation of where she came from might have been easier to deal with if she'd been confident that, if she got out of this alive, she had Xavier to depend on.

A day ago, she had believed she had. But hour after hour stuck in this small, concrete room, dwelling on nothing but the knowledge that her whole life had been about lies had her doubting everything. Xavier had promised her before that he would never give up on her, yet he had. Okay, maybe it had been her fault, she'd pushed him to it, but still, facts were facts, and the facts were that he'd walked away.

What if he did it again?

Could she really blame him if he did?

After all, she was the child of a killer.

For all she knew, her mother had been just as evil as her father.

Or maybe her mother had been a victim of her father.

Annabelle wasn't sure which was worse.

She wasn't sure of anything anymore. She wasn't even sure she wanted to go home. She had no life anyway. She pushed away anyone who was stupid enough to try to get close to her. Other than work, she had nothing, and it wouldn't be hard to replace her at the center. How could living alone in this tiny room be any worse than living alone in the big, wide world. In the end, alone was alone.

She sank down against the mattress. Her head hurt. She hadn't eaten or drank anything since Jeremy left. All she had done was sit here and attempt to comprehend everything. Annabelle knew she should keep up her strength. Eat, drink water, sleep, keep herself going so she was still alive when Xavier and the others found her. But right now, she just didn't care.

"Hello," a voice singsonged as the door to her room opened.

Her father was back.

"Wakey, wakey, Annabelle. We have a lot to do."

Jeremy sounded positively chirpy. That couldn't be a good thing. And what could they possibly have to do? It wasn't like he was going to let her go, was he? Cautiously, she opened her eyes and sat up. Jeremy was setting his phone up on the table, using a little stand so that it pointed at the bed. Roman had made a video recording of her with his phone and sent it to Xavier. Was Jeremy planning on doing the same thing?

"Thought you'd want to say goodbye," he explained, casting her a glance.

Goodbye? To Xavier? Why would Jeremy want her to do that? If Xavier knew she was alive, he would never stop looking for her. Jeremy had to know that.

As if reading her mind, he said, "Don't want that pest of a cop boyfriend of yours vowing to hunt me down because he thinks I've got you squirreled away someplace. Better he knows the truth," he explained.

The truth? Her mind was working sluggishly at the moment.

What truth was he talking about? Didn't he intend to keep her locked away in this room for the rest of her life?

He laughed at her puzzled expression. "Honey, if I'd wanted a daughter, I wouldn't have let Kathy keep you all these years. But I trusted my sister once before, and when I claimed what was rightfully mine, she threatened to turn me into the police to get you back. But she had more. Proof I'd done a lot more than simply kidnapping you. She didn't hand it over to the police under the condition that I stayed away from you. But Kathy's dead now and you have all her stuff, which means you have the proof, and I can't let you use it. If you weren't involved with a cop, I would have just taken you out and the proof right along with it. Instead, I had to wait for an opening and grab you when you were alone and vulnerable. Well, I have you now, and I'm going to make sure—once and for all—that you can't take me down."

Annabelle knew her mind wasn't functioning quite right at the moment when the only thing that Jeremy had just said that stood out to her was that her mother had wanted her back. Her imminent death hadn't even penetrated yet.

Apparently finishing with the phone, Jeremy started to move toward her. Finally, her common sense kicked in. Kathy and John might not have been her biological parents, but Kathy had blackmailed her own brother to keep her safe. Xavier may have let her down, but only after she'd let him down too. They could sort things out and she could have the family she had always dreamed about, a family in whose love she felt confident and safe.

She scrambled off the bed when Jeremy reached for her, paying no mind to the blanket that flopped to the floor, leaving her naked body fully exposed. Her father wasn't a threat to her sexually. He probably just figured having her naked would make her body easier to dispose of, less chance fibers or hair or anything would be left behind.

"I'm not in the mood for games, Annabelle." He spoke to her as one would a disobedient child. "Thanks to that idiot Roman,

I'm all out of time. He led the cops right to him, and therefore, right to me. I've wrapped up everything else. You're my last loose end and I don't intend to leave you hanging around."

"You can't kill me ... I'm your daughter," she sputtered, backing away from the man and wondering if she could make it to the door before he caught her. Chances were probably not. Jeremy had closed the door, but she hadn't seen him lock it. Even if she made it to the door and got through it, she had no idea where she was. She could be out in the middle of the woods someplace like before, and between the cold and the fact that she had no clothes or shoes, hadn't eaten or drank anything in twenty-four hours, and she didn't know where she was, her chances of outrunning Jeremy were zero.

Jeremy merely shrugged.

Deciding she had nothing to lose by making a run for it—her father was going to kill her anyway—she faked left, then darted to the right and bolted for the door. Jeremy caught her before she reached it, grabbing her shoulder, and yanked her back and up against his chest.

"I didn't appreciate that, Annabelle," he snapped. "I'm not taking pleasure in this. I'm merely doing what needs to be done." With an arm around her stomach, he hitched her a little higher against his body and carried her to the bed, tossing her down onto it.

Annabelle immediately tried to roll away, but Jeremy pressed his knee into her stomach, effectively pinning her in place. Not that that stopped her from struggling with every ounce of strength she possessed.

"You are as wriggly as a worm," Jeremy complained, taking hold of one of her wrists and securing it to the bedpost, then doing the same with the other.

She went completely still.

Wriggly as a worm.

When she was a little girl, in the mornings she would creep

into her parents' room and into their bed, snuggling up at her mother's side. She'd never been able to stay still though. Crawling about from here to there, squirming and fidgeting until her mom would pull her into her arms and say, "Annabelle, you are such a wriggly little worm."

Annabelle hadn't thought of that in years.

Maybe her grandmother had said that to Kathy and Jeremy when they were small.

Jeremy yanked on her chin, snapping her back into the moment. "Don't want to hear any more whining and crying out from you," he said in way of explanation as he shoved a balled-up scarf into her mouth and then tied another around her head to secure it in place.

For some reason, Annabelle felt surprisingly serene. She was about to die, yet she wasn't panicked or scared or even sad. Instead, she felt at peace.

Jeremy climbed onto the bed and straddled her, his hands moving to encircle her neck. Then he paused, a look of something, surprise perhaps, flashed across his face. "I don't want to see your eyes as you die," he mumbled, pulling another scarf from his pocket.

As it was tied around her eyes, plunging her into darkness, Annabelle's false sense of calm vanished.

The hands around her neck squeezed tighter.

Although she knew it was useless, Annabelle screamed as loudly as her gag allowed and thrashed as madly as her bonds let her.

* * * * *

11:57 P.M.

"This is a nightmare," Xavier snapped from the back seat. "He's about to kill her. How much farther away are we?"

"A couple of minutes," Jack replied patiently for what had to be close to the hundredth time.

They had wasted hours trying to find the place where Jeremy was holding Annabelle. Jack, Ryan, and Kate had been extremely patient with him. He'd ranted, he'd been depressed, he'd paced, he'd read and re-read Kathy's diary entries in the hopes that something would come to him. And then elation had hit him as they finally received the break they'd been waiting for.

Annabelle had been legally adopted by Kathy and John. It had taken a while to get access to her original birth certificate, but once they had it, they knew the name of her biological mother.

Cassidy Ramsey, aged nineteen, had disappeared about ten months before Annabelle was born. She'd been travelling across the country, her car had broken down, she'd been seen hitchhiking. Then she was simply gone. Until she had turned up at a hospital, in labor, and given birth to Annabelle. Xavier didn't know how Jeremy had coerced her into keeping quiet while they were at the hospital. Maybe he'd promised her he wouldn't kill her, and she could raise her baby. But she hadn't said a word about who Jeremy really was. She hadn't reported that she was a kidnap victim and hadn't caused a stir, and then once she and the baby were released from the hospital, she simply disappeared again. Her body had never been found, but Xavier knew she was dead.

Once they knew about Cassidy Ramsey, they found a house in her name in a secluded location. It hadn't changed hands in twenty-nine years. Annabelle was twenty-eight. That meant that Cassidy had acquired the house while pregnant. Xavier was positive it was the house where Jeremy was holding Annabelle.

As soon as they located the house, they had jumped in the car.

Where he had completely lost it when he'd received another live streaming link.

Xavier hadn't expected another video since Roman had been apprehended. Shock had quickly morphed into pure terror when

Annabelle had appeared on the screen.

He had watched, paralyzed by fear, as Annabelle scrambled off a bed.

She'd been naked.

For a moment, that was all he'd seen.

But then his common sense kicked in. There had been no signs that Annabelle had been sexually assaulted when Jeremy had kidnapped her the first time. Hopefully, that meant that he wouldn't touch her that way this time either.

Jeremy had been frustrated that Annabelle was being uncooperative and she had protested that she was his daughter and he couldn't kill her. Xavier had been immediately relieved that Jeremy had told Annabelle the truth about her parentage because he didn't think he could bear breaking the news to her. And then he had been furious at Jeremy for springing it on her when she had no one who loved her there to support her and help her deal with it.

At least it seemed that Annabelle was still fighting hard for her freedom. She'd tried to make a break for it, only to be caught by Jeremy, who had immediately carried her back toward the bed.

Annabelle had continued to fight until Jeremy had muttered something to her that had sent her into some sort of trance. By the time she snapped out of it, he had already secured both her wrists to the bed.

"We're here," Kate announced.

Ripping his gaze away from his phone, Xavier found they were parked in the driveway of a freshly painted white farmhouse. It had a big porch, painted blue to match the shutters. The lawn was recently mowed, and neatly organized flower beds framed the front of the house.

"You wait in the car," Jack ordered.

That was so ridiculous, it didn't warrant a response.

"You're injured, Xavier." Jack countered his silent objection. "And you're too emotionally involved. Annabelle is in there."

"I didn't see you standing back at the cemetery when Malachi was holding Laura hostage," he challenged.

Unable to come up with an argument to that, Jack simply scowled but didn't object further as they all climbed from the car. "At least hang back, let me or Ryan or Kate lead things."

"No," he said simply, already heading for the front door, gun in hand. He wasn't putting Annabelle's fate in anyone else's hands but his own.

Glancing at his phone, he saw Jeremy had put a gag and blindfold on Annabelle and was now straddling her, his hands around her neck. He dismissed the possibility that they were already too late. He couldn't lose Annabelle while he was this close to getting her back.

"Basement," Ryan whispered as they all entered the house. He pointed at the phone. "No windows," he added.

The smell of death was strong as they descended the basement stairs. Xavier wasn't surprised to find that the small room at the bottom of the steps contained a dead body. Four, to be exact. Ava Burns was tied to the table they had seen in the videos Roman sent them. Faith Smith, Ruby McBrady, and Mackenzie Willows' dismembered bodies were scattered about on the floor. Blood was everywhere. This was Roman's kill room.

But the stench of blood went deeper. It was older, more ingrained, as though this room had been absorbing death for a long time now. This was where Jeremy had been holding, raping, and killing his victims for years. If he had to guess, Xavier thought there were probably bodies buried somewhere on the property.

"Door is unlocked, remember," Kate whispered. "Otherwise Annabelle wouldn't have made a run for it."

Xavier nodded, took a deep breath, and turned the knob.

NOVEMBER 15TH

12:09 A.M.

Jeremy tightened his grip a little. Annabelle had stopped struggling beneath him, but he didn't think she was dead yet, merely unconscious.

It had surprised him that looking into her eyes—his eyes—as he had started to strangle her had bothered him. It shouldn't. He had killed before. Many times. Many, *many*, times. Never before had he felt even an ounce of guilt. Maybe something about Annabelle being his daughter had touched him somehow. Not enough to make him let her live, though.

He'd been blackmailed before. He wouldn't allow it to happen again. When Kathy had split all those years ago, the night she'd found him with his first dead body, he hadn't realized she had taken the time to take photos. If he had, he would have stopped her.

Would he have killed her? His own sister? Jeremy wasn't sure, but he did know he wouldn't have allowed her to possess anything she could later use against him. And use against him, she had. Twice.

The first time to force him to let her and John adopt Annabelle.

The second time to get Annabelle back.

Still, his sister had loved him. Enough to not send him to prison even for kidnapping Annabelle, the child she thought of as her daughter. She had tracked him down, shown him copies of the photos, told him she'd turn him into the police if he didn't leave Annabelle alone. Once he'd left, she had faked a note from the "kidnapper" and given it to the police, who had swooped in and rescued little Annabelle.

Kathy hadn't been able to turn him in. A part of her still loved him, despite who and what he was.

As kids, they'd been close. Did everything together. Had only each other to rely on. But then they'd started down two very different paths. Kathy had wanted to be better than their druggie parents. She'd wanted a job, a husband, children, a normal life. He, on the other hand, had simply wanted to pay back the world for giving him such a rotten life. So he had taken his anger out on women. Picking up hitchhikers then bringing them back to his house, raping them, and making them pay him to let them go. When that was no longer enough, he'd gone on to killing.

Killing Annabelle was different from that. His preference would have been to let her live, but his own self-preservation was paramount. As evidenced by the fact that he had worked with Roman Tallow.

The man was, simply put, insane.

Completely insane.

Jeremy had known that from the second they'd met. Roman's insanity had made him the perfect partner. The man was a ticking time bomb just waiting to explode. He hadn't needed much of a push to get off and running. For the most part, Jeremy had been happy to let Roman do what he wanted. So long as he ended up with Annabelle, it hadn't really mattered.

Roman had nearly messed that up though. Going after Sofia Xander instead of Annabelle. What an idiot. Jeremy had thought his instructions had been perfectly clear but Roman had gotten it wrong, almost abducted the wrong woman. Thank goodness that had been interrupted, although Sofia Xander was a very beautiful woman and having her around for a while might have been fun. No matter though. There were thousands of pretty girls out there ready for the picking and he'd gotten Annabelle, which was the most important thing.

It should be almost done, Annabelle should be dead or just about.

"Let her go, Jeremy."

The voice startled him.

Releasing Annabelle, he spun around to find four cops, including Annabelle's boyfriend, standing in the room. He must have forgotten to reset the alarm. How stupid was he? And unless Annabelle was already dead, he didn't stand a chance at killing her now. He had no weapons on him so he couldn't kill her quickly, and if he made a move to finish strangling her, one of the cops would shoot him. He should have gone with his first instincts and killed her as soon as he brought her here from the woods. Only sentimentality had somehow got in the way, and he hadn't been able to bring himself to do it.

Jeremy weighed up his options.

Death or prison seemed to be the extent of them.

Prison was out of the question. He wouldn't survive being caged up like some sort of animal just because society wasn't able to deal with him.

That only left death.

So, death it was.

Standing, drawing himself up to his full seven feet one-inch height, he shot his best glare at Detective Xavier Montague and the others. If he'd been a better father, or even a father at all, he would have made his last words a threat to this man that if he ever caused Annabelle any pain, he'd be sorry. But that would be pointless. In mere seconds he would be dead, and he couldn't deliver on any threats he made.

Instead, he let out an almighty roar and charged at the detectives.

All four fired.

Death was instantaneous.

* * * * *

12:18 A.M.

"Annabelle."

Who was calling her name?

Was she dead?

Was this heaven? Or hell?

"Belle, it's Xavier, wake up now. It's over. Jeremy is dead. You're safe."

Then she was still alive.

Xavier must have found her before Jeremy had succeeded in killing her. The last thing she remembered was the world around her fading away as her father's hands on her neck cut off the blood supply to her brain and she slid into unconsciousness.

"Ambulance is on the way," someone announced. Jack Xander maybe, and she felt the pressure in her arms release as he must have untied her, then began to rub her hands to restore circulation.

She gave a little moan at the fiery pins and needles that assaulted her limbs as blood flow resumed.

"Annabelle, are you awake?" Xavier asked as he removed the scarf from her mouth.

"Yeah," she answered, her voice nothing more than a scratchy rasp. Her throat ached horribly, worse than when she'd had strep last year.

Xavier let out a relieved breath. "Hold on, we'll get you out of here."

"Don't be ridiculous, you can't carry her. Did you forget you're injured?" Jack said, presumably to Xavier.

"Okay," Xavier murmured, reluctantly. Then she could feel his lips hovering above her forehead, pressing a kiss to it. "I love you, Belle," he whispered.

Wrapping her arms around his neck, she clung to him. Never in her life had she been so grateful to be alive. She wanted to tell

Xavier everything she was thinking and feeling, but her throat was so bruised and sore that she didn't think she'd be able to get the words out.

"Come on, let's get you out of here." Jack gently untangled her arms from around Xavier's neck and picked her up. "I'm going to leave the blindfold on until we get you outside," he informed her.

Until that moment, she hadn't even realized that she was still wearing it, but now that it had been drawn to her attention, she desperately wanted it off. She didn't want to be trapped in the darkness any longer. She was reaching for it when Jack's voice stopped her.

"Annabelle, leave it. Trust me, you don't want to see this," he told her.

"I need it off," she protested, not being able to see was making her start to panic.

She pulled it off, and it took a moment for her eyes to adjust.

Once they did, Annabelle wished she had listened to Jack's advice and left the blindfold on.

The room adjoining hers was a blood-streaked mess.

There were bodies on the floor.

They had been chopped into pieces.

And a body was tied to the table.

It was Ava.

Jeremy had killed Ava while she was right next door. She had heard the woman's screams of terror when she had realized she was about to die.

She had spent time with Ava, talked with her, gotten to know her, tried to work together to escape.

And now Ava was dead.

Killed by her father.

Who would have killed her, too, if Xavier hadn't turned up when he had.

That she had been mere seconds away from death hit her like a blow to the head.

Annabelle had held it together this far, but now the barrier she had been keeping erect by sheer force of will was quickly crumbling.

Tears were coming, she knew it, but she didn't wanted to cry until she was in Xavier's arms. And Xavier was looking in way worse shape than she was right now. His face was bruised and swollen. He walked stiffly, favoring one side. She couldn't be in his arms right now.

She tried to hold them back, keep her tears inside until later, but she couldn't. They burst out in a noisy sob. Embarrassed, she tried to wiggle out of Jack's arms. She didn't really need to be carried anyway, other than her neck she wasn't hurt, she could walk on her own.

"It's all right, Annabelle," Jack soothed, refusing to set her down.

"Give her here." Xavier reached for her.

"You can't carry her," Jack reminded him.

"I can," Xavier contradicted.

"If you say so." Jack sounded doubtful but handed her over to Xavier.

The second she was in his arms, her barriers crashed. Her tears began to flow more freely, in a near hysterical flood. Her arms clutched tighter at Xavier, her body pressed as closely against his as it could, needing physical contact with him to reassure herself that she was really alive.

Alive.

She was still alive.

Somehow, she had survived two serial killers back to back.

Now she just had to survive learning the truth about who her father was.

Right now, though, she didn't care about that. She didn't care about anything. All she wanted to do was hold on to Xavier and never let him go.

NOVEMBER 16TH

Paige had never felt so content in her life.

"It's so quiet here," she whispered, resting her head on Elias' shoulder.

Yesterday, after Annabelle had been found and taken to the hospital, she and Elias and the girls, and Ryan and Sofia and their kids, had driven up here to this gorgeous log cabin in the woods. Xavier and Annabelle were going to join them later today since Annabelle had only been released earlier this morning, and Jack and Laura were planning on coming up tomorrow when Rosie was released from the hospital. Mark and his family would be here the day after that.

The view from the cabin was even more beautiful than the cabin itself. The trees reached up to the sky, the last of the fall leaves were bright splashes of red, orange, and yellow in an otherwise brown and green landscape. The sky had been a clear blue since they arrived.

Ryan and Sofia had taken Sophie, Hayley, and Ned to explore the woods. Paige had wanted to go with them, but she wasn't strong enough yet to go hiking, even an easy one. So instead, she was curled up on Elias' lap, wrapped in two blankets. It was cold out and her recent bout of hypothermia had left her extra sensitive to the cold. Baby Arianna was in her arms and as stunning as the landscape was, it couldn't even come close to comparing to her delightful little girl.

"I wish we could stay here forever," she sighed. She didn't want to go back to her regular life. She wanted to stay right here with her family and friends in this serene place that made her forget all about the mess Bruce Daniels had left her life in.

"Me too." Elias pressed a kiss to her temple and tightened his hold on her. "But we can't. We can enjoy every second that we're here, but in two weeks we have to go back home. And that means that you are going to have to deal with what happened. I mean *all* of it," he added gently. "You know that, right?"

Unable to stop the shudder that swept through her, Paige knew exactly what her husband was referring to. And she knew that he was right. She also knew that she wanted so badly to never think about it again. But if she didn't, if she just pretended she hadn't been raped, then how would she be able to do her job? It was inevitable that at some point she was going to come across a victim of sexual assault, and a perpetrator of a sexual crime. If she didn't dealt with her feelings about her own assault, how would she be able to cope with that?

"Paige?" Elias prompted, jostling her a little.

"Yeah, I know. I don't want to, but if I don't and I fall apart later it affects more than just me and you now. Now it would affect our daughters, and I won't let that happen. I'll work with Charlie Abbott for as long as I have to," she promised.

"I love you, Paige. I am here for you one hundred percent, and so is everyone else. Don't push us away. You don't have to do this alone, okay?"

Paige tilted her head back so she could kiss him. "Okay. I love you too, Elias. So much. I'm so thankful that we finally have a family." Her gaze returned to the little baby in her arms. She still couldn't quite believe that this precious child was really hers.

"Mommy, Mommy."

Looking up, she saw Hayley running across the small clearing between the edge of the woods and the cabin, a handful of flowers held out in front of her. Ryan and Sofia were just behind her. Sophie was running at Hayley's side, and Ned was trailing the two girls, running as fast as his little toddler legs could go.

310

"Hey, sweetheart," she said as the child reached her. "Did you have fun with Uncle Ryan and Aunt Sofia?"

"Uh-huh." Hayley nodded. "I picked these for you." She held out the bunch of daisies. They were a little wilted, and a lot of the petals had fallen off, but they were without a doubt the most beautiful bouquet of flowers she'd ever been given in her life.

"I love them," she gushed.

"Mommy, are you crying?" Hayley asked, her blue eyes creasing in concern.

"I'm just happy, baby," she assured the little girl.

"Aunt Paige, you don't usually cry so much," Sophie piped up.

"Aunt Paige is a little emotional because she's been sick," Ryan told his daughter.

"Oh." Sophie nodded like that explained everything.

"Come here, honey." Paige took hold of Hayley and lifted her up onto her lap, cuddling both of her little girls. "Hayley, I want you to understand something. Uncle Ryan is right. I'm a little emotional at the moment because I've been sick, but you and Arianna and Daddy make me the happiest person in the world, okay? Even if I cry," she added.

"Okay." Hayley smiled at her and then cuddled close.

As she sat in her husband's arms, their two daughters on her lap, Paige felt more tears brimming in her eyes. She felt like the luckiest person ever.

* * * * *

4:11 P.M.

He cast a glance at Annabelle, who was asleep in the passenger seat of his car. Xavier was glad she was getting some rest. After what she'd been through the last week, she needed it.

Yesterday morning when they had walked into the dungeon and he'd seen Jeremy's hands around Annabelle's neck, he'd thought they were seconds too late and Annabelle was already dead.

He had expected to talk to Jeremy, attempt to talk him into giving himself up.

It had been a complete shock when Jeremy had charged them.

All four of them had fired.

It was clear Jeremy had committed suicide by cop.

By the time they'd established that Jeremy was dead, Annabelle still hadn't been moving.

The rush of relief when he'd pressed one hand to her chest in search of a heartbeat, the other to her neck to feel for a pulse, and he'd felt both had almost made his knees give way.

Although she'd been alive, her neck had been badly bruised. She'd been kept in the hospital under observation overnight, so her doctors could monitor her and make sure the swelling in her neck didn't become so severe that it blocked her airways. He had spent the night there with her, sleeping in a chair beside her bed, comforting her when she woke from nightmares.

The doctors had checked him out at the hospital too. Carrying a hysterically sobbing Annabelle in his arms had aggravated his cracked ribs. Not that anything in the world would have stopped him from doing it. Annabelle had needed him, and he was never abandoning her again.

He was so proud of her. She was amazing. So strong that she left him in awe. Xavier had told her so when she had awakened this morning.

Annabelle had smiled at him, told him she had to fight because she had a lot to live for; him. They'd spent some time talking through some of their issues and he was now confident that he and Annabelle were going to be able to make being a couple work.

Before they'd left to join Ryan, Sofia, Paige, and Elias they had visited Jack, Laura, and Rosie. Annabelle had oohed and ahhed over the baby and had actually seemed comfortable with Jack and

Laura. He'd never seen her so relaxed with people.

Now they were most of the way to the cabin and he was enjoying listening to Annabelle's quiet snores. He was feeling so positive about everything. Not that he thought things were going to be smooth sailing from here on out. Annabelle still had a lot to deal with. He did too. He still had unresolved issues of trust stemming from his marriage to Julia. And Annabelle had to come to terms with her true parentage.

Thinking of which, he had something he needed to tell her. He wished he didn't have to, but he didn't want to keep it from her; she had a right to know.

Wanting to get it over and done with, and since they were almost to the cabin, Xavier decided to wake her. Keeping one hand on the wheel, with his other he reached across and gently shook her shoulder. "Annabelle," he called quietly.

"Mmm?" she murmured, then yawned and stretched.

"We need to talk."

Raising a questioning brow, she asked, "Is something wrong?"

"Not wrong, exactly." He was stalling, and he knew it.

By the look she shot him, Annabelle knew it too. "What do you need to tell me?"

He decided it was better to just do it. Like ripping off a Band-Aid, the faster the better. "Did Jeremy tell you anything about your mother?"

Vulnerability bloomed in her pale eyes. She was still on shaky ground when it came to her biological parents. "No. When I asked he refused to answer me."

"We ended up finding you by getting your mother's name from your birth certificate and then looking for any properties she owned. Her name was Cassidy Ramsey. Jeremy abducted her when she was nineteen," he informed her gently. Xavier slowed the car, so he could take a closer look at her to monitor how she was handling the news and make sure she was ready for what he had to say next.

"Did Jeremy kill her after I was born?" she asked quietly. She was fighting to keep it together; her face was calm, but her eyes were a mess of emotion.

"No. They stayed together. She was in the house, hiding in an upstairs bedroom. She was found after we rode to the hospital in the ambulance," he broke the news as gently as he could.

"She knew what he'd been doing? She knew he was killing women in their basement?" Annabelle posed both as questions, but he knew they weren't.

"We believe she's suffering from Stockholm Syndrome," he explained. "Jeremy abducted her, kept her isolated and locked up while she was pregnant, threatened her with you when he took her to the hospital to give birth. She was a victim of Jeremy's, too, Annabelle."

"She knew what he was doing," Annabelle countered. "That makes her an accomplice. Maybe she even helped him do it." Catching something in his expression, her eyes widened until they seemed way too big for her face. "Did she?"

"Maybe," he reluctantly acknowledged. "She wouldn't admit it, but Jeremy and Kathy worked scams together when they were children, so it's probable he made Cassidy help him too."

"So, both my parents are killers. Jeremy and Cassidy." Annabelle brushed at the tears falling down her cheeks, but they were streaming so quickly that as soon as she brushed some away more took their place.

"That has no bearing on you, Annabelle," he said, a little sharper than he'd intended, but he wasn't going to have her thinking that meant she had the potential to become a killer too.

"Pull the car over," she begged.

He did so immediately. As soon as he'd come to a stop, Annabelle flung open her door and threw herself out. She ran a few yards away, then tilted her face to the sky and took big gulps of the fresh air.

He knew there was nothing he could say to help her right now.

Annabelle had to come to terms with who her biological parents were on her own. But he would be right there, right beside her every step of the way.

For now, he just pulled her into his arms, holding her tightly, rubbing her back, and murmuring consolations he wasn't sure she was listening to into her hair.

"I don't know who I am." She cried into his chest.

"I do." He took hold of her chin and tipped her face up, so she had to look at him. "You're Annabelle Englewood. You're smart and kind and strong ... and the woman that I'm in love with." Releasing her, he reached into his pocket and pulled out the small box containing the engagement ring he'd bought almost two years ago. Annabelle had turned him down the two other times he'd proposed, but he knew she wouldn't this time.

"Xavier ..." Her eyes darted from the little velvet box up to his face.

Dropping down onto one knee, he took hold of her left hand. "Annabelle Englewood, I love you. I want to spend the rest of my life with you, I want to have a family with you and grow old with you. Will you marry me?"

A huge smile broke out on her face, and like the sunshine on a rainy day, it cleared away her tears. "Yes," she giggled. "Yes, yes, yes, yes, yes!"

Xavier slipped the ring on her finger, then stood and slipped his arms around her waist, settling her back against his chest. "I love you, Annabelle."

Putting her arms around his neck, she pressed herself closer. "I love you, Xavier."

Then they kissed.

A deep, passionate kiss.

A kiss that promised many years of kisses ... of hope ... of support ... of enjoyment ... of the best life had to offer.

A kiss of love.

Jane has loved reading and writing since she can remember. She writes dark and disturbing crime/mystery/suspense with some romance thrown in because, well, who doesn't love romance?! She has several series including the complete Detective Parker Bell series, the Count to Ten series, the Christmas Romantic Suspense series, and the Flashes of Fate series of novelettes.

When she's not writing Jane loves to read, bake, go to the beach, ski, horse ride, and watch Disney movies. She has a black belt in Taekwondo, a 200+ collection of teddy bears, and her favorite color is pink. She has the world's two most sweet and pretty Dalmatians, Ivory and Pearl. Oh, and she also enjoys spending time with family and friends!

For more information please visit any of the following –

Amazon – http://www.amazon.com/author/janeblythe
BookBub – https://www.bookbub.com/authors/jane-blythe
Email – mailto:janeblytheauthor@gmail.com
Facebook – http://www.facebook.com/janeblytheauthor
Goodreads – http://www.goodreads.com/author/show/6574160.Jane_Blythe
Instagram – http://www.instagram.com/jane_blythe_author
Reader Group – http://www.facebook.com/groups/janeskillersweethearts
Twitter – http://www.twitter.com/jblytheauthor
Website – http://www.janeblythe.com.au

sic enim dilexit Deus mundum ut Filium suum unigenitum daret ut omnis qui credit in eum habeat vitam aeternam

CPSIA information can be obtained
at www.ICGtesting.com
Printed in the USA
BVHW041701040523
663608BV00019B/123

9 780994 538086